War among Gods and Men

– The Wisdom of Tao –

 A Blasphemous Pilgrimage

Hong-Yee Chiu

info@EHGBooks.com

Library of Congress Cataloging (applied for)

ISBN- 13:978-1478315698
ISBN-10: 1478315695

Contents – Vol. I

Figure Captions

Acknowledgements and Credits

I would like to thank Linda Pei-lin Yang for her interest in this work and to introduce me to Chen Tian-nian, Professor of Art in Shanghai, who provided much of the illustrations. Grateful thanks is due to China Economic Website for providing the illustrations of Parn Goo and Woman Wa. I would like to thank the Chiugo Publishing Company which first published the Chinese work in Taiwan. Support of Nonny Li-chen Hsueh in various matters is greatly appreciated. I would like to thank my wife Tung-ai for her understanding while writing this work.

War among Gods and Men

The Lost Wisdom of Tao

In the beginning, it was darkness. "... 'Let there be light', and there was light." Light is energy. Energy can create matter. This was how the Universe began billions and billions of years ago, so we were told. Since the beginning of the Universe, Energy has always played a dominant role as a chief driving force for all courses of events.

Yet far more powerful than energy is the wisdom of Tao. Tao is the nameless and the formless, the gateway to all subtleties, the law of laws of nature, the most profound of the profound, the guidance of Energy. Tao permeates everywhere, but only in ancient times were there real masters who could grasp the essence of Tao.

Many astounding events, human and otherwise, have taken place since the Universe began, but most of these early events were forgotten and few were recorded. Nevertheless, some events taking place during the dawn of civilization in the Middle Kingdom were captured in annals. One such set of annals detailed a series of inexplicable feats achieved through the wisdom of Tao.

These enigmatic feats were accomplished by the few who had mastered the wisdom of Tao. At the end of this period of history, under a decree of peace, Taoists of the three Sects agreed never to become involved with human affairs again and they all sequestered to remote mountains to continue their pursuit of Tao. The wisdom of Tao thus became lost and has not been recaptured since.

Quite accidentally I came upon this set of unusual annals which gave a detailed depiction of events during that period. The annals were cryptically written in the ancient language of the Middle Kingdom. Armed with the knowledge of this ancient language (which I learned from distant disciples of the great master teacher Confucius), I managed to accomplish the difficult task of deciphering the mystifying messages embodied. Incredible as these narrations may seem, they did take place, as contended by the annals. However, since these events took place such a long time ago, only scattered (though numerous) artifacts of that period were preserved and found. It will probably take a few more centuries; at least, for historians and archeologists to reconstruct the lost wisdom of Tao from these artifacts, if ever. In the meantime, I decided to make the only depictions of the power of the wisdom of Tao known to the world.

During the wee hours when I struggled to decipher the cryptic messages of the annals, I often developed the strange feeling that I could feel the presence of the Great Master of Tao, Lao Tzu, a Yoda of his time. In the hopes of my heart, perhaps one day this Great Master will once again come upon us to reveal the wisdom of Tao.

Hong-Yee Chiu

The Creation

Space has an unknown number of dimensions; maybe ten, or even twenty-six. *Time* does not exist because *Time* has not been created yet; *Space* has no need for time. Indeed inside *Space* there is nothing but stillness – no, stillness is not the word. Stillness means the absence of activities such as sound, light, or others, thus implying their existence. No, not here. *Space* has only void, a void without any tactile structure. No sound, light or any other activity is yet known to *Space*; they are not needed and hence not created. *Space* has no need to create them, for *Space* always enjoys Its existence in the purest abstract form.

Space has many subspaces. The smallest unit of a subspace is a coordinate, an intangible, pretentious and fickle line, an element of *Space*. All coordinates are equal and hence they are symmetric with respect to each other. These coordinates are only permitted to wander among Its countless patterns, for no other activities are allowed, and the coordinates do wander from one pattern to another, sometimes kaleidoscopically. The roving takes place effortlessly, elegantly and gracefully in all dimensions and at their pleasure; on some occasions the coordinates wander from one pattern to another concertedly, on others individually and on still others almost chaotically. *Space* enjoys the kaleidoscopic wandering of Its coordinates, too, for the aimless roaming allows *Space* to soar amidst an infinite variety of eternal and ever-changing patterns.

Yet *Space* is not perfect. During the timeless roving of Its coordinates among the endless patterns, ripples and kinks develop spontaneously and unpredictably. Along the patterns of fiducial lines of coordinates, waves and bends pop up here and there. Helplessly, *Space* has to endure these ripples and kinks. Amidst these small disturbances,

3

Space manages to keep the immeasurable patterns upon which the coordinates rove conspicuously and perpetually similar, though never identical.

On rare occasions, ripples and kinks occur in more than one coordinate's dimensions. Still rarer is the occasion when kinks occur in four different coordinates. During the uncountable aimless roaming sessions of Its coordinates, this has not happened, yet.

*

It is happening now. Inexplicably, a kink in a four-dimensional subspace has developed. Unlike many other kinks in subspaces of lesser dimensions, which are timidly dissipated, this kink is not going away. This happening was strong enough to cause a disturbance in remaining coordinates. *Space* has been perturbed; It has always been the Law, now Its authority has been challenged. It is feeling a crushing force upon all Its coordinates; some coordinates are actually being crushed out of existence. Helplessly, *Space* is undergoing a hitherto unknown transfiguration. *Space* will never be the same again.

The timeless patterns the coordinates have been roaming about are also undergoing transformations, as one of the coordinates has suddenly made an unprecedented transfiguration into an entity called *Time*. *Space* can no longer enjoy Its existence in the purest abstract form. From now on, *Space* must accept activities It so much detested. *Space* must accept the existence of *Time*, even to the extent of accepting the control exerted by *Time*. *Time* is different from *Space*, but there are still many similarities. Under certain conditions, *Space* and *Time* are interchangeable and the combination of a three-dimensional *Space* and a one-dimensional *Time* can be regarded as an inseparable entity called the *Space-Time Continuum*. The advent of *Time* also introduces other changes. Indeed, *Space-Time Continuum* will no longer cherish the timeless existence *Space* once enjoyed; in the so far very remote future, both *Time* and *Space* may also disappear altogether and forever. However, at the present epoch of *Time* there is no need to worry or even to think about this possibility. At least not in the aeons of time to come.

Space is suffering more changes than merely the loss of Its coordinates and Its submission to *Time*; the collapsed *Space* with three spatial and one temporal coordinate is no longer abstract or still. A new entity that *Space* never experienced before now permeates everywhere, however remote. This new entity is *Energy*. The destiny of *Space-Time Continuum* is now determined by the very relationship between *Energy* and *Time*.

This *Space-Time Continuum* whose destiny is controlled by the energy it contains is the Universe. This Universe was born during the *ksana*, or the indescribably short instant during which some coordinates of *Space* were crushed out of existence. This newly born Universe was extremely small, so small that even mathematicians who are used to infinitesimal quantities regard it as small, but ever since its birth the Universe has been at a state of rapid expansion. Soon the shape of the Universe became discernible; it is a rapidly expanding sphere in the four-dimensional *Space-Time Continuum*. It contains a nearly infinite amount of energy. Its temperature is extremely high, so high that even physicists who are used to unwieldily high energy view the temperature as high.

The forever-expanding sphere in the four-dimensional *Space-Time Continuum* is what we call our Universe.

*

War among Gods and Men

Parn Goo feels extremely constrained and confined. He feels that he is too restrained in his perfect, symmetric, spherical form. It is also too hot, unbearably hot. He struggles and struggles to free himself from this spherical, symmetrical bondage, but all his efforts are futile; at most he only succeeds to deform infinitesimally from the confines of the sphere. He feels extremely frustrated, so do the constituents inside his body. All over him he can feel the vigor within to struggle against the unknown power of restraint, and shares with him the frustration, the despair that he might not be able to overcome. But he does not give up. Unceasingly his whole body continues to exert vigor to fight against the invisible and intangible force of confinement. He has not succeeded yet, but he does not give up. He and his within continue and continue the struggle to free himself.

As the struggle continues, he suddenly feels the growth of a concerted effort. He begins to feel the power of unity and he decides to join in. As he and his body rhythm in unison against the unknown, he also feels a rapid growth in himself, accompanied by a gradual decrease of the intolerable heat. As time passes, he feels more and more comfortable. He feels his growth and he feels hope as the intangible external constraint that confines him to his spherical form continues to wane.

First he can only bulge his spherical form ever so slightly and only for a short while before the united effort collapses, returning him back to his spherical bondage. Then he feels a concerted effort towards a particular direction. In unison, they push, push, and push and a distinctive bulge begins to take shape. Despite the efforts of suppression of the invisible external constraint, this bulge not only manages to sustain its irregular form, but also grows into a protrusion. The protrusion quickly takes the shape of an arm. The strength of this arm grows rapidly; soon it becomes strong enough to overcome completely the external, invisible constraint. This arm is now permanent.

The war is won! Symmetry is now broken! The invisible external power has been subdued! The genesis of his second arm comes almost without effort. Then his head emerges, his legs extend, and finally Parn Goo is free! Free at last! Parn Goo is no longer constrained to his symmetrical, spherical bondage.

Yet he still cannot stand up straight. Above him, he finds a light but strong cover. Beneath him, he finds a thin crust of embodiment, still somewhat fragile. Carefully he pushes, and the light cover above yields to his efforts and begins to rise. Meanwhile, the thin crust of the embodiment beneath begins to thicken. Parn Goo continues to push, push and push, and he continues to grow, grow and grow. For aeons and aeons of time, he keeps on pushing while growing. As Parn Goo grows and pushes, the Universe expands and heaven and earth are pushed farther and farther apart.

Eventually his growth slows down to a trickle. The light cover is now far, far above him. Beneath him, the thin crust of embodiment has become so thick that it no longer grumbles under his heavy footsteps. Parn Goo is very happy now. He is very happy about his breaking away from the enslavement of symmetry; he is very happy about his ability to push the light cover to an enormous height; he is also very happy that during his growth the crust underneath his feet has thickened and solidified, and now supports him comfortably. Now he can rest. After a lifetime of hard work that has lasted the entire history of the Universe, he deserves a good rest. He lies down and prepares to sleep. He loves his creation so much that, before he falls into his eternal, dreamless slumber, he wills his body to the world he just helped to create.

*

Figure I- 1. Creation by Parn Goo

The final transformation begins almost immediately. Parn Goo's eyes are the first to pop out of his body, rising to the height of heaven to become the Sun and the Moon. His four limbs, which first broke the symmetry of his spherical bondage, become the source of vitality of the

8

world he created – four invisible but discernible forces. His bones are transformed into stony mountain ranges, his muscles crumble to become black soil covering the barren earth. Under the scrutiny of his eyes in the sky, his hair turns green and begins to ensconce the black soil. His veins become rivers in which flows his blood, now clarified into a pure, almost abstract form, as *Space* always liked. His internal constituents are deposited deep underground, stowed away safely for the future. Finally, his head disintegrates into thousands and thousands of pieces, each carrying some of his wisdom, his vitality, his unwillingness to compromise with any bondage, and his desire for a world of harmony. These pieces begin to multiply. As time goes by, of the multiplied millions, each acquires an embodiment of its own. Most become mortals, some good, some evil, some ferocious, some gentle, but some are transcended to become deities residing high above, close to heaven, and some fall down to become the lowest form, demons. In between, a wonderful spectrum of life-forms thrives on earth. During the aeons, these life-forms generate many activities which, for better or for worse, alter the appearance of the world that Parn Goo created. Among these life-forms is one species called Human, the most intelligent among all lesser than deities. Human has wonderful qualities that would have placed him among the rank of deities. At the same time he also has those qualities that would have degraded him among the lowest of life forms, the demons. So Human is eternally destined to be at strife between qualities of deities and desires of demons. Occasionally Human achieves a place among deities, but in many instances he also joins the rank of demons.

During the countless millennia after Human first appeared in the world, several reigns of terror passed by; a number of fiendish life forms, with their enormous strength, were able to overpower easily the tiny creature of Human. As a result, for most of the time Human had to hide in dark caverns; only the bravest among them dared to venture outside under the open sky.

Fire was first discovered by such a daring Human by the name Sui Ren, the Flint Human. He taught his fellow Human the use of fire and he became a leader of Human. Using fire, beasts were subdued; friendly ones became subservient company of Human, while fiendish ones escaped to the wilderness away from Human.

As danger gradually subsided, Human began to enlarge his vista. A wise Human by the name of You Chao, the Nest Human, invented shelters fashioned after the nests of flying creatures. Human no longer had to live inside dim caverns. Now Human could live in the open, sheltered by the new invention, called house. He kept herds of subdued beasts and creatures around his house; these beasts and creatures and Human became permanent partners. Human fed and used these partners for many purposes to suit his needs and these partners relied on Human for their continued existence.

Human's search for food continued to be his main activity. Another Human appeared, Shen Nong, the Magical Agriculture Human. Instead of searching for food in wildness, Shen Nong learned from nature how to generate food from food. With this new knowledge, Human finally settled down, sheltered by the invention of You Chao, the Nest Human, warmed and lighted by the discovery of Sui Ren, the Flint Human, secured from hunger by the clever idea of Shen Nong to regenerate food from food, and surrounded by a large assemblage of once wild beasts and creatures. Human felt secure and prosperous. He even had the leisure time to do some unnecessary chores, like carving patterns on stone tablets and building houses which served no practical purposes. He even learned to use his voice to arouse the attention of his fellow

Human, to tell others what he wanted. He had learned how to communicate with his voice; he had invented Language.

Yet Human was not satisfied. Communication via voice lasted only while the sound could be heard. Human wanted to have a way to express his voice without sound. One day, the answer came to a wise Human by the name of Chang Jei. He was looking at tracks left by birds and animals, which for aeons of time had been used by his fellow Human to track his prey. Perhaps each voice could be associated with a mark or symbol like those left by birds and animals, thought Chang Jei. As each type of track would lead to a different bird or animal, so could each type of mark or symbol be used to mean a different voice. He assembled a number of symbols and he taught his fellow Human the use of them to supplement their voices. Some of his symbols bore the likeness of objects, like a fish, a bird, or a horse, but very soon he found out that there were also voices which had no material forms, such as his fondness for his mate, or his fear of certain animals, such as snakes. He taught his fellow Human that the world was not made of only objects they could see; there were also many things that could not been seen nor sensed but could only be felt. With these new symbols, Human learned how to pass his experience to another fellow Human without uttering a voice. With this new tool, Human was definitely many steps superior to other creatures of the world. Human had developed a culture that could be passed along from one Human to the next, from one generation to the next, even from one to another far, far away.

Even as Human learned to better his life, his life was still filled with uncertainties. When he hunted, he did not know if he could bring home a prey; when he planted food according to the instructions of Shen Nong, he was never sure he would be able to harvest, because the Sun might shine too much, or too little, and rain might not come in time. His life was always shrouded in a veil of uncertainty. A man, by the name Fushi, discovered the use of three broken lines to make predictions about the outcome of hunting or agricultural activities. He invented a set of eight trigrams which could be used to make predictions. Sometimes the predictions came true, sometimes not, but Human felt much more comfortable and secure because he could relieve his uncertainty through the use of the eight trigrams. Fushi thus became the leader of Human.

Even in the beginning, Human was not alone. During the time of the Flint Human, parallel to his activities to elevate himself from drudgeries of survival, many life forms, some of which bore the likeness of Human, some not, also acquired similar abilities. Yet Human was the most successful one. Envious of Human's success, these competing life-forms often raided Human of his subdued beasts and creatures, sometimes even drove Human from his shelters or even killed him. Human learned how to fight off these enemies, or to tame them to become Human. During Fushi's time, an extremely powerful and diabolic life-form attacked Human. Human had to fight day and night against this powerful enemy. Many a fellow Human died in fending off this attack, but finally Human won. Most of the invading life-forms were killed, but their leader, Gong Gong, survived. He was viciously mad at his unsuccessful attempt to subjugate Human to himself and his fellow life-forms.

In his last attempt to subdue man, Gong Gong charged and jolted his head against Bu Zhou, a pillar that supported heaven in the southwest corner. Gong Gong was very powerful, and he succeeded in causing the pillar to collapse partially into a huge mountain and, as a result, heaven cracked. The attack was so fierce that, despite his powerful strength, Gong Gong himself was fatally injured. As he lay on the ground dying, he laughed hard at his last feat, for he had caused heaven to crack, and the world that he could not conquer would soon end.

The world was in grave danger now. A crack of cosmic dimension appeared at the southwest corner of heaven. Through this cosmic crack, debris of the primordial fire fell onto the world; this was the fire that Parn Goo had found so intolerable during his struggle to free himself from his spherical bondage. Through this cosmic crack, essences that made the beautiful world possible also began to dissipate. The world would soon end.

Human was in peril. Human would soon die and vanish from the wonderful and magnificent world that countless predecessors had helped to build and to perfect. Fushi, the leader of Human at that time, was unable to mend the crack, and he helplessly watched the world withering day by day.

The sister of the ruler Fushi, Woman Wa, was from her birth a curious woman. She had searched the depths of the deepest caverns, she had explored the bottom of unfathomable canyons, she had ascended the tallest of mountains, and she was familiar with almost every form of rock and stone. Once upon a time she came across a collection of colorful stones, carefully piled and stowed, as if purposely left there a long time before. She left this pile alone, for she knew that it had been left there to fulfill a destined purpose in the future.

The world was in deep peril now. Woman Wa again trekked from one corner of the world to the next to search for a way to mend the fatal cosmic crack. Once again she came across the pile of colorful stones, which had been somewhat disturbed by recent shakes of the thick crust of earth. A debris leaked through the cosmic crack had left an intense cosmic fire burning nearby. Woman Wa observed that some colorful stones had, under the effect of this cosmic fire, transformed into a liquid which soon became hardened into a new substance. This substance was strong, and was capable of binding two stones into one through its magic power of unbreakable bonding.

"Perhaps the time has come," thought Woman Wa. She took some more of these colorful stones and threw them into the intense cosmic fire. The stones were instantly transformed into liquid, which soon solidified to form a strong bond.

"The time has come." She took as many colorful stones as she could carry, and ascended the partially collapsed Mountain of Bu Zhou. She patched the cosmic crack with colorful stones, and used cosmic fires to train the colorful stones into liquid, which soon filled all the crevices of the cosmic crack and solidified. An unbreakable bond was created and the cosmic crack was mended; essences of the world no longer leaked through the crack. The world was delivered from extinction by a legacy left by Parn Goo; Woman Wa had fulfilled another last wish of Parn Goo. The world had been saved and would become more prosperous in time to come.

Human rejoiced: Woman Wa was his savior. At the request of Human, Woman Wa became the permanent custodian of heaven. She ascended high above clouds to the height of heaven to reside among deities. She constantly inspected heaven and carried out the tedious work of mending all cracks. She had become the guardian of heaven and also of Human. Thanking her for her protection, Human built a temple to honor her. Human asked for and was granted a holographic image of Woman Wa, in her exact likeness. Each year the leader of Human would go to the temple to speak the wishes of his subjects to Woman Wa, who would listen and would make the wishes come true.

Figure I- 2. Woman Wa mending Cosmic Crack

After the failed attempt of Gong Gong to subjugate Human, there came a period of peace. As activities of Human widened, groups of Human became consolidated into larger groups, and into still larger groups. Finally, there were only two groups left, one led by Huangdi, the Yellow Emperor, and the other by Chi You, the Ugly and Ignorant.

Chi You was of a beastly build, mighty, and was endowed with magical power. As the two groups grew in size and strength, conflicts took place frequently. These two groups of Human clashed at times, but eventually a major engagement took place. By virtue of Huangdi's wisdom, Chi You, who depended on his physical strength, was the apparent loser. In desperation, Chi You applied his magical power. Dense fogs were summoned around battlefields. Using his magic, projectiles of balls of fire were thrown at Huangdi's followers. During the next several clashes, Huangdi's followers suffered severe losses; they could not fight against the projectiles of balls of fire, nor could they find their way in the dense fog that Chi You summoned.

Huangdi and some of his wise Human worked out a scheme for defense. From the colorful stones left by Woman Wa, one was found that always pointed in the southward direction. A large piece of the stone was acquired and hung from a pole. Even in densest fogs this stone would keep on pointing in the southward direction. Huangdi's followers would never become lost again, no matter how dense the fog was. Next, Huangdi instructed his followers to bend tree branches and to tie both ends with strings. Sticks sharpened at one end could be launched to great distances by pulling the string and then releasing it. The sharp projectiles could inflict severe wounds on an enemy, and the projectiles could be aimed with greater accuracy than the wanton balls of fire thrown by Chi You. In the next engagement, because of the south-pointing stone, Huangdi's followers did not lose their way in the dense fog summoned by Chi You, and they could fell their enemies with their sharp projectiles at distances beyond the reach of balls of fire. Chi

You was defeated and killed. Henceforth the world would be reigned by only one single group knwon as Human.

Huangdi was succeeded by another ruler, who was succeeded by still another, and another. Some of the rulers of Human were good, some evil, and some mediocre. Occasionally wars had to be fought to rid evil rulers. Through the symbols – written languages – Human could learn from his predecessors, and in turn Human could pass along his learning to his successors. Thus Human could acquire and accumulate knowledge. Never since the beginning had the world seen more activities than after the epoch of written languages.

While Human fought wars and built civilization, Woman Wa continued her eternal task as the guardian of heaven. During the aeons of time since creation, Human and deities had always lived apart. Except for Woman Wa, deities were not concerned with Human, neither would Human be concerned with deities. If not for a small incident that eventually caused a close encounter between deities and Human, they probably would never have been brought together. Because of this small incident, a dynasty fell, and during the ensuing battles deities and Human were involved in mixed engagements, sometimes fighting together and sometimes against each other. A war of immense scale ensued. After the war was over additional deities were appointed to become gods and goddesses to take care of affairs of Human.

The story of this war that is about to be narrated happened during the reign of the last emperor of a period known as Shang, the reign of Emperor Zoe. In the annals of history, his reign took place from 1081 to 1046 B.C.

War among Gods and Men

1. The Pilgrimage

Sou was the third prince of Emperor Yi. One day, when Emperor Yi was touring his royal garden with his three princes, a corner of a pavilion suddenly collapsed and the whole structure was in danger. Prince Sou immediately leaped forward, and with his miraculous strength he lifted up the collapsed corner to allow workers to repair the broken pillars to prevent further damage. Impressed with the strength of Prince Sou, Premier Shang Yon and other high court officials later petitioned Emperor Yi to designate Prince Sou as the successor to the throne, a request that Emperor Yi readily consented to. After the death of Emperor Yi, Prince Sou succeeded to the throne and was titled Emperor Zoe.

Emperor Zoe had an assemblage of extremely competent court officials. Premier Shang Yon, who with unquestioned fealty had served the two previous emperors before Emperor Zoe, was an experienced statesman. Wen Zhong (Imperial Teacher), who taught Prince Sou during his youth and was designated Prince Regent during the early reign of Emperor Zoe, excelled himself in all aspects of literary as well as military talents. He proficiently guided the operation of the government. Nobleman Huang Feihu (Flying Tiger), the invincible commander-in-chief of the army holding the title of Master Lord of National Poise, formidably oversaw the safety of the country. In addition, the regime was loyally supported by feudal lords of different ranks, which consisted of four dukes, North, South, East and West, who each ruled 200 feudal lords of lesser ranks. Under a decree established during the founding of the Shang dynasty which created these fiefs and titles, upon succession each lord or duke was required to renew and reaffirm his fealty to the emperor in reign, in this case Emperor Zoe. The country thus thrived well. It appeared that nothing but prosperity could take place.

One day during the seventh year of the reign of Emperor Zoe, as the daily court session was about to end, Premier Shang Yon asked permission to submit a request. The permission was granted. Shang Yon conveyed to Emperor Zoe: "Tomorrow is the holy birthday of Lady Goddess Woman Wa. Since ascension to the throne, Your Majesty Emperor has not yet paid respect and tribute to her. Your Majesty Emperor should use this opportunity to do so on behalf of the country and people."

"Who is Woman Wa? What has she accomplished to deserve my respect and tribute," asked Emperor Zoe.

"Your Majesty Emperor, you grew up in the Palace and you have not made many contacts with the common people to know the names of their goddess. Lady Goddess Woman Wa is the guardian of heaven. During early days of the history of human civilization on the earth, a defeated barbarian monster, Gong Gong, jolted his head against a pillar which supported heaven in the southwest direction and caused it to collapse. A large crack developed in heaven and the world was in grave danger. It was Lady Goddess Woman Wa who extracted colored stones from depths of the earth and infused these stones with fire to mend the cosmic crack. She prevented heaven from collapse and saved the world from extinction. People built a temple many years ago to thank her for her great and merciful deeds. After she saved them, she was appointed the guardian of heaven and of people. Your Majesty Emperor must go to her temple and offer incense and sacrifice to pay tribute and respect to her!"

Figure I- 3. Emperor Zoe

"In this case I must go. Prepare to visit the temple of Lady Goddess Woman Wa tomorrow," responded Emperor Zoe, and the court recessed.

The next morning, the procession of worship started early towards the temple of Lady Goddess Woman Wa. Inside the magnificent temple the icon of Woman Wa stood majestically behind a thin veil. Offerings were made accordingly and Emperor Zoe presided over the ceremony

21

to honor the birthday of Woman Wa. When the ceremony was just over, a gentle wind lifted up the veil to show a clear view of the lifelike holographic image of Woman Wa. She was of exquisite beauty. By comparison, suddenly the harem in the palace of Emperor Zoe which included several hundred beautiful concubines, looked like a collection of paper dolls.

Aroused by her beauty, Emperor Zoe asked his attendant to bring him a brush pen and ink. He quickly composed a poem and copied it onto the wall of the temple of Woman Wa. The poem read:

> *Your beauty is like a pear blossom,*
> *Covered with pearls of rain droplets.*
> *Surrounded by peonies, veiled behind a thin smoke,*
> *Your beauty is flawless and without comparison.*
> *I wish I could have you,*
> *Serving me for my pleasure.*

Premier Shang Yon was shocked. "Your Majesty Emperor! Lady Goddess Woman Wa is the most righteous goddess in heaven. You are desecrating your guardian goddess! Your serf Shang Yon respectfully begged Your Majesty Emperor to come here to pay tribute and respect to Lady Goddess Woman Wa, so that the country and people will continue to receive blessing from her. Now Your Majesty Emperor composed a poem explicitly manifesting your luscious desire, thereby blaspheming Lady Goddess Woman Wa and desecrating her house in the human world. When common people see this, they will consider you an evil emperor not worthy of their respect. May your serf Shang Yon respectfully beg your Majesty Emperor to issue an order to erase what you have written?" he pleaded.

"No! I am only expressing my appreciation of the beauty of Woman Wa. I want to let the world know how much I admire beauty. Say no more," responded Emperor Zoe.

Shang Yon retreated sadly. Upon the return trip no one dared to say a word, but the fear and displeasure were obvious.

On her birthday, Woman Wa went to visit three sage kings of the past. She stayed in the palace of the three sage kings until dusk. Before she returned to her palace in heaven, she went to her temple to see what people wished her to do. Upon entry to her temple, she saw the poem on the wall and she was extremely enraged. "This poem is an insult to womanhood and a desecrating act against me. I must display my power to punish him." She then returned to her palace and asked her attendants to prepare her chariot to carry out her punishment.

Woman Wa's chariot glided smoothly and swiftly over the clouds. As she approached the capital of Shang, the city of Chow Go (Morning Song), the passage of the chariot was blocked by an array of red light rays. Using her power of prognostication, she quickly discovered that Emperor Zoe still had about 28 years of reign left and nothing could be done until then. The array of red rays of light warned Woman Wa that the time was not ripe for her to carry out her punishment.

Returning to her palace, she asked her attendants to take out a gold gourd bottle from storage. She then descended to her temple in the human world. She uncorked the bottle, and a giant white flag with the inscription, "Elves, sprites, gather ye here!" popped out and flowed amidst high winds. Messages were swiftly sent to all elves and sprites to gather in front of the temple of Lady Goddess Woman Wa. Soon the open ground in the front of the temple was filled with elves and gremlins of all sizes and shapes. She selected three female elves and sent the rest home. The three female elves selected were: a female fox elf who had lived over a thousand years and had already acquired a human form, a nine-headed female pheasant elf, and an elf transcended from a jade Pee-Pa (a stringed musical instrument). Woman Wa gave the three elves instructions for her punishment: "You three elves must assume human female forms of exquisite beauty and at opportune occasions, you must enter Emperor Zoe's palace to gain his favor and trust. In time, you must destroy his empire. However, you must be careful not to hurt common people. After you have accomplished your mission according to my instructions, I shall reward you by transforming all of you to fairies in real human form and assign you appropriate ranks in heaven."

The three female elves knelt down and thanked Lady Goddess Woman Wa. Quickly they came up with a plan to carry out their new mission. Unknown to Emperor Zoe, his careless, inconsiderate and lewd act would not only destroy his empire, but also changed the course of future events in heaven as well as on earth.

2. Homage of Feudal Lords

After returning from the pilgrimage, Emperor Zoe could not keep his thoughts away from the beautiful image of Woman Wa. He became bored with the several hundred beautiful women whom he already kept in his harem. Meanwhile, Imperial Teacher Wen Zhong had to depart in haste as the commander-in-chief of an army to suppress rebellion in the North Sea. Emperor Zoe felt lonely, so he befriended two court officials, Fei Chung (Fei the Corrupt) and Yu Whenn (Yu the Adulator), known for their corruption and adulatory eloquence. Emperor Zoe mentioned his boredom to the two officials, who immediately seized the opportunity to offer their evil advice: "Your Majesty Emperor, the most omnipotent of the World, the richest of the Four Seas! With your power, you should be able to acquire all things Your Majesty Emperor desires. Let your serfs make a humble suggestion: Tomorrow Your Majesty Emperor shall issue an Imperial Order to ask each dukedom and its subordinate subdivisions to submit one hundred most beautiful girls for you to pick from. With so many fiefs under your reign, you surely will find some one to your desire." This suggestion fit Emperor Zoe's itch so well that he decided to carry it out the next day.

During the court session the next morning, Emperor Zoe announced that an imperial order to demand beautiful women from feudal lords was already drafted and was ready to be sent out. Upon learning the contents of this order, Premier Shang Yon interceded. "Your Majesty Emperor, let your longtime serf make an appeal. An ancient sage said: 'If the virtue is with the ruler, gladly common people submit their obedience and fealty.' You already have three palaces and six estate mansions, each of which is filled with beautiful women ready to serve you at your pleasure. You should be satisfied. You must not carry out this repulsive act, especially now, ecause the country is already spending heavily to support the military effort of Imperial Teacher Wen Zhong to suppress rebellion in the North Sea. You should not, for the sake of your carnal desire, cause people to suffer unnecessarily. Please think thrice."

After a long silence, Emperor Zoe said, "You are right. I will cancel this order."

During the next year, the eighth year of reign of the Emperor Zoe, arrived the rare occasion of Homage Happening, during which all eight hundred feudal lords would gather around the capital to pay homage and respect to the reigning emperor of Shang. While waiting for an audience with the Emperor (during which the main function was to iterate their fealty and to present gifts they had brought as tokens of their submission), they also would use this rare occasion to socialize among fellow feudal lords and with court officials. Fei the Corrupt and Yu the Adulator were named the liaison officers for this rare and profound affair. Knowing the wretched personalities of the pair, most visiting lords offered expensive gifts and bribes to the two. One lord, a righteous man, Soo Hoo (Soo Defender) regarded it below his dignity to deal with the two corrupt officers and he offered neither gifts nor bribes. Not finding the name of Soo Defender among the names in their private bribery and gift list, the two were enraged and decided to retaliate.

The ceremony of Homage Happening took place on the New Year's day. The court session of Emperor Zoe was held early. All lords gathered outside the Gate of Wu (Gate of Noon) waiting to present their New Year's wishes and salutations to the Emperor. Premier Shang Yon suggested: "Your Majesty Emperor should personally interview the four dukes, North, South, East and West. After the interview, Your Majesty

Emperor may then appear at the terrace above the Gate of Noon to exchange greetings with the remaining lords as a group." Emperor Zoe was pleased at this suggestion. After the interview and the appearance of Emperor Zoe at the Gate of Noon, all lords were invited to a banquet inside the Palace. After the banquet and the grand interview, the ceremony of Homage Happening was complete. All lords prepared to leave.

Before the lords left, an idea occurred to Emperor Zoe. He summoned Yu the Adulator and Fei the Corrupt to his court for consultation. Emperor Zoe said: "My thoughts are still with the beauty of Woman Wa. Can you go to the lords on my behalf, asking them to search for beauties in the lands of their reign, and send the girls of their finding to me?"

Seizing this opportunity to carry out their devious scheme of retribution, Fei the Corrupt responded: "Premier Shang Yon already persuaded you to rescind this order. Your Majesty should keep your words. However, I heard that one of the lords, Soo Defender, has a daughter who has the reputation of being delicately and exquisitely beautiful. Instead of getting other lords involved, you may simply order Soo Defender to deliver his daughter to your palace. It is within your mighty power to issue such an order. Your Majesty can have your desire fulfilled without disturbing your country and your people."

Emperor Zoe was extremely pleased at this suggestion. An urgent imperial order was sent to summon Soo Defender to the court.

After listening to the wish of Emperor Zoe, Soo Defender responded: "Your Majesty already has a harem encompassing three palaces and six estate mansions, each of which is filled with beautiful women. Why do you need an extra one? Besides, my daughter has never been trained to serve as a courtesan. Your Majesty should immediately execute the two evil officials for their ill suggestions. Instead of placing your mind on women, Your Majesty should concentrate your effort to rule the country with justice and mercy. I will not send my daughter to your palace."

Enraged at the response of Soo Defender, Emperor Zoe immediately ordered his execution.

Fei the Corrupt interceded. "There are eight hundred lords outside, each carrying a substantial army. Execution of Lord Soo might cause a rebellion which may tumble this regime. May I suggest that you order Soo to go back to the land of his reign and to bring his daughter immediately to you. If he does not obey your order, you can send an army to subdue him. By that time all lords will be back home and they will not likely be incited to riot against you." Yu the Adulator seconded this proposal.

The life of Soo Defender was thus spared, but he was under an urgent imperial order to return to his land to bring his daughter back to the capital, Chow Go, city of Morning Song.

Returning to his temporary residence, Lord Soo Defender was furious. After discussing it with his own officials, who pledged loyalty and support to him, he decided to cease his fealty to Emperor Zoe. He wrote a poem on a wall in his temporary residence, explicitly expressing his frustration:

> *The Emperor is destroying moral values,*
> *I, Soo Hoo of the City of Chi,*
> *Vow never to pay homage again.*

As soon as Soo Defender returned to his county of Chi, he ordered preparation for the defense of the walled city of Chi against anticipated attacks from Emperor Zoe.

Aggravated at the poem, Emperor Zoe ordered one of his generals, Ru Shun (Brave), to assemble an army of 200,000 to march to the city of Chi to subdue Soo.

Sympathizing with Soo, Ru Brave tried to shed this unpleasant job. "It might not require Your Majesty's own effort. You may ask one or two lords who have not gone back to carry out your order."

Fei the Corrupt agreed. "It is a good idea. Please ask Duke North, Tsung Hohu to head the force of subjugation, since the city of Chi is within his duchy."

Knowing the ferocity, greed and cruelty of Tsung Hohu (Migratory Tiger), Ru Brave realized that all people along the route of the attacking force lead by Duke North would suffer greatly. He counterproposed that, instead of Duke North, Duke West, Chi-Chang (otherwise known as Wen Wang or King of Literature), who was respected for his concern of the welfare of common people, should be given the task.

Emperor Zoe pondered a while and then decided to adopt both suggestions, so both Dukes of North and West were summoned to the court.

Duke West, Chi-Chang, who ruled the vast duchy by the name Zhou, raised objections against the campaign, citing that Soo Defender was a good lord, that it would not be appropriate for Emperor Zoe to use the army to subdue a lord merely for the purpose of seizing a woman, especially his daughter. Emperor Zoe insisted that his order could not be modified, an opinion heartily supported by Yu the Adulator and Fei the

Corrupt, and also by the greedy Duke North. Duke West, outnumbered, reluctantly consented to the order, but he decided to hold off military action at first, so he told Duke North, "You may start the campaign right away. It will take me some time to prepare my army for action. You go first, I will join you later."

The next day Tsung Migratory Tiger led an army and marched towards the city of Chi, and days later they arrived at the vicinity of their destination. The army stopped and encamped at a distance of ten li from the city wall. Tsung Migratory Tiger sent a messenger to the city of Chi, challenging the defense of the city.

The next day, Soo Defender, accompanied by his warriors and an appropriate number of soldiers, emerged from the main city gate to face the invading army. After making a perfunctory salute to Duke North, his lord superior, Soo Defender said: "Your Lordship should not engage in this war for an immoral cause. Please return to your territory so that both of us may continue to live in peace."

Eager to display his power and authority, Tsung responded angrily, "I am under an imperial order to come here to subjugate you!" Turning around towards his warriors, Tsung Migratory Tiger said, "Which brave warrior among you will volunteer to capture this rebel for me?"

An arrogant warrior by the name Mei Wu, wearing a bright red robe under his golden armor, a helmet decorated with pheasant feathers, and armed with a huge battle-ax, responded. Riding a bluish horse, Mei Wu charged forward towards the defense line of Soo Defender. Without even waiting for a formal order, the son of Soo, Chun Chung (Loyal), rode forward to face the challenger. Armed with a two-pronged spear, Soo Loyal met Mei Wu midway. After twenty rounds of weapon clanking, Mei Wu began to weaken under the heavy thrust of the two-pronged spear. Finding a slip in the weapon play of

Mei Wu, Soo Loyal pierced him and Mei Wu fell dead. Amidst drums of victory, Soo's army launched a fierce attack against that of Tsung. Under the heavy assault, Tsung's army was defeated, and retreated by a distance of ten li. Satisfied with his success, Soo Defender returned his army to the city of Chi.

Riding on the crest of his daytime victory, Soo Defender schemed a night sneak attack. Hoofs of warhorses were covered with soft cloths and the bells on the reins silenced. Dressed in black, each soldier was ordered to muffle his mouth to prevent any inadvertent noise. Veiled under total darkness, Soo Defender's army quietly marched towards Tsung's encampment.

When Tsung's camp was within sight, cloths were removed from horses' hoofs and torches were lit. Tsung's army, having suffered a humiliating defeat during the day, was resting, warriors drinking, cursing the day's misfortune. Suddenly, Soo Defender's army appeared as if from nowhere. With torches they set everything in sight on fire, while slaughtering Tsung's army mercilessly. Tsung's warriors had scarcely enough time to scramble onto their horses to escape, and many of them did not even have a chance to pick up their fighting equipment. Tsung himself was wounded by Soo Loyal; his left leg armor was lifted off by the young Soo's two-pronged spear, barely sparing his leg. Chased by the army of Soo Defender, Tsung's army retreated by another thirty li.

At this moment an army of unknown origin appeared, but this army of 3000 – called the Soaring Tiger army – was a friendly one. It was the army of Tsung Heihu (Tsung Black Tiger), a brother of Tsung Migratory Tiger. After Black Tiger was told of his brother's defeat, he agreed to help Migratory Tiger launch a counterattack.

War among Gods and Men

When scouts reported that Tsung Black Tiger had reinforced his enemy, Soo Defender was scared. He knew that the Black Tiger of his youth had gone to study sorcery from a master Taoist on a high mountain, and from this Taoist he had acquired magic power. Suddenly, right after his victory, he was now facing an unknown element. A challenge from Black Tiger to talk to Soo Defender was received. Disregarding his father's warning that Black Tiger might be an enemy too capable for him, Soo's son, the Loyal, impatiently volunteered to face the challenge.

The thirty rounds of fighting quickly tired the Black Tiger, whose use of a short battle-ax was a disadvantage compared to the long two-pronged spear of Soo Loyal. Retreating under the constant thrust of the spear, the Black Tiger found an opportune moment and opened the lid of a red gourd bottle which he carried on his back and conjured a spell. Lo and behold, a black smoke arose from the gourd bottle; the black smoke materialized into a gigantic iron-beaked magical eagle. It attacked Soo Loyal from all sides with its iron beak and caused his horse to tumble, throwing Soo Loyal to the ground. He was quickly captured by foot soldiers of the Black Tiger.

Tsung Migratory Tiger wanted to have Soo Loyal executed immediately to avenge his defeat. The Black Tiger persuaded his brother to delay the execution, reasoning that once Soo Defender agreed to yield his daughter to Emperor Zoe, Soo Defender would automatically become a royal relative and the unwarranted execution of the son of a royal relative might bring him misfortune. Soo Loyal was therefore imprisoned instead.

Having lost his brave son to the enemy, Soo Defender was in great distress. At this time his military supply officer Tsen Ren (the Humming Tsen) showed up, after having escorted the delivery of a fresh supply of

32

food grain and other necessities as scheduled. Following a debriefing of the most recent misfortune, the Humming Tsen volunteered a combat against the Black Tiger. Soo Defender felt dismally insecure, for he was afraid that he might lose another good warrior. However, the Humming Tsen assured Soo Defender that he, too, possessed invincible magical powers.

Riding his Fiery-Eyed Golden Pupil Beast and carrying two long pestles, the Humming Tsen and his three-thousand-man army – the Black Crow army – met the challenge of Black Tiger and his Soaring Tiger army. The two long pestles danced in the two rapidly moving arms of Humming Tsen and Black Tiger once more was forced to retreat. However, before Black Tiger could open the lid of his red gourd bottle, Humming Tsen suddenly closed his eyes and after conjuring a spell, two white stunning rays emerged from his nostrils, immediately felling Black Tiger to the ground. The Black Crow army quickly captured Black Tiger and dispersed the Soaring Tiger army.

Soo Defender had met Black Tiger before, and they had been friends at one time. As a gesture of friendship, Soo Defender personally untied Black Tiger from his bondage and apologized for the rough treatment he had received. Black Tiger responded to the hospitality and explained that the purpose of his intervention had been to try to arrange a peaceful settlement of this conflict. However, before he could have a chance to make his intention known, he was already being challenged to a combat against Soo Loyal. Black Tiger told Soo Defender that his son was only imprisoned and no harm had been done to him. He wanted to discuss with Soo Defender a way out of the current state of unnecessary war. A banquet of reconciliation was thus arranged while the discussion of peace proceeded.

At the same time, the encampment of Migratory Tiger was in great disarray. Their savior, Black Tiger, was captured and his fate was unknown. The promised help from Duke West was still yet to come. Just at this moment, a messenger from Duke West arrived. His name was San Yeesen (Felicitous). Migratory Tiger was extremely angry and he accused Duke West in front of San Felicitous that, in the presence of Emperor Zoe, Duke West had promised to send an army to assist him, but now the only reinforcement he got was a mere messenger.

San Felicitous responded: "My Duke did not want to send an army because, wherever an army passes by, there are bound to be disruptions which may cause great discomfort to the people. My mission is to persuade Soo Defender to yield his daughter willingly to Emperor Zoe without the use of force. I am confident that I can accomplish my mission."

At this self-assured statement Migratory Tiger laughed loudly. "This is a new trick that I never heard before. I do not think it will work. However, to show respect to my dear friend Duke West, at least I should give you a chance to try." An escort was thus dispatched to accompany San Felicitous to the city of Chi.

Hearing that a messenger from Duke West had arrived, and knowing that Duke West had always been just, merciful, and thoughtful, Soo Defender personally greeted San Felicitous at the city gate and escorted him inside the city. A banquet of welcome was readily arranged. Towards the end of the welcoming banquet a letter from Duke West was presented to Soo Defender. The letter read:

To the Lord of the City of Chi, the Honorable Soo,

With all compliments and salutation from Duke West, this letter is humbly submitted under the respectable flag of your command:

I plead you to give serious consideration to what you should do to diffuse the current situation. You have already violated the code of fealty by disavowing your Emperor. A serious offense has been committed. You will still be able to remedy your rebellious acts by delivering your daughter to Emperor Zoe.

The advantages are:

Your daughter will enjoy all luxuries of the palace and you will be honored as a royal relative. On top of this, you will have spared many innocent lives in the forthcoming war, and you will also spare the people of Chi the horror of siege and threat of death. This is a sacrifice to you, your daughter and your family, but I think as a wise lord you will agree with me that this is a small price to pay to maintain peace in this region.

Waiting for you to make a wise decision, best wishes and highest salutation to you.

Dutifully yours, Duke West.

Soo Defender read the letter several times over. He began to realize that he was putting his welfare above that of the people of his fief. He told San Felicitous that after he consulted with his family, he would be ready to submit an answer the next morning. To show his good will, he sent both San Felicitous and his captive, Tsung Black Tiger, back to the encampment of Migratory Tiger.

Soo Defender went to see his family. His wife was in great distress, for she was afraid that her daughter, raised in tender care, must now face the unknown to serve an Emperor in the capacity of a courtesan in a palace far away. However, his daughter, Dar-Gee, was of a different mood. She told her parents: "I already heard and I knew what is the cause of the current conflict. I am distressed that lives have been lost on my behalf. You have raised me in comfort and educated me well. Now is time for me to repay you these favors. I have learned from the book of sages that one must sacrifice oneself for the sake of peace. Let me go. I will do my best to restore wisdom to Emperor Zoe."

"Brave girl! People of the city of Chi and I are indebted to you for your selfless sacrifice! I am proud of you. I am sorry that my power cannot stop what is about to befall on you. I will personally escort you to the city of Morning Song. Be prepared to leave tomorrow."

The next day the party left as scheduled. However, Soo Defender did not realize that he was to lose his filial, thoughtful, and selfless daughter Dar-Gee forever, even before their arrival at the capital. Destiny had already been cast.

3. Dar-Gee

Upon returning to the camp of Tsung Migratory Tiger, Black Tiger angrily reproached his brother. "You portrayed Soo Defender as a traitor who defied the imperial order of Emperor Zoe, but you did not tell me the content of the imperial order, nor did you tell me the truth of the reason for his disobedience. You are a liar. You should be ashamed of yourself. You should have at least made a genuine effort to resolve this matter peacefully first. Instead, you brought your army here to subjugate Soo Defender by force and you suffered defeat as well as casualties. Now, with the help of Duke West, this matter has been resolved peacefully. I will never have anything to do with you or your evil doings in the future. Before I go, I must repay Soo Defender for his kindness." Turning to the guards, he ordered: "Release Soo Loyal immediately." After Soo Loyal was released and sent back to the city of Chi, the Black Tiger led his 3000-strong Soaring Tiger army back to his reign, the fief of Tsao.

Meanwhile, inside the city of Chi, Dar-Gee bid her final farewell to her mother. Although she had a firm determination to serve Emperor Zoe for the sake of the people of Chi and her father, she could not help but feel an apprehension of sadness, a premonition that she would never see her mother again. From the cheeks of Dar-Gee flowed freely tears of sorrow, which were joined by those of her mother, who was about to see her daughter depart for a long and uncertain journey without any apparent prospect of reunion in the future. The pearly tear-drops on the red cheeks of Dar-Gee only sadly multiplied the already exquisite beauty of her lovely countenance. Finally, as the sun was rising high, the procession started.

War among Gods and Men

Using her telepathic power, Elf Fox had been watching the development of Emperor Zoe's court diligently. After Soo Defender was ordered to yield his daughter, she moved to the neighborhood of the city of Chi and she monitored the development of the war intensively. As the procession moved towards the city of Morning Song, she knew her opportunity had arrived.

Smoothly the procession reached the first official guesthouse without any incident. The guesthouse, operated by the central government, already had been warned of the arrival of Soo Defender and his daughter. Rooms were cleaned and meals prepared. After a long day's journey over rough roads, all went to sleep early.

Soo Defender could not sleep. Carrying his weapon, a semiflexible steel whip, he went around and inspected all suspicious spots until he was satisfied with the security of the compound. Still he could not sleep, so he went back to his room, reading a book under a flickering candle light.

Dar-Gee slept alone in a room adjacent to that of her maid attendants.

"This is a golden opportunity to carry out my mission," thought Elf Fox. Transfiguring herself into a small fly, she flew into Dar-Gee's room through a crack between the window frames. Transfiguring back to her fox form, she speedily suffocated Dar-Gee. After a faint struggle, Dar-Gee was dead. Immediately, Elf Fox exited her fox body and entered the body of Dar-Gee. From then on, the body of Dar-Gee was under the control of the Elf Fox. The Elf Fox became Dar-Gee and Dar-Gee was Elf Fox. The real Dar-Gee was dead.

The slight disturbance during the death of Dar-Gee alerted Soo Defender. He rushed to Dar-Gee's room. At this moment, Dar-Gee (Elf

Fox) cast a spell to her discarded fox body, changing it into a half-fox, half-human form, which then charged towards Soo Defender. With a single strike, using his steel whip against the assailant figure, Soo Defender cracked the skull of the half-fox half-human form. "Are you all right, my dear," Soo asked his daughter.

Dar-Gee answered wearily, "Yes, Father. I had a bad dream that a monster was about to attack me."

"It is over now, I already killed the monster. Go to sleep while I have this mess cleaned up."

The trip continued without further incident, and days later they reached the city of Morning Song. Soo Defender sent a messenger to the court to announce that he and his daughter had arrived.

Still angry at Soo Defender, Emperor Zoe wanted to put him to death immediately, an order that was quickly seconded by Yu the Adulator and Fei the Corrupt.

Without waiting for permission to speak, Premier Shang Yon rushed forward. "Your Majesty, you wanted Soo Defender's daughter. You now have his daughter. As an Emperor, you should keep your words and you should not punish Soo. You will lose your credibility among all lords!"

Emperor Zoe hesitated.

Seeing that they were against a well-respected statesman, the two evil officers immediately changed their tone: "May we suggest that you take a look at Soo's daughter Dar-Gee first? If she is as beautiful as claimed, you can then pardon Soo. Otherwise, the order of execution should be carried out." Emperor Zoe thus ordered that Soo's daughter be brought to his presence immediately.

39

With her delicate steps, her walk towards the Emperor was like a heavenly dance. With part of her pitch-black, long hair flowing around her neck to her back, and wearing a sad countenance like a pear blossom after a rain-storm, she slowly moved forward and knelt down facing the Emperor. She stopped at a distance far enough to show her respect for the Emperor but close enough for him to recognize her exquisite beauty. In compliance with the proper protocol of the court, she knelt down, before him, but raised her face just enough to let him have an almost complete view. With an almost musical tone, she begged him to pardon her father.

For a few moments, the Emperor was mesmerized by what he saw. When he came back to himself, he was more than pleased. Dar-Gee bore a likeness to the holographic image he had seen in the temple of Woman Wa. "My long search has come to a satisfactory end," thought the Emperor. Forgetting his status, he left his throne instantly to help Dar-Gee rise from her kneeling posture and asked her to sit by his side. Not only was Soo pardoned, he was also given a state banquet of celebration in his honor, together with an increase of his annual stipend. All conscientious court officials were unhappy that Emperor Zoe was putting his carnal desire above the interest of the country, but no one dared to say anything.

Dar-Gee had never expected that the bait would be so easily bitten. She carefully planned her next strategy to win favor from the Emperor. As the daughter of a lord and thus heavily protected from the outside world, she must show an initial shyness and modesty. She must not be too eager to use her tricks of charm. She must pretend to let her emotion and her experience slowly grow. In truth, she still had to learn how to use the beautiful body she had so newly acquired. A real human body was so much different from a transfigured human form. There were so many delicate qualities of a human body that she still had to experience and to learn how to use. Now she understood why the rewards Lady Woman Wa had promised her and her elf companions were real human bodies. A human body was definitely superior to her animal form. She began to enjoy her new experience and her new job.

Figure I- 4. The Shy Dar-Gee

War among Gods and Men

The court was adjourned almost immediately following Dar-Gee's appearance, as Emperor Zoe was eager to return to his residential palace with his new possession. Still shy from her first experience in the court, Dar-Gee kept her head down as she rode with the Emperor on a sedan chair moving slowly towards the residential ward of the palace. Occasionally she peeped at the surroundings of the palace, and only in her boldest moments did she dare a glance at the Emperor, who sat next to her with his eyes transfixed on her.

Each time his eyes met hers, the Emperor could not help smiling with a pride and a sense of triumph as if to tell the icon of Woman Wa that finally he had realized his dream. He gently took her hand and placed it on his lap.

Dar-Gee, having never been in contact with a unknown man in her life, blushed and sank her head down, giggling slightly.

After arrival at the residential palace, the Emperor spent the entire afternoon walking around with her, showing her the palace and his garden. He showed her his collection of exotic flora and flowers, his aquarium pond which was filled with water lilies of exquisite colors and shapes, and the little zoo which housed a collection of beautiful, unusual fauna, given to the Emperor as token of submission to his power by various feudal lords. Dar-Gee listened to the Emperor responsively but without uttering a word. No words needed to be spoken, as her countenance was filled with an unmistakable expression of admiration, appreciation and adoration which the Emperor could not have missed.

Soon darkness fell and a dinner banquet was set. Emperor Zoe devoured the well-prepared repast heartily, but Dar-Gee ate like a bird. She sipped wine gently, and the movements of her fingers were so delicate that the beautifully decorated food plates appeared to be a perfect setting for her performance. Emperor Zoe offered her the best from the plates, but Dar-Gee bit only a small portion. After sipping some more wine, her shyness melted away somewhat and her face was filled with curious and inquisitive looks as if she wanted to ask some questions. Finally her shyness disappeared to the extent that she could even gather enough courage to thank Emperor Zoe when another piece of food was placed on her plate. The Emperor, having drunk several large cups of wine already, was greatly pleased. The dinner lasted for several hours; Dar-Gee was a slow eater, but Emperor Zoe was in no hurry to hasten the completion of the meal. He already had won his prey and he enjoyed watching her almost every seemingly exalted and pleasing movement.

Finally the dinner was over. As was the custom, she had to be bathed first before she was allowed to be approached by the Emperor. She was brought by ladies-in-waiting to the bath room, which was a large room equipped with a fairly large sunken tub in the middle, surrounded in its walls by shelves stocked with a supply of bath items in an abundant variety. Emperor Zoe wanted to stay to watch her taking her first bath, but Dar-Gee refused to undress in front of him. An experienced lady-in-waiting whispered in the ear of the Emperor the suggestion that he should recede to a neighboring room where he could still peep through curtains. After Emperor Zoe left, ladies-in-waiting helped Dar-Gee undress. First the colorful silk rope which was used as a belt was untied, then the beautiful robe she wore in the morning in the court was unwrapped, exposing another translucent silk robe which was her undergarments. The mystery of a naked beauty behind the translucent screen reminded Emperor Zoe of the thin veil covering the exquisitely beautiful icon of Lady Goddess Woman Wa. He extremely aroused.

Figure I- 5. Dar-Gee taking bath

The translucent silk robe was removed next and with the help of ladies-in-waiting Dar-Gee stepped into the tub. Gently and expertly two ladies-in-waiting bathed her. First her long hair was curled up over her head and kept in place with a long jade needle. Then a soft cloth soaked with extracts of a natural soap seed, mixed with perfumes, was rubbed around her neck, her breasts, her arms, her legs and her underside. This done, another water-soaked cloth was used to rinse her and to wash away the soapy mixture. The gentle procedure of bathing was repeated over her entire body. Finally she was helped out of the bathtub while the two ladies-in-waiting dried her with towels. As she stood there, completely naked, Emperor Zoe could not believe his eyes at the delicate texture of her skin, the well-formed breasts, the gentle and slightly folded arms, the beautiful proportion of her body, the pitch-black hair curled and kept in place by a jade needle, and the daintily shy expression on the extremely pretty face.

Finally she was rubbed with an ointment all over her body, giving a delightful fragrance. A loosely fitted silk robe was wrapped around her. The robe was bound with a silk rope tied with a simple knot that could be easily untied with a pull. This was to be her nightgown. She was now ready for the Emperor.

Another lady-in-waiting guided her to the sleeping chamber of the Emperor, who was already waiting impatiently. As soon as she came to the vicinity of the bed, Emperor Zoe stood up and greeted her.

Taking her gently by her arm to the edge of the large bed, he said, "My beautiful fairy, your beauty is beyond words of description. Please sit down."

Shyly, without saying a word, she sat. Again she sank her head down, as if to avoid the Emperor. He gently lifted it. He started to kiss her, first around her neck, then at the back of her ear, then at her lips. Dar-Gee blushed. A beautiful shade of redness filled her face. As he forced his tongue into her mouth, she first resisted slightly but quickly gave in. She soon offered the Emperor her tongue. As he kissed her and she kissed him, he began to disrobe her.

Without resisting him, Dar-Gee melted in his arms and said softly in a sweet and pleading tone: "Your Majesty Emperor, please excuse me for my inexperience and please be gentle..."

War among Gods and Men

In her animal form, she had done this many, many times before. However, as her newly-acquired human body was being used for the first time, even as an experienced elf, Dar-Gee could not bear the initial pain of penetration, and she moaned. As her pain quickly subsided, she began to enjoy her new experience with a human body. This experience was so much different. This was so exquisite, and so fulfilling. As the Emperor continued to thrust his body against hers, she could feel the exchange of emotion between her and the Emperor. She embraced Emperor Zoe, tightly and emotionally. She moved her hands around him, probing every part of his body. For the first time in millennia she learned about love, an experience unique to the human race. As animals it had been an instinct, whose sole purpose was to propagate the species. There was much more in this than a mere propagation of race. She was elated, she was exhilarated, she was aroused, and she experienced the fullness of excitement. To be a human was much more precious a quality, an asset, than she had ever dreamed of before. She suddenly realized what kind of prize she had won. She was not the captive of Emperor Zoe; Emperor Zoe was her captive. She must continue to keep him her captive. He was hers, exclusively hers, and no one could take him away from her.

Both were completely exhausted from the invigorating act, to her, a new experience as a human, to him, the fulfillment of a dream as well as a wish. Both slept late. The Emperor ignored several wake-up calls by his attendants to get up and ready himself to open the daily court session. Finally, at noon, a messenger was sent to the court to inform all the officers who had waited all morning, since the first rays of the sun struck the city, to go home. The Emperor had proclaimed that there was nothing of importance that needed to be discussed that day.

Having been exposed to the quality of a human body and having learned its abilities, Dar-Gee was instantly addicted to the pleasure it could bring her. Being an experienced elf, she combined her charm and her animal sexual instincts in combination with her exquisite body to please Emperor Zoe. After her first taste of human love, she orchestrated her animal instinct and her newly-acquired human experience into a charm that Emperor Zoe had never experienced in his life, nor could he resist.

Countless women had, more or less under orders, submitted their bodies to the Emperor for his pleasure, but there had never been one who had responded with the same intensity of desire and love as this one. He, too, learned about love. This was the first time that he had experienced the sensation of being loved. It was equally a new experience to Emperor Zoe as it was to Dar-Gee.

She quickly learned how to use her shyness to arouse the Emperor, she also learned how to use her bold desire to please the Emperor. Soon court sessions were no longer held. Night after night, orgies went on and on. Official documents from the 800 feudal lords piled up high, waiting for action from an Emperor who no longer showed any interest in the affairs of the country. Two months passed by, and not a single official dared to disturb the Emperor from his orgies with Dar-Gee.

Finally three high officials, Premier Shang Yon, Vice Premier Bee Gahn, and Chief of Officers Mei Po decided to bring Emperor Zoe back to his senses. They rang all the signal gongs and banged all the signal drums in the palace to arouse the attention of the Emperor to come to the court to commence a court session that had been overdue almost since the arrival of Dar-Gee. Under the pressure of these officers, Emperor Zoe reluctantly left his residential palace to go to the court.

War among Gods and Men

Looking at the height of several piles of documents that needed to be reviewed, and being fatigued by nights and nights of orgies, drinking and feasting, Emperor Zoe was immediately discouraged and he instantly expressed his desire to terminate the court session almost as soon as it was forced upon him. Premier Shang Yon pleaded with the Emperor to stay on to take care of at least some urgent matters, but Emperor Zoe kept pushing things off, citing that Shang Yon and other officials could make the decisions on his behalf. While they were disagreeing in the court, a guard at the Gate of Noon reported that a traveling Taoist claiming to be a demigod wished to see Emperor Zoe.

A demigod, known by his Taoist name Son of Clouds, had happened to pass by the city of Morning Song during one of his frequent over-the-sky treks. Finding the city enshrouded in an elfin smog, he decided to investigate. He traced the elfin smog to the palace, so after some preparations he descended in front of the Gate of Noon and asked to be admitted to see Emperor Zoe.

Wishing to divert the argument between himself and Premier Shang Yon, the Emperor readily granted the request of the Taoist. In a few moments Son of Clouds entered into the court. He wore a turquoise colored scarf over his head and a robe decorated with astrological symbols and Taoist talismans. Carrying a bamboo basket which was covered with a piece of cloth on one arm and holding on the other a holy duster, which symbolically conveyed the intention to dust away all worldly temptations to elucidate the truth of the universe, he glided effortlessly towards the Emperor without any apparent foot motion. With a typical Taoist salutation of moving his fingers to emulate a kowtow but without actually submitting himself to the ground as was usually done, Son of Clouds approached the Emperor with a perfunctory greeting: "This humble Taoist hereby salutes the great Emperor."

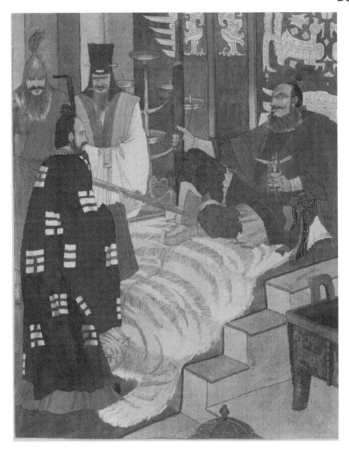

Figure I- 6. Son of Clouds and Emperor Zoe

Emperor Zoe was both impressed and annoyed at the carefree spirit and the impudent manner of Son of Clouds. Thought Emperor Zoe: "This Taoist, though normally outside my reign because of his vow to give up all worldly enjoyments, pleasures, honors, and possessions, and living in a cavern in a remote mountain beyond my reach, nevertheless is now in my court and thus under my dominion. I must punish him for his insolence.... Wait! I must not be rash. If I do so without a cause, my

49

officers will certainly remonstrate me for unjustifiably punishing him because I have no disposition of tolerance. Let me ask him some questions and let me hear his answers first." So the Emperor said, almost equally rudely: "Where do you, Taoist, come from?"

"I come from clouds and water."

"This is really an unusual answer," thought Emperor Zoe. Without even thinking, he responded with a rhetoric query: "Where are clouds and water?"

Son of Clouds did not answer directly, instead he recited two verses:

> As white clouds wander,
> My heart floats aloft.
> Like water,
> My aspiration flows, east or west.

The Emperor, being an intelligent person, suddenly realized that this was no ordinary Taoist. He quickly responded with another rhetoric: "When clouds disperse, and water parches away, whither shalt thou go?"

"When clouds disperse, the moon shall appear bright; when water parches away, brilliant pearls shall abound."

The Emperor, satisfied with the conversation, granted Son of Clouds a seat.

Without thanking the Emperor according to the usual court protocol, Son of Clouds merely sat down and started to sing the verses:

> The Son of Heaven only knows his eminence,
> He knows not the supreme knowledge
> Of three Sects and their origin.

"What is the supreme knowledge of the three Sects and their origin?" Emperor Zoe had become curious now.

"Let me sing a song for you."

A devoted Taoist am I.
Never bow to the vanity of Lords,
Never submit to the power of Kings.
I only succumb to the wisdom of Tao.
Reside in a cavern,
Sequester in a remote mountain,
Harbor a simple life.
I wear no hat or shoes,
Stars and the sky are my cover,
Flowers and grass my cushion.
Demigods I befriend,
Taoist companions are my chessmates.
Taking a small hoe,
Off to gather herb medicine I go.
I save my fellow humans wherever I come.
When I am hungry,
I pace to cities to beg,
But I only take enough to keep me alive.
Walking barefoot,
Or wearing a pair of straw sandals,
I dance steps according to Tao,
To remove elfin smogs in the world of dust,
Or to show the preponderance of the three Sects.
Two steps forward and then a side step,
A spell or two I cast, then I wait
For my incantation to come true.

> *Of the three Sects,*
> *The most supreme is their wisdom of Tao.*

"You are great," said the Emperor. "I already feel I am above this world of dust, and all worldly wealth passes me by like floating clouds. Where do you come from? Why do you want to see me?"

"I am Son of Clouds, residing in the Cavern Jade Column in Mount End South. As I was gathering herb medicine from high mountain peaks, I saw an elfin smog enshrouding the city of Morning Song. I traced this smog to your palace. I am here to eliminate it."

"You are wrong," laughed the Emperor. "Nothing could have penetrated the walls of my palace without my knowledge."

"Of course. If you know what is evil, evil will not be with you." Son of Clouds also laughed in return. "But evil can be disguised. Let me give you a device I have prepared to eliminate this elf." Uncovering his basket, Son of Clouds took out a wooden sword carved from pine wood, which was inscribed all over with Taoist talismans. Presenting it to Emperor Zoe, Son of Clouds requested the sword be hung at the interface gate between the residential palace where Dar-Gee resided and the main hall of the court where they now stood.

Emperor Zoe ordered the sword hung as directed by Son of Clouds. "How much should I compensate you," he asked.

"Nothing," responded Son of Clouds.

The Emperor insisted. "With your magical power, I shall be greatly benefited by your presence. Why do you have to cloister your ability and secret your name in the wildness? Please come to serve in my court. Just name your price."

"I am extremely grateful to Your Majesty for your offer." This was the first time Son of Clouds had used this complimentary title to address the Emperor. "But I am a wild man happily residing in the environment of untamed nature. My wants are few and my style of life is not compatible with that of the court. I walk barefoot, but I live to my heart's desire. I can sleep until the sun is high in the sky, and whenever I like, I trek mountains and ford streams in ragged clothes. When I am tired, I sleep on high peaks. In my dreams I attend banquets of deities, eating celestial food and drinking nectar among gods. What more shall I need? I bid you farewell now."

"Bid Son of Clouds farewell," commanded the Emperor. All officials of the court murmured good wishes. A basket of gold and silver ingots was presented to Son of Clouds, but he declined to take any. After making a Taoist salutation to the Emperor to bid his final farewell, he glided swiftly out of the palace and soon disappeared among the clouds.

Feeling tired, Emperor Zoe terminated the court session right after the departure of Son of Clouds. Not finding his favorite Dar-Gee to greet him when he went back to the residential part of the palace, he went directly to her room. To his surprise he found his beloved concubine lying in bed sick, her face whitened and lips lifeless. "What happened? This morning when we parted, you were as beautiful as a flower. Now you are withered. How did you become sick?"

"I was strolling towards the court to wait for your return, then suddenly I saw a sword hanging high at the gate. As I approached, this sword flew down to attack me. I had to run back to the palace and I am now scared to death. I do not think I will live long. I am not afraid of death but I regret not being able to serve you further and enjoy your company and your love. I am dying now and I bid you my last farewell." Dar-Gee spoke feebly, in an almost inaudible, shaky tone.

"It must be the sword of Son of Clouds! He told me there was an elf in the palace, but there are no elves! The sword is now killing my favorite girl." Turning to a nearby attendant, he ordered, "Remove the sword and burn it immediately."

The sword, being carved out of wood, burnt into ashes in no time. Son of Clouds, still in the vicinity of the city of Morning Song, sighed when he sensed the burning of the wooden sword he had given to Emperor Zoe. "I merely wanted to eliminate the elf to prolong the reign of the Shang dynasty. It looks like the end of the dynasty is unavoidable. Since I am already here, I may as well issue another warning to the regime." Taking a brush pen, he wrote the following verses on the wall of the residence of the Chief Imperial Astronomer:

> An Elfin smog now enshrouds the Palace,
> And a revolution is about to start in the West.
> Blood shall flow in the city of Morning Song,
> On the day of the third Celestial Stem,
> And the seventh Earthly Branch,
> In the first year of a new sexagenary cycle.

The next morning a few passersby discovered these verses and began to read them. They were puzzled by the cryptic message conveyed by the verses, so they discussed it among themselves. Soon a throng gathered and joined the discussion. The noise of the chitchat became louder and louder as one theory was put forward only to be dwarfed by another. Then the Chief Imperial Astronomer Du Yuansee, after carrying out a full night of observations, returned home and was aroused by the loud noise. He asked his attendants about the cause of the noise, and they reported that a Taoist had left verses on the wall but the message was cryptic, so the passersby were discussing the meaning of the verses.

The Chief Imperial Astronomer ordered the crowd dispersed and he went to the wall to read the writings himself. Du Yuansee could not understand the meaning of the cryptic lines either. He copied the verses on a piece of paper, then asked his attendants to wash away the writings. Alone in his study, he tried to decipher the enigmatic message. The day of the third Celestial Stem and the seventh Earthly Branch should be the ninth day of the third lunar month, or another sixty days beyond. What did it mean? He pondered and pondered. He speculated that it might be Son of Clouds who had left the verses, issuing an warning on an imminent danger to the country. He thought: "This Taoist Son of Clouds visited the Emperor, citing the presence of an elf in the palace. As a matter of fact, my observation of the heaven also indicated an unusual elfin nebulosity around the imperial constellation of Tze-Wei. This nebulosity appears to be related to the elfin smog that Son of Clouds talked about. Emperor Zoe has not attended his court for several months; he spends all his time in orgies with his new concubine Dar-Gee. She might be the source of this elfin smog and elfin nebulosity. All responsible officials of the court are concerned. As the Chief Imperial astronomer, maybe I should use this opportunity to draft a court communique to the Emperor warning him of the imminent danger."

After he finished the communique, he carried it himself to the court for presentation. To his delight he found that it was the turn of Premier Shang Yon to be in charge of reading all incoming documents. After presenting his salutation to the Premier, Du the Imperial Astronomer said: "Distinguished Premier and Statesman, last night as I observed the heaven I found a faint elfin nebulosity around the imperial constellation of Tze-Wei. As you know, the Emperor is now engaging in an orgy spree with his new concubine queen and he sinks himself deeply among wine and women. This country and the royal temple of Shang are now in grave danger. I have prepared a communique to the court warning him of this imminent danger. Would you please transmit this document to the Emperor for me?"

"As you know, the Emperor has not presided over court sessions for several months and it is difficult for me to relate your communique to him personally," responded Premier Shang Yon. "On the other hand, I can go with you to his residential palace to present this document to him. We can try to reason with him. Let's go."

Arriving at the residence palace, the duo was stopped by a guard. "This is the residential palace of the Emperor, don't you two know that you are not allowed here?"

"Of course I know, but please report that Premier Shang Yon is waiting to see His Majesty."

It was somewhat unusual for a court official to ask to see an emperor in his residential palace. "What is his purpose in coming here? It is highly irregular for him to come here directly. On the other hand, since he served two emperors before me with unquestioned loyalty and fealty, maybe he has something important to say. Let him in," Emperor Zoe ordered.

"What is the urgent matter that you want to see me about," the Emperor impatiently asked.

"The Imperial Astronomer Du Yuansee reported that during his observations last night he observed a faint elfin nebulosity around the imperial constellation of Tze-Wei. Du the Imperial Astronomer has been a loyal officer serving three generation of emperors, including you. Since in these days you do not come to court to take care of affairs of the

56

country, we decided, at the risk of offending Your Majesty, to come directly to you for action. A communique has been prepared."

"Let me take a look at his communique," Emperor Zoe said. The communication read:

To His Majesty of Ten Thousand Years and with all salutations!

This serf officer learned from his books that, when a country falters, elfin phenomena appear. Last night, your vassal observed the heaven diligently and saw a faint elfin nebulosity in the imperial constellation of Tze-Wei, and the position of this elfin nebulosity corresponds to the inner palace, near the imperial residence. Earlier, when you presided over the court, a Taoist demigod, Son of Clouds, warned you against an elf in your court. Ever since Soo Defender delivered you his daughter, you have not presided over many court sessions. Your loyal officers are disappointed and concerned. May this vassal beg Your Majesty to meet your officers more often, so that the peace and prosperity we are enjoying now can continue to thrive.

With all respects to Your Majesty,
Your serf officer Du Yuansee.

"His words are good and sincere. However, he mentioned Son of Clouds. Because of this damned Taoist, my beloved Dar-Gee nearly lost her beautiful life. Heaven blessed me that she recovered after I ordered the destruction of the wooden sword. Now he mentioned elfin smog in this palace. I do not want to have a repetition of the near disaster," thought the Emperor.

Ever since she had nearly lost her life because of the magic wooden sword of Son of Clouds, Dar-Gee had been on the lookout for possible dangers. She knew almost all the court officers were against her. After she had developed a taste of human love, she developed a taste for power, too. She saw the awe and fear commanded by the Emperor upon officers, upon attendants, upon ladies-in-waiting, and even upon his Queen Consort and other queens. She observed very carefully, and soon she learned how to manipulate the powers.

When the officers came, she exited the room and stayed behind a curtain, as it was against the normal protocol of the court for the Emperor's women to be in the presence of court officers. However, she monitored the conversation very attentively. She constantly watched the facial expressions of the Emperor, and she caught a few key words as he read the communique. She began to realize the severity of the matter. As the Emperor was reading the communication, a rage rose within Dar-Gee. "This old fool and stupid idiot! Because of that evil Taoist who called himself Son of Clouds, I nearly lost my life. I nearly lost the luxury of the palace and my human body. Now this old fool is arguing to persuade the Emperor to eliminate me. I must protect myself. To set an example, I must have him executed!" thought Dar-Gee.

She then lifted up the curtain and reentered the room. When Emperor Zoe saw her, without even thinking, he turned to Dar-Gee and said: "Du Yuansee mentioned an elf in the palace. Why?"

Dar-Gee took the communique and read it. In response to the question of the Emperor, she said, with a charming but determined tone, "We all know that Son of Clouds is a crackpot; he created rumors to destroy people's confidence in you. Du Yuansee furthered this groundless rumor." She then cast a look at the Imperial Astronomer. "Your country is strong and not faltering," she said deliberately. "However, if you do not stop rumors, then your country will really be faltering. I suggest that you execute this liar, lest more rumors should abound. Once rumors abound, your country and especially you will be in danger." She paused for a moment. Then she said to Emperor Zoe: "Execute him!"

Although Emperor Zoe had a miraculous physical strength, he was not particularly strong in his reasoning power. Indeed, he had been carefully guided throughout his earlier years of reign by loyal and capable officers like Shang Yon and the Imperial Teacher. After his acquisition of Dar-Gee, the Emperor had spent all his time indulging in pleasure-seeking activities, and he no longer wanted to hear words from those capable advisors whom he had listened to throughout his reign; now he wanted to enjoy the constant pour of sweet words of adulation and praise. "What a great opportunity to give these loquacious, self-righteous officers a good lesson," the Emperor thought.

Avoiding the eyes of Shang Yon, the Emperor ordered: "Dar-Gee is right! Good! Execute Du Yuansee immediately for promulgating wild rumors. After his execution his head shall be displayed in public to discourage future propagators of rumors."

Shang Yon pleaded with tears. "No! Please listen: Du Yuansee has been a loyal officer and he has served flawlessly three emperors, including you. He is only reporting to you what he saw in the heaven and if he does not report, he fails his duty and according to the laws of Shang, he will be punished. You cannot punish Du Yuansee for what he was ordered to do. It is easy to execute Du Yuansee, but Your Majesty will generate a fear among other court officers. Please pardon Du."

"No! I must follow the suggestion of my faithful Dar-Gee. I must stop all rumors and unwarranted criticisms." The Emperor refused to listen any further and he waved his attendants to escort Shang Yon out of the residence palace.

Du the Imperial Astronomer was already tied up and ready to be executed when Premier Shang Yon was escorted out. At this moment, the Chief of Staff Officers Mei Po dropped in. Startled at the imminent execution Du Yuansee, he asked Premier Shang Yon for the reason. After he learned what had happened, he insisted that Premier Shang Yon should accompany him to see the Emperor immediately, to try to reason with the Emperor.

The Emperor was still angry. The Chief of Staff Officers Mei Po said to him in a pleading and remonstrating tone: "Your Majesty is violating laws laid down by the founding emperor of Shang and you have ignored the dictums of sages. Du the Imperial Astronomer is an honest, loyal and faithful officer who consummates the responsibility bestowed to his rank by the founding emperor of Shang. You must release Du the Imperial Astronomer immediately."

Dar-Gee intercepted: "Your Majesty, you do not have to follow dictums of sages. Your words are dictums and you are the law. You must punish this insolent man."

"I am the law and my words are dictums." Emperor Zoe repeated the words of Dar-Gee. He then added, "You are a co-conspirator of the Imperial Astronomer Du. However, because of your previous valuable service to me, I shall only banish you from the court to the countryside as a menial laborer."

Dar-Gee said, "No! We must make Mei Po an example to the rest of the court officers and to the people of the country. Mei Po must be punished by death, but not now. I will devise a method of execution that will henceforth discourage the remaining court officials and people of this country from criticizing you, inciting rumors against me, and believing in the groundless elfin smog theory. Bring me your engineers."

The court engineers came. Dar-Gee gave detailed instruction for the construction of an execution machine. It would be known by the name of Pao-Lo. It was a twenty-foot long bronze tube, with three chambers in which an abundant quantity of burning charcoal could be placed. During operation, the bronze tube would be heated to red-hot. The prisoner to be executed would then be tied to the bronze tube via iron chains. Within moments, the body of the prisoner would be rendered to ashes. Dar-Gee ordered that twenty such machines be built and placed in the meeting hall of the palace.

Realizing that the situation was no longer under his control, Premier Shang Yon approached the Emperor, begging him to allow him to retire. "I have already served three emperors with loyalty. I am old now, my bones are bending, my eyesight is failing, and my muscle is growing weak. May I ask Your Majesty to allow me to retire to my country home to live the rest of my life as a private citizen?"

"Indeed you are a loyal officer. I am sad to see you go, but I see that you are determined to retire. I shall grant you a life time pension and an estate for you to live comfortably on for the rest of your life. Attendants! Prepare a three-day banquet of farewell for Premier Shang Yon."

All the court officials were sad to see Shang Yon, a just, merciful and competent statesman, leave. They walked with him to the Ten Li Pavilion, a traditional place to speak the final words of farewell. Seven high officers, including the two elder brothers of Emperor Zoe, sobbed: "You are returning to your home village with honor and glory, but how could you give up your responsibility to your country?"

"My usefulness is over now. At my age, I do not mind dying for my country, but my death would be just a meaningless sacrifice. Let me drink to your health. I promise I will not forget you. We shall meet again." With these words, Premier Emeritus Shang Yon departed, trotting his horse slowly towards his village.

The Pao-Lo execution machines were completed and were installed as specified. Emperor Zoe ordered the prisoner Mei Po brought in. "Do you know what this is," asked the Emperor.

"No, I do not know."

"It will burn your bones out, but it will burn your tongue first to punish you for your criticism against me."

Knowing that his fate was sealed, Mei Po suddenly became very brave and his voice became very angry and very determined. "You are not torturing me to death, you are torturing your country and the Shang dynasty to death. Do you think you can silence your critics by torture? I do not pity my fate, but I pity the fate of this country."

The execution was carried out, and within moments Mei Po was reduced to nothing but ashes. All the court officials were stunned by the cruelty of the execution of a loyal and honest officer. No one dared say anything.

Emperor Zoe was very pleased. Premier Shang Yon had already volunteered to leave his service. He had silenced two of the most outspoken critics of the court. He went back with Dar-Gee to the residential palace continuing their activities of drinking, feasting and orgies. "From now on, no one under my reign will dare criticize me. What a great way to silence my critics!" the Emperor concluded.

4. The Queen Dethroned by Murder

After watching the torturous death of Mei Po in cold blood at the instrument of fire designed by Dar-Gee, Emperor Zoe said to her: "My beauty, you have supplied me with an extremely effective method to mute my critics. From now on no officer shall dare utter a word of objection; even the most eloquent will stutter. What a great way to rule my country! Let's rejoice." Turning around, he said, "Attendants! Prepare a banquet to celebrate the brilliant work of my beauty!" So off to Sou Sian Palace (Longevity Palace) they went, where the two feasted amidst music and dancing.

This was around eight o'clock by our reckoning. Normally by this hour, unless there was a special occasion or festivity, most activities in the palace would have ceased in order to allow palace servants a rest and to prepare for another day, which was usually filled with busy activities. Thus the night was quiet in most parts of the palace except Longevity Palace. While the Emperor and Dar-Gee indulged themselves in merrymaking, the sound of loud music, dancing and laughter permeated the still air of the night and reached the Middle Palace, where Queen Consort Jiang resided. She was not asleep yet, so she asked: "What is this noise?"

"There is a celebration in Longevity Palace. The sound is from the music and dancing lauding the completion of a new torture machine and its first use to execute a court officer." An attendant then narrated the whole story of the torturous death of the Chief of Staff Officers Mei Po to Queen Consort.

War among Gods and Men

Queen Consort sighed. "I have heard numerous reports recently that the Emperor has taken quite a lot of ill advice from Dar-Gee. He is putting his throne at risk if he applies this kind of cruel and unjustified punishment to kill his loyal officers merely because they offer advice that displeases him. I must remonstrate with him, asking him to restrain himself and to place affairs of this country above his activities of merrymaking." As if she wanted to convince herself, she continued: "No, I am not jealous of his other queens; I have accepted his privilege to have more than one woman other than myself. I accepted my duty as Queen Consort when I became his queen, to place my duty to my country above all. I have submitted myself to the system. My chief concern is the welfare of this country and of the future of Shang dynasty." She then spoke to her attendants. "Prepare my sedan chair for passage to Longevity Palace."

The procession arrived at Longevity Palace shortly. Informed that the Queen Consort had arrived, with his drunken eyes half-closed, Emperor Zoe said, "I have not seen my Queen for some time. It is opportune that she chooses this occasion to come; I will ask her to enjoy with me the music and dance of Dar-Gee." The Emperor then dispatched Dar-Gee to welcome Queen Consort. After the usual protocols were exercised, Emperor Zoe announced to the joyous party: "Queen Consort just arrived. Let the party continue. Dar-Gee, sing a song and accompany your song with a dance to entertain the Queen!"

Dar-Gee left her seat and stepped to the open space in the middle of the hall. Court musicians then played a soft, pleasant and seductive music. After a short of overture, Dar-Gee began her performance. She danced gently, heavenly, gracefully, and erotically.

Queen Consort had never seen this kind of dance nor heard this kind of music before. It was heavenly, but at what cost! she thought.

64

She was in an ambivalent mood. Indeed, Dar-Gee was talented. But what was this music and dance used for? To celebrate the creation of a torture machine and its initiation by inflicting horrendous pain and cruel death upon an honest and loyal officer of the court, for no other guilt than his honest remonstration with his emperor for a good cause! Queen Consort sighed, and spoke in a sad tone to the Emperor. "So this is how my Emperor has spent his days and nights. What has become of your responsibility to your country, your ancestral emperors, and Shang dynasty? Your Majesty should spend more of his time looking after affairs of his country, and only in his spare time should he indulge in luxuries of the world like these." As she was finishing speaking, she pointed her finger at the court musicians and Dar-Gee.

"My dear Queen, you do not understand," replied Emperor Zoe. "Life is short, the present is but an instant and time flows like water in a river, never to return. If I do not catch the present moment to enjoy myself, soon my life will be over. The exquisite quality of dances and songs by Dar-Gee is rare. Be merry while you may – why do you look so sad at the dainty sight and rare sound?"

"The dances and songs of Dar-Gee are indeed rare and dainty, but not precious."

"Why? What could be more dainty and more precious?"

Queen Consort Jiang replied: "As a woman who is married to the system, I must display my loyalty to you, to this country and to the people. I have read from the writings of sages that a good emperor must rank virtue over material wealth and must distance himself from adulation and skin-deep beauty. These are the qualities of an emperor of the people. You just asked me what is more dainty and more precious. Daintiness and treasure in the heaven are the sun, the moon, and the stars. Those on the earth are the fields that produce the five grains to feed the people, the gardens and forests that enrich them. The treasure of a household is its harmony and filial offspring. The treasures of a country are her contented people, and the assets of a court are its loyal and righteous officers. If Your Majesty continues to disregard your duty as an emperor to indulge in lewd music and erotic dances, orgies and decadence, to execute your loyal officers because of their honest opinions and advice against your selfish wishes, your throne and the Imperial Ancestral Shrine of Shang are in grave danger. The words of women of pleasure command no authority and respect, yet you have replaced the voices of loyal dissent in your court with these coos. I, a woman of the court as well as your Queen, sincerely wish that Your Majesty will reform, to distance yourself from adulatory and corrupt officers, to refrain yourself from indulging in drinking, orgies and erotic performances, and to pay more attention to affairs of the country. If you do so, people will soon forgive your past misgivings, mistakes and errors, and their loyalty shall return. I may have infracted upon the proper protocol in expressing frankly my criticism of you and I ask you to forgive me for my impudence. However, I sincerely wish that you will correct yourself of your misbehavior and pay more attention to business affairs of this country. The country and her people will rejoice. Now I bid you good night." She stood up and left.

The drunken Emperor Zoe was mad. "Out of kindness I asked her to join me to enjoy the heavenly dance of Dar-Gee, in return she criticized me for my enjoyment of life. If I could, I would like to kill her right away, here," thought the Emperor. As he was thinking, his facial expression became more and more vicious. None of the facial expressions escaped the careful scrutiny of Dar-Gee. Finally he turned to her and commanded: "Continue to dance, Dar-Gee."

Dar-Gee was overjoyed at the change of mood of Emperor Zoe, but she hid her joy. "What a great opportunity!" she thought. She immediately responded to Emperor Zoe's command, "No, I must not dance any more since the mistress of the palace criticized me for my inappropriateness."

"Nonsense! I am the master of the palace. If Queen Consort continues to criticize me or you, I will find a way to get rid of her and make you the Queen! Continue your dance," the drunken Emperor said casually. However, even though these words were spoken casually out of his momentary anger, the statement left a strong imprint in the mind of Dar-Gee that she *could* become Queen Consort. As she continued her dancing and singing, she kept on deliberating the idea in her mind. The joy-making activities continued until dawn.

A few months passed by. During the autumn moon festival, according to the prevailing court protocol, other queens would go to the Middle Palace to present their greetings to Queen Consort. Queen Jiang was attended by the two queens Huang (the sister of Huang Flying Tiger) and Yang when Dar-Gee came to pay her the ceremonial visit as a part of the ritual. Queen Jiang was told that the visitor was Dar-Gee. She then remembered the incident in Longevity Palace and she thought this might be a good occasion to reprimand her. She said to Dar-Gee: "The Emperor spends day and night in orgies with you, indulging himself in worldly pleasures. He has stopped tending affairs of the country. You have not uttered a word to encourage him to go back to his duties. Instead you continued to join him and encouraged him in his pleasure-seeking activities. You are his new favorite. For the sake of the country you should use your charm to persuade the Emperor to pay more attention to affairs of the country. I am not jealous of you, but you should know your place in this palace – the country needs a ruler who

67

actively pays attention to affairs of the country, and not one who indulges himself in pleasure-seeking activities. I will punish you if you do not reform. Now leave."

This reprimand was made in the presence of Queens Huang and Yang. Although Queen Jiang did not mean to embarrass Dar-Gee in front of other queens, nevertheless Dar-Gee felt greatly humiliated, especially in the presence of two other queens. She vowed vengeance as she left in disgrace. As she returned to her palace, a lady-in-waiting, Hsiang, who was also a court musician and often accompanied Dar-Gee in her singing and dancing, greeted her. Hsiang noticed that Dar-Gee was upset and asked why. Dar-Gee related her encounter with Queen Consort, and vowed vengeance. "Queen Consort made me lose face in front of the two other queens. I must avenge this insolence."

Hsiang consoled her. "The Emperor promised some time ago that one day he will make you his Queen Consort. Once you are Queen Consort, you can easily avenge your embarrassment."

"No, it is not that easy. Queen Jiang must be overthrown, but how can this be done? I need a perfect scheme and some one must carry out the scheme. Can you help me?"

"We are all women residing inside this gigantic palace." Hsiang evaluated the situation. "Any scheme we devise may not work because we are not familiar with the system and we do not have the confidence of court officers. Besides, we do not have anyone who will do the legwork. In my humble opinion, we must invite an officer of the court to help us. If we have outside help, we can certainly succeed."

After pondering for a while, Dar-Gee agreed. "Your idea is fine, but usually no court officer is allowed inside the residential palace. Further, even if he gets in here, there are so many attendants and anyone can leak out our secret. How can we get an officer whom we can trust into the palace to discuss this matter with him?"

Hsiang thought for a moment, then suggested: "I have noticed that the Emperor likes and trusts Fei Chung. He is known for his ability to devise schemes. Tomorrow the Emperor is scheduled to inspect his royal garden. You can send a message to Fei Chung to come to the palace. I can prepare an unsigned order and deliver it to him, to ask him to devise a scheme to overthrow Queen Jiang. You can promise him a promotion and a doubling of his salary if he succeeds. He will like that."

"What happens if he refuses my request and informs Queen Consort or the Emperor of my plan?" Dar-Gee said.

"Don't worry. In the first place, it will be an unsigned order so in the case the scheme was discovered, you can deny any knowledge. He knows I am your trusted attendant, so if I tell him that although this order is unsigned, it comes directly from you, he will believe the authenticity of this order and he will discreetly carry out your instructions, because he knows your power. Secondly, it was he who recommended you to come to the palace in the first place. I know his personality. I am sure he will not turn down this job provided there is an adequate reward. Besides, he is a favorite of the Emperor," Hsiang replied.

"Good, carry on," Dar-Gee told her.

The next day, Hsiang forged an imperial order to summon Fei Chung to the residential palace of Dar-Gee. Hsiang handed Fei Chung a sealed envelope and said, "Here is a secret order from Lady Dar-Gee. If you can accomplish this task, you will be amply rewarded. You must not reveal this order to anyone."

After Fei Chung returned to his residence, he opened the envelope in a secured room. After he read the order, a fear suddenly descended upon him. "Queen Jiang is the official wife of the Emperor. Further, her father is Duke East, Jiang Huan-Chu, ruling East Ru and he is the commander-in-chief of an army one hundred thousand strong with hundreds of fierce warriors. Her eldest son Jiang Wen-Huan is a warrior known for his ferocity. I will be in great danger if they find out I scheme against them. On the other hand, if I do not carry out her secret order to overthrow the Queen, all Dar-Gee needs to do is to say something bad about me to the Emperor during their moments of intimacy, then my head will roll." After a whole day of pondering, Fei Chung still could not come up with a perfect scheme.

At it happened, while sitting in the main hall of his house sipping tea and pondering, one of his servants passed by. This servant, of muscular build, was of the name Jiang Quann, of the same surname as Queen Jiang, and he came from East Ru, the fief of Duke East. An idea suddenly occurred to Fei Chung. He summoned Jiang Quann to his study and said, "How long have you been in my household?"

"Seven years, My Lord."

"Are you loyal to me?"

"Absolutely. I am ready to die for you at any time."

"Very good, you need not die. Here is an errand you can do for me. I will guarantee you absolute safety. You will be amply rewarded with wealth and fortune after the mission is accomplished. Now do this ..." Fei the Corrupt whispered his command to Jiang Quann.

One day during the usual feasting, amidst dancing and music, Emperor Zoe appeared to be bored. Seizing this opportunity, Dar-Gee suggested: "Because of me, you have been neglecting affairs of the

70

country. I suggest you call a court session tomorrow morning to tend to affairs. This should satisfy those court officers who complained that you have neglected your duties."

Emperor Zoe was surprised at this suggestion, but consented right away. "This is great advice! Your quality surpasses that of all queens of sage kings I have read about!" So a court session was scheduled for the next morning.

The next morning, as the procession marched towards the hall where the court session was to be held, an armed man holding a sword dashed out from behind a bush and charged towards Emperor Zoe, shouting, "Under the order of my mistress, I shall execute this immoral emperor." Needless to say he was immediately subdued and arrested. Emperor Zoe was extremely angry that any assassin could have so easily sneaked inside the palace, which was heavily guarded. When he came to the main hall of the court, he immediately announced that an assassin had just been captured inside the palace. The Emperor said, "Who was in charge of security of the palace last night?"

General Ru Brave responded: "It was I, and I personally led the security force to inspect the entire palace ground. I did not find anything unusual. Let me question him ..."

Before Ru Brave could finish, Fei the Corrupt interceded. "Your serf Fei Chung will volunteer to take charge of the inquisition of the assassin. I will find out who is the architect behind this hideous act of treason."

In no time Fei the Corrupt obtained a confession from the alleged assassin and he reported back to the Emperor. "I have found out the truth, but I do not dare to report it to you."

"Why?"

"You must pardon me first before I dare reveal the mastermind behind the plot against you."

"You have my pardon. Now go ahead," the Emperor said.

"The assassin confessed that he is a member of the household guards of Duke East, Jiang Huan-Chu, and he was under the order of Queen Jiang to assassinate you. The purpose of their plot is to institute Duke East as the Emperor after you are dead. By your own blessing, the assassination plot failed. I have obtained a full confession. Please summon all officers and royal relatives to your court to discuss this matter."

In a great rage, Emperor Zoe slapped his palm hard at a tea table on his side and shouted, "She is my wife and she plotted against my life! This is a domestic affair. There is no need to consult anyone. Ask Queen Huang to come here to take charge of the investigation." After giving the order, the Emperor went back to Longevity Palace.

In the meeting hall, all the officers who had come to attend the court session discussed among themselves this rather incredible plot. A few believed that there was a plot, but many more expressed their doubts. A senior officer, Yang Zen, spoke to Huang Flying Tiger in private. "The reputation of Queen Jiang is flawless. She is virtuous, kind, benevolent, and she rules the palace with a good conscience. According to my humble opinion, there must be some unusual intricacies which we do not know. This assassination attempt must be a plot against the Queen."

Huang Flying Tiger agreed. He announced to all: "My fellow officers, do not go home yet. Stick around. Let us hear what comes out of the investigation of Queen Huang."

The Queen Dethroned by Murder

A messenger delivered an imperial order to Queen Jiang. The message read:

Decreed as follows: Queen Consort reigns in the Middle Palace, supports the Emperor, enjoys the grandeur of the world. She must consider her position an endowment from heaven. Instead, she contrives treason, as follows: She orders an armed warrior Jiang Quann to attempt to assassinate the Emperor. Because of blessing from heaven, the assassin was caught right away at the spot. He was questioned and he confessed that Queen Consort conspired with her father and ordered him to assassinate the Emperor. The Emperor orders this messenger to arrest Queen Consort and to deliver her to West Palace to be questioned by Queen Huang.

After this imperial order was read, Queen Jiang was almost paralyzed by the shock. She cried loudly, "Grievance! Miscarriage of justice! It must be the plot of a devious scoundrel to frame me! As the Queen of this palace I have always been industrious, I have ruled internal affairs with justice, care and diligence. I have not done a single wrong. Now without finding the truth the Emperor has charged me with this hideous crime of plotting his assassination and he wants to send me to West Palace to face trial of a crime that I never even dreamed of!"

The messenger consoled her: "There must be some mistake, Your Highness. Please follow me to West Palace. Queen Huang is a fair and just lady. She will not allow any miscarriage of justice."

In tears, Queen Jiang followed the imperial messenger to West Palace. Queen Huang placed the imperial message on an offering table. On behalf of the Emperor, she began her duty as a prosecutor to question Queen Jiang. Queen Huang said: "This is an extremely serious charge. You must tell the truth!"

War among Gods and Men

The Queen knelt down in front of the offering table and said: "I have been a faithful wife and a loyal subject. Now some one set up a scheme to frame me for a grotesque crime. You, Queen Huang, have known me for a long time. Please use your judgment, help me and vindicate me!"

Queen Huang said: "This imperial order charges you with treason, that you ordered Jiang Quann to assassinate the Emperor so that you can seize the throne for your father, Duke East, Jiang Huan-Chu, that you intended to topple the dynasty of Shang. This is extremely grave. If the charges are true, not only have you betrayed the Emperor, you also have severed the husband-wife relationship!"

Queen Consort Jiang replied: "My dear sister, I am Duke East's daughter. My father is the ruler of East Ru and the head of two hundred lords. He has the highest rank possible in the country. In addition, he is a royal relative of the highest distinction. I am Queen Consort, whose rank is higher than that of the four dukes. I have two sons, and the eldest one has been designated the crown prince. He shall succeed his father as the Emperor should such a day come. I shall then be the dowager Queen. I cannot achieve a higher position than my current one; even if my father were to become the Emperor, as his daughter, my position would be far below what I have now, much below that of the mother of an emperor. Why would I plot to kill my husband, the Emperor in reign? Although I am a woman, I am not that stupid not to realize the situation. I am wrongfully charged! Please vindicate my innocence! Further, there are eight hundred lords in this country. If I am punished for crimes that I did not commit, these lords shall revolt on my behalf. Please relate my message to the Emperor."

Queen Huang was convinced of the innocence of Queen Jiang. At this moment, another messenger came by asking for the result of the questioning. Queen Huang went with this second messenger to report to the Emperor.

"Has this criminal woman confessed yet," asked the Emperor.

Queen Huang replied: "Under your order I cross-examined Queen Jiang. I have found no substance in the charge against her. She is your Queen Consort and has served you many years as a virtuous wife, as an impeccable mistress of the palace. She bore two princes for you, and the eldest has been designated the crown prince. Eventually he will succeed you. Then she shall be the dowager queen. What more could she have gained by assassinating you? Queen Consort is an intelligent woman. I do not believe she is that stupid to give up her position as Queen Consort. As such, she will be worshiped in the Imperial Ancestral Shrine of Shang after her death. To become the daughter of an emperor would only lower her status. Even the most stupid person realizes the situation. In addition, ever since she became Queen Consort, she has been industrious and ruled the palace business with justice, care and diligence. Further, her father, Jiang Huan-Chu is Duke East, ruling the vast, fertile region of East Ru, and he is also a royal relative of the highest distinction. He has already achieved the highest rank possible. What more will he stand to gain by assassinating you? There is no reason that he should try to do so. The assassin must be sent by someone else. You must send another officer to question him. He could not have been sent by Queen Jiang. It must be a crafty plot to frame her."

After listening to these arguments, Emperor Zoe was swayed in his opinion and he began to be convinced of the innocence of his wife. He thought, "Yes, Queen Huang made it very clear that this assassin must be part of a devious plot to discredit Queen Jiang, to frame her. I must not fall into this trap. Let me find another officer to question the assassin."

As he was pondering, Dar-Gee watched his facial expression attentively. After some thought, she cast a sarcastic smile. The Emperor noticed and said, "Why are you smiling?"

Dar-Gee replied: "Queen Huang has been fooled by Queen Jiang. No criminal ever confessed that he or she did wrong. The assassin Jiang Quann has already confessed that he was sent by her father. Of all women in the court, why should he confess that he was sent by Queen Jiang and not by others? The only way to extract the truth from her is by using torture. This is a matter of utmost importance. You must exert the right judgment!"

"My beauty is right." The opinion of the Emperor was again swayed to the opposite.

Queen Huang interjected: "Dar-Gee, you must not talk nonsense. Queen Consort is the legal wife of the Emperor, mother of the nation. During the entire human history, no Queen Consort had ever been subjected to torture or execution, no matter what the offense. At most she would be imprisoned or banished. There is no precedent to torture Queen Consort."

Dar-Gee retorted: "Law has been instituted by the Emperor in reign for his convenience. My Emperor, you should order an executioner to West Palace. If Queen Jiang does not confess to her crime, pull one eye out of her. This is the most painful punishment. She would confess to any crime if you threaten to pull her eye out." Emperor Zoe agreed to her suggestion and he refused to listen to the pleading of Queen Huang. An executioner was ordered to carry out this horrendous torture.

Queen Huang quickly returned to West Palace. Upon seeing Queen Jiang, Huang said in tears: "Disaster! Dar-Gee is your sworn enemy! She persuaded the Emperor to send an executioner to West Palace to torture you if you do not confess. The executioner is ordered to pull one of your eyes out if you do not confess! Please listen to my humble opinion. Confess to the charge even if it is not true. After your confession we all will persuade the Emperor to spare your life and to imprison you instead. Later we can try to reclaim your innocence."

Queen Jiang replied in tears: "My dear sister, I know you are trying to help me. But I have been raised according to the discipline to adhere strictly to truth and honor. I will never confess to such a hideous charge, to demean my name in posterity. If I confess, my father shall forever be known in history as a perfidious duke, and I shall be known as a traitorous and untrustworthy wife. My son who is now the crown prince shall never be recognized as a legitimate heir to the throne. I would rather die an honest woman. Death and suffering last but an instant, but the reputation of my name shall prevail forever ..."

Before she could finish, the executioner arrived and yelled, "If you do not confess, I must carry out the imperial order!"

Queen Jiang cried, "I would rather die than to confess to a crime that I did not commit."

Another messenger arrived to oversee the questioning. After Queen Consort steadfastly refused to confess, the executioner used a knife and dislodged one eye from Queen Jiang. Yelling in great pain, she fainted. Queen Huang and her ladies-in-waiting applied bandages to her eye trying to stop the blood flow, which had already soaked the dress of Queen Jiang.

The executioner presented the eye to Emperor Zoe. Queen Huang arrived moments later. "Did this swine woman confess," the Emperor asked.

"No. She did not commit the crime, so how could she confess? An eye has been pulled out of her," replied Queen Huang.

Upon seeing the bloody eye, Emperor Zoe felt guilty. She had been a faithful wife queen for many years, and the memory of those years of love and tender care came back to him. Now because of his momentary anger, he had committed an act that could never be undone or remedied. In a regretful mood, he turned his head to Dar-Gee. "I mistrust your words. Now her eye has been pulled out, and she did not confess. Probably she did not commit the offense. Now what shall I tell my court officers? What shall I tell Duke East?"

Dar-Gee replied, "We have no choice but to extract a confession from her. Without a confession, all court officers shall side with her. In addition, Duke East is a powerful lord. We must extract a confession, otherwise Duke East will rebel against you."

Torn between his emotion and the political difficulties ahead he would soon face, Emperor Zoe sank his head. He had already committed a repulsive and horrendous act. He had made a very serious mistake. What else could he do? How could he face his court officers as well as Duke East? After pondering for a long while, he asked Dar-Gee: "Now what shall I do?"

Dar-Gee replied: "Now we have to carry the questioning one step further. We have to extract a confession. If we fail to extract a confession, this matter will never be settled. I suggest that we continue to torture her until we obtain a confession. I have a scheme. Heat a copper iron to red-hot. If she does not confess, burn both her hands. She will confess."

Emperor Zoe said, "According to the account of Queen Huang, she did not commit the crime. I already committed a severe mistake by pulling her eye out. Now you advise me to torture her with an even more cruel scheme. What happens if my court officers know about this? What happens if she refuses to confess?"

Dar-Gee replied, "Never mind the truth. Your situation is like the dictum: You are riding a ferocious tiger – you cannot get off easily. You must use torture. Even if she did not commit the crime, you still have to extract a confession from her. Otherwise you will offend all your court officers and all lords!"

Unwillingly, Emperor Zoe ordered the preparation of the next torture. Queen Huang immediately went back to West Palace and informed Queen Jiang, who was lying amidst a pool of blood. Queen Huang cried in sympathy: "What did you do in your last life to deserve this kind of hideous treatment and torture! My dear sister, please confess. Otherwise they will burn your fingers with a red-hot iron."

Queen Jiang cried in tears and blood and replied: "You be my witness. I must have committed serious offenses against heaven in my previous life, but please be my witness: I did no wrong."

At this moment, the executioner came. "If Queen Jiang does not confess, her fingers will be burnt!" Queen Jiang stubbornly refused to confess the crime she did not commit. The executioner applied the red-hot iron to her hand, instantly charring the flesh to the bone. In a shriek of pain, Queen Jiang fainted again.

Queen Huang went to report to Emperor Zoe. In tears, she said, "You have applied the most cruel torture to her and she still did not confess. She did not commit the crime that she was accused of. The plot is more serious than I thought. Even your life might be in danger."

Emperor Zoe was in shock now. He complained to Dar-Gee: "It is you who asked me to apply cruel tortures to extract confession. There is no confession. What should I do? What should I do?"

Dar-Gee replied, "Do not worry. We still have the assassin Jiang Quann. We can bring the assassin to West Palace and let some other officers cross-examine Queen Jiang in front of him. We can extract a confession when the assassin is brought face-to-face with Queen Jiang."

Two warrior generals, Zhao Tien (Field) and Zhao Lei (Rumble), were ordered to bring the assassin to West Palace. Queen Huang told Queen Jiang, "Your enemy is here now."

With her remaining eye, she saw Jiang Quann and cursed: "Who paid you to frame me? You dare accuse me to plot to murder the Emperor. God will never spare you!"

Jiang Quann replied, "It was you who ordered me to commit the act of assassination. Do not deny it. This is the truth."

Queen Huang cursed in anger: "You thing! You devious thief! You caused Queen Jiang to suffer the most cruel torture! Look what you have done!" Turning her head to the sky, she continued, "God of heaven and earth, you must kill this ghastly, spiteful and malicious crook!"

Meanwhile the two princes Yin Jaw and Yin Hong were playing a game of Wei-Chi (Go) in East Palace. An attendnt, Yang Yon, ran in and reported: "Master lords, disaster!" The two princes, who were of ages fourteen and twelve, were not concerned and continued their game of

Wei-Chi. Yang Yon reported again: "Master lords, please stop playing Wei-Chi! Disaster in West Palace! Your mother is in deep trouble!"

The two princes then stopped their game and asked, "What do you mean?"

Yang Yon reported in tears: "For an unknown reason your mother was accused of an assassination plot to murder the Emperor. She denied the charge. The Emperor ordered her to be put under extremely cruel tortures in order to force her to confess. First one of her eyes was pulled out. Then her hands were burnt by a red-hot iron to the bone. She still denied the charges. Now she is being cross-examined in the presence of an assassin. Please go there to save your mother Queen!"

The two princes, shouting in grief, ran to West Palace. They saw their mother in a pool of blood, her hands burnt beyond recognition. The two princes knelt next to her and cried: "Mother, why are you being tortured? You are Queen Consort, how can anyone torture you like this?"

Queen Jiang heard her sons' voices, and struggled to open her remaining eye. She cried: "My sons, look at me! I have been tortured for a crime I did not commit. This Jiang Quann accused me of the master plot to murder the Emperor. Dar-Gee calumniated against me and impelled the Emperor to torture me. Please vindicate me. I gave you life, now please give me back my innocence." Suddenly a spasm overcame her, and she expired.

Crown Prince Yin Jaw became undescribably furious at his mother's torturous death. He asked Queen Huang: "Who is Jiang Quann?" Queen Huang pointed her finger at the assassin. The crown prince was now mad. He saw a sword hanging on the wall. He took it down and cursed at Jiang Quann: "You thief! You dare tell lies to frame my mother Queen!" With a single strike, he cut Jiang Quann into two halves. The crown prince then yelled: "I am going to kill Dar-Gee! I am going to avenge my mother!" Then he ran out with the sword.

The two warrior generals Zhao Field and Zhao Rumble had not exactly seen what had happened; they saw one of the two princes cut Jiang Quann into halves and they caught the word "Kill!" They immediately ran back to report to the Emperor.

Queen Huang was also in shock. She told the younger prince: "Chase after your brother and get him back here!" This was done. She then reprimanded the two princes. " You have destroyed your only chance to clear your mother's name. We could have burnt his hands, too, to force a confession from him. Now he is dead and there is no way for us to extract a confession to vindicate your mother. If the two warrior generals Zhao Field and Zhao Rumble tell the Emperor that you have killed Jiang Quann, and that you intend to kill Dar-Gee, you two will be in serious trouble!"

Surely enough, Zhao Field and Zhao Rumble reported to the Emperor: "The crown prince killed Jiang Quann and they chased after us with swords in their hands! They claim they will come here to kill Dar-Gee!"

The Emperor became enraged. "These two rebel sons! Queen Jiang plotted to murder me, now they are coming with swords after me. Like mother, like son! They are rebels, and must be killed." Taking out his own sword, he passed it to Zhao Field. "Use my sword to cut off the heads of the two rebel sons!"

A palace attendant rushed to West Palace to report to Queen Huang: "The Emperor ordered the two Zhao warriors to kill the two princes."

Queen Huang went to the main gate of West Palace and waited. As the two Zhaos attempted to enter, they were stopped by Queen Huang at the entrance. "Why are you here in West Palace again?"

"We have been ordered by the Emperor to execute the two princes for their rebellion against the Emperor," the two Zhaos replied.

Huang angrily shouted at the two: "You idiots! The two princes chased you out of the West Palace, then they left. They are not here. Why don't you go after them in the East Palace? That is where they live! Why do you come here? I know you two evil things are abusing your authority, using this excuse to roam around the palace to look for women for your pleasure. If it were not for the imperial order from the Emperor, I would have you both executed right here. Now get out and get lost!" Upon these words, the two Zhaos felt extremely embarrassed and scared, so they immediately went to East Palace to look for the two princes.

As soon as the two left, Queen Huang hurried inside West Palace and summoned the two princes. "This idiotic Emperor first killed his own wife, now he wants to kill you both. He sent two warrior generals here. I tricked them away, but they will certainly return. You cannot hide here. Go to Hsin Chin Palace where Queen Yang resides. You can probably stay there for a couple of days. Meanwhile I will contact high court officers to persuade the Emperor to pardon you."

The two princes knelt down and thanked Queen Huang. "Aunt Queen, how can we repay you for your effort to save us? Our mother is dead now; please arrange for her to be buried properly. This is the only request we have."

"Don't worry. Please go. I will take care of her burial."

The two princes rushed to Hsin Chin Palace. Queen Yang was leaning against the gate, hoping to hear some good news about Queen Consort. The two princes saw her and immediately knelt down and in tears they begged her to save their lives. Queen Yang was startled. "What happened to Queen Consort?"

Yin Jaw narrated in tears: "My father Emperor listened to the evil words of Dar-Gee, and believed in the truth of the confession of the thief Jiang Quann that our mother Queen paid him to assassinate the Emperor. Our mother denied the charge. To extract a confession from her, the Emperor ordered one of her eyes pulled out. She still refused to confess. Then he ordered her hands burnt by a red-hot iron to the bone, but she still refused to confess. She is dead now. In a rage I killed the assassin Jiang Quann. The Emperor again listened to the words of Dar-Gee and wanted to have both of us killed too. We were advised to come here. The two Zhaos are looking for us now. Please save us."

Before the two princes could finish, Queen Yang was already in tears and she said to the two: "Come in quickly. Stay here for the time being. I will take care of the two Zhaos."

Queen Yang reckoned that when the two Zhaos could not find the two princes in East Palace, they would come to her palace to look. So she stood by the palace entrance, waiting. Surely enough, soon the two Zhaos rushed towards her palace, like two hungry wolves searching for prey.

Upon seeing the two, Queen Yang ordered the attending eunuchs: "Arrest these two intruders. This is the inner palace where women

84

reside. No strangers or court officers are supposed to be here. Execute both of them!"Zhao Field moved forward and hailed Queen Yang. "Salute to the Queen! We are Zhao Field and Zhao Rumble, under a direct order of the Emperor to look for two princes. We have the Emperor's sword as token of his authority."

Queen Yang looked at the sword to check its authenticity. She then shouted: "The two princes reside in East Palace. They have no reason to be here. What is the purpose of you two here? Get out. If it were not for the order of the Emperor, I would have you both executed here! Now get out!"

The two did not dare argue, so they left. After some more futile searches, they talked among themselves and decided to give up. "We have been unable to locate the two princes in all three palaces. Instead we have offended two queens. We are totally unfamiliar with the layout of the palaces. Maybe we should go back to report to the Emperor that we cannot find them." The two thus left.

After making sure that no pursuers would come, Queen Yang went inside Hsin Chin Palace. The two princes came out of hiding and thanked her. She said to the two: "This is probably not a safe place for you to hide. There are many attendants and I do not know whom I can trust. The Emperor has become stupid, idiotic, and irrational. He killed his own wife and now he wants to have both of you, his own sons, killed also. He ignored all moral principles. You two must leave here, and the safest place is probably the main hall of the court. The court session is not over yet. The two uncles of the Emperor as well as other royal relatives, Vice Premier Bee Gahn, and the commander-in-chief Huang Flying Tiger, are still there. These are all straight and honest officers. They can protect you much better than I can." The two princes thanked Queen

Yang for her help and her advice. Queen Yang escorted them to the gate leading to the main hall of the court, then went back to her palace.

After she went back she thought to herself: "Queen Consort Jiang was the wife of the Emperor. She was framed for a hideous crime by some evil officers. Even she, in her lofty position, could not escape the deplorable treatment she received. I am only a queen, a concubine. Now Dar-Gee has gained all favor from the Emperor and she has poisoned and bewitched the mind of the Emperor. He does not even care about his own crown prince. He even ignores the most important and basic father-son relationship. If anyone reports that I escorted the two princes to escape from the palace, ill fortune shall descend upon to me. How could I take such cruel torture as Queen Jiang did? I cannot expect to escape from this miserable fate. Besides, although I have been a queen for a number of years, I still do not have any children. There is nothing for me to linger for in this world. Moral codes have been broken and great disaster shall befall this country." She thought and thought, and finally she decided to end her life.

The next day, attendants reported to the Emperor that Queen Yang had hanged herself. He asked for the reason. No reason could be attributed. There were no suicide notes, either. The Emperor ordered her buried.

After leaving Hsin Chin Palace where Queen Yang resided, Zhao Tien Field and Zhao Lei Rumble had gone directly to Longevity Palace to report to the Emperor that they had failed to locate the two princes. Meanwhile, Queen Huang had also arrived. The Emperor said, "Did Queen Jiang confess?"

Huang reported: "No, she died of your torture. But before she died, she told me: 'I have served the Emperor faithfully and dutifully for sixteen years, and bore him two princes. I have been in charge of East

Palace, and I have been careful not to commit any wrong or offense against the Emperor. I have not been jealous of other women of the Emperor. I do not know who wants to frame me. This person ordered an assassin to lay blame on me, accusing me of high treason. I have been subjected to intolerable tortures. All my contributions to the regime as Queen Consort, my contribution to my husband in the procreation of two sons, evaporated like floating clouds and all love vanished like fog. I die a death not even befitting an animal. I have no way to vindicate my grievances. I can only hope posterity will absolve me of the unjust accusation.' She asked me to transmit this message to you, then she perished. Her body still lies in West Palace. I plead to you, her Emperor and her husband, to grant some sympathy upon your relationship with her, her procreation of your princes, and to allow her to be buried properly as Queen Consort. This will at least stop court officers from criticizing you that you have no virtue." The Emperor granted Queen Huang her request.

He then turned to the two Zhaos. "Where are the two princes?"

"They are not in East Palace," the Zhaos replied.

"Are they in West Palace?"

"No, they are not even in Hsin Chin Palace."

The Emperor then said, "Then they must be in the main court hall. Go and arrest them. Execute them right away." The two Zhaos thus continued their search for the two princes.

In the main hall of the court, officers eagerly awaited news of Queen Consort Jiang. While they were waiting, Flying Tiger heard hurrying footsteps. He then saw the two princes running towards the main hall, in a desperate mood. "What happened?" Flying Tiger said.

Upon seeing Flying Tiger, the two princes rushed forward and grabbed his sleeves, and begged: "Please save our lives." Flying Tiger was astonished, so the elder prince briefly recounted the sad events of their mother and continued: "Then Queen Huang was questioning the assassin Jiang Quann. It was my fault to grab a sword and kill the assassin before we could extract the truth from him. Afterwards out of rage I threatened to kill Dar-Gee and I chased the two Zhaos away. They went to report to our father Emperor what we have done. Now the Emperor has issued an order to put both of us to death. Please save us." Then the two princes started to cry pathetically.

All the court officers grieved at the tragedy. One of them suggested: "We must ring the gong to summon the Emperor here to ask him to vindicate the innocence of Queen Jiang and pardon the two princes."

Before these words were finished, voices from the west side of the main hall roared: "The Emperor has lost his mind. He slaughtered his wife by torture and he is ready to kill his own princes. He established the cruel torture machine Pao Lo. He stopped the good and righteous from speaking. We cannot stand the grief over the death of Queen Consort and the impending execution of the innocent princes. Something must be done to help the current situation. As the saying goes, a wise bird chooses the right branch to make a nest and a virtuous officer selects a good king to serve. Now the Emperor has committed perverse deeds and violated moral principles. He is no longer fit to be the Emperor. We are ashamed to be his officers. All of us must abandon this irrational Emperor, leave this court for another country!"

These words were from two brothers, Fang Hsian and Fang Bee, who were captains of the palace guards. Seeing that a rebellion was brewing, Flying Tiger quickly reacted. He shouted at the two: "Of what rank in the court do you think you are? You are not qualified to comment on matters of this importance! Shut up or you will be punished!" The two brothers lowered their heads and retreated to the side.

Although Flying Tiger reprimanded the two, he sympathized with their opinion. The matter was certainly extremely serious. He, too, sank his head into a sad mood. All the royal relatives ground their teeth and sighed deeply without being able to come up with a scheme to resolve the current crisis. An officer dressed in a red robe moved forward and addressed them all: "Current affairs are nothing but the fulfillment of the presage of Son of Clouds of Mount End South, that an elfin smog has enshrouded the palace. There is an old saying: 'If the king is not righteous, evil officers will dominate the court.' Now the Emperor has unjustifiably executed Imperial Astronomer Du Yuansee, established the hideous Pao Lo machine and burnt Chancellor Mei Po to death. Today he just murdered his wife and now he intends to kill his own princes. The schemer of this devilish plot only laughs at the stupidity of the Emperor. I am afraid the Shang regime will soon be toppled over and replaced by another. The Imperial Ancestral Shrine of Shang will soon be rendered ruins." The officer who made this statement was Yang Zen, also a chancellor.

Flying Tiger sighed, "I am afraid you are right."

At this time, the same voices roared again: "This repressive Emperor has committed evil deeds that will terminate the Shang dynasty. We are going to leave the capital and go to East Ru to borrow an army to eradicate the moronic Emperor!" Upon these words, the two Fangs each grabbed a prince and placed them on their backs, then pushed officers aside and ran out of the palace.

All the officers were startled. This was a mutiny, a crime of treason, a serious offense, but Flying Tiger pretended that he saw nothing. Vice Premier approached him and said: "General Huang, Fang Hsian and Fang Bee mutinied against the Emperor. Why are you silent? Don't you have anything to say?"

Flying Tiger replied: "It is a pity that of all the civilian and military officers around, none anywhere comes close to having the loyalty of the two Fangs. They are two unpretentious bullheads, yet they cannot stand to watch the prevalence of injustice that has befallen Queen Consort, mother symbol of the country, and they were disturbed by the death sentence imposed on the two princes, so they carried the two princes to escape from this court. However, if they are caught, these two will be executed along with the two princes. It is a useless struggle, but they did it for the sake of justice. My sympathy is with them." Before the court officers could respond to Flying Tiger, the sound of a chasing party was heard.

It was the two Zhaos who ran to the main hall. They first showed the officers the sword of the Emperor to indicate their authority. They then said: "Respectable officers, have you seen the two princes? We are under an order of the Emperor to take the two princes prisoner."

Flying Tiger replied: "Yes, they were here complaining about the unjustified torturous death of their mother and their unwarranted death sentence. Two captains of the palace guards, Fang Hsian and Fang Bee, mutinied against the injustice, so they each carried a prince and escaped. They are not far away. Since you have been ordered by the Emperor to catch them, go and chase after them."

The Zhaos were scared out of their wits. Fang Bee and Fang Hsian were both over eight feet tall and were known for their enormous physical strength. The two Zhaos could not even take one single punch from them, how could they capture the two? "Flying Tiger is putting a hot potato in our hands" Zhao Field thought. He then said: "If this is the case, I will go back to report to the Emperor."

Zhao Field went back to Longevity Palace and reported to the Emperor: "We went to the main hall. Many civilian and military officers were scattered around. We could not find the two princes among them. We overheard from some officers that the heads of the guards, Fang Hsian and Fang Bee, sympathized with the two princes so they mutinied. They each carried a prince on their backs and they intend to escape to East Ru to borrow an army to avenge the death of Queen Consort. This is what we have found."

The Emperor was again enraged. "Go and arrest the two Fangs."

Zhao Field pleaded, "The two Fangs are known for their physical strength. I do not have the ability to catch them. Please send Flying Tiger instead." The Emperor consented. Thus, the hot potato was sent back to Flying Tiger. An imperial order was hastily drawn and given to the two Zhaos.

Zhao Field brought the order to Flying Tiger. Flying Tiger laughed, "This hot potato is back to me." He accepted the order and the sword of the Emperor from the two Zhaos. He then went back to his official residence to prepare himself for the pursuit. His four sworn brothers, Huang Ming, Zhou Chi, Long Quan, and Wu Chien, wanted to follow him. Flying Tiger refused. He mounted his riding beast, Five Color Godspeed Ox, and left by himself.

The two Fangs ran for thirty li before they stopped for a rest. The two princes thanked the Fangs: "How are we going to repay you?"

Fang Bee replied: "This humble officer cannot tolerate the injustice that is about to befall you, so we mutinied against the Emperor rashly. Now we have to sit down to draft an escape plan." While they were discussing this, they saw Flying Tiger approaching on Five Color Godspeed Ox. The two Fangs were worried. "We left in a great rush and had not made up an escape plan. Now we are about to be caught. What are we going to do?"

Figure I- 7. Flying Tiger and two princes

Before anyone could say a word, Flying Tiger arrived. The two princes asked him: "General Huang, are you going to arrest us?"

Flying Tiger dropped from his ox and bowed to the two princes. "Please forgive me for my intrusion."

"May I ask what is your business here?" the elder prince said.

"I am under an imperial order to come here to ask you to kill yourselves with the sword the Emperor gave me. I have no other choice because I am under an imperial order. Please decide it upon yourselves."

Yin Jaw pleaded: "You must know that we mother and sons have been framed for a crime we never committed. My mother already died unjustifiably of a torturous death. If we die, then her innocence will never be vindicated. Please spare us. We will never forget the great benevolence you bestow upon us."

Huang Flying Tiger also pleaded: "I know the grievances of your mother, and yours, too. However, I am under an imperial order. I do not wish to carry out this order. If I let you go, I will be charged with the crime of treason. If I arrest you, I cannot bear the weight of my conscience. I do not know what to do." They all stood in silence, for there seemed to be no good way to get out of the dilemma.

Crown Prince Yin Jaw finally decided: "All right, may I make a suggestion that will fulfill your obligation to the imperial order?"

"Please go ahead," Huang Flying Tiger replied.

Yin Jaw suggested: "Kill me and bring my head to the capital to show to the Emperor. Let my brother go. This will at least leave the possibility open for a vindication of my mother and us."

Yin Hong immediately stopped his brother. "No, please. He is the crown prince and I am nothing but a lord. I am young and ignorant.

Please kill me and bring my head back to the capital and let my brother go. He will be able to go to either East Ru or West Branch to borrow an army to vindicate my mother."

The two then argued who was going to die, and the argument ended up with everyone in tears. The two Fangs cried and pleaded to heaven: "God, please help us!"

Huang Flying Tiger, who had never been very willing to carry out the order in the first place, decided that he must do something. He said, "Stop lamenting. Only five of us know that I have caught up with you. If this secret leaks out, all my family and I will be executed.

"Now, Fang Bee, you take the elder prince to East Ru to see the father of Queen Jiang, Jiang Huan-Chu. You, Fang Hsian, take the younger prince to see Duke South, Er Tsong-Yu, telling him that I send you and the younger prince to him. Ask the two dukes to vindicate the innocence of the Queen. I will go back to report to the Emperor that I lost you over a fork junction."

Fang Bee thanked Flying Tiger. Then he said, "We did not expect we would be on the run. We did not bring money with us. Do you have any money with you?"

Flying Tiger said, "Unfortunately I do not have any money with me, either. However, I carry with me a piece of jade with gold lining. It must be worth something like one hundred pieces of silver. Sell it and divide it among yourselves. Unfortunately this is all I can contribute now. Farewell. I will report back to the Emperor that I cannot find you."

By the time Flying Tiger slowly trod his ox back to the capital, the sun was setting. All the court officers were still waiting patiently at the Gate of Noon, eager for news of the two princes. They were delighted to see Huang Flying Tiger came back empty-handed. "What happened?" Vice Premier Bee Gahn said.

"I cannot find them. They must have escaped on a different path," replied Flying Tiger. All were relieved and went home.

Flying Tiger went inside the palace. The Emperor said, "Did you catch the mutineers and rebels?"

"No, I did not. I came upon a fork junction. I asked passersby and local residents if they had seen the fleeing party, but none had. I was afraid if I continued to search you might feel uneasy, so I decided to come back."

The Emperor commended him: "Thank you for your efforts. It is too bad that they escaped. All right, go home. We will discuss this problem tomorrow."

Dar-Gee was greatly perturbed that the two princes had not been caught. She further advised the Emperor: "Your Majesty, if the two princes escaped to the territory of the Queen's father, Jiang Huan-Chu, an invading army will be on its way to attack us soon. We are already at war; Imperial Teacher Wen Zhong is still engaging in a distant expeditionary mission to squash rebels. We cannot afford to have another invasion against us. Ask the two warrior generals Yin Po-bei and Lei Kai to lead a light cavalry of three thousand to catch the two princes." An imperial order was instantly drafted and dispatched.

After Flying Tiger went back to his official residence, he pondered the fate of the regime. "The actions of the Emperor are certainly irrational. Grievances are mounting. What shall I do?" As he pondered, his attendants reported: "Two warriors Yin and Lei are here to see you."

The two were admitted and the imperial order was presented. After Flying Tiger read the order, he thought, "These two are evil and have no concern about justice. If they catch the two, all my efforts to save them will be in vain. I must try to delay their pursuit." He then told Yin and Lei: "It is too late to assemble a cavalry for you now. Come back tomorrow morning." The two, being subordinates of Flying Tiger, did not dare complain.

After Yin and Lei left, Flying Tiger turned to one of his warrior generals, Zhou Chi, and said: "I have received an order from the Emperor to issue Yin and Lei a military command together with a cavalry of three thousand. Next morning, go to the barrack of the Left Guard and select three thousand weak, old and meek cavalry men together with equally old and weak horses and assign them to the two." Zhou Chi understood what Flying Tiger meant and this was done. In the morning, the military command, as well as the three thousand cavalry, was turned over to Yin and Lei. The two were disappointed at the condition of the cavalry, but they did not dare complain or argue. Yin and Lei marched the light cavalry out of the south gate of the city. Naturally this light cavalry marched slowly.

Two days after Fang Bee and Fang Hsian escorted the two princes out of the city of Morning Song, they came upon a fork junction. The two Fangs stopped and conferred with each other. "We have no money, and although we have the jade given to us by Flying Tiger, we cannot sell it because people might become suspicious. We should point the way to the two princes and let us go separate ways." Fang Bee then told the two princes: "We are unsophisticated military soldiers with few schemes in our heads. We got you out of the court on our emotional outbursts, but we do not have any escape plan. The best scheme we can think of at present is for us to split up. You two can mingle easily with merchants and travelers to go to your destinations. It is safer for all of us this way." The two princes agreed, and so the party split.

Yin Jaw told his brother: "I will go eastward to East Ru. You will go southward." After bidding each other farewell, they departed on their separate ways.

Yin Hong, a prince who was raised in a delicate environment, was not used to the hardship of a pedestrian traveler. After walking for around twenty li, he felt both hungry and tired. He passed by a family eating their meal outdoors. He approached and asked: "May I have some food?" He still wore his red robe from the palace. The head of the family saw his silk robe and perceived that this young lad must be from a prominent background. They saluted to him and offered him food.

After the prince was fed, he thanked the host and asked the way to the territory of Er Tsong-Yu, Duke South. Then he continued his southward trek. Being an inexperienced traveler, he did not even realize that he needed a lodging for the night. By the time he was tired, he was already in wilderness and the sun was setting fast. He panicked, but he was lucky and saw an old temple ahead, so he entered. This temple worshiped Huangdi, the Yellow Emperor. After praying to Huangdi to protect him, he lay down underneath the altar and soon he fell fast asleep.

Yin Jaw was a little luckier. He walked forty li and passed by a large estate mansion, which bore a large sign: "Residence of First Officer." "This must be the home of a retired high officer. He must know me. I can ask him to let me sleep here for the night." As he entered the yard, he heard a poem being chanted:

A loyal heart laments without avail,

War among Gods and Men

> *Years of efforts rendered vain*
> *By elfin evils in the palace.*
> *Populace turned into apparition,*
> *A poor soul of wilderness*
> *Finds no way to reach the Emperor's heart.*

Yin Jaw waited until the chanting stopped, then he said, "Is there anyone there?"

"Who are you?" said the voice that chanted the poem.

"A traveler. May I oblige you the hospitality to allow me to stay under your roof until tomorrow morning?" the crown prince said.

"Your accent seems to be of the city of Morning Song. Are you a native around that city," the voice asked.

"Yes, indeed I am," replied the crown prince.

"Are you a resident inside the city or outside," the voice asked again.

"Inside the city," the crown prince replied.

"Please come in. I want to ask you some questions," the voice invited.

Upon entering the hall, the crown prince was astonished and uttered a cry of surprise. "It is you! Premier Shang Yon!"

Equally surprised, Shang Yon said, "It is you! Crown Prince! Please forgive me for not being able to welcome you at the door." He then continued, "You should be in East Palace. Why are you here?"

In tears, the crown prince reported the cruel death of his mother, and told Shang Yon the imperial order to execute him and his brother and their subsequent flight. After the crown prince had finished, Shang

Yon yelled in grief: "I never expected this idiotic Emperor to be so cruel, so compassionless to his wife and his own offspring. Although I, an old man, have retired myself from the court to roam among trees and springs, my heart is still with the country. Why are there no officers to intercede, to argue against the Emperor? Please rest your mind. I will prepare a communique and I will present it to the Emperor myself to argue for your cause." Shang Yon then turned to his attendants. "Prepare a banquet of welcome for the crown prince."

As for his pursuers, the old and sick light cavalry moved slowly. On the first day they marched not even thirty li. Three days later, they had only marched a total distance of around one hundred li. Then they came upon a fork junction. Lei Kai stopped the cavalry and conferred with Yin Po-bei: "Partner, let us station our cavalry here. At this rate we will never catch them. I suggest we select one hundred of the strongest cavalry and we split at this fork junction. We each lead fifty to chase the two princes. You go eastward towards East Ru and I go southward towards South Capital."

Yin Po-bei agreed. "You are right. These soldiers are indeed too weak and some of them too old. They can march only thirty li a day. At this rate how are we going to catch them? Your idea is great. We will rendezvous here after we catch them." Lei agreed. So Yin and Lei went their separate ways, each with fifty of the strongest horsemen.

The two parties chased at top speed. Lei's party took the southern route. By the evening, there was still no trace of either of the two princes. Lei ordered: "Let us stop here and have our meal. Afterwards we will continue our pursuit at night." This was done and the pursuit continued. By eight o'clock of our reckoning, the entire cavalry was dead tired and several of them dozed off, nearly falling down from their

99

horses. Lei thought, "My men are tired. Also, at night we might miss the prince. In that case all our efforts will be in vain. Let my men have a rest. Tomorrow morning we can continue our pursuit." He then ordered: "Go and find a village. We will ask the local residents to accommodate us for the night." The entire cavalry, dead-tired, were more than eager to look for a place of rest. They hoisted their torches high above their heads, and looked around. In the thick of the pine trees ahead, they saw the faint silhouette of a building. By the time they arrived at the site, they realized it was but an old temple.

The scout reported: "We cannot find any village, but there is an old temple ahead. We can rest there for the night." Lei agreed. Upon opening the door of the temple, they saw none other than Prince Yin Hong sleeping soundly underneath the altar.

"Heaven blesses me! Had I forced the cavalry to move ahead, I would have missed him." Waking the prince up, Lei said, "Your Highness, I am under the order of the Emperor to ask you to go back to the capital. Court officers have prepared a communique, to present themselves as guarantors on your behalf. You can rest your fear."

Prince Yin Hong replied, "You need say no more. I already know that I cannot escape from my fate. However, I have been walking along and I cannot take it any more. Please lend me your horse."

Lei was more than pleased to know that there would be no resistance. He quickly consented. "Your Highness, please ride my horse. I will walk behind you." Lei and his 50 horsemen then trekked back towards the fork junction.

Meanwhile Yin Po-bei and his cavalry trotted along the road towards East Ru. Two days later, they passed by a small town by the name of Wind Cloud. Ten li later, they passed by an estate mansion bearing the sign "Residence of First Officer." Yin Po-bei knew it was the retirement residence of ex-Premier Shang Yon. As Yin Po-bei had served under Shang Yon, he decided to pay him a visit. He reckoned he probably could get some information about the whereabouts of the princes. Being an old acquaintance, he was recognized by attendants of the household and was admitted without them first reporting the arrival of a guest to the ex-Premier. As he entered the hall, he saw the crown prince eating a meal with ex-Premier Shang Yon. "It is my day of luck!" thought Yin Po-bei. He then presented himself to the two. "Premier Shang Yon, Your Highness, I am under an imperial order to ask the crown prince to go back to the capital."

"You come here just at the right time!" Shang Yon asserted angrily. "Out of four hundred civilian and military officers of the court, none dares express his dissent against the ill wishes of this idiotic and irrational Emperor. They are all silent. What has the world come to?" In his anger, he would not allow Yin Po-bei to take the crown prince.

The face of the crown prince turned pale. Tears flowed down his cheeks like water. He said resignedly in a trembling voice, "Premier, please do not be angry. Since General Yin is here under an imperial order to arrest me, I must face my fate."

"Rest your worry. I have not completed my communique yet. Let me finish it first. Then I will go with you to see the Emperor myself," Shang Yon replied. He then turned to his attendants. "Prepare my horse and pack my bag. I will be leaving for the capital soon."

However, Yin was afraid that if he allowed Shang Yon to come along with him and his captive, he might be reprimanded for placing his private relationship above the imperial order. "May I ask the Premier for a favor?" Warrior Yin said. "I am under an imperial order to ask the crown prince to go back to the capital. May I go back with the prince first? You can show up separately. Otherwise I may be implicated in placing my private relationship above the imperial order."

Shang Yon laughed. "I know you are afraid that you might be reprimanded for letting me come along with you. All right, Your Highness, please go back to the capital with General Yin. I will follow you shortly." The crown prince hesitated before leaving and turned to look at Shang Yon from time to time, as if he could not bear to leave with Yin Po-bei.

Shang Yon summoned Warrior Yin back. "The crown prince is alive and well as he leaves here. Do not harm him in any way. I will see you in the capital."

"Your order shall be obeyed." Yin bowed.

The crown prince thus left with Yin Po-bei. However, on his way back, he kept on wishing, "My life may be gone, but my brother may still be able to carry out the mission of vindication."

A couple of days later, Yin and his captive arrived at the fork junction. When Prince Yin Hong saw Crown Prince Yin Jaw, he could not help but grieve that the last chance of vindication of his mother's cruel death was gone. He held the hand of his brother and cried to heaven: "God, what kind of offenses have we two brothers committed against you? You have placed both of us in the path of death. You have terminated our hopes of vindication of our mother!" The cavalry of three thousand, though under an imperial order to arrest them, could not help lament the anticipated ill fate of the two princes.

After the princes were delivered to the capital, Yin Po-bei and Lei Kai went to the palace to report their capture to the Emperor. The

Emperor ordered: "I do not need to see them. Execute them right away, then bury them."

Yin Po-bei replied, "We do not have an order of execution, how dare we execute the two princes?"

The Emperor immediately took a brush pen and wrote on a note, "Execution ordered," and passed the note to the two. Yin and Lei took the order and emerged outside the Gate of Noon, ready to carry out the execution.

After Flying Tiger had issued the military command to Yin and Lei, he was also concerned with the fate of the two princes, so he sent scouts to spy on the chasing party. His scouts reported to Huang Flying Tiger the capture of the two princes. Master Lord of National Poise was enraged. "These two rascals. For the sake of gaining favor from the Emperor, you two scamps have no regard for the lineage of the Shang dynasty. I shall see to it that you will never enjoy your reward." He asked Huang Ming, Zhou Chi, Long Quan, and Wu Chien, his four sworn brothers and comrades in arms, to summon all royal senior relatives, Vice Premier and other important court officers to the palace. Flying Tiger then rode his Five Color Godspeed Ox directly to the Gate of Noon. By the time he arrived, all the officers and senior royal relatives had already come and were waiting outside the Gate of Noon.

Flying Tiger first saluted to all of them. He then said, "My respectable officers and seniors. I am a military officer and I have only a limited influence in civilian matters. The outcome of the events of today hangs upon you civilian officers."

Just then, a group of executioners escorted the two princes to the front of the Gate of Noon. The two princes pleaded to all: "Our lives are in your hands. Please help us."

One royal uncle, Wei Chuchi, said, "All officers have submitted communiques to pledge to be your guarantors. Presumably everything should be all right." But Yin and Lei showed the waiting officers the imperial order of execution.

Flying Tiger grew so angry that he blocked the passage of the Gate of Noon and shouted to the two: "Yin and Lei! Congratulations to you for capturing the two princes. You two will be promoted, but I do not think you will stay in your promoted positions for long!"

Before he could finish, civilian officer Zhao Chi grabbed the order of execution and tore it into pieces. He then said, "It is bad enough that this idiotic and irrational Emperor has lost his mind, but it is even worse that he is aided by these rascals. Who dares execute the two princes of East Palace? Who dares kill the crown prince? My fellow officers, the front of the Gate of Noon is no place to discuss matters of this importance. Let us go to the main hall and ring all gongs to ask the Emperor to come to attend a court session. All of us must speak out for the sake of justice and the country!"

Yin and Lei had not expected that they would encounter such violent reactions from the court officers, civilian as well as military. They were stunned by the situation. Flying Tiger then asked his four sworn brothers to stay with the two princes to prevent the order of execution from being carried out. Meanwhile all of them entered the main hall and all the gongs were rung to ask the Emperor to come to the main hall. This was usually done when there was a matter of utmost importance that needed to be taken care of right away.

The Emperor heard the sound of the gongs and the roll of drums. As he was about to inquire, an attendant reported: "The entire assembly of civilian and military officers has gathered in the main hall to ask for your presence to discuss a matter of utmost importance."

The Emperor said to Dar-Gee, "These officers must have gathered to plead for the lives of the two disloyal sons. What shall I do?"

Dar-Gee suggested: "Issue another order to execute the two princes immediately. Meanwhile issue an order to all court officers gathered in the main hall to delay the court session until tomorrow. By tomorrow, the crisis will be over."

A messenger soon arrived at the main hall, carrying an imperial message. The message read:

By order of the Emperor,

It is an established rule of the court that if an emperor summons any person, he must leave at once without even waiting for his horse to be ready. If an emperor orders a person to die, he must not live. This is the supreme law of the land. My disloyal son Yin Jaw together with his brother Yin Hong totally disregarded the law of the land. They killed the assassin Jiang Quann to try to eradicate the evidence of their murder plot. They then tried to kill two officers dispatched by me, and they attempted to assassinate me. They have violated laws, trespassed against moral principles of the country and acted against ancestors of Shang. Now I have both of them captured. They are to be executed today in the front of the Gate of Noon. All of you are ordered not to interfere. If you have matters of importance to discuss with me, come back tomorrow.

The officers were stunned by the tone and intention of the order. They conferred among themselves but they could not come up with a concrete plan to save the two princes. They did not dare leave the meeting hall, either.

During this critical moment, two demigods, Son of Naked Essence, of Cavern Lofty Clouds in Mount Supreme Splendor (Tai-Hua) and Son of Cosmos Feat, of Peach Cavern in Mount Nine Demigods, happened to pass by the city of Morning Song on one of their frequent over-the-sky treks. They were blocked by two arrays of red light. The sources of light were traced to the air of carnage surrounding the two princes. Upon prognostication the two demigods concluded that these two princes were destined to be involved in engagements in the near future. Son of Cosmos Feat spoke to Son of Naked Essence. "My Taoist brother, the reign of Shang is about to come to an end. The King of People has emerged in West Branch. These two are destined to be involved in the forthcoming war. Let us take them back to our mountains to train them as our disciples. I will take one and you will take the other. At an opportune moment, we will send them back to the world of dust to fulfill the preordination." Son of Naked Essence agreed. Two Yellow Turban Muscle Men were then dispatched to take the two princes away from the executioners.

Just when the executioners were struggling with the crowd of protectors who attempted to prevent the execution of the two princes, strong gusts of wind commenced, blowing dust and pebbles from the ground. The sun was blocked by the blowing dust and the sky darkened. Everyone had to shield their faces with their sleeves against the bombarding pebbles and sand particles. By the time the winds subsided and the sky cleared, the two princes were gone without a trace. Yin and Lei searched among the crowd, but could not locate them. Finally they gave up the search and reentered the palace to report to the Emperor that, after a strong gust of wind blew, the two princes seemed to have disappeared without a trace.

The Emperor was equally perplexed. "It is extremely strange that the two princes disappeared amidst a strong gust of wind. Who could have caused the disappearance?"

As Premier Shang Yon arrived at the city of Morning Song, he heard people discussing the strange incident. He was also extremely perplexed. Upon arrival at the Gate of Noon, he saw a huge crowd outside amidst a throng of soldiers in combat armor and arms. Shang Yon entered the gate, crossed the Nine Dragon Bridge and was greeted by a band of officers. After an exchange of salutations and pleasantries, Shang Yon said: "Senior officers, senior royalties: I have resigned from affairs of the court and retire myself to the countryside, to befriend birds and wild lives in forests. Although I have not been away long, I already have heard much disappointing news from the capital. The Emperor seems to have lost his mind, for he has murdered Queen Consort by torture and he even intends to kill his own sons, one of them his heir. You all have been receiving salaries from the court of Shang, therefore you must also bear the responsibility of the welfare of this dynasty. Why has there been not even one officer who dared risk his life to remonstrate with the Emperor about the dangerous consequences of his irrational acts?"

Flying Tiger replied: "Premier, the Emperor stays inside his residential palace and he does not come to the main hall often to discuss with us affairs of the country. We have to communicate with him through written messages delivered by messengers. We hardly get any chance to talk to him face-to-face. Today the two princes were captured. They were tied up in front of the Gate of Noon, waiting to be executed. A high officer, Mr. Zhao, tore up the order to stop the execution. All of us came to the main hall to try to start a court session. We rang gongs to summon the Emperor to the court. Instead of coming to the court, he sent a message stating that he would attend a court session tomorrow. Meanwhile he ordered the execution of the two princes to be carried out right away. Fortunately a strong gust of wind was sent from heaven, blowing dust and pebbles from the ground, and the sky darkened. After the gust of wind was over, the two princes had disappeared. Yin Po-bei has just gone inside the palace to report this strange incident to the Emperor. Let us wait for him to come out."

Just then, Yin Po-bei emerged. Shang Yon went to meet him and said angrily, "But for the will of heaven to make the two princes disappear amidst a gust of wind, you would have executed them both! Congratulations to you for your high accomplishment! You will soon be granted a land to become a lord!"

Yin bowed and apologized. "Please forgive me! I am only following my orders."

Shang Yon then turned around and spoke to all the officers present. "I, an old retired man, decided to come to the capital to fulfill my last obligation to the late Emperor Yi whom I served with loyalty. I am prepared to die to fulfill this obligation. Today I will remonstrate with the Emperor about his wrongdoings. I must speak without reservation." Shang Yon then asked the officer in charge to ring gongs to summon the Emperor to the court and to blow horns, which usually announced the imminent arrival of the Emperor.

The Emperor was already deeply upset by the disappearance of the two princes. He heard the ringing of gongs and the blowing of horns. He was very angry, but he decided to go to the hall to face the officers. After the Emperor ascended his throne and all officers of the court presented the proper salutations, he said, "Is there any communique you want to present to me?" Shang Yon came forward with a communique. Emperor Zoe saw a man in plain dress standing in front of him, obviously not an officer. He said: "Who are you?"

Shang Yon raised his head and replied, "The ex-Premier Shang Yon is here to present his salutation to Your Majesty."

Emperor Zoe was astonished. "You already retired to your country abode. Now you are back in the capital. I have not sent an order to summon you here. Why do you come? Don't you know that you have violated protocols of the court?"

Shang Yon walked towards the Emperor and pleaded: "I have heard that you have indulged yourself in wine and women and have acted contrary to moral codes and standards. Please listen to my remonstrations with you about current affairs. I have prepared a communique to this effect. Please pay attention to my suggestions." He then presented his communique. The communique read:

To Your Majesty, a faraway subordinate of the court speaks with the utmost sincerity:

Because of recent irrational events, moral principles of the society are violated and this country is in grave danger. I often heard that an emperor must rule the country with reason and govern people through virtue. Attention must be paid to all matters concerning the country and her people. This will ensure the longevity of the dynasty, securing the Imperial Ancestral Shrine. Unfortunately Your Majesty listened to evil and deviant subordinates, indulged yourself in wine and women, and has fallen into their traps to kill your Queen Consort and ordered execution of your own princes, thus terminating the lineage to your throne. The righteous and honest officers were tortured to death by the Pao-Lo machine. No tyrant emperor of the past has done more than you have. I, a loyal subordinate officer of the Shang dynasty, risk my life to give you the following advice: First remove Dar-Gee and order her to commit suicide, then vindicate the Queen Consort and the two princes. People will look upon you as a great emperor, and civilian and military officers of the court shall regain their faith in you. Please forgive me for my impertinence to speak frankly without reservation.

Dutifully yours, Ex-Premier Shang Yon.

The Emperor had already ben enraged when he unwillingly went to the court; he was fuming after he finished reading the communique. He tore it into pieces and ordered his guards: "Take this old rascal outside the Gate of Noon and hammer him to death!"

The guards were about to move forward to seize Shang Yon when he stood up and yelled: "Who dares seize me! I was a prince regent and I have served three emperors of Shang dynasty!" He then turned to Emperor Zoe. "You brainless, asinine and fatuous Emperor! You pamper yourself in wine and women, waste your life in sensory pleasures. You have no consideration of the hardship of your ancestral emperors to develop this great country to the present state of prosperity and to establish laws to govern people in justice and in accordance with moral principles! You have angered gods of heaven and earth. You have murdered Queen Consort, mother symbol of the country. You have believed the words of a worthless woman Dar-Gee to kill your own princes. You have tortured righteous officers to death by the Pao-Lo machine. I only pity the Shang regime! The great efforts of your ancestral emperors to establish this great country will be rendered vain

110

and the Shang dynasty shall be toppled by your own hands! When you die, how are you going to face your ancestral emperors?"

At this statement, the Emperor became so enraged that he slapped the table repeatedly in front of him with his fist and yelled, "Hammer him to death right here! Hammer him to death right here!"

Shang Yon shouted back, "I do not lament my own death. I pity you and I bemoan the fate of Shang!" Turning his head towards the sky, he cried, "Emperor Yi! I have failed in the responsibility you delegated to me on your deathbed. Shang dynasty shall end within years!" At the end of this lament, Shang Yon smashed his head against a stone pillar, instantly cracking his skull. Blood splashed all over the hall. A brave officer of the court of Shang had just sacrificed his life for the sake of his dynasty at the age of 75.

All the officers looked at each other, not daring to speak a word. The Emperor was still angry: "Throw the body of this old rascal outside the city and let it wither away in wilderness without a burial!" This was done. However, at night, common people who held high respect for the ex-Premier stole the body and buried him in a secret grave.

Zhao Chi, the civilian officer who had torn the imperial order for the execution of the two princes, was so aggravated by the situation and so frustrated by the inaptness of the four hundred civilian as well as military officers present, that he left his rank and protested in sympathy for the late Shang Yon, because even his dead body had been desecrated through the rage of the Emperor. "I, Zhao Chi, cannot tolerate the irrationality of the Emperor. I want to join Premier Shang Yon in the underworld!" He then pointed to Emperor Zoe and yelled, "You senseless Emperor! You think with your evil power you can suppress words of righteousness and sit on your throne forever? The days are numbered before you will be overthrown by the people!"

The Emperor was so angry that he ground his teeth and again whacked his palm at his desk. "Send this scamp to the Pao-Lo Machine." Soon the Pao-Lo machine was fanned to red-hot. Within minutes Zhao Chi was rendered ashes. The foul odor of burnt flesh soon filled the main hall of the court. Having vented his anger, the Emperor ordered the court adjourned and returned to his residential palace. The officers of the court also returned to their homes, scared and with leaden hearts.

5. Emperor Tricks the Four Dukes

Dar-Gee received the Emperor warmly. Emperor Zoe was still angry. He told Dar-Gee: "Today I have been insulted by two rascals. Even with a torture machine as harsh and brutal as Pao-Lo, there are still officers who are not scared. Can you devise some other more effective means to silence my critics?"

Dar-Gee replied in her charming voice: "Give me some time and let me think it over."

The Emperor then added: "I will appoint you Queen Consort soon. However, I am afraid that the father of Queen Jiang, Duke East Jiang Huan-Chu, may avenge the horrible death of his daughter. He may rebel against me and lead the two hundred lords under him to attack the capital. Imperial Teacher Wen Zhong is still deeply engaged in his campaign against rebels in North Sea. What shall I do?"

Dar-Gee replied: "I am a woman residing inside your palace, secluded from the outside world and I have very little knowledge of affairs of the world. I cannot offer you much advice. I advise you to summon Fei Chung to the palace to consult with him." The Emperor agreed. Soon Fei the Corrupt arrived and was brought to the presence of the Emperor.

"Queen Jiang is now dead. If Duke East knows about her death, he may start a rebellion against me. Do you have any scheme to maintain peace in that area?"

Fei the Corrupt replied: "With Queen Consort Jiang dead, the two princes disappeared, Shang Yon having killed himself, and now Zhao Chi

113

put to death on the Pao-Lo machine, nearly all the officers are discontented. I am afraid sooner or later someone will dispatch a messenger to inform Duke East of affairs in the capital. Then he will rebel against you. I suggest that we send messengers right away to recall the four dukes to the capital. Kill all of them when they come. The eight hundred lords of lesser ranks will be without effective leadership. The leaderless lords will post no threat to you."

Emperor Zoe was very delighted at this suggestion and he commended him. "Dar-Gee was right to recommend you. You do have ingenious schemes to pacify the country." Thus four secret imperial orders were dispatched to the four dukes, Duke East, Jiang Huan-Chu, Duke West, Chi-Chang, Duke North, Tsung Migratory Tiger, and Duke South, Er Tsong-Yu.

The messenger dispatched to deliver the order to Duke West traveled through towns and villages, scaled mountains and crossed streams. Finally, 70 li beyond West Branch Mountain, he arrived at West Branch City, the capital of Fief West, or Zhou Dukedom. He was extremely impressed by the sight he saw. People were well-to-do, store stocks were bountiful, lives were leisurely but industrious. Passersby on streets conversed in polite manners, merchants transacted their business honestly, and the city was ruled with an impeccable atmosphere of justice and neatness. The signs of prosperity were everywhere. The messenger sighed, "I have long heard of the orderly rule of the West. Now I finally get to see this sight myself." He then went to the official guesthouse and reported that he brought a message from the Emperor for Duke West.

The next day a court session was heard and the message of the Emperor was delivered and read:

The Imperial Order from the Emperor posts:

Rebellion activities in North Sea have intensified, causing people of that area to suffer. Civilian and military officers of my court have produced no useful schemes to pacify that region. I am recalling you, the four dukes to the court to discuss this matter with me. When you receive this order, you, Chi-Chang, Duke West, must prepare to depart for the capital immediately, to help relieve my worry. When the great deed is accomplished, I shall reward you with promotion and additional land. Obey this order. I shall not renege.

As was the custom to thank a messenger who had traveled afar to deliver a message, Duke West Chi-Chang entertained the messenger with a banquet and presented him a gratuity of gold and silver. He then told the messenger: "Your Highness Imperial Messenger, please go back to inform the Emperor, that as soon as I finish packing my bag, I shall be on my way to the capital city Morning Song." The messenger thanked Duke West for the hospitality and then departed.

Duke West then summoned a court session. He first told the court officers: "I have been recalled to the capital for consultation with the Emperor. During my absence I delegate Chancellor San Felicitous to deal with internal affairs of the fief. I delegate Generals Nangong Gua the Swift, Hsin Chia, and Hsin Mian to deal with external events." He then summoned his crown prince Yikao to his presence and said: "Yesterday right after I received this imperial order, I prognosticated my own fortune. Adversity awaits me. Even though I may not be physically harmed, I shall encounter many hardships and shall face seven years of imprisonment. I delegate you administrative responsibilities of this fief. You must continue my policy of benevolent rule. You must obey laws of the land, and do not change the current system without a good reason. Do not act upon selfish impulses. Do not send anyone to secure my freedom. After the seven years of adversity are over, I shall return on my own. Do not forget what I have said."

Yikao, the crown prince, pleaded to his father: "If you know you are facing seven years of adversity, may I beg you to let me go on your behalf? A filial son must place his father's safety above his own."

Duke West replied: "If the adversities were avoidable, wouldn't I try to elude it? I cannot escape from this fate. It is the wish of heaven. If you stay here and perform your duty well, then you have already more than fulfilled your filial duty." The court session was adjourned.

Duke West went to his residential palace to bid his mother farewell. His mother, Tai Jiang, said, "I have prognosticated your fortune. You are destined to suffer through seven years of hardship."

Duke West replied, "Indeed so. After the messenger from the capital delivered the imperial order, I prognosticated my fortune and I know there are seven years of hardship awaiting me. However, I shall not lose my life. I have just delegated internal affairs to Chancellor San Felicitous, external affairs to Generals Nangong Swift, Hsin Chia and Hsin Mian, and general administrative responsibilities to Yikao. I come here to bid you farewell, for I shall depart for the capital Morning Song tomorrow morning."

Tai Jiang said to her son, "When you are away, be careful and do not rush into rash acts."

"I shall obey your advice," Duke West replied.

The next day, all court officers accompanied Duke West to Ten Li Pavilion – a traditional place to bid the last farewell on a long journey. A banquet of farewell was arranged. At the end of the banquet, Chi-Chang patted the shoulder of Yikao. "I shall see you seven years from now.

Maintain peace among your brothers." Duke West and his attendants then departed.

A few days later, Duke West and his entourage came upon the foot of Swallow Mountain. The sky darkened and thick clouds gathered. Duke West told his company, "thunderstorm will commence soon. Let us find a shelter." There were no villages nearby. The storm soon came. The group found shelter in a thick forest to dodge the heavy shower. Half an hour later, thunder roared. As the storm was subsiding, a bright red flash splashed its light against the cloud-darkened sky and a loud thunder blared. Duke West ordered his attendants: "Look for a star general."

The attendants were puzzled. "What does he mean by a star general?" As they were looking, someone heard the crying of a newborn baby and soon they located a baby boy next to an old tomb. One attendant said, "This must be the star general. Let us take him to the duke."

He was an extremely magnificent baby boy. Duke West was very pleased. "Although I have many sons, he is so lovely. I will adopt him," he thought. He told his attendants: "Take care of this baby. When we come to a village ahead, we will find a family to foster him until my return."

Twenty li ahead, before they reached the next village, they saw a Taoist carrying a commanding disposition waiting in the middle of the roadway. This Taoist approached and saluted to the Duke with a Taoist bow: "Salutation to my Lord."

Duke West, impressed by the poise of the Taoist, got off his horse and returned the salutation. "I am Chi-Chang, Duke West. May I ask from which mountain you come? May I hear what you wish to tell me?"

The Taoist replied: "I am Son of Clouds, of Cavern Jade Column, in Mount End South. I have been looking for the star general whom you just found after the thunder and the red flash of light. I am glad you have found him." Duke West asked his attendants to show the Taoist this baby. "Star general, finally you have arrived at this world!" Son of Clouds said. He then turned to Duke West. "May I take this baby to my cavern in Mount End South to train him as my disciple? When you come back to West Branch seven years hence, I will return him to you. Will you consent to this request of mine?"

Duke West was immensely impressed by the ability of the Taoist to forecast the seven years of predicament which he had prognosticated. "This Taoist has some unusual abilities. This baby boy shall learn a lot of the wisdom of Tao from him," Duke West thought, so he readily consented to the request. "I trust you. It is all right with me for you to take him as your disciple. However, how do I know him when I see him again?"

"Let me give him a name so you will know when you meet him again. Let me see. He was born of thunder. I will name him Lei Tsen the Thunder. In the future, if someone with this name shows up, then it is him." Duke West agreed. So Son of Clouds took Lei Tsen (Thunder) with him to Mount End South, where he raised the baby boy among his other disciples and taught him the wisdom of Tao. As if destined by fate, seven years later when Duke West was released from his imprisonment, it was Lei Thunder who would deliver him to his fief.

Duke West and his entourage continued their trek. Without incident they passed through the five frontier passes, Ming Pond City,
118

crossed Yellow River at Meng Gin and finally arrived at the capital Morning Song. He went to directly to the official guesthouse. The three other dukes had already arrived. It was late when Duke West arrived and the three dukes were already eating and drinking. After an exchange of greetings, the dinner table was reset into a banquet of welcome, and feasting and drinking resumed.

As drinking continued towards midnight, Duke South, Er Tsong-Yu, became half-drunk. Duke North, Tsong Migratory Tiger, had a reputation of being a greedy person, and he had befriended the two toadies of the court, Fei Chung the Corrupt and Yu Whenn the Adulator. Because of this relationship, he had been assigned the task earlier to construct a tall building called Starplucker Pavilion for the Emperor, and he had amassed a huge fortune from pilfering during the construction project. Er Tsong-Yu suddenly recalled this incident. He said to Tsong Migratory Tiger: "My dear Duke. We four are leaders of all other lords and they look at us as their role models. However, I heard you have committed many evil deeds. When you were in charge of the construction project Starplucker Pavilion, you profited from this venture. You imposed upon common people forced labor, and you exempted those who bribed you. People were taxed heavily to fund the construction project and you pilfered from the taxes collected. May I advise you to have some consideration for common people? You have already amassed enough fortune. You should consider doing some good deeds instead!"

Tsong Migratory Tiger was enraged. "We are of the same rank. What makes you think you can inflict insult upon me?" He knew that he had two important friends in the court, Fei the Corrupt and Yu the Adulator, so he was not going to let Duke South impose upon him. Half-drunk, he stood up, ready to engage Duke South in a fistfight.

119

War among Gods and Men

Duke West pointed his finger at Tsong Migratory Tiger. "What Duke Er said is true. He merely wants to remonstrate with you about those evil deeds. You should listen to him."

Meanwhile, Duke South became mad at Tsong Migratory Tiger. Grabbing a wine carafe, he threw it at Tsong Migratory Tiger, and hit him squarely at his face. The Migratory Tiger got up and moved forward to grab Er Tsong-Yu, but he was separated from him by Jiang Huan-Chu, who shouted: "You are all dukes, the highest rank in the Emperor's court. Where are your manners? Duke Tsong, it is late at night. Go to sleep."

Outnumbered, Tsong Migratory Tiger left the banquet and went directly to his bedroom to sleep. The three other dukes, having not seen each other for a long time, decided to continue to chat. Around two o'clock in the morning by our reckoning, a servant of the guesthouse sighed to himself, "Your highnesses, tonight you drink to your hearts' delight. Tomorrow your blood shall flow in the streets!" He only mumbled, but the air of the late night was extremely still and quiet.

Duke West heard every word that was spoken. He asked the servants: "Who has just spoken?" None of the servants in the guesthouse admitted that anyone had spoken. Duke West said: "I just heard someone saying, 'Tonight you drink to your hearts' delight. Tomorrow your blood will flow in the streets!' Who said this?" All the servants denied it. Dukes South and East had not heard these words spoken. However, Duke West insisted that he had heard it clearly. He then called in his guards and threatened: "Execute all of them, one by one, right here."

As the guards moved forward to seize the servants, the truth emerged: "It was Yao Fu."

120

Duke West then sent away his guards and retained Yao Fu. "What is the meaning of what you have just said? You had better tell the truth this time."

Yao Fu replied: "I regret my loud mouth. There is a secret scheme against you. Queen Consort Jiang was framed and tortured to death in grievance. Two princes vanished amidst a gust wind just when they were supposed to be executed. The Emperor and Dar-Gee secretly plan to kill all you four. Tomorrow when you go to see the Emperor, he already plans to order all of you executed without giving you a chance to speak. I feel sympathy for you, that is why I sighed and spoke these words to myself."

Duke East, Jiang Huan-Chu, said, "What happened to Queen Jiang?" Yao Fu told them what he knew regarding the circumstances surrounding the death of Queen Consort Jiang and the disappearance of the two princes.

Jiang Huan-Chu fainted. After he was revived, he cried, "I have never heard of or seen such cruel and inhumane acts against anyone! My poor daughter! My poor daughter!"

Duke West consoled him. "We cannot revive the dead, but we can help you to vindicate the innocence of Queen Jiang. We will prepare a communique to the Emperor to argue the innocence of your daughter."

Jiang Huan-Chu thanked them and said: "I appreciate your efforts, but since it is my misfortune, I must present the communique."

Dukes West and South said: "You may send in your own communique, but we three will submit another one on your behalf."

The treacherous Fei the Corrupt learned that the four dukes had arrived and were residing in the official guesthouse. A spy he posted in

121

the guesthouse informed him that the four dukes had learned the truth from one of the servants. He secretly went to the palace to see the Emperor. "The four dukes have arrived and they have learned what happened. They are preparing communiques to be presented to you when they are in the court. May I suggest that you order all of them executed without even reading their communiques. This is the best plan." Emperor Zoe was extremely pleased and commended him.

On the day of discourse, the court session commenced early in the morning, not long after sunrise. Officers in charge of the entry to the main hall reported: "The four dukes have arrived." The Emperor ordered them sent in.

After the four dukes entered the hall and presented their salutations, Duke East, Jiang Huan-Chu, handed a communique to the Emperor. Without even looking at the communique, Emperor Zoe said, "Jiang Huan-Chu, do you admit your guilt?"

Jiang Huan-Chu replied: "I have been head of East Ru Duchy and I have obeyed all laws of Shang. I have committed no crimes or offenses. However, you have tortured your Queen Consort to death and you have attempted to slaughter your own sons. You place your trust on the evil woman Dar-Gee. My ancestors received great dispensations from Shang Emperors, and I myself from the late Emperor Yi. I have the moral duty to remonstrate with you against your evil deeds. I have done no wrong against you. Please vindicate the dead of their innocence!"

Emperor Zoe was easily enraged at any criticism against him, but this time, partly due to his guilty conscience, he was angrier than usual and he cursed: "You with your lame excuses! You ordered your daughter to assassinate me. Your guilt is beyond the height of a mountain!" He then ordered armed guards of the palace: "Take him outside the Gate of Noon and chop him into pieces." The guards then
122

tied Jiang Huan-Chu up and removed all insignias of his rank. Jiang Huan-Chu cursed violently as he was taken out.

Dukes West, North, and South all left their ranks and came forward to speak to the Emperor: "Your Majesty, we have a joint communique to present to you. Jiang Huan-Chu has committed no crime or offenses against you. You did not even read his communique before you order his execution. The Emperor is the leader of officers, and officers are arms of the Emperor. If Your Majesty orders execution of an officer without even reading his communique, you shall be accused of being atrocious. Civilian and military officers will never submit their fealty towards you. You must listen to us."

Vice Premier Bee Gahn opened the communique submitted jointly by the three dukes. The communique read:

Faraway subordinate officers of Shang, Er Tsong-Yu, Chi-Chang and Tsong Houfu present to Your Majesty:

Sage kings do not indulge in wine and women, but concentrate to rule the country with justice and benevolence. Since you succeeded the throne of the late Emperor Yi to rule Shang, we have seen little benevolence in your reign. You have indulged in wine and women, distanced yourself from righteous and honest officers. Queen Jiang was a virtuous Queen and she had committed no offenses, but she was tortured to death. Dar-Gee has tarnished the palace with her evil schemes and deeds. She has advised you to construct horrendous torture machines like Pao-Lo to silence your loyal remonstrators, executing the Imperial Astronomer when he told you the truth. We wish you, the omnipotent Emperor of the world, to distance yourself from toadies like Fei Chung and Yu Whenn, and execute Dar-Gee to vindicate the virtuous Queen Jiang.

Otherwise peace may not be with this country and this regime for long. We have risked our lives to remonstrate with you about the danger that may erode the foundation of this country. Please listen to us.

Upon finishing reading this communique, the anger of Emperor Zoe was beyond description. He tore the communique into pieces and ordered: "Execute these rebel officers." Armed guards then tied up all three dukes and pushed them towards the Gate of Noon. The Emperor ordered General Ru Brave to supervise the execution.

At this moment, two officers left their ranks and spoke to the Emperor. These two were Fei Chung the Corrupt and Yu Whenn the Adulator. They pleaded: "Indeed the four dukes are guilty, but please have mercy on Tsong Migratory Tiger. He is an honest and loyal subordinate officer of yours. He successfully constructed the Starplucker Pavilion in time. We have known him for a long time. Please pardon him."

Both Fei the Corrupt and Yu the Adulator were favorites of Emperor Zoe. Besides, it was through the stratagem of Fei the Corrupt that he had succeeded to lure the four dukes to the capital. Being a person with inconsistent opinions, Emperor Zoe instantly proclaimed: "Tsong Migratory Tiger alone is pardoned. The other three lords shall be executed right away."

This arbitrary exercise of justice annoyed Huang Flying Tiger, as well as other royal relatives including the two uncles of Emperor Zoe and Vice Premier Bee Gahn. They all left their ranks and pleaded: "Jiang Huan-Chu has conquered East Ru region on your behalf. He has been a loyal officer all along. There is no evidence that he attempted to assassinate you. Chi-Chang has always been loyal to you; he is highly respected and is known as the Sage of West. Er Tsong-Yu has been instrumental in fencing off barbarians from the south. Please pardon them all. All of us will gladly serve as guarantors of their behavior."

After some thought, the Emperor replied: "Jiang Huan-Chu committed the crime of treason. Er Tsong-Yu and Chi-Chang sided with Jiang. They all deserve to die. You should not endanger yourselves to pledge as guarantors of these rebels!"

Huang Flying Tiger pleaded: "Jiang Huan-Chu and Er Tsong-Yu are well-known for their contributions to the stability of your dynasty. Chi-Chang is a conscientious gentleman who has committed no crimes against you. Besides, Chi-Chang is known for his ability of prognostication. If you execute them for no justifiable charge, how can people have trust in your justice system? Besides, they all are in charge of hundreds of thousands of armies as well as hundreds of fierce and ferocious warrior generals. If their people learn that their leaders have been executed for no good cause, rebellion will commence. Imperial Teacher Wen Zhong is still in the midst of a campaign against rebels in North Sea. You cannot afford additional rebellions in the country. Please have pity on these three and pardon them."

Emperor Zoe was swayed by the argument of Huang. In addition, his seven royal relatives including two of his uncles kept pleading with him to spare the lives of the three. After pondering for a while, he finally decided: "I have often heard the good name of Chi-Chang. Although he is wrong to side with traitors, I will spare his life on account of your pleading. However, I cannot release him otherwise if he rebels against me in the future. You all will be responsible. As for Jiang Huan-Chu and Er Tsong-Yu, the evidence of their treason is so strong that I cannot pardon them. Have them executed right away! Speak no more." Another imperial order was sent: "Spare the life of Chi-Chang."

The two dukes were executed right away. Chi-Chang thanked the seven royal relatives and in tears he said, "Jiang Huan-Chu and Er Tsong-Yu were executed for no justifiable cause. From this day on there will be no peace in the east and south!"

The royal relatives replied, also in tears: "We will ask the Emperor for permission to collect the bodies of the two dukes and to bury them properly."

Attendants of the two dukes immediately escaped back to their dukedoms and reported the deaths of their masters to their heirs.

The next day, Vice Premier Bee Gahn asked the Emperor for permission to properly bury the bodies of the two, and to release Chi-Chang back to his land. Emperor Zoe, having discharged his main worry, generously consented. An imperial order was issued to this effect. Vice Premier Bee Gahn took the order and went out of the palace to oversee its execution.

As soon as Bee Gahn was gone, Fei the Corrupt said to the Emperor, "Chi-Chang presents himself as an honest person, but he is actually scheming and treacherous. He knows how to distort facts to fool others to follow him. If you let him go back to his land, he can scheme against you with the heirs of the two dead dukes. As the saying goes: You will regret it if you release a dragon to sea or free a ferocious tiger back to its mountain habitat."

The Emperor said, "I have already issued a written order, how can I renege upon it?"

Fei the Corrupt suggested, "I have a scheme to eliminate Chi-Chang." The Emperor asked him how, and Fei Chung replied, "Chi-Chang has been honorably released. According to custom, he is obliged to present himself to the Gate of Noon to express his thanks. He has many friends in the court. They are bound to send him off with a big banquet. I will join them to find out his intentions. If he is really loyal, you can pardon him. Otherwise you can execute him for treason."

The Emperor agreed. "You are right. Go and find the truth."

As soon as Vice Premier Bee Gahn left the court, he went to the guesthouse to visit Chi-Chang. "I have obtained an imperial order to release you back to your land, and to bury the two dukes properly."

Chi-Chang bowed and thanked him, "How can I ever repay you for your kindness and dispensation?"

Vice Premier approached Chi-Chang and whispered: "There is no law nor order in this court. For no reasons at all two officers of the highest rank were executed. Tomorrow after you have presented your thanks to the Emperor at the Gate of Noon, you must leave right away. Do not linger. Things can change at any moment."

Chi-Chang thanked Vice Premier again. "I will never forget you."

Early the next morning Chi-Chang went with his attendants to the Gate of Noon and performed the ritual. Afterwards he immediately departed with his guards and attendants. He and his entourage exited the west gate of the city. Upon arrival at the Ten Li Pavilion, Chi-Chang saw most of the court officers already there waiting for him. The leading ones were the royal relatives, Vice Premier Bee Gahn and Huang Flying Tiger. Evidently the group had been waiting for some time. Huang Flying Tiger and the representative of the royal relatives, Wei Chu, came forward: "Today the lord of highest esteem shall return home. We have prepared a modest feast to send him off, and we are offering a goblet of wine to salute to you. We also have a few words, if you care to listen to us."

Chi-Chang bowed. "At your service."

Wei Chu said, "Although the Emperor has done wrongs against you, please have consideration upon the greatness of the late Emperor and do not lose your virtue as a dutiful and loyal subordinate. If you can make this promise to us, we officers of the court and people of the land are much obliged to you."

Chi-Chang immediately removed his hat and bowed. "I owe my life to you all. How can I have any idea other than to unceasingly continue my loyal service to my Emperor as a vassal?" Feasting and drinking then began. Chi-Chang was known for his capacity to hold drink and he emptied one goblet after another as all the officers filed in front him wishing him the best of fortune. As they were drinking and feasting heartily, they saw two horsemen approaching, followed by an entourage of attendants. They were Fei the Corrupt and Yu the Adulator.

Chi-Chang thanked the two, "What have I done to deserve the favor of your presence here?"

Fei the Corrupt replied, "We apologize for being late. Please forgive us." The entourage of the two then set up their own banquet table. Although all the officers extremely disdained the two, they did not want to offend them, for they could not afford to. On the other hand, they did not want to socialize with the two, either. With one excuse after the other, all the officers left, since their objective to bid farewell to Chi-Chang had been accomplished.

Finally only the three of them were left. Chi-Chang, being a gentleman, did not suspect the purpose of the visit of the two and amidst toasts he drank heartily. Fei the Corrupt said, "We are drinking with small goblets. It does not satisfy me." He then ordered: "Fetch large goblets here." After toasting a large goblet of wine to Chi-Chang,

Fei the Corrupt complimented, "My Lord, I heard that you are an expert of prognostication. Is it true that you have never been wrong?"

Not suspicious of any stratagem against him by the two, Chi-Chang replied: "Some things in the world have been ordained since creation. However, there are many uncertain events in life. Prognostication only works with preordained events. A wise man can usually avoid disasters if he knows beforehand."

Fei then continued, "If the Emperor has done wrong deeds, as many court officers have asserted, may we learn about the future course of events of this country?"

By this time, Chi-Chang was half drunk and had totally forgotten the warning given him regarding the two. He sighed. "The fate of this country is not bright. This dynasty shall end with his reign, and the Emperor shall not die a natural death. The Emperor chooses to disregard the opinions of others and does whatever he pleases. He is accelerating his fall. As a subordinate officer, I have no heart to describe what shall befall him." His head drooped, and he sank into a sad mood.

Fei Chung continued probing. "When shall the end come?"

Chi-Chang replied: "Within twenty-eight years, on the day of the third Celestial Stem and the seventh Earthly Branch, in the first year of a new sexagenary cycle."

The two pretended to sigh and drinking resumed. After a while, the two asked Chi-Chang: "How about us? Can you prognosticate our fate?"

Chi-Chang did not suspect that the two were trying to trick him for information. He took out several gold coins, threw them to the air and let them fall. He took the patterns and prognosticated accordingly.

Looking perplexed, he pondered for a while, then said, "This is extremely strange."

Fei and Yu laughed and said: "What is so strange about it?"

Chi-Chang replied, "Most people die of illness or other human actions such as imprisonment or execution. However, you two will die a strange death."

Fei and Yu asked: "What kind of strange death shall we die?"

Chi-Chang replied, "I do not know how to describe it. You two shall die amidst frozen snow and ice."

The two looked at each other, then burst into laughter, and Fei Chung said, "As the saying goes, a person was born of destiny and shall expire according to his providence. Let us not worry about it."

Fei and Yu then lured Chi-Chang to say more. "How about yourself?"

Chi-Chang replied, "I shall die a natural death."

Fei and Yu flattered Chi-Chang: "You were born with blessing from heaven." After a few more drinks, using the excuse that they had to attend matters in the court, the two bid farewell and left.

On their way back, the two cursed Chi-Chang: "This old swine! His life is in our hands and he claims that he will die a natural death. He then decried us to die amidst frozen snow and ice." They went directly to the palace.

The Emperor asked: "What did he say?"

The two replied: "Chi-Chang is speaking nonsense. He insulted you with fatuous words. He is guilty of rudeness to his Emperor."

Emperor Zoe became enraged: "This old rascal! I pardoned him so that he can go back to his fief. Now he has insulted me! What fatuous words did he say?"

The two told him: "He said he had prognosticated the fate of this country. He said that it is not bright. Within twenty-eight years this dynasty shall fall within your reign. Then he said that you will not die a natural death."

Emperor Zoe cursed. "Did you ask him how his life shall end?"

The two answered: "Yes, we did. He claimed that he shall die a natural death. Of course he is speaking nonsense. His life is in your hands, now he says that he will die a natural death. Isn't that a self-deception! We two also asked him to prognosticate our fate. He said that we shall die amidst frozen snow and ice. Not mentioning the fact that we are under your blessing, even common people do not usually die amidst frozen snow and ice. This is sheer nonsense! We cannot tolerate a person like him spreading wild rumors."

Emperor Zoe then issued an order: "Ask Zhao Field to arrest Chi-Chang and bring him back here for execution."

After Chi-Chang remounted his horse, he began to realize that he had spoken words he should not have. He ordered his attendants: "Let us leave right away. Things change rapidly around here." As they moved along, Chi-Chang was perplexed. "I prognosticated my fate, and I came to the conclusion that I was to be imprisoned for seven years. Now I am safely on my way back. Was I right? Maybe whatever I said to the two will cause trouble for me."

As they were moving along, Zhao Field arrived. Galloping his horse after Chi-Chang, he yelled, "Stop! The Emperor has just issued an order to summon you back to the capital."

Chi-Chang replied, "Yes, I know." He then turned to his guards and attendants. "This is my fate. You go back as soon as possible. Tell them not to worry, I shall be back safely in seven years." Chi-Chang then followed Zhao Field back to the capital.

As Zhao Field and Chi-Chang approached the Gate of Noon, a scout reported the return of Chi-Chang to Huang Flying Tiger. He was startled. "He is back so soon! Maybe the two treacherous toadies slandered Duke West or planned some scheme to frame him with some trumped-up charges." He told Zhou Chi, "Quickly, summon all royal relatives to the Gate of Noon." By the time Huang Flying Tiger arrived at the Gate of Noon, Chi-Chang was still waiting there for the Emperor to receive him. Flying Tiger said: "Why are you summoned back?"

Chi-Chang replied: "I do not know." Just then, an order from Emperor Zoe arrived to admit Chi-Chang. All the officers accompanied him into the meeting hall in the palace.

Upon entry, Chi-Chang said to Emperor Zoe, "May I ask what Your Majesty wishes to see me for?"

Emperor Zoe cursed: "I spared your life. Not only are you not grateful, you also insinuated insults against me. What did you do with your prognostication?"

Chi-Chang replied: "This method of prognostication has been passed down from generation to generation, since the time of the two sage kings, Shen Nong and Fushi. Through time, this method evolved into the use of eight trigrams. I cast my prognostication in strict accordance with these ancient rules; how dare I insinuate insult against Your Majesty?"

Emperor Zoe said, "All right, now cast another prognostication about this country."

Chi-Chang replied, "I have done this already. I told Fei Chung and Yu Whenn about my conclusions. It was not a good fortune, but I did not say anything against you or form any adverse opinion."

Emperor Zoe stood up and shouted, "You said that I shall not die a natural death. You boasted that you shall die a natural death. Isn't this an insult to your Emperor? You are spreading wild rumors to fool the masses. You are a source of future trouble, if not now." He then issued the order: "Execute Chi-Chang right away!"

While the guards were readying to take Chi-Chang prisoner, a group of officers and royal relatives, led by Huang Flying Tiger, intervened: "Your Majesty, you must not execute Chi-Chang. Everyone in the country knows that you have pardoned him. People rejoice over your benevolence and kindness. Chi-Chang based his projection on the ancient art of prognostication passed down by Sage King Fushi. The predictions were obtained according to ancient rules. He did not make up the results. He is not a treacherous person."

The Emperor said, "He uses his elfin magic to insinuate insults against me. How can I pardon him?"

Vice Premier Bee Gahn explained: "We are asking you to pardon Chi-Chang on behalf of this country. If he is executed because of his art of prognostication, people will revolt against you, because the accuracy of his prognostication is well-known. We can test him. We can ask him to cast a prognostication for the next few days. If he is right, pardon him.

If he is wrong, you can charge him with the crime of spreading reckless rumors."

Figure I- 8. Duke West

Chi-Chang made a prognostication for Emperor Zoe

The Emperor could not find an excuse not to listen to the highest officers of his court. He consented to the request.

Chi-Chang took out his three coins and prognosticated. He was startled at his result. "Your Majesty, tomorrow there will be a fire in the Imperial Ancestral Shrine. Quickly remove all sacred tablets of ancestral emperors from the Shrine to protect them from fire. Otherwise the foundation of this dynasty may be wrecked!"

Emperor Zoe said, "When shall this fire commence?"

Chi-Chang replied, "Tomorrow at noon." Emperor Zoe then ordered Chi-Chang imprisoned until the next day, to test if his prognostication was true.

After all the officials left, Emperor Zoe consulted with Fei the Corrupt, "Chi-Chang said that tomorrow a fire shall commence in the Imperial Ancestral Shrine. Do you believe it? What happens if it turns out that he is right?"

Yu the Adulator replied, "Just issue an imperial order to ask the keepers of the Imperial Ancestral Shrine to take extra precaution. No incense must be burnt. No fire of any sort will be allowed around or inside the Shrine. I want to see how a fire can start from nothing."

The next day, Huang Flying Tiger and the seven royal relatives gathered in his official residence, waiting eagerly for the predicted fire in the Shrine at noon. A time keeper reported: "It is noon now." There was no fire. All were worried. Suddenly, thunder and lightning commenced, shaking the ground.

While Emperor Zoe and his favorite toadies were conferring in the main hall in the palace, the keeper of the Shrine reported: "The sky darkened and lightning commenced. A ball of fire descended from the sky and ignited the Shrine."

The Emperor and his two toadies were dazed. Emperor Zoe said to the two: "His prognostication turns out to be true. What shall we do?"

Figure I- 9. Royal Temple caught fire
A ball of lightning struck the royal temple and ignited it

Yu and Fei conferred with each other for a while, then said: "Although the prognostication of Chi-Chang was correct, it might still just be a coincidence. He cannot be released upon one single merit. If you do not want to face the high officers of the court who remonstrate with you against the execution of Chi-Chang, you can issue an order to banish him to the village of Yeau. Release him from banishment only when peace prevails in this country."

After the order of banishment was received, Vice Premier Bee Gahn consoled Chi-Chang. "Please be patient. After a month or two we will try to persuade the Emperor to release you back to your land."

People in the village of Yeau, whose name meant Guidance to Goodness, were overjoyed at the arrival of such a great man in their neighborhood. Chi-Chang thus became their teacher and counselor. Under his guidance, villagers became educated and the village prospered. A good order was established. In his leisure time, he reviewed the ancient method of prognostication by Eight Trigrams, which had been passed down from generation to generation since their invention by the Sage King Fushi. As a man of good disposition, Duke West Chi-Chang expressed no complaint against his fate. He merely quietly and patiently waited for the conclusion of the seven-year banishment which he had prognosticated before he left his fiefom.

After the execution of the two dukes and the banishment of the third, Emperor Zoe became even more irrational and arrogant. One day, it was reported to Huang Flying Tiger: "The new Duke East, Jiang Wen-huan, has mutinied to avenge the death of his father and his sister. He led an army of one hundred thousand to attack the frontier pass Drifting Spirits. The new Duke South, Er Shun, also commanded an army of two hundred thousand to attempt to overtake the frontier pass Three Mountains."

Out of 800 lordships of the country, 400 had already mutinied against Shang. Huang Flying Tiger sighed in grief: "This is the beginning of the end! Peace shall never be with us!"

War among Gods and Men

6. Taming of Pearl of Wisdom

One day, inside Golden Ray Cavern in Genesis Mountain, as Demigod Tai-Yee (Great Unity) was just about to lecture Tao to his disciples, messenger boy White Crane of the Palace Jade Abstraction in East Kwen Ren Mountain Range arrived with a letter from his teacher-mentor Primeval, the Patriarch of Sect Elucidatus. After presenting the letter, White Crane said, "The Patriarch wishes that the Pearl of Wisdom be incarnated to the human world as soon as possible, since he will be needed to serve as a vanguard in the forthcoming revolutionary army of Jiang Sarn."

"Yes. Please tell the Patriarch that everything shall be done according to his wish."

*

In his youth, Li Gin (Militaris) went to remote mountains to study Tao to become a demigod. However, being born under the wrong star, he was not able to embrace the elusive wisdom of Tao, although he did master the basic training. His teacher eventually told him that the most he could accomplish was wealth and power in the human world. Accepting his fate, he returned to the world of dust, and had since accomplished much in military matters. He served the Shang Empire and now held the rank of Sentry Commander, in charge of Chien Tang Frontier Pass.

He already had two sons; the elder one was named Suvarnata, the younger one Moksa. Now his wife was pregnant for the third time. Oddly, this pregnancy had lasted three years and six months, without any sign that a birth was about to take place. All the doctors she

139

consulted with confirmed the conception, but no one seemed to know why the pregnancy lasted for such an unusually long period.

One night in her dream she met a Taoist. In his commanding tone, he told her: "Now is the time for your son to be born. Take this." Before she could find out what she was given, she woke up.

The next morning, she gave birth to a rather strange thing, a ball of flesh without any resemblance to a human baby. Angry at this "thing," Li the Militaris cut the ball of flesh in half with his sword. To his surprise, a child emerged, unharmed, and quickly grew to the normal size of a baby. His waist was wrapped in a piece of red cloth and on his right wrist was a golden bracelet. Unlike other newborn infants, this child immediately ran around the room, exploring everything he could find. Surprised but pleased, Li Gin held the boy up. Finding him otherwise absolutely normal, he quickly developed an affection for the newborn. However, the strange circumstance of his birth still bothered him and his wife.

The next day, disguised as a traveling Taoist, Demigod Great Unity went to visit the frontier pass and asked to see Li Gin. Being an ex-Taoist himself, Li Gin had a liking for Taoists, so Demigod Great Unity soon found himself in the reception hall. After an exchange of pleasantries, Demigod Great Unity spoke. "I know you have just acquired a son. Unfortunately, as your son was born at the evil hour of Chou, he shall commit carnage after carnage. He will be a great warrior but he could also cause you a great deal of trouble. With your permission, I shall accept him as my disciple. When the need arises, he knows where he can seek help from me."

Impressed by Demigod Great Unity, who seemed to have a formidable command over people, Li Gin responded: "I comply with your request. Now please stay over for a vegetarian banquet in your honor."

But the offer was politely declined. "Thank you, but I must go now. Your son knows where to find me when he needs me." Then Demigod Great Unity vanished.

Years went by without any incidents. Heeding the advice of Demigod Great Unity, Nata was always kept within the compounds of the official residence. Though he was only seven years old now, Nata had already grown to a formidable height of six feet, and he was a naughty one.

In the meantime, messages were received from Emperor Zoe's court that rebellion had started in the South and the East. Orders were given to Li Militaris to drill his warriors and soldiers to become war ready, in the case the Frontier Pass should be invaded. Military exercises were held almost daily. Getting bored of watching these military exercises, Nata decided to sneak out of the official compound to explore the never-never land that had been barred to him since his birth.

One day, amidst the excitement typical of a military exercise, Nata quietly slipped out of the compound through a side door. Not far from the official compound was a river. Having never seen a river in his life, Nata got very excited. This was so much bigger than his tiny bathtub. It must be a fun thing, he thought. He immediately stripped himself and jumped to dip himself in the water. He then used his red birth cloth as a towel to dry himself. Now this was no ordinary cloth, nor was the golden bracelet ordinary he wore at his birth. The red cloth – Skycover Cloth – was a remnant left over from the heavenly material that was used to make the robe of the Jade Emperor of the Heaven Palace. The bracelet he wore was the Bracelet of Zion, a dharmaratna, or magical fetish, given to Demigod Great Unity by his teacher-mentor Primeval as a mascot of his cavern. Both items carried immense magical powers. To make things worse, the river Nata had gone to swim, called Nine Lagoon River, happened to be one of the several gateways to the palace of the Dragon King of East Sea.

The washing of the Skycover Cloth generated such a huge underwater wave and disturbance that the palace of the Dragon King of East Sea was shaken. A two-horned sea monster patrol, a *yaska*, was dispatched by the Dragon King to investigate. This yaska was accompanied by a small group of giant crab soldiers, and was dispatched to the surface of the river to investigate. Seeing that the disturbance came from a child, the monster sped forward with a battle-ax he was carrying and shouted: "You little devil, you have caused great disturbance to the palace of the Dragon King. You had better stop your disturbance and get out of here before I, a Yaska in the service of the Dragon King, kill you!"

Seeing a monster shouting threatening words and charging towards him, Nata instinctively threw his Bracelet of Zion at it. Unleashing its magical power, the Bracelet of Zion homed towards the sea monster and marked a direct hit, knocking him dead. Nata laughed: "What an incompetent fool! Now my Bracelet of Zion is stained with his blood. Well, let me wash it in the river."

The washing of the Bracelet of Zion produced even more underwater disturbances than the Skycover Cloth had. The giant crab soldiers accompanying the yaska fled back to report his death to Au-guang, Dragon King of East Sea.

The third prince, Aubin, being an accomplished warrior, volunteered to investigate. The dragon prince Aubin transfigured himself into a human form and mounted a dolphin. Accompanied by an entourage of several giant shrimp and crab soldiers, he surfaced to investigate. Skipping over water waves, he coasted swiftly towards the

Nata. Seeing the disturbance was from a child, he slighted his opponent. He raised his two-pronged spear, combat-ready, and shouted, "Who killed my patrol?"

"Me." Raising his head slightly to look at Aubin, Nata had answered casually, then he continued washing the Bracelet of Zion.

Figure I- 10. Nata killed the Dragon Prince

"Who are you," Prince Aubin asked.

"The third son of Li Militaris. My father is the regiment leader of this frontier pass. I am swimming peacefully here; it was your monster yaska who provoked me by charging towards me with a deadly weapon. I had to kill him in self-defense."

"You, the audacious scoundrel and murderer! I am going to teach you a lesson," shouted the dragon prince Aubin. He then charged towards Nata with his two-pronged spear.

Without any weapon to defend him, Nata threw the Skycover Cloth at Aubin. The magical power of Skycover Cloth was released. It grew in size, and as it descended it bundled up Aubin, forcing him off his dolphin. Dragging the bundled-up Aubin ashore, Nata tapped him with the Bracelet of Zion. The magic of transfiguration was destroyed and the dragon prince was back to his dragon form. Realizing that he had captured a real dragon, Nata was very excited and he said to himself, "My father raised me since I was a baby, and I have never been able to repay him with anything. Now I have captured a rare dragon. Let me make a gift out of this dragon for my father to show my gratitude." He thus knocked the dragon dead and skinned it to remove its tendons, and wove the tendons into a waist belt for his father's court dress. After he finished his task, he returned to the official residence.

His mother, in extreme anxiety over the disappearance of Nata, was relieved to find him safe and sound. "Where did you go, my dear son?"

"Just around," responded Nata.

"Go to your quarters and wash up," ordered his mother, so Nata went back to his quarters.

The entourage of giant shrimps and crabs of Aubin escaped back to the dragon palace and reported the mishap. Extremely mad at Li Militaris, whom he had met when Li was studying Tao, Dragon King of East Sea, Au-guang, vowed vengeance. Transfiguring himself into the form of a human scholar, he went to visit Militaris and was admitted to the reception hall.

Li Militaris found his old acquaintance in a mad mood of rage. Without even a perfunctory exchange of pleasantries, Dragon King Au-guang accused him: "Your son is a murderer."

The surprised Li Gin responded: "My dear old friend, I have only three sons. Both my first and second sons are now studying Tao in high mountains under reputable demigods. My third son has always been kept within the compound of my official residence. You have made a mistake to accuse any of them as a murderer."

"I have made no mistakes," responded the Dragon King. "Your son was swimming in the Nine Lagoon River, and by some magical trick he caused a great disturbance in my undersea palace. I sent my patrol, a yaska, to investigate the source of the disturbance. He was killed by your son. My third son then went up to investigate the death of the patrol. Not only was he killed, the murderer also skinned him and removed his tendons." Wiping his tears with his sleeves, the Dragon King shouted, "And you still deny it!"

Li Militaris replied, "My eldest son Suvarnata is now studying Tao in Five Dragon Mountain, my second son Moksa in Mount Nine Merits. The third son Nata is only seven years old, and he has never been allowed outside the compound of my residence. Where did you get the idea that any of them committed such a serious crime?"

"It is exactly your third son who did it," the Dragon King replied.

"I will ask him to come here to see you and he will verify his innocence." Li Militaris personally went to find Nata.

He found Nata in his room. "What did you do today," asked Li Militaris.

Nata responded, "I went out of the compound to play. Then I saw a river. The weather was hot in the afternoon so I decided to take a dip. Shortly afterwards a sea monster appeared. He first shouted insulting words at me then he came at me with an axe, so in my self-defense I threw my bracelet at him. The useless fool was killed instantly by the bracelet. Later, another so-called prince riding a dolphin appeared. He too shouted insulting words at me, and before I could explain to him, he also charged at me with a two-pronged spear, so I bundled him up with my Skycover Cloth and brought him to the shore. I tapped him with my Bracelet of Zion, and he turned out to be a dragon. I thought this would be a good opportunity to show my gratitude to you, so I skinned the dragon and from his tendons I knitted a waist belt as a gift to you. Here is the dragon tendon belt for you to use with your court dress."

Li Militaris was stone-silent. Minutes passed. "You have caused a disaster!" the shocked and trembling Militaris finally said. "The Dragon King is a god officer appointed by the court of Heaven Palace, to take charge of rain, rivers and seas. He is no ordinary god. Go to talk to him yourself."

Nata went to the reception hall. He apologized to the Dragon King. "It was a mistake. I apologize for my overreaction. Now let me give you back the dragon belt."

The presence of the belt only intensified the grief of the Dragon King. "You murderer!" he shouted. "Both my son and my patrol are

146

appointed officials of the Court of the Jade Emperor. You have killed them both. This is an offense against the Jade Emperor. Tomorrow I am going to the court of the Jade Emperor of Heaven to file charges against you. You'd better prepare yourself for punishment."

Li Militaris was scared, for what the Dragon King had said was true and the offense was definitely a serious one. Li and his wife were crying, grieving that severe punishments were to come.

Seeing this sad scene, Nata responded: "I am no ordinary child, either, I am a disciple of Demigod Great Unity. He left words that I should see him when I am in trouble. Now I am in trouble. I will seek help from him. Let me go."

According to the teaching of Tao, there are five basic forms in the universe: metallum, wood, water, fire and terra.[1] One basic training of Tao is to learn how to manipulate the five basic forms, including the skill to transmute any one form into another. Thus, a capable Taoist can transmute oneself into one of the basic forms, say terra. Once transmuted into a basic form, this Taoist can fully utilize the properties of the form to his advantage. For example, a Taoist standing on terra firma can apply the transmutation process to himself, then disappear into the ground. He can then add energy, the driving force of the universe, to his transmuted terra form. The added energy will drive his transmuted terra form to travel as a soliton wave. Unlike other waves, a soliton wave retains its identity and its integrity as it propagates. Whenever he wishes, he can also apply the reverse process of

---

[1]This differs from the ancient Greeks, whose four basic elements are earth, wind, fire and water. In the teaching of Tao wind or air is not regarded as a form or element, probably because water can evaporate to become 'air', so air or wind is regarded as another paradigm of water.

transmutation to restore himself to his original form. In other words, using the Tao of transmutation, a Taoist can travel swiftly inside terra firma. This mode of transportation is called terra-trekking. Other modes of trekking are possible, such as metallum-trekking, wood-trekking, hydro-trekking, and fire-trekking. However, because of the abundance of terra and water, trekking inside these two media is the most common.

Although Nata had been incarnated into human form, he still retained his basic training of Tao, so he terra-trekked to Cavern Golden Ray. Demigod Great Unity was surprised to see him, and asked: "Why aren't you in Frontier Pass Chien Tang?"

"May your disciple report to you a disaster?" Nata said. "Yesterday I went out of the official compound for the first time, and I took a swim in Nine Lagoon River. I was confronted by a sea monster and then the third prince from the Dragon Palace. In my self-defense I killed them both. Now Dragon King wants to file charges against my parents in the court of the Jade Emperor. Please pardon me for my ignorance and please save my parents and me."

"Well, I anticipated this kind of predicament, because you were born in the wrong hour. It was wrong for you to kill them, but it was equally wrong for those two to attack you first without provocation. It is true that the Dragon King is an appointed officer of the court of the Jade Emperor, but he should not use his official position to force a settlement. Come. Remove your shirt, I will pass along some magical power to you. Use this magical power to bring the Dragon King back to the Frontier Pass and try to reason with him. You must not be arrogant this time."

Nata then went directly to the main gate of Heaven Palace of the Jade Emperor and patiently waited. He saw Au-guang the Dragon King of East Sea approaching, fully dressed in formal court attire. The magical power granted to Nata by Demigod Great Unity was invisibility. When Nata saw the Dragon King in court attire ready to file charges against him and his parents, he suddenly became outraged and he cursed: "This old rascal really wants to use his position to impose upon my family!" In his rage he completely forgot the advice of his teacher. The invisible Nata went behind the Dragon King and knocked him down to the ground with his Bracelet of Zion. Nata then twisted his arms back and forced him to lie facedown.

The Dragon King yelled in pain and he turned his head around, then he saw Nata. In great humiliation he shouted, "You rascal, you have already committed a horrendous crime. Now what do you think you are doing in front of the court of the Jade Emperor?"

This remark further enraged Nata and he suddenly had the urge to kill the Dragon King, too, but he was afraid that he might cause further trouble. He shouted back, "You old eel! Let me tell you, I am no ordinary child. I am the Pearl of Wisdom, disciple of Demigod Great Unity of Cavern Golden Ray, Genesis Mountain. Under an order from Palace Jade Abstraction, I was incarnated as the son of the regiment leader, Li Militaris, waiting to join the revolutionary army as a vanguard under the command of Jiang Sarn, against the tyrant Emperor Zoe. I was only taking a swim in Nine Lagoon River when your patrol and your son attacked me without provocation. I killed them both because they threatened my life. They provoked me first and I killed them in self-defense. I apologized to you already for overreacting to their provocation. Yet you still want to use your official position to file ludicrous charges against my father and me. This matter could be resolved among ourselves and my parents. My teacher told me that if you want to continue to press absurd charges, I can kill you, too."

"I dare you, you idiot youth of insolence!" cursed the Dragon King.

"All right, you asked for it." Nata punched him forcefully until Au-guang the Dragon King started to yell in pain. "I know how to teach you a proper lesson, you eel with scales." As he spoke, Nata started to tear the court dress apart, exposing the golden scales of the Dragon King. He then started to tear the scales of the dragon piece by piece. The pain inflicted on the Dragon King was so intense that he soon begged for mercy. "All right, I will spare you if you come with me peacefully to Frontier Pass Chien Tang and settle the dispute. Wait, you may try to escape. Now you must transfigure yourself into a small snake so that I can carry you in my sleeve." Under the forceful fist of Nata and the threat that more scales would be pulled out, the Dragon King unwilling accepted the humiliating order to transfigure himself from a dignified King into a little snake. Putting the little snake in his sleeve, Nata rode on the clouds and soon arrived at Frontier Pass Chien Tang.

"Where have you been," Li Militaris asked wearily.

"I have just gone to Heaven to ask uncle Dragon King to cease filing charges against you," Nata replied.

"You liar! You have no rank to go to the court of the Jade Emperor ..." reprimanded Li Militaris.

"Please believe me, I did not go inside the Court, but I did wait at the gate and I did bring Uncle Dragon King back with me."

"You are still fabricating lies. Where is your uncle Dragon King?"

"Here. He is inside my sleeve." Nata shook his sleeve and a small snake fell out, which immediately transfigured back to its human form, in his torn court dress stained with blood from his wounds where the scales had been pulled out.

"What happened to you?" Li Militaris said in full astonishment.

In raving anger, Au-guang the Dragon King recounted the incident of how he was repeatedly beaten by Nata, and he showed Li Militaris his bloody wounds where scales had been torn away. "I am going to gather the three other Dragon Kings from North, West, and South Seas and we will file a joint charge against you." Then the Dragon King vanished amidst a whirling wind.

"Now you have made things worse. What shall we do?" Li Militaris said.

"Don't worry, father and mother. I will get my teacher Demigod Great Unity to help me," Nata consoled his parents. Although impressed by the magical power of Nata, Li Militaris was still worried. His wife asked Nata to go back to his room while they tried to sort things out.

Nata was disturbed, too. He did not go back to his room, but strolled aimlessly around until he came to the exhibition hall. Among items of exhibit, he found a bow inscribed with the name Zion, and three arrows inscribed with the name Thunder. He asked around, and one of the attendants told him that the Bow of Zion and the three Arrows of Thunder were war relics from Huangdi's period. Reputedly the weapons had been used by one of Huangdi's mightiest warriors to conquer the last barbarian of that period, Chi Yu. The Bow of Zion was so taut that no one had ever been known to be able to pull a dent on the string, not to mention shooting an arrow with it. The bow and arrow set had been designated the mascot of the frontier pass. Challenged by a feat considered to be impossible, Nata thought, "My teacher told me that one day I shall hold the rank of vanguard in the revolutionary army of Jiang Sarn, but I do not have any military skill yet. Maybe I can use this bow and arrow set to practice archery." Nata then placed an Arrow

151

of Thunder on the Bow of Zion and pulled the string. Lo and behold, effortlessly, the bow was bent and the arrow disappeared through the clouds, leaving a trail of red glow in the sky for some time.

Unknown to Nata, the Bow of Zion had a range of several thousand li and the Arrow of Thunder had the ability of homing at a designated target. Through a bug in the Tao during the construction of the Bow of Zion and Arrows of Thunder, if a target was not designated, the Arrow of Thunder would automatically find a target when it was near the end of its range. As it happened, the Arrow of Thunder had been wantonly aimed in the direction of Cavern White Bones located in Skull Mountain, the home of Lady Stone Watershed. A maiden disciple of the Lady was out gathering herb medicine. The Arrow of Thunder, having not been given a target, and now near the end of its range, homed at the throat of the poor maiden and instantly killed her. In response to the disturbance, Lady Stone Watershed came out of her cavern to investigate and found her maiden disciple shot dead through the throat. She removed the arrow and saw the inscription, "Sentry Leader Li Militaris." She became very angry because when Li Militaris was pursuing his Taoist career, she had done him a favor and now an arrow bearing his name had been used to kill one of her disciples. She immediately dispatched her Yellow Turban Muscle Man to fly to Frontier Pass Chien Tang.

Using the magical Kerchief of Eight Trigrams, the Yellow Turban Muscle Man bundled Li Militaris up and carried him back to Cavern White Bones moments later.

Li Militaris was surprised to be captured by his old acquaintance without cause, but he was even more puzzled by her anger. Learning that one of the Lady's disciples had been killed by the Arrow of Thunder in his possession, he tried to explain. "The Bow of Zion is so taut that no one has ever been known to be able to pull even a dent on its string. I do not know who did it, but I promise you that I will find out, otherwise I will come back here to face the blame." Lady Stone Watershed gave Li Militaris three days to find the culprit. Li then hurriedly terra-trekked back to Frontier Pass Chien Tang.

Scared by her husband's sudden disappearance, Li Militaris' wife was relieved to see his safe return. However, his grinning face indicated that something was wrong. "I have been the sentry leader here for twenty-five years, and I knew of no one who could pull the string of the mascot Bow of Zion to shoot an Arrow of Thunder. Now the Bow has been used and a maiden disciple of Lady Stone Watershed has been killed. If I cannot locate the culprit in three days, my life will be in danger," sighed Li Militaris.

"Maybe it is the doing of Nata," suggested his wife.

"Maybe, but first let me inquire." Li Militaris then asked a servant to fetch him. The boy came. "Do you know archery? It is an important skill that you might need for your future mission in Jiang Sarn's army," said Li, trying to probe for the truth.

"Oh, yes. I have been practicing. I saw a bow and arrow set in the exhibition hall, so I tried, but the arrow disappeared through the clouds, leaving a red trail behind. Pity a good arrow was lost," Nata proudly replied.

"So it is you! Another disaster! Do you know that the arrow you just shot killed a maiden disciple of Lady Stone Watershed? She wants me to find out the culprit and to bring him to her, otherwise my life will be in danger."

"I will go with you to see Lady Stone Watershed and explain to her," responded Nata. They both terra-trekked to Cavern White Bones. A lad disciple was outside. He became startled and was about to shout for help when Nata threw the Bracelet of Zion at him, knocking him down.

Lady Stone Watershed heard the noise and she came out of her cavern to investigate. Nata threw the Bracelet of Zion at her, but she caught it effortlessly. He threw his Skycover Cloth at her, and she caught it also. Now without any weapons, Nata started to run away. Capitalizing upon this opportunity of confusion, Li Militaris immediately escaped and terra-trekked back to his Frontier Pass.

With Lady Stone Watershed chasing behind, Nata ran as fast as he could and having no place to go, terra-trekked to Cavern Golden Ray. He asked his teacher, Demigod Great Unity, for help.

Great Unity emerged from the cavern to greet Lady Stone Watershed.

"Your misbehaving disciple just killed my disciple. I want to kill him as punishment," Lady Stone Watershed charged.

"The unfortunate killing was a true accident, but no malice was intended. We must reason among ourselves to reach a reasonable punishment," replied Demigod Great Unity.

"No, absolutely no. I want his life to avenge the death of my disciple," insisted Lady Stone Watershed.

"You cannot do this. As you know, the three Sects have already agreed that after the forthcoming revolution, deities will be appointed. Anyone, including demigods, who gets involved in the forthcoming revolution may risk having his or her name included in the Roll of Deities.

Once included in the roster, he or she is destined to die! This is a very important mission and the Pearl of Wisdom is instrumental in its fulfillment. Neither I nor my teacher-mentor will allow your vendetta," argued Great Unity.

Without further words, Lady Stone Watershed charged forward with her sword. Demigod Great Unity retreated to his Cavern, and took out his sword and a magical device. Before he went out to face his challenger, he knelt down in the direction of East Kwen Ren Mountain Range where Palace Jade Abstraction was located and where his teacher-mentor and his Patriarch Primeval resided. Great Unity prayed: "Your disciple apologizes that today he has to break his vow of abstinence from carnage." After this short prayer, he emerged from the cavern. He spoke to Lady Stone Watershed. "Your level of Tao is very shallow and I advise you to leave now. When you come to your senses we can then discuss a proper punishment or compensation."

"No, I want him to pay for his crime with his life." Lady Stone Watershed charged forward. Again, the Kerchief of Eight Trigrams was cast.

Demigod Great Unity did not move; he silently chanted an incantation. Then he pointed to the Kerchief. "Come down". The Kerchief floated harmlessly down to the ground.

Blushing at her failure, Lady Stone Watershed charged forward to engage Great Unity in a sword to sword combat. Avoiding her swords, Tai-Yee took out a dharmaratna, Capsule Nine Dragons of Divine Fire. With a simple incantation, Lady Stone Watershed vanished and was enclosed inside the Capsule.

"What a great magical device! Had you given this one to me when I was incarnated, a lot of trouble could have been avoided," sighed Nata.

"Not at this time. With this powerful device, he could only cause more trouble and mischief. I will give this device to him only after Jiang Sarn is appointed as the commander of the revolutionary army," thought Great Unity.

"Go back quickly. Dragon Kings of Four Seas already have an imperial order from the Jade Emperor to arrest your parents. Go now. Heed this advice ..." Tai-Yee said, and off Nata went.

Clasping his hands, Demigod Great Unity ordered the nine fire dragons inside the Capsule to spew fire. An hour later, Lady Stone Watershed was reduced to her original form, a piece of rock that, in its original habitat of a watershed, had managed to gather the essence and spiritual power of the sun and the moon through millennia of time, acquiring a life and the wisdom of Tao of magic power so as to be able to assume a human form. Unfortunately the rock had overstretched her luck, and thus perished as a result of stubbornness typical of a rock. Demigod Great Unity then ordered the fire dragons to stop spewing fire. After retrieving the Bracelet of Zion and the Skycover Cloth, he returned to his cavern and all the magical devices were properly stowed away.

Arriving at the Frontier Pass Chien Tang, Nata found that the four Dragon Kings had already taken his parents prisoner. In a stern tone, he spoke to the Dragon Kings. "My parents are innocent. I am the only culprit. I will be solely responsible for my own actions. But I am no ordinary person; I am the Pearl of Wisdom incarnated as the third son of Li Militaris. Let us settle this way: You will let my parents go and I will immolate myself as punishment. I shall perform hara-kiri, returning my bones and flesh back to my parents. If you disagree with me then I will kill you all. Afterwards I will go to the Jade Emperor's to face whatever punishment I shall deserve. Do you agree with me on my terms?"

After conferring among themselves, the four Dragon Kings agreed. With a sword in his right hand, Nata first cut off his left arm, and removed fresh and bones from his body. The hara-kiri was performed. Satisfied with their vengeance, the four Dragon Kings left. Li Militaris and his wife buried their dead son accordingly.

Being the Pearl of Wisdom, Nata's spirit did not disperse. Now floating in the void, Nata had no place to go, so he went back to Cavern Golden Ray. Demigod Great Unity told Nata's spirit: "In time, you will be revivified. Meanwhile, you cannot stay here, but you may go back to tell your mother in her dreams that you need a place to stay. Ask her to build a temple for you. I have located a lot in Green Screen Mountain. It is a half day's horse ride from the Frontier Pass."

So Nata went back to the Frontier Pass and conveyed this message to his mother in her dreams. The same message was conveyed several times and his mother was convinced that the message was real. She related her dreams to Li Militaris, who, being happy to have gotten rid of this mischievous kid, refused to comply with the request. He did not want to have any memory of his unpleasant experience. However, Nata kept on casting the same dream over and over to his mother, so finally she gave in. She took her private savings and secretly built a temple at the designated location.

One day, during his military exercise, Li Militaris passed by Green Screen Mountain and saw a crowd of people in front of a temple. He said: "What is this temple?"

"It is the Temple of your deceased son Nata. It was built by your wife. People adore Nata because he always grants the righteous wishes of the worshipers."

Still enraged at his son, Li Militaris angrily cursed: "You disturbed your parents when you were alive, and now after your death you still fool people with your magical power." In his angry mood Li Militaris ordered the temple demolished and he personally knocked down the icon of Nata. He ordered the worshipers: "This is no god, and no one is allowed to worship him." The temple was burned down to the ground.

Returning to his official residence, Li Militaris blamed his wife. "While alive, your son was the cause of a great deal of trouble. Now he is dead and you built a temple to honor him. Don't you know that the court of Emperor Zoe is now controlled by Fei the Corrupt and Yu the Adulator? I have never sent them any gift. If they knew that my wife built a temple without authorization from the Emperor, they could seize this opportunity to destroy my career and perhaps to have both of us imprisoned or killed. You will not build any temple again!"

Coming back from a hunting excursion, Nata found his temple burnt down to the ground. An errand ghost reported what had happened while he was away. Nata was enraged. "I have already returned my bones and flesh back to my parents; I owe them nothing. What makes my father think he has the right to destroy my temple?" He went to see his teacher immediately.

"You already punished yourself for your mischievous acts. Your father was wrong to destroy your temple. All right, since Jiang Sarn will be appointed to his commander post soon, I will now revivify you to a physical existence. Follow me," Demigod Great Unity said.

They went to the back of Mount Genesis, to a pond by the name of Five Lotus. Demigod Great Unity asked a disciple nearby to gather two lotus flowers, three lotus leaves with stems. First he broke the stems of the lotus leaves into three hundred and sixty pieces, then he laid the broken stems among lotus flower petals to form a Tao pattern of three talents. The stems would become Nata's bones and the lotus flowers would become his body. Demigod Great Unity then positioned the three leaves in locations according to a design of heaven, earth, and man. A ball of golden decoction was then placed in the middle of the pattern. Using his wisdom of Tao to extract the essence of heaven, and controlling his breath according to the nine methods of separation, he pushed Nata's spirit into the center of the pattern of lotus leaves and stems. An incantation was recited. Lo and behold, suddenly a lad of seven feet sprang up, his face still retaining the pinkish white color of the lotus flower and his lips the color of cinnabar, which had been used during the preparation of the golden decoction. Great Unity gave Nata a set of clothes he had brought.

After Nata was dressed, he knelt down and thanked Demigod Great Unity for revivifying him back to a physical existence. Nata then said, "I must punish Li Militaris for his inconsideration."

Demigod Great Unity said, "Yes, he is indeed unreasonable. Follow me to the peach garden." Taking a fire-tipped spear from among a rack of weapons, Demigod Great Unity taught Nata the Tao of spear. Nata, who was incarnated from the Pearl of Wisdom, learned the Tao of spear play in no time. "I will give you additional dharmaratnas," said Demigod Great Unity. A pair of Wheels of Wind and Fire were given to Nata for transportation, together with a leopardskin bag which contained the following items: The Bracelet of Zion and the Skycover Cloth that were originally given to Nata, and a boomerang Golden Brick.

War among Gods and Men

Riding the Wheels of Wind and Fire, Nata soon arrived at Frontier Pass Chien Tang. He shouted, "I want Li Militaris."

Soldiers guarding the Frontier Pass reported to Li Militaris: "Your third son is back! He is calling your name, ready to combat against you!"

"Nonsense! I never heard of dead people coming back to life! Nevertheless let me investigate who has the audacity to pose as my dead son." Mounting his war horse and carrying his two-pronged spear, Li Militaris went out to face his challenger. He was both surprised and angry. He shouted: "You thing! You have caused me great disasters when you were alive, now you are back to life to cause more trouble!" He then charged forward to combat against his son.

"Since I have already returned my flesh and bones to you, I am no longer your offspring. Why did you destroy my temple and my icon? You have no reason to do these dreadful things. You will now pay for your irrational action." After these words Nata also charged forward.

Li Militaris was no match for Nata's spear play, nor for his strength. In a short while he began to retreat under the forceful thrust of the fire-tipped spear. As his escape route back to the Frontier Pass was blocked by Nata, Li Militaris had to dismount his horse, and escaped via terra-trekking.

Chasing Li Militaris on his Wheels of Wind and Fire, Nata soon caught up with him at Five Dragon Mountain. At this moment, a Taoist lad strolled by, intercepting the path of pursuit between Li Militaris and Nata. The lad began to sing a song as he approached the two:

Reflection of the bright moon by a clear pond,
Beautifies peach flowers along a dike.
A different flavor of clarity,
Is revealed by the glowing clouds.

Li Militaris stopped and listened. Then he recognized this young Taoist. It was his second son, Moksa. Meanwhile Nata also arrived. Seeing that Li Militaris was talking to a lad clad in a Taoist robe, wearing a loose scarf over his head and a pair of sandals knitted from flax on his feet, Nata stopped and asked: "Who are you?"

"You infidel offspring! You are now trying to murder your father. I, Moksa, the second son of Li Militaris, have been instructed to wait for you here."

Nata stopped, and narrated to the brother he had never seen in his life all that had happened, including the incident of the burning of his temple on Green Screen Mountain.

Moksa yelled, "Nonsense! Parents can never do wrong things."

Nata retorted, "I already returned my flesh and bones to him; I am no longer his son."

"You infidel offspring! Let me take care of you." With these words, Moksa charged forward with his sword.

Eager to continue his pursuit of Li Militaris, Nata took the boomerang Golden Brick out of his leopard skin bag and threw it at Moksa, knocking him off balance. Retrieving the Golden Brick, Nata continued his pursuit. Soon he almost caught up with Li Militaris.

Li Militaris sighed, "Let me kill myself so that I will not face the humiliation of being killed by my own son."

"Wait. Let me help you." This voice of relief came from a demigod by the name of Grand Bodhi Manjusri, the teacher of Li Militaris' eldest son, Suvarnata. "Go inside my cavern, I will take care of Nata. Your eldest son Suvarnata is inside waiting for you." So Li Militaris slipped into Cavern Cloud Tips.

"Did you see an armed warrior passing by," asked Nata.

"Yes, I just sent him into my cavern," replied Manjusri.

"He is my enemy. If you do not send him out, I will pierce you with my spear," threatened Nata.

"This is my territory; behave or get out," Manjusri calmly said.

"I am Nata, a disciple of Demigod Great Unity. Give me Li Militaris or I will kill you," Nata threatened again.

"I know Great Unity quite well, but I never heard of him having a disciple by the name of Nata. If you do not behave, I will have you thrashed." Manjusri also threatened, but in a lighthearted way.

Not taking this threat seriously, Nata charged forward. Grand Bodhi Manjusri took out a device called the Pole of Dragons. Suddenly, Nata found his two arms, his neck, and his two legs bound onto a golden pillar by three gold rings. "Suvarnata, come out and give Nata three hundred thrashes." Suvarnata, the elder brother of Nata, obeyed the order of Grand Bodhi Manjusri and gave Nata, who was now helplessly bound to the Pole of Dragons by the three gold rings, a good thrashing. Finally, the Grand Bodhi Manjusri said, "Let him stay here and let us go inside the cavern."

At this time, Demigod Great Unity also arrived. "Save me, my teacher!" Nata pleaded. Pretending not to see Nata, Great Unity passed by the Pole of Dragons and went into Cavern Cloud Tips to visit Grand Bodhi.

"Your disciple is here now, receiving punishment for his imprudence," said Grand Bodhi Manjusri.

"I know. He is short in his temper. I am using your punishment to tame his temperament. Li Militaris is wrong to have burned Nata's temple. My intention was to ask Nata to humiliate his father, but not to kill him. Nata overreacted." Replied Great Unity. They then sat down and chatted.

Figure I- 11. Nata confined
Nata was confined to the Pole of Dragons as punishment

After a while, Manjusri said, "I think he has already learned enough lesson." He then turned to Suvarnata, " Let Nata off the Pole and bring him here." After Nata was brought in, Manjusri spoke to both Li Militaris and Nata. "Now that the two of you have vented your anger, it is time to reconcile. From now on, you must respect each other and there will be no further conflict." In the presence of his teacher Demigod Great Unity, Nata had to consent to reconcile with his father.

"Li Militaris, you may go now. Nata, you wait around while my friend and I play a game of chess," said Demigod Great Unity.

Eager to continue his pursuit of his father, impatiently Nata scratched his head and paced up and down. Great Unity and Grand Bodhi Manjusri pretended not to notice. Finally, Great Unity said to Nata, "You may go home now."

Quickly mounting his Wheels of Wind and Fire, Nata lost no time in resuming his pursuit. Soon he found himself catching up with his father. "Now I will get you, you helpless Li Militaris!" he shouted.

Just at this moment, another Taoist appeared in between Nata and his father. Intercepting Nata, this Taoist asked him for the reason of his hot pursuit. Nata related what had happened, including the reconciliation in the Five Dragon Mountain.

"Now you are wrong. You have already agreed to a reconciliation, so you should keep your promise and you should not restart another conflict," said the Taoist.

"No, I want to have a combat with him," insisted Nata.

"All right, he is yours," said the Taoist, but before he let Nata go, he slapped Li Militaris gently on his back.

The Taoist had somehow magically increased the strength of Li Militaris, for, while Nata had had the upper hand before, now, under the powerful thrush of Li Militaris's two-pronged spear, he began to retreat. "You evil Taoist, it is you who gave Li Militaris his strength. Now I will pierce you with my spear." Nata turned to the Taoist.

The Taoist hopped aside to avoid the spear. Then he took out a small pagoda from his sleeve. Throwing the pagoda up, it grew in size and it descended upon Nata, completely enclosing him. With a simple incantation, fire started to spew upon Nata from all sides. His life was now in danger.

"All right, I will honor my promise of reconciliation." pleaded Nata.

"I will let you go if you keep your promise."

"Yes, I will." So Nata was released.

Finding himself unharmed, Nata told himself: "It was nothing but a cheap trick. He did not have any real power." He then continued his attack on Li Militaris. Once more the pagoda was thrown and again fire spewed from all sides upon Nata. The fire was as real as any fire could be. Nata pleaded again that he would respect his truce with his father. He was once again released, unharmed. Under the threat that the pagoda would be used again, unwillingly, but without any other option, Nata reconciled once again with Li Militaris.

"Li Militaris and Nata, both of you listen: Both of you are needed in the forthcoming campaign of Jiang Sarn. You two must absolve any enmity between you since you both shall serve in the same court as colleagues. Li Militaris, let me give you this pagoda and teach you its Tao to protect yourself in case Nata wants to restart a conflict again. To cool things down, Nata, you had better go back to Cavern Golden Ray to continue your study of Tao for a few more years and to learn to tame your temperament. Li Militaris, the revolutionary campaign will commence soon. You will be in an awkward position then if you continue to hold your present post. I suggest that you resign from your position now and live in seclusion with your wife to improve your Tao until the moment arises for you to join the revolutionary army." With these words, the Taoist departed. This Taoist who had saved Li Militaris was Light of Lantern, and would reappear several times during the revolutionary war.

Nata then went back to Cavern Golden Ray to continue his study of Tao under Great Unity. Li Militaris followed the advice of Light of Lantern and resigned from his post. He and his wife lived in a small farm in a nearby mountain, where he continued his study of Tao, but she died a few years afterwards. The father and son would meet again and would fight as comrades against common enemies during the forthcoming revolutionary war against the supporters of Emperor Zoe.

Although he had finally reconciled with his son, Li Militaris was still wary of a repetition of this unpleasant experience. From that day on, to protect himself, he never let the little pagoda, Thirty-Three Heaven Pagoda, out of his sight. After the successful revolutionary campaign, because of their important contributions, Li Militaris, Nata and his two brothers ascended to heaven to become gods, and the pagoda was never used. However, to this day icons of Li Militaris, who acquired the title of Devaraja, still show him with the little pagoda on his left hand as a reminder to Nata that he was under the constant protection of the mighty power of Light of Lantern. Li Militaris has since been known as the Palming Pagoda Devaraja Li.

Figure I- 12. The Palming Pagoda Devaraja Li

War among Gods and Men

7. Jiang Sarn

At the time of this saga, there were three Sects devoted to the study of the wisdom of Tao of the universe and life. They were: Anthropodus, Elucidatus, and Interceptus. All three Sects would play various important roles during the forthcoming revolutionary war. At this moment, let us pay attention to Sect Elucidatus.

The Patriarch of Sect Elucidatus was Primeval and the seat of the Sect was Palace Jade Abstraction, located on a high peak in East Kwen Ren Mountain Range. Primeval had 12 most senior disciples. One of them was Jiang Sarn.

One day Primeval dispatched his messenger boy White Crane to summon Jiang Sarn to his presence.

"Jiang Sarn, how long have you been here," the Primeval asked.

"Your Excellency, I have been here for forty years. I came here when I was thirty-two, now I am seventy-two," replied Jiang Sarn.

"I think you have studied Tao in this Palace long enough. As you were born under the wrong star, you will never achieve the status of a demigod. Nevertheless you are destined to be a great man, enjoying wealth and power in the world of dust. You shall lead a revolutionary army, to assist an emperor to deliver people from suffering and to establish an empire, commencing a great period of history. You are also destined to undertake the important task of appointing deities to serve in Heaven Palace. For the time being, however, your time in Palace Jade Abstraction is up. You must now return to the world of dust."

Jiang Sarn was shocked, and he pleaded, "But I enjoy my life here. My determination to study Tao is firm and sincere. I do not care about wealth and power in the human world. Please let me stay and continue my study of Tao under you. Even if I cannot become a demigod, at least let me have the fulfillment of being among the rank of accomplished Taoists."

"No, you have a mission to accomplish. You have your own destination. You do not belong here." In a determined tone Primeval waved his hand in a gesture to leave. "Have no fear. While you are in the world of dust, I will constantly watch over you and you can come to me at any time if you have any difficulty that you cannot overcome. This is not a farewell; we will meet again. But you must leave here now."

In a sad mood Jiang Sarn bade farewell to his fellow Taoists, with many of whom he had spent 40 years of his life. After packing his simple belongings and bidding farewell once more to the familiar mountain, Jiang Sarn began his return journey from the high mountain peak to the world of dust. As he slowly walked the first leg of his return trip towards Precipice Unicorn, he pondered: "Where should I go? I left the human world of dust forty years ago. When I came to this mountain, my parents were long dead and my relatives were few and aging. Presumably they are all dead now. All my friends probably have already forgotten me ... Wait, I had a very dear friend during my youth, Sung Remarkable. He used to live near the capital city Morning Song. Maybe I can look him up."

Without further ado, Jiang Sarn terra-trekked to the vicinity of Morning Song. Arriving at the Village of Sung, he asked a passerby lad who was riding an ox if Sung Remarkable was still around.

"Sure, he is only five houses down that way." The lad pointed in a certain direction.

Sung Remarkable was in the middle of doing accounting, but when he heard the arrival of Jiang Sarn, he put down what he was doing and immediately went out of the house to greet his old friend.

"My dear friend, where have you been during all these forty years? Why haven't you written me? I often thought of you. I have been married for some time now. Come in and let me introduce you to my wife." Sung Remarkable could not hide his pleasure at seeing a friend he had long admired.

"Let us have dinner. Tell me what you have done in the last forty years," Sung Remarkable suggested, after an informal welcome.

"I have been studying Tao in Palace Jade Abstraction, in East Kwen Ren Mountain. My teacher-mentor said that I was born under the wrong star and I could never achieve the state of a demigod. He said that my future is in the world of dust, so he sent me back." Still embarrassed at his dismissal by his teacher-mentor, Jiang Sarn presented his brief narration in a timid tone.

"Indeed! Look at what you've missed all your life! I must insist that you share with me my modest residence for as long as you wish. You have already missed a good part of your life. Waste no more! Let me find you a wife first then I will do my best to help you settle down," insisted Sung Remarkable.

Sung Remarkable was true to his words. The next day, the first thing he did was to introduce Jiang Sarn to his neighbors and his friends. While Jiang Sarn was familiarizing himself with the world that he had missed for 40 years, Sung Remarkable scouted around to find a suitable wife for him. He went to the village of Ma, and looked up an old friend of his, Squire Ma. Remarkable knew that Squire Ma had an unmarried daughter at the age of 68. Sung thus proposed marriage on behalf of Jiang Sarn. Four ingots of silver were presented to Squire Ma as a part of the betrothal gift. The proposal of marriage was accepted.

A day of fortune for marriage was selected according to proper procedures of Tao. The newly-weds were invited heartily by Sung Remarkable to stay in his household for as long as they wished.

Several months quickly passed by. One day Ms. Ma — it was the custom then in ancient Middle Kingdom to address a married woman by her maiden name with a title like this — suggested to her husband that they should not plan to stay in the household of Sung forever. Jiang Sarn should start to build a career of his own, like starting some kind of business so that they would eventually become financially independent, a suggestion that Jiang Sarn quickly consented to. However, throughout his 40 years of studying of Tao, Jiang Sarn had never learned any trade, and the only craft he'd ever learned was how to knit bamboo skimmers. Cutting a quantity of bamboo from the backyard of Sung's residence, Jiang Sarn worked for several days to knit enough bamboo skimmers to start his business.

Carrying a load of two basketfuls of bamboo skimmers on a shoulder pole, Jiang Sarn traveled to a market place in Morning Song. He selected a spot and set up a stand to sell his merchandise. However, during the entire day no one showed any interest. Having learned his skill in the lofty Palace Jade Abstraction, which had not made contact with the human world for millennia of time, his knitting style was naturally way out of fashion. No one wanted to buy a strange looking skimmer. Completely demoralized, he returned home, dead-tired from the long trip. As soon as he saw his wife Ms. Ma, he threw the shoulder pole as well as the load of bamboo skimmers to the ground and complained loudly: "You suggested I make these bamboo skimmers. For

172

the whole day no customer appeared. I wasted my time and I am dead-tired for nothing!"

"Maybe you do not know how to sell merchandise in a market," retorted Ms. Ma.

The quarrel continued and the noise soon attracted Sung Remarkable and his wife Ms. Sun. After he was told of the unsuccessful business venture of Jiang Sarn, Sung Remarkable was upset. "I am not rich, but I can afford to have you both as my houseguests for as long as you wish. You're a genius; you're only wasting your time knitting bamboo skimmers yourself! If you want to go into business, you should ask for my help. I have plenty of helping hands here. Come to think about it, I also have plenty of wheat in storage. I can ask my workers to grind wheat into flour to make noodles that you can readily sell."

A few days later, Jiang Sarn, carrying a load of two basketfuls of freshly made raw noodles on a shoulder pole, again marched to Morning Song. "Bamboo skimmers may be out of style, but people have to eat and noodles will never go out of style," thought Jiang Sarn. Again, Jiang Sarn's star was not shining on him, for during the whole morning as people passed and passed by his stand, no one showed any interest in buying noodles. Finally, around noon time, a man came by. He examined and examined the pile of noodles, and finally decided that he could use some. "Give me a penny's worth of noodles, you noodle monger." Well, at least a sale of a penny's worth was still a sale, so Jiang Sarn started to measure a penny's worth of noodles for his precious customer.

"Watch out, runaway horse!" shouted a soldier, chasing a horse which had just run loose. "Watch out ..." Before these words were repeated again, the speeding horse narrowly missed Jiang Sarn but knocked down his basket, spreading the entire content of fresh noodles on the ground. To make things worse, the rushing wind of the passing horse scattered dust all over the pile of noodles. Now even this customer decided that he could do without a penny's worth of dusty noodles, so he left.

Sadly, Jiang Sarn returned home with his empty baskets. Both Sun Remarkable and Ms. Ma were happy to see all the noodles gone. Joyfully, Ms. Ma congratulated him. "You are really great! You sold all the noodles in only half a day."

"No, all the noodles are lost. I stayed in the marketplace for hours without a customer. Eventually a man came by asking for a penny's worth of noodles. At that time a runaway horse kicked my basket, so all my noodles were lost."

Hearing Jiang Sarn's misfortune, Sung Remarkable suggested another idea: "You do not have to learn a trade the hard way. I own twenty restaurants. I can rotate you as the manager of the day among them. In exchange, you can have the profit of that day. You will quickly learn how to operate a restaurant. If you agree with my suggestion, I can pick a choice site for you. Tomorrow a military exercise has been scheduled. I have a restaurant along the route to the exercise field. Upon returning from their exercise, soldiers and warriors are hungry and they will usually generate a huge volume of business." Jiang Sarn was very grateful and he accepted this offer.

Appropriately dressed as a restauranteur, Jiang Sarn went to the suggested site to take charge of the restaurant. A quantity of food was prepared. Unfortunately, it rained all that morning and only by noon did the sun creep out of the clouds. No exercise took place and because of the heavy rain even the usual customers did not show up. Facing the huge pile of steamed buns, roast pork, goose, mutton and other

174

perishable food which would spoil in the next day or so (the time of Jiang Sarn was around 1100 B.C. and refrigeration would not be invented for another 3000 years, give or take a century), Jiang Sarn sighed. "Why didn't Primeval let me stay in his mountain? Why did he banish me to suffer in the world of dust? Where are the wealth and power he promised me?" He then turned to the employees of the restaurant and offered: "My dear workers, finish as much as you can since the food will spoil if not eaten." Once again Jiang Sarn sadly returned home.

"Don't worry! This happened to me before also. You should not blame yourself. You are an accomplished Taoist, and it is my fault to suggest you take up common trades. You should use your talent. Meanwhile, you can take a break while looking for other opportunities." The never-discouraged, all-faithful Sung Remarkable consoled Jiang Sarn.

But Jiang Sarn was discouraged. In his depressed mood, he strolled aimlessly around the property of Sung. Wandering through cultivated fields, patches of tall bamboos, he eventually came upon open ground. Being a Taoist who knew geomancy, or feng-shui, well, he immediately recognized the profundity of the fortune associated with this location. It would be an excellent site for a business building – the serendipity and blessing associated with the site would bring great prosperity and wealth to the owner. Telling this to Sung Remarkable, Sung replied: "Yes, many geomancers told me the same thing, too. However, each time a construction work was started, by the time the main beam was to go up, some gremlins would show up and they would burn down the structure. After several trials, I gave up the idea."

"Don't worry. During my study of Tao, I mastered exorcism. I know how to catch and subdue gremlins. According to my divination, the third day of the next month will be a day of providence to start construction work. By the time the main beam is about to go up, I will personally come to the construction site to subdue the evil gremlins."

So construction work began. On the day when the main beam was about to be set, Jiang Sarn put on his Taoist robe and his sacred scarf. Writing a Tao talisman of five thunders on his left palm and curling up his fingers to make a fist and taking a sword made of peach wood inscribed with Taoist talismans, he waited by the bare structure of the building. As the gremlins – there were five of them – showed up, Jiang Sarn opened up his left fist and aimed his palm in the direction of the five gremlins. Lo and behold, streaks of lightning emerged from his palm, directed at the five gremlins, and accompanied by loud thunder. The gremlins were knocked down to the ground. Waving his sword of Tao, Jiang Sarn went to the five fallen gremlins, ready to pierce their hearts.

The gang leader of the five gremlins pleaded: "Please spare our lives. We will never do this again. We will swear our fealty to you and we will be your vassals for life. We have been studying our elfin Tao for centuries, and if you kill us, all our efforts will be in vain. Spare us, reform us, and we will never rebel against you!"

"Maybe they can be of some use to me in the future. At least I can use their muscle power for my future construction projects," thought Jiang Sarn. He then commanded the five: "All right. I will spare your lives, but you must obey my orders. Now go to a mountain and hide there. When I need you, I will summon you and you must come immediately. From now on you must not disturb or harm any person, otherwise I will use my Tao to kill you." The five gremlins agreed and they were released from their bond. They then went to hide in a remote mountain. Later, true to their promises, they did help Jiang Sarn in many of his construction projects.

The building was completed and no gremlin ever appeared again. The loyal friend Sung Remarkable was extremely pleased as well as impressed. However, there were not enough gremlins around to generate a steady business for Jiang Sarn as an exorcist. An idea occurred to Sung: As an accomplished Taoist, Jiang Sarn must be good at prognostication – a skill that was needed at all times, and eventually this skill might even evolve into an extremely lucrative business such as financial forecasting. So why not let Jiang Sarn start from the bottom, as a fortune-teller?

The next day a suitable location was found. Jiang Sarn, pleased at this suggestion, wrote himself a couplet outside his fortune-telling business:

> *Subtle and astute are my prediction,*
> *Never a word without becoming conviction.*

In his little office, the following couplets were hung:

> *A mouth of ironclad projection*
> *Forebodes all welfare and evil of human essence,*
> *Two eyes of penetrative vision,*
> *Observe prosperity and regression of the earth.*

Yet his luck did not come by so easily. Half a year went by without a customer in need of his power of prognostication showing up in his little office. This time Jiang Sarn was less discouraged, however, for at least he could use his spare time to review his Tao, and besides, it was much easier work than knitting and selling bamboo skimmers, peddling noodles, or supervising restaurants.

One day, his luck turned around. A firewood monger by the name of Liu, who had lost a great deal of his meager earnings on fortune-tellers without any of the predicted wealth coming true, and who had since become an agnostic, saw the couplet outside Jiang Sarn's door. He decided to teach this fortune-teller a lesson. Putting his load of firewood down, he went in to ask Jiang Sarn to forecast his fortune. "How much do you charge for telling a fortune?"

"It depends on whether it is a long-term forecast or a short-term forecast. A long-forecast costs fifty coppers, while a short-term forecast costs only twenty coppers."

"All right, I want a short-term forecast. Tell me my fortune for this day. If your prognostication comes true, I will pay you. Otherwise I will knock down your fortune-teller sign."

Even without his penetrative vision, Jiang Sarn knew that this customer was a tough one. However, having mastered the Tao of divination, he was confident. From an array of folded messages piled vertically in front of him, he asked Liu to pick one. Randomly selecting one, Liu handed it over to Jiang Sarn. Opening it up, the folder contained nothing but Taoist symbols and inscriptions. Meditating for a minute or two, Jiang Sarn told Liu: "Unless you can promise me to adhere strictly to my instructions, this prognostication will not be fulfilled."

"Yes, I will follow your instructions to the T."

"Good. Go south. Under a willow tree, an elderly man is waiting for you to buy the entire load of your firewood for one hundred twenty coppers. In addition, he will entertain you with two bowls of wine and four steamed buns."

Half-believing, Liu went south with his load of firewood. "This fortune-teller must be crazy. All throughout my life as a firewood monger, I have never been entertained by my customers with wine and

178

food," Liu thought as he carried his heavy load of firewood on his shoulder pole southward.

Surely enough, an elderly man was sitting under a willow tree, sipping tea. Seeing Liu approaching, he beckoned him to stop. "We are short of firewood now. I want to buy your entire load. How much?"

Liu was impressed and astonished, but he was not willing to let the prognostication come true so easily. "One hundred coppers," said Liu, undercutting his price.

"The price is very reasonable. Bring the firewood over."

Being a neat person, Liu piled the firewood into an orderly stack and with a broom, he swept any loose leaves and branches to a corner. Moments later the elderly man came out, apparently pleased at the neatness of the firewood monger. He handed over one hundred twenty coppers to Liu and said: "You are a very neat person. The extra twenty coppers are a reward for your tidiness. Tomorrow we will have a birthday celebration and we have prepared much food. We would like you to share the celebration with us. Here are a bowl, a carafe of wine, and four steamed buns. Sit down and enjoy yourself."

"A real demigod this fortune-teller is!" thought Liu in amazement. "Well, it looks like a small carafe. Let me pour a full bowl of wine, so that the second bowl will not be full. This discrepancy will discredit the fortune-teller." However, he soon found out that the carafe was bigger than he had thought, so that the second bowl was also full.

Returning to Jiang Sarn's fortune-telling business, Liu was very impressed and he repeatedly congratulated Jiang Sarn for his power of divination. However, twenty coppers was still a lot of money – his whole morning's earnings were only one hundred twenty coppers. An idea occurred to him. Liu went out of the door and randomly grabbed a passerby, who happened to be a tax collector, apparently in a hurry.

"Let me go. I have important official business," yelled the tax collector.

"No, you need fortune-telling. If you do not come in with me, I will drag you to the river and we will jump into the river together," threatened Liu.

Just to get rid of this rascal, the tax collector agreed to an unnecessary fortune-telling. "How much do you charge for a short-term forecast," asked the tax collector. Before Jiang Sarn could open his mouth, Liu interjected, "Half a silver piece."

"I never heard of such an expensive fortune-telling," complained the tax collector.

"It is worth it, every copper of it. Do it, otherwise I will drag you to the river."

Unwillingly, the tax collector took out a half silver piece, and picked up a folded message from the pile. "What do you want to know," asked Jiang Sarn.

"I have been trying to collect tax from a delinquent taxpayer. Unfortunately I could never find him. My supervisor thought I had conspired with him to evade the tax. Where can I find him?"

After a few moments of meditation, Jiang Sarn replied, "He just came back from a long business trip and he already has the money for you, one hundred and three ingots of silver."

Half an hour later, the tax collector ran back. "Thank you, Taoist Jiang Sarn! You are absolutely remarkable and you are a demigod! Sure enough, he was waiting for me with his back taxes, all one hundred and

180

three ingots of silver! Your fee of half an ounce of silver is extremely reasonable!"

By word of mouth, Jiang Sarn's business prospered. Appointments had to be made in advance to obtain his prognostication. "Well, not bad. Although the wealth and power promised by the Primeval have not come true yet, at least I am making a decent living and I have already saved some money," contended Jiang Sarn.

Meanwhile, the two other elves that had been commissioned by Woman Wa in her punishment plot against Emperor Zoe still hung around, waiting for an opportune time to enter the palace. After visiting Dar-Gee on the previous night to discuss how to enter the palace formally, on the next day, during her trip home, the elf Jade Pee-Pa passed by Jiang Sarn's fortune-telling business. Out of curiosity, she transfigured herself into a woman in mourning and went over to investigate. Seeing her in mourning dress, out of sympathy, people who were waiting outside Jiang Sarn's small office to have their fortunes told let her go in first, even without an appointment. Jiang Sarn immediately realized that the woman in mourning was nothing but an elf. Asking to see her right hand, he immediately grabbed it with his left. Using three fingers to control the three veins which were the sources of her magic power, and using his penetrative vision to transfix the spirit of the elf so that she could not escape, he hit her head with a heavy stone ink stand and immediately killed her.

"This fortune-teller just murdered a woman. He must have tried unsuccessfully to rape her. Let us get the authority to arrest him," shouted the crowd, while surrounding the little office to prevent Jiang Sarn from escaping. Meanwhile, Vice Premier Bee Gahn passed by and the crowd asked him to arrest Jiang Sarn.

Jiang Sarn emerged from his small building, dragging the body of the woman in mourning with him while still holding her left hand. He told the Vice Premier: "This is no woman in mourning, she is an elf and I just caught her."

"Let her go, we will take care of it," said the Vice Premier.

"No, I cannot release my hand. I have transfixed her veins. If I let my hand go, she will escape," replied Jiang Sarn.

"All right, let us take you and the dead woman to the Emperor's court to settle this matter." Thus Jiang Sarn and the body of the dead woman were taken to the Emperor's court. During the trip, Jiang Sarn firmly grabbed her hand to prevent her from escaping.

Emperor Zoe, having heard so many elfin theories in the last few years, decided to investigate this case himself. "If you can prove that this woman is an elf, I will reward you. Otherwise, you will be punished as a murderer with intent to rape."

"Bring me a brush pen, ink, and paper." Using his right hand, he quickly drew appropriate Taoist inscriptions on three sheets of paper, transferring his power of Tao onto the three sheets of otherwise ordinary looking paper. Pasting one sheet over the woman's head, one over her heart, and one on her back and reciting an incantation to seal the spirit of the elf within the woman's body, Jiang Sarn then released his left hand. "Bring firewood and burn her," he ordered.

Two hours went by, but the intense fire could neither burn the woman's body nor her clothes. Surprised and scared, Emperor Zoe asked Jiang Sarn, "What do we do now?"

Jiang Sarn replied, "The elfin Tao of this elf is very strong. She can only be destroyed by the Fire of Samadhi. It is a fire that can only be generated by intense contemplation. I acquired the power to generate this fire during my training in Palace Jade Abstraction under the personal instruction of Primeval. I will burn her to revert her to her original form."

Figure I- 13. Jiang Sarn and Jade Pipa
Jiang Sarn reduced Jade Pipa to her original form

War among Gods and Men

Jiang Sarn sat down in a lotus posture. Closing his eyes, he concentrated his mental power. Suddenly, from his eyes, nostrils and mouth came long and narrow spiritual flames of Samadhi. The spiritual flames not only burned material objects, but also spiritual evils. The dead woman suddenly came to life. She sat up and pointed her finger at Jiang Sarn. "Why do you want to kill me? I meant no harm." Meanwhile, Dar-Gee sadly and helplessly watched her companion burn to death. Within minutes, the spiritual flame of Samadhi reduced the elf to her original form, a jade Pee-Pa, a stringed instrument. Extinguishing his spiritual fire, Jiang Sarn ordered the jade Pee-Pa brought to the Emperor. Dar-Gee hid her sadness and managed to congratulate the Emperor in a natural voice for his good fortune that an elf was finally found and disposed of. She also asked the Emperor to give her the jade Pee-Pa on the pretext that she could restring it and use it as a musical instrument. Subsequently Dar-Gee kept the jade Pee-Pa inside the Starplucker Pavilion on an offering table and constantly worshipped it with burning incenses. From time to time she would contemplate a way to revivify her companion, an effort in which she never succeeded.

Needless to say, Dar-Gee vowed vengeance against Jiang Sarn. To keep him under her power so that she could plan vengeance, she suggested that he should be given a position in the court. Extremely pleased at Jiang Sarn's ability, the Emperor consented to the suggestion. Thus Jiang Sarn was appointed to the rank of Imperial Astronomer, the old job of Du Yuansee, who had been executed for reporting to the Emperor his detection of an elfin nebulosity around the imperial constellation.

Finally Jiang Sarn was a step closer to achieving the goal of glory and wealth in the human world, as prophesied by Primeval. This pleased Ms. Ma very much.

One day Dar-Gee and Emperor Zoe were feasting in the Starplucker Pavilion. Suddenly she was in the mood to entertain the Emperor, so she asked the band to play music and she danced. Ladies-in-waiting applauded, but quite a few ladies-in-waiting did not applaud. Instead, their eyes were filled with tears. Dar-Gee noticed and asked her chief lady-in-waiting to investigate. She was told that these ladies-in-waiting had formerly served Queen Consort Jiang and they could not bear their grief when they saw the new Queen dance. Dar-Gee was in a rage. "Still owing loyalty to their old mistress! I cannot trust any such persons. I swear I will eliminate them."

During another opportune time, she told Emperor Zoe about her findings. He was very angry and wanted to put these ladies-in-waiting to death instantly, but Dar-Gee said, "I have a better idea. Such disloyal persons deserve torturous death in order to make an example of them. Let me handle it."

She issued an order, in the name of the Emperor, to demand that each of the ten thousand fief families in the capital city hand in four snakes, poisonous or not. She then ordered a huge pit dug, 200 feet in diameter and 50 feet deep by our measurements, in an empty lot inside the Palace compound. The scheme was to fill the pit with snakes and then throw those ladies-in-waiting who exhibited loyalty to Queen Consort Jiang into the pit. The pit was appropriately named Yu Basin, or Scorpion Basin.

Announcements were posted on all major roadways as well as on the four city gates, so that no one could have missed them. The announcement demanded that each fief family in or around the capital submit four snakes to the palace within a month of time. Those who disobeyed the order would be severely punished.

War among Gods and Men

As is well-known, snakes dislike cities and wherever cities are built, snakes move away. The city of Morning Song was a well-developed one and had a long history at the time of this saga. How could that many snakes be found near the capital? A snake-catching business suddenly boomed as many snake-catchers went to desolate, unpopulated regions to trap snakes. The cost of catching snakes was high, and the price of snakes even higher. Poor families had to pawn their meager belongings in order to purchase the required four snakes per family.

Officers soon found out about the snake affair but none of them, except Jiao Li, dared to venture to persuade the Emperor to stop this irrational order. Jiao Li begged the Emperor to rescind his order for snakes, but the Emperor refused to listen. When Jiao Li insisted again, the Emperor became mad and the officer was put to death. From then on no one dared to say a word against the Emperor's berserk decree to order each family to deliver four snakes to the Palace.

All the snakes were finally delivered. The 40,000 snakes were all dumped into the Scorpion Basin. The clothes of the ladies-in-waiting, 70 odd in number, were stripped and they were thrown into the snake pit, one by one. As piercing screams and cries for clemency rang through the entire Palace, Emperor Zoe watched with intense pleasure while caressing the back of Dar-Gee. "My dear love, you are a genius."

Dar-Gee, using her charming and delicate voice, responded, "Without this kind of punishment, I do not know how I can assure the loyalty of the ladies-in-waiting to you." Servants of the palace who watched the terrible scene were extremely saddened by the cruel torture, but they could not but hide their tears, lest they should also be punished by the same torturous death.

Figure I- 14. Orgies
Young men and women made love in the garden of wine and meat

Sensing the Emperor's pleasure for orgies, Dar-Gee devised another scheme to please him. She ordered a garden to be built near the Starplucker Pavilion. The garden consisted of an artificial mountain and an artificial fountain. On the manmade mountain a number of posts were planted. At Emperor Zoe's pleasure, the fountain in the pond would spew out wine and the posts would be packed with racks of roasted meat. This was the historically famous "Meat Forest and Wine Pond" in Middle Kingdom. Young men and women were sent to the garden naked. They were ordered to chase each other in the open areas of the garden, and when they caught each other, they would engage in lovemaking acts in the open, and when they were hungry they would eat meat hung on the posts and drink wine from the fountain. Whenever Emperor Zoe and Dar-Gee liked, they would order orgies held and they would watch the group lovemaking activities for their pleasure.

One day, as they were enjoying the scene of the orgies, Dar-Gee suddenly saw the Jade Pee-Pa displayed on a nearby offering table, with incense burning. "The sad death of my sister colleague must be avenged," determined Dar-Gee. A scheme came to her mind and she secretly prepared a set of drawings. One evening, after the usual entertainment of watching orgies, torturing a few innocent palace ladies-in-waiting, feasting, drinking and dances, Emperor Zoe was bored. Seizing this opportunity, Dar-Gee ordered the set of drawings to be brought in and she showed one of them to the Emperor. This drawing depicted a magnificent tower pavilion with a number of stories. It was drawn with tiled roof and engraved pillars. The ceilings in the interior were lined with pearls, walls inlaid with agates, rubies and semiprecious stones, and the hanging lamps were decorated with exquisite sea-shells.

"What is it, my dear," asked Emperor Zoe. "I did not know you could draw!"

"A special design of mine, which will please your Majesty tremendously. Its name is Elk Tower. It will be such a magnificent building that heavenly gods, exquisitely beautiful goddesses and fairies

188

will visit you just to see this tower. You will enjoy the ultimate luxury of the human world, and I will faithfully serve you forever," persuaded Dar-Gee.

"It is, however, an immense project. Who would be able to take charge of its construction?" the Emperor thoughtfully said in half-believing tone.

"Jiang Sarn, of course. Did you see the other day his great ability to reduce an elf into her original form? Nobody else but Jiang Sarn can do it," Dar-Gee the Elf Fox, ready for her vengeance, eagerly recommended.

"Yes, of course. Why did I never think of it! As always, you are right, my dear Dar-Gee. I will summon Jiang Sarn here to see me tomorrow," agreed the Emperor.

During his daily mental exercises, Jiang Sarn often prognosticated his own fortune. After he received the imperial order for an interview, he prognosticated. He immediately sensed that his life would be in danger, although he had only a vague idea of what the danger would be. He quickly formulated an escape plan. He secretly went to visit Vice Premier Bee Gahn and told him: "Tomorrow I shall have an interview with the Emperor. I know my life will be in danger, but I have an escape plan."

"Your life is in danger? You have done nothing wrong. Maybe I can accompany you to see the Emperor and use my influence to save you." Bee Gahn was very astonished.

"Thank you for your kindness, but you cannot help me out of this predicament. If you come you might get yourself unnecessarily involved," Jiang Sarn politely declined.

"It is a pity that you have to leave. The court needs an honest and capable man like you. Although we have not known each other for long, we share many similar views and between us we have developed a long-lasting friendship. I am sad to see you leave. But — how can you escape?" Bee Gahn lamented.

"Do not worry. I have a plan." Jiang Sarn was sad to leave Bee Gahn, too. "I have prognosticated your fate, too. Your life will be in danger in the near future. Let me leave you an envelope. When you face danger, open it and read the instructions. It might save your life. Take care of yourself. Farewell."

The next day, Jiang Sarn promptly presented himself to the palace and he was readily sent to Starplucker Pavilion where the Emperor held meetings with court officers now, if he needed any of them. As Jiang Sarn entered, he saw Emperor Zoe examining a set of magnificent drawings. He asked Emperor Zoe: "May this serf be of service to Your Majesty?"

"Yes. You have been recommended to head the construction team to build this Elk Tower for me. A set of diagrams has been provided by my Queen Dar-Gee. Please examine it carefully and tell me how long it will take you to complete the construction project and how much it will cost."

Jiang Sarn examined the set of diagrams thoroughly. It was certainly an immense project, and its cost would be monstrous. He estimated that forced labor would be imposed on almost every able body around the capital and taxes would be raised so high that people might not even be able to survive. As he was about to finish his examination, his mind was made up. He thought: "I have been here for some time already. This court does not look like the kind of place promised by Primeval. Maybe this court is not my destiny. Let me try to reason with this Emperor; if he can be reasoned with, then I will stay. Otherwise this might be a good time for me to leave to search for another opportunity." When he finished his examination, he backed away from the drawing and turned to the Emperor. He shook his head and sighed. "An extremely elaborate and grand construction."

"How long will it take you to finish it," Emperor Zoe impatiently asked.

"I want to be honest with you. With the current budget situation, without taxing people to starvation, this project will take thirty-five years to complete," replied Jiang Sarn.

"My Queen and my love," the Emperor said, turning to Dar-Gee,. "Jiang Sarn said it will take thirty-five years to complete the project. Time flies and years go by. We cannot be young for long. This will take too much time and too much taxation. I think I will have to give up this project."

"The opportunity for vengeance has finally arrived," thought Dar-Gee. "Your Majesty," she quickly responded, "no, it will not take that long to construct it. Jiang Sarn is a liar. He in an incompetent Taoist and he lies to you. I have estimated that it will take no more than two or three years to complete. Jiang Sarn should be charged with the capital crime of purposely deceiving his Majesty. He should be immediately put to death at the Pao-Lo execution machine."

"You are absolutely right. Guards, prepare for execution." The indecisive Emperor had readily changed his mind.

"Wait! Let your serf submit an advice for your consideration. Rebellions have started all around you. Drought and flood now occur frequently in our fertile lands, and our treasury is about to be depleted.

War among Gods and Men

Your Majesty should take measures to conserve national resources and to strengthen the economy of the country. For a long time you have indulged yourself in wine and women, distanced yourself from good officers and become intimate with corrupt and adulatory ones. You have lived in your world of self-admiration and deception. Loyal officers were executed for their honest opinions. Your regime is already in grave danger. Now you want to listen to words of a woman of your pleasure, to start an immensely expensive project at her suggestion, without regard to the welfare of your country! The taxation required to build this Tower in two or three years will be so enormous that the economy of this country is certainly going to be wrecked, and the people will starve. More people will join the already rampant rebels. Please, may Your Majesty listen to your serf, to stop this project and to start thinking of ways to revive the economy of this country! I humbly request your kind consideration," pleaded Jiang Sarn.

"You idiot! You ungrateful clod! You dare criticize His Majesty! Guards, arrest him and put him to death on the Pao-Lo machine immediately." Without waiting for the Emperor to respond, Dar-Gee had impatiently issued the order.

Before the palace guards could come forward, Jiang Sarn had already run down the steps of Starplucker Pavilion and sped away. Emperor Zoe laughed: "Look at him! He thinks he can escape by running. No one ever escaped from my palace by running away! Guards! Get him!"

Guards started chasing after Jiang Sarn. The chasing party grew in size as others joined in. As his pursuers were closing in, Jiang Sarn stopped by a bridge over a moat and said: "You need not chase me any further. I will die here." He then jumped into the rapidly flowing water in the moat. There was not even a splash, and he vanished. There was no trace of him, except a soliton wave which rapidly moved away to the river which fed the moat. No one paid any attention to the seemingly ordinary water wave. Guards then reported to Emperor Zoe that Jiang Sarn had committed suicide and his body had vanished amidst the rapidly flowing water.

Unknown to the chasing party and the Emperor, Jiang Sarn had escaped to the Sung village via hydro-trekking. He restored himself near the household of Sung. As he appeared at the door, Ms. Ma greeted him. "Congratulations, my lord. You are back from your post in the capital today."

"I have resigned," Jiang Sarn said.

"Why," the startled Ms. Ma asked.

"The Emperor listened to his evil Queen Dar-Gee and wanted to build an extremely luxurious tower for his pleasure, called the Elk Tower. I was commissioned by the Emperor to head the construction project. As I see it, the construction of this Tower will exhaust the treasury; heavy taxation and forced labor will be imposed upon the people, causing great suffering. I advised the Emperor of the evil aspects of this project. He agreed to drop the project, but the evil Queen Dar-Gee accused me of lying. The irresolute Emperor changed his mind immediately and became very angry. He fired me from my post on the spot. I have thought it over. This is not the place that my teacher Primeval promised me. I have heard that West Branch City, the capital of Duchy Zhou, is ruled by a very capable duke. Maybe that is the destiny my teacher promised me." Jiang Sarn then tried to persuade his wife to go with him. "Come with me to West Branch City. There I shall find fulfillment of the promise of wealth and power. There I shall also find the opportunity to apply what I have learned to serve my country and my people. Come with me."

Ms. Ma was frustrated. The little advance in life achieved by her husband through her persistent efforts had suddenly evaporated. She was angry. In desperation she cursed: "You never really studied to become a man of literature; you said you studied Tao, but to be frank with you, you only know sorcery! Heaven blessed you that you finally were appointed a court officer. The Emperor was kind enough to offer you an opportunity to show him your ability so he could promote you to a higher rank. The Elk Tower is a good project. In addition you would be in charge of high finance and you could easily profit from this project. Soon we could have had our own houses, gardens and servants had you taken this project! Offering advice to the Emperor! Ha! What rank do you think you hold in the court? You think you are qualified to offer the Emperor advice! You were born to be a rotten sorcerer! You were born and destined to be poor!"

Jiang Sarn retorted, "My dear wife, you do not understand. Here I will never get to achieve what I am destined to become. Please pack up and leave with me for West Branch. One day, when I acquire wealth and power, you will be a lady of rank. You will wear a pearl crown and a cape embroidered with jade, with the designation of Lady of the First Rank."

"My husband, you are dreaming. You are giving up the bird in hand, and to search for birds in a fictitious forest! You want to be an honest and straight officer, but look around. How many straight officers are there? They all pilfer," disagreed Ms. Ma.

"You do not know the outside world. This regime is now crumbling and it is only a matter of time before it will be toppled over. Come with me to West Branch," pleaded Jiang Sarn again.

Indeed Ms. Ma was frustrated. In her society, men were always dominant; the life of a woman was always tied to that of her husband. She could not have a career of her own, so her only hope was for her husband to advance his career and she wanted to help. Since her marriage to Jiang Sarn, she had tried to help him establish a profession or a career. With her limited knowledge and education, she had tried her best. Yet she had met no luck, but disappointments after disappointments. "It was my fate and destiny that I was married to him. As a woman I have to accept the reality," she had often thought. Finally, luck seemed to have struck her: For the first time since her marriage, her husband had seemed to be able to establish a profitable and successful business – fortune-telling. By sheer luck he caught an elf and as a result he was recognized by the Emperor and appointed an officer of the imperial court. She was elated and she had let her hope grow. It was not the highest position, but at least her husband was now among elites. If he could have stuck with his position, in time he would have established seniority and he would have advanced in rank. She could have had everything a woman wanted: financial security and social prominence. Now suddenly, out of the blue sky, he threw away this opportunity and thus punctured her bubbles of hope – and it was not through any evil luck, but because he refused to serve the Emperor to head a construction project. Why would he do such a thing? She searched her mind and she could not find an answer. Maybe he knew nothing about construction, maybe those worthless sorcery tricks were all he knew. As her thoughts piled up, she became more and more frustrated. She was angry at the ineptness of her husband, and that fate had destined her to be a woman, to be a wife. As a wife, she could not do anything about the situation but must accept as a matter of course any destiny that would befall her. Now he wanted to leave her neighborhood to venture into a strange, foreign country! What did he know about that strange country other than rumors, gossip and hearsay? He seemed to have made up his mind. He seemed determined to do so, searching for fortune in an alien nation merely because of a vague promise from his teacher whom she had never met nor ever heard of.

Indeed throughout her entire life she had never left this area; she'd grown up in her father's household and after her marriage she lived in the household of Sung Remarkable, in a neighboring village. Save for a few trips to Morning Song, she had spent her entire life around the local area. She was used to it and she liked it. She had often dreamed of having a house of her own. Even this dream was now shattered. Now she was asked to give up her native land, the familiar setting, her alliance with this area, and in fact almost everything of her life, to follow her husband to an unknown destination. It was now to be a decision between her husband and her native land. "No, I shall never leave my native land to search for a vague and perhaps unfulfillable promise," she finally decided.

In tears, Ms. Ma spoke, in a determined tone that Jiang Sarn had never heard before. "I was born in the area around Morning Song. This is my home, and this shall be my burial place. I will never leave my home land to go to a foreign country. If you want to go, you go alone and I want a divorce."

"My madam, we are married and we should stick together. This is no place for me, I must go to a foreign land to search for my fortune. I shall acquire the wealth and power promised by my teacher Primeval."

"I do not want to leave here. I do not want to go to West Branch. My star of fortune probably destines me to be an ordinary country woman, and I shall be content with it. I will not go. You can go and

196

marry someone else with a better fortune. I want a divorce right now," insisted Ms. Ma.

"You will regret it later. Please follow me to the city of West Branch."

"No –" At this moment, aroused by voices of argument, Sung Remarkable and his wife dropped in. After listening to arguments from both sides, and seeing that Ms. Ma was firm on her determination to want a divorce, he and his wife joined in to persuade Jiang Sarn to grant her a divorce. As was the custom of that time, the divorce proceeding was very simple; all that was required was for the husband to write and sign a decree to inform the wife that he wanted to terminate the marriage relationship.

After Jiang Sarn finished the divorce decree, he told his wife once more, "The divorce decree is now in my hand. Once it is passed to you, the divorce proceeding is complete and there will be no other recourse. Let me reiterate: I do not want to divorce you. Please think it over."

"Just give me the decree and it will be done."

"I beg you to think it over."

"No, my mind is already made up. Let us not waste any more time. Give me the decree."

Thus Jiang Sarn and his wife, Ms. Ma, were divorced. Ms. Ma then went back to the home of her father. Subsequently she married an ordinary peasant and lived a reasonably stable, happy, though not wealthy, life.

A few days later, Jiang Sarn was ready to leave. After packing his few belongings and the silver he had saved, he bid farewell to Sung

Remarkable and his wife Ms. Sun. "Jiang Sarn will forever be grateful to you for your unceasing support, enduring friendship, consideration, kindness and faith. I do not want to leave you, my best friend in my life, but if the Emperor learns I am hiding in your household, you may be in great trouble. I must go now."

After a farewell banquet, Sung Remarkable accompanied Jiang Sarn to the Ten Li Pavilion. He then asked him: "Have you changed your mind? Where are you heading?"

"To the land of Duke West, West Branch."

"Please send me a message if anything good comes out of your venture, just to relieve my anxiety." With these words, they parted.

Jiang Sarn first went through the city of Meng Gin, where he crossed Yellow River. Then he went through the city of Ming Tze (Ming Pond), and finally headed towards Frontier Pass Tong [a city that bears this name still exists today]. Beyond Tong lay four more frontier passes through which he had yet to go; these four passes were known by the names Lin Tong, Penetrating Clouds, Boundary Marker and Vast Water. Beyond Vast Water lay Duchy Zhou, the land of freedom and prosperity.

As Jiang Sarn approached Frontier Pass Tong, he saw a company of 800 odd people, in ragged clothes, sitting on the ground and crying. Jiang Sarn inquired. He was told that they were citizens of Morning Song, that they had escaped the mandatory hard labor and heavy taxation recently imposed by Tsung the Migratory Tiger who had been commissioned by the Emperor to construct the Elk Tower. The sentry leader of the frontier pass, Chang Fung (Phoenix) refused to let them out of the pass, and an imperial order was expected soon to take the refugees back for punishment. The sentry commander Chang Phoenix was merely waiting for the arrival of the imperial order to arrest them.

"I served in Emperor Zoe's court before. Maybe I can persuade him to let you go," Jiang Sarn consoled the pitiful refugees. When the guard in the frontier pass reported that a court officer Jiang Sarn wanted see the sentry commander, Chang Phoenix thought it might be a convenience to have a friend in the court, so an interview was granted.

Chang Phoenix was surprised to see Jiang Sarn in Taoist attire and not court dress. Jiang Sarn informed him that he had recently resigned his post to go to West Branch City, and begged Chang Phoenix to let these poor people out of Frontier Pass Tong.

"You are also a deserter from the service of His Majesty. I should have you arrested, too. However, since we served together in the same court before, as a favor to my former colleague I will let you go this time. If I ever see you again I will have you arrested and sent back to Morning Song to face punishment." In anger, Chang Phoenix ordered: "Throw this one out!"

Jiang Sarn was thrown out in disgrace. The refugees became even more sad, because their last hope was gone. As the frontier pass was part of a system of a long, great wall of defense, to scale the high and heavily-guarded wall was out of the question. An idea came to Jiang Sarn. He told the refugees: "There is a way out. However, there is danger involved. But if you are willing to take the risk, I can get you out."

Jiang Sarn was thinking of the art of terra-trekking. But there were unknown dangers. The Tao of terra-trekking had been developed primarily for personal transportation. It was rarely used as a means of moving masses of people. Even when used as a means of personal transportation, there were risks; only those with the most accomplished Tao used it regularly. Many Taoists, including Jiang Sarn, used this art

199

only in dire need. This was the reason why he had taken the overland route to reach the frontier pass instead of applying the Tao of terra-trekking to go to West Branch directly. Now it seemed that this was the only way to get the 800 odd refugees out of the frontier pass, so he decided to take the risk.

"Gather here and do not leave. At dusk I will come back. When I ask you to close your eyes, you must do so immediately. Whatever noise you may hear, ignore it. If you open your eyes, you will die," ordered Jiang Sarn.

He went to a nearby mountain and sat on a piece of rock. He then took out a book of incantations from his pack, and reviewed the complete procedure. Basically speaking, in the process of trekking the person to be transported was temporarily transmuted to one of the five basic forms of the universe – metallum, wood, water, fire or terra – and through the power of Tao the transmuted form was moved in the same medium as soliton waves, which could propagate at a fantastic speed. At the destination, the transmuted form was restored to the same person. Terra-trekking was the most common mode of trekking, mainly because earth was abundant and could be found almost anywhere. The dangers involved in terra-trekking occurred during the initial transmutation and the final restoration processes, and obstructions by other forms during the propagation of the soliton wave. After reviewing the entire process again, Jiang Sarn became a little uncomfortable. However, a promise had already been made and these poor people were dependent on him to deliver them to safety. Besides, short of a miracle, this was the only route of escape. "Success or failure, I must do it!" Jiang Sarn said to himself.

At dusk, he returned to the site where his "passengers" were waiting. Kneeling towards the direction of East Kwen Ren Range, Jiang

Sarn prayed to his teacher-mentor and his patriarch, Primeval of Palace Jade Abstraction. "Please help me and my poor people. We have to get out of here and the only way is via terra-trekking. I am not confident that I can accomplish this, but I have to do it. You promised to help me when I am in difficulty. Now I am in difficulty. Help me and help these people." After his prayer, he cast a series of incantations.

Jiang Sarn's order of closure of eyes was strictly obeyed. The 800 odd people heard strong and strange noises, and they felt cold, but they did not open their eyes. The convoy traveled over 400 li beneath Frontier Passes Tong, Lin Tong, Penetrating Clouds, Boundary Marker and Vast Water. Finally Jiang Sarn stopped his incantation and announced: "You are safe now, open your eyes."

"This is Ridge Golden Rooster, just outside Frontier Pass Vast Water. You are now safely in the territory of Duke West. You are now on your own. Farewell."

After these words, Jiang Sarn left. He had made the decision to West Branch, but he did not know anyone there. During his time it would be awkward and unbecoming to introduce himself to the ruling Lord. He must be "discovered", so to speak. Therefore he went to the village of Parn Chi (Rocky Creek), and decided to live in seclusion as a hermit, while making himself known in the local region that he was a learned scholar with great abilities. He chose to live in a hut near Wei Water, a tributary to Yellow River. He did not realize that it would be another seven years before he would be discovered as a talent.

Walking another 70 li, the 800 odd refugees arrived at the city of West Branch. A communique describing their hardship was prepared. An elderly man was elected as their leader and was sent to present the communique to Chancellor San Felicitous. After reading the communique, he ordered that fertile land and enough starting silver pieces be given to those who were strong and capable so that they could begin farming to support themselves and their families. For those who were weak and meek, a list was compiled so that the government could issue them monthly rations of food and other necessities. The principle of public aid, as laid down by Duke West, was to get able bodies to stand on their feet in the shortest time possible, and the government would be responsible only for the livelihood of the meek and weak who could not support themselves.

8. Duke West and Jiang Sarn

Since his banishment to a remote village, Duke West had spent his days educating the people of Yeau and passed his idle time wisely, concentrating his efforts mostly on perfecting his methodology of prognostication as passed down by the Sage King Fushi. Instead of using three coins as was the prevailing way, he expanded the ancient Eight Trigrams into sixty-four patterns. Three whole and broken line segments were stacked into eight groups from which sixty four patterns and three hundred and sixty combinations were formed. These diagrams, patterns and combinations were then used in divination. After the establishment of the Zhou Dynasty following the successful revolutionary campaign, this method was further developed to become the main body of the *Scripture I* or *I-ching* (*Book of Changes*). Over the ensuing millennia this method of prognostication has since been further developed and is still in use today by ardent followers of the art. A divination with this new technique portended that, after seven years of imprisonment, Duke West was to be freed soon, but before he would be freed he would lose his eldest son.

The arrival of refugees from Morning Song prompted officials of West Branch to renew their efforts to seek the release of their duke. Crown prince Yikao decided to go to the capital to seek the release of his father. He discussed with Chancellor San Felicitous his idea to try to persuade Emperor Zoe to release his father. Chancellor San did not like the idea. He tried to dissuade the Crown Prince and he said, "When your father left seven years ago, he said that one day he would return on his own and no one should venture to save him. You must not disobey your father's words. If you feel uneasy, you can always dispatch an emissary to find out about his well-being. You must not risk your life to do so."

But Yikao was very determined, and replied, "My father is now imprisoned in a strange land, without any loved ones. As a dutiful son, I must save him. I will bring three precious gifts to Emperor Zoe to please him, so that my father may be released." He then disregarded further words of Chancellor San and decided to bring the gifts and to volunteer himself in place of his father for imprisonment.

After bidding farewell to his mother, Yikao soon departed for the capital city of Morning Song. As gifts to the Emperor, he brought with him the following items: a south-pointing cart that derived its magic power through a colored stone, a war relic reputedly used during the campaign of Huangdi, the first emperor of the Middle Kingdom, against a mighty barbarian leader, Chi You; a sobering mat – to relieve hangovers from overindulgence of wine and spirits; an albino orangutan trained to chant songs and play music on a lute. In addition, he brought with him ten beautiful young women trained to dance and sing.

After arriving at the capital, Yikao first visited Vice Premier Bee Gahn. Bee Gahn was not too pleased to see these gifts of indulgence. However, since he sympathized with Duke West, he reluctantly brought Yikao to the Emperor's presence in Starplucker Pavilion.

"I, son of Duke West, plead to Your Merciful Majesty to accept my humble gifts to redeem the offenses of my father," Yikao said.

"You are a filial son, and I am moved. Rise." sympathized the Emperor. "I will reconsider his offenses. Meanwhile, let me take a look at the gifts."

At this moment, behind a pearl screen, Queen Dar-Gee noticed the presence of Yikao, who was a young man of extreme handsomeness, elegant manner, and unmatched eloquence. She was immediately aroused. "I must have this young man," she thought. Against the protocols of the court at that time, she emerged from behind the pearl screen to join the Emperor. She looked at Emperor Zoe inquisitively, so that he was compelled to introduce Yikao to her. "I have long heard that you are a master of the art of Goo Lute. Can you play one tune for me," asked Dar-Gee.

"Your Majesty Queen, I have not played any tune since my father's imprisonment. My heart is too broken to enjoy the pleasure of the sound of strings. Please forgive me," responded Yikao.

"Play a tune as the Queen requested, Yikao. If your skill on the lute is as good as your eloquence, I will pardon your father," promised the Emperor. Yikao immediately consented.

A Goo Lute was brought to the Emperor's presence. Yikao sat on the floor, cross-legged, in a lotus posture. Placing the Goo Lute on his lap, he first tuned the strings, then he played a short folk tune called "Winds of Daybreak." He sang as his long and slender fingers plucked the strings:

> Tenderly, weeping willow twigs
> Flirt with fragile winds of a cold morning,
> Blooming buds of peach blossoms
> Shine red charm over the sky,
> Gentle blades of grass and flowers
> Blaze the ground with shades of colors,
> While horse carts busily move men of dust east and west.

The skill of Yikao was heavenly. Although he had not touched the strings for several years, as soon his fingers touched them, it was like old friends had met. The ten fingers danced on the strings and a beautiful melody of dainty timbre emanated. The melodies of the song carried a flavor of melancholic sweetness typical of most folk songs, and were expressively woven into the brilliant crispness of the pitches of Goo Lute. The melody of the song was beautiful to begin with, but the way Yikao played made it even more beautiful.

Dar-Gee was a good musician and a good dancer, and she loved music and dance. She immediately became inebriated by the music and song, and irresistibly aroused by Yikao. Her ears were mesmerized by the music and her eyes became transfixed on him, gazing at his every movement. The more she looked at him, the more she was attracted and aroused by his stately and majestic manners. In her state of inebriation, she reminisced about the days when she was an elf. During those numerous occasions when she had transfigured herself into a female human form, she had had many unforgettable lovemaking experiences with numerous handsome men. Of course, then she still possessed the substance of an animal body and could not enjoy the kind of orgasm that only a female human body could. Even so, she still remembered how alluring, magnificent, and splendid those human males were! No animals — not even those who had mastered the art of transfiguration and were familiar with the human culture — could match the least! She stole another look at Yikao. What a handsome young man! His outline, how beautiful, especially the attentive disposition when he played the Goo Lute. His long and slender fingers, how delicately they moved to pluck the strings! Yet how swiftly they shifted! A person who could play such beautiful tunes must be very intelligent. She then cast a look at Emperor Zoe — his obese body, his clumsy movements, the fat tissues on his face, and his murky head. She wanted to have Yikao by her side, so she could caress him while he played the Goo Lute, and then enjoy love making with him afterwards. But she already had ample experience in the court of the most powerful Emperor to realize that this was but a dream. Yet, she thought, if she could manage to keep Yikao inside the palace for a while, she might find an opportunity to fulfill her desire. Being a person of such refined disposition, he must be warm and tender, considerate. He must have a better understanding of a woman's need than the Emperor, and he must be able to bring a greater pleasure to her... While she was relishing her sexual fantasies, she was making pragmatic schemes to keep Yikao in the palace so that her fantasy could be realized.

Dar-Gee was suddenly awakened from her trance by the words of the Emperor. "You are a great lute player. You and your father are pardoned."

Dar-Gee quickly reacted. "The music is superb, and rarely heard," she agreed. "However, once Yikao and his father are gone from the capital, so is this heavenly music."

"Indeed so," lamented the Emperor.

"May I make a suggestion?" Embracing the Emperor's sentiment, Dar-Gee offered: "May I suggest to Your Majesty that Yikao stay here to teach me how to play Goo Lute until I have learned how to play the lute as well as he can?"

"You really want to learn how to play Goo Lute? Can you learn to play as well as he?" The Emperor was surprised.

"Of course," Dar-Gee answered. "It is not difficult to learn to play Goo Lute. You can ask Yikao." She then cast a look at Yikao. Under the pressure, the powerless Yikao had to nod, even if grudgingly.

"You are both intelligent and thoughtful, my lovely wife Queen," Emperor Zoe commended. He then turn to Yikao. "Yikao, you stay here and give instructions to Queen Dar-Gee." Yikao could not but say yes.

Dar-Gee was overjoyed. "Let me get the Emperor drunk, then Yikao will be mine tonight," she thought. Then she suggested to Emperor Zoe: "Your Majesty, if you want Yikao to teach me how to play Goo Lute, we must revere him as a teacher. We must prepare a banquet for him. This is the normal protocol to start a new teacher student-relationship."

"Agreed." The Emperor then turned to Yikao again. "You stay here for a banquet." Yikao could not possibly decline, so he stayed.

The protocol of banquets in ancient Middle Kingdom called for separate tables for guests and hosts. A table was set as the centerpiece of the hall for the Emperor and Queen Dar-Gee, facing the southward direction, and a guest table was set at the west side for Yikao, facing the eastward direction. While the banquet went on, Dar-Gee only touched wine with her lips from a small goblet while she persuaded the Emperor to finish every drink she poured for him, that is, "bottoms up" in the language of Middle Kingdom. Emperor Zoe was very pleased that his Queen Dar-Gee would learn how to play Goo Lute and he never had any thought that there was a ploy behind her enthusiasm, so soon he was dead-drunk. Dar-Gee then ordered servants to help Emperor Zoe back to his sleeping chamber and to attend to the Emperor's sleep.

As soon as Emperor Zoe left, she began preparing the next step of the seduction. Her mood changed suddenly. Her facial expression became alluringly charming. She slightly twisted her splendid waist, then lightly swayed her impeccable neck, and her dainty hair responsively undulated, as if being blown by a gentle wind. She then used a soft, seductive, almost pleading voice and asked Yikao: "Can we begin our lessons tonight?"

As soon as Emperor Zoe left, Yikao began to feel uneasy. In the first place, in ancient Middle Kingdom men and women were always kept socially apart, unless they were from the same household. Rarely were guests of opposite sexes mingled together, unless the females were courtesans. Now Yikao had been left alone with the beautiful Queen, and the disposition of Dar-Gee had suddenly become seductive and the tone of her voice erotic. He tried to excuse himself, so he said: "His Majesty has gone to sleep. Is it too late to begin lessons tonight?"

"Not late at all," Dar-Gee quickly responded. She then further flirted, casting a suggestive look at Yikao: "Besides, when the Emperor is not around, we can talk more freely. It is better for the instruction of Goo Lute." She thus ordered two Goo Lutes brought in, one in front of her and the other in front of Yikao. Thus Yikao had no other choice but to give instructions.

First Yikao explained the construction of Goo Lute and the basic techniques of playing. "Goo Lute has a total of five internal and external profiles. It can play six scales and the melodies consist of five basic tones. The left fingers press the strings against the supports and the right fingers pluck the strings to produce the five tones. There are eight basic techniques to pluck the strings." Yikao then demonstrated the eight different techniques. Pleasing melodies were heard.

After demonstrating the basic techniques, Yikao tried to terminate the instruction for the night, so he said: "Normally there are six proscriptions and seven abstentions in the playing of Goo Lute."

"What are these proscriptions and abstentions," asked Dar-Gee curiously .

War among Gods and Men

"Playing Goo Lute is proscribed under the following six emotional conditions: bad news, grief in the heart, preoccupation with other matters, anger, erotic desire and fright.

"The seven situations that call for abstentions are: thunderous and stormy weather, great distress, improper attire, intoxication, debauchery, unappreciative audience, filthy surroundings. Goo Lute is different from other types of musical instruments. It was invented during the reign of sage kings and handed down from generations to generations as an instrument for the most refined music. It can play eighty-one major and fifty-one minor tunes, and thirty-six melodies of different qualities. It is therefore the sublimation of the most refined musical instruments. If it is not played with the utmost dedication and concentration, the music will not be pleasing and it does no justice to such a refined and venerable instrument. Throughout the ages, masters of Goo Lute have observed the rules of six proscriptions and seven abstentions, to show their respect for the art."

But Yikao certainly had failed in his attempt to hint that, under the circumstances, learning how to play a difficult instrument like Goo Lute would be futile. Dar-Gee completely disregarded his advice and continued to pluck the strings. She was interested in music, but at this particular moment her mind was preoccupied with the fulfillment of her sexual fantasy, thus violating the rules of proscription and abstention, so her playing was naturally poor. Despite her efforts, not one tune she plucked was pleasing. While she plucked the strings, she constantly cast pleasant dumb looks at Yikao, as if to blame him for not getting closer to correct her fingering. Dar-Gee wished, because of her poor performance, that Yikao would come closer, using his long and slender fingers to help hers pluck the strings. If she could get Yikao to touch her fingers, then

210

she could use the opportunity to touch his body, to embrace him, to coo her words of love, to bill her attentive caress, then he would be hers ...

Yet Yikao paid no attention to her flirtations, but continued to give instructions from his guest table, using words to describe where Dar-Gee did wrong. Yikao's sole intention was to finish the instruction of how to play Goo Lute as quickly as possible so that he and his father could return home.

After a while, the instruction had gone nowhere. Yikao still maintained his posture at his guest table, and only gave instruction in words. Dar-Gee was not able to lure Yikao to leave his seat. She decided to change her tactics. She put down the Goo Lute and said to him: "Goo Lute is difficult to learn. Well, let us continue to eat. Yikao, you come here and sit by my side." In the time of ancient Middle Kingdom, especially in upper-class societies, the differentiation between the host and the guests was very distinctive. Even when the host and the guests were very intimate friends, in formal banquets they were seated at different tables, each served by one or more servants. Unless there was an intimate relationship between a male and a female, they usually did not mingle socially, not to mention eating around the same table.

Yikao knew that Dar-Gee was Emperor Zoe's favorite. Because of her, Emperor Zoe had already killed his original Queen Consort. He even ordered the execution of his two own sons, one of them the Crown Prince, just to satisfy Dar-Gee. Dar-Gee was indeed extremely beautiful and coquettish, but she was also very wicked. If for the sake of carnal pleasure he established a relationship with her, and should Emperor Zoe learn about the affair, not only his own life would be in danger, even his father's would be in jeopardy – and to seek his father's safe release was the primary purpose that he had risked his life to come to Morning Song.

211

Besides, he was of the line of a prominent family with a long history. The earliest members of his genealogy could be traced back to the reign of Emperor Yao, the emperor who succeeded the first emperor, Huangdi, the founder of the Middle Kingdom who successfully defeated the last barbarians to establish the Middle Kingdom. His earliest ancestor had served as an agricultural officer in the court of Yao. Several tens of generations had passed by, and each generation had produced none but straight and honest scholars and officers. He would never tarnish his family's name by having an illicit relationship with Dar-Gee, no matter how fiery her desire was, no matter how beautiful she was. Not under any circumstances.

So he stood up and bowed to Dar-Gee. "Owing to the great favor of Emperor Zoe, Yikao is fortunate enough to be here to redeem the sins of my father. How can I forgo the proper court protocol to sit with Her Majesty Queen on the same table?"

Dar-Gee still would not give up. "What you said were right if you were here in the capacity of an officer. But you are not. You are here in the capacity of a teacher, and I am your student. There is nothing wrong in a teacher and student sitting together."

Yikao again bowed and declined as politely as he could. Despite Dar-Gee's insistence, he would not go over. Dar-Gee finally gave up, and said: "All right, let us continue the instruction." By now Dar-Gee was so aroused that she had really lost her concentration. If she had pretended not to be able to learn how to play Goo Lute earlier, she was really distracted by her desire now. She could not even pluck the right musical scale. Indeed, the fifth proscription, erotic desire, took full effect. Each time she looked at Yikao, she was aroused more. The young man she was infatuated with was no more than ten feet away, yet he was as untouchable as the moon. It was so different from the days when she was still a freely roaming elf. "How free was I then!" she sighed to herself. "I wholeheartedly present my love to him, but he completely ignores me! Let me try another scheme." So she told Yikao: "Your table is too far from mine. I often cannot hear clearly what you have said." Without waiting for Yikao's response, she ordered ladies-in-waiting to move his table closer. This time Yikao did not object. "Ha! There is still hope!" she thought.

Figure I- 15. Dar-Gee and Yikao
Dar-Gee tried to seduce Yikao while Emperor Zoe slept

Although Yikao was closer, he was still as unreachable as before. After a while, there was still no progress, in either getting closer to her desire or to her Goo Lute playing. Yikao still concentrated in giving out instructions, completely ignoring the flirtation of Dar-Gee. Probably because of the encouragement of the most recent success to get Yikao to move closer, her passion grew stronger and stronger. Finally, she reached her limit. She suddenly put down the Goo Lute and said: "This way I will never learn how to play Goo Lute. I am sitting here and you are sitting down there. We are too far apart. This is the reason why I always pluck the wrong strings or push the strings at the wrong locations. We are going to waste a lot of time and I still cannot make progress. I have a perfect scheme. We can be closer and I can learn faster."

Yikao answered, "It is not possible to learn playing Goo Lute in one or two days. One must constantly practice. After a while one then masters the intricacies and the interplays of different techniques of how to play the instrument. Your Majesty Queen must be patient."

Dar-Gee said, "It is easy for you to say so. But if I do not learn how to play Goo Lute well, tomorrow when the Emperor asks me, what answer shall I give? My suggestion is, you come to my table and sit here. I will sit on your lap. You hold my two hands and guide my fingers to play. It will not take long for you to teach me how to play Goo Lute. Why should we waste any more time?" As she said these words, her face slightly blushed with the excitement of her fantasy thoughts, making her even more erotically tantalizing.

These words could not possibly have expressed Dar-Gee's thoughts more explicitly. Yikao's face turned pale and he did not know how to respond. After a while he slowly murmured, "Your Majesty Queen, please forgive me. I cannot follow your order. You are the most noble woman of the court, mother symbol of the country, respected by feudal lords, worshiped by common people. If for the sake of learning how to play Goo Lute, you sit in my lap, and if someone spreads this rumor around, people will say I debauch Your Majesty Queen, even if nothing really happened. Who will believe our innocence? The reputation of Your Majesty Queen will suffer irreparable damage and I, Yikao, shall be known in history as a deviant person. Your Majesty Queen, please show respect to yourself and please be patient."

These words were spoken in front of ladies-in-waiting. Dar-Gee immediately felt abashed and humiliated. She had nothing to say for a while. Her desire had been turned into disgrace. Restraining her anger, in the best tone she could utter, she told Yikao: "You may go now. We will continue the lesson some other time." Thus exited Yikao.

After Yikao left, she was still angry.

> *I commit my heart to the moon,*
> *But the moon turns me down and*
> *Prefers shining on earthen trenches.*

Reciting these verses from an ancient poem, Dar-Gee vowed vengeance. Her intense infatuation suddenly turned into a maddening hatred. When she returned to the sleeping chamber, the drunk Emperor Zoe was already sound asleep. It was not even possible to use Emperor Zoe, whom moments ago she had regarded as ugly and obese, to satisfy her unfulfilled fantasy. Frustrated, she went to sleep.

The next morning Emperor Zoe asked Dar-Gee the Elf Queen, "How did the lesson go last night?"

"Don't mention it. As I was learning, Yikao tried to make a pass at me."

"Get Yikao here as soon as possible. I want to see him immediately," the Emperor angrily commanded. In no time Yikao was brought to the presence of the Emperor.

"What is the matter in your delay to instruct how to play Goo Lute?" Since it would have been rather embarrassing to accuse Yikao of making pass at his Queen, the Emperor decided to use an indirect method of questioning.

"It is extremely important for the student to exert the utmost concentration to learn anything," replied Yikao. "To learn playing a difficult instrument like Goo Lute well especially requires immense concentration. One must vacate one's mind of all other worldly thoughts so that one can exert the utmost concentration to learn how to play Goo Lute. This is the only way to learn."

"Learning how to play lute of Goo is not difficult, if the instruction is clear. Your instructions were not clear; your instructions were too vague," retorted Dar-Gee, trying to shift to another tactic.

The Emperor did not quite understand the contents of the argument and his mind had shifted to another direction. He did not care about the ongoing arguments, but he enjoyed Goo Lute music, so he wanted to hear another tune. Brushing aside the argument between Dar-Gee and Yikao, he asked: "Yikao, play another tune if you will."

Yikao was glad to be able to get out of the embarrassing situation. "Yes, I will," he responded. He then sat down in a lotus posture, cross legged, and sang these words as he plucked the strings:

> A loyal heart tries to reach heaven,
> Wishing his emperor longevity without bound.
> Forestalling evil lucks forever,
> Timely wind and rain abound,

216

Enriching the land and her people.
Endlessly shall this country endure.

The song was sung with a sprightly melody and appropriately repeated several times at places. Listening to the verses carefully, Emperor Zoe could not detect any indication of disloyalty; all he heard were voices of fealty and earnest wishes for an auspicious future for the country. Sinking his head, the expression of his countenance showed the sign of forgiveness.

Dar-Gee watched the facial expression of Emperor Zoe intently. Not wanting to miss her chance at vengeance, she tried to delay the Emperor's decision. So she suggested that the albino orangutan should be brought in to sing songs, hoping that another opportunity would arise.

The orangutan was brought in. Dressed in brilliantly-colored court dress, he was a magnificent animal. He saluted to the Emperor according to proper court protocol. Emperor Zoe was extremely pleased and he granted the orangutan the same status as a human. "Sing a song," ordered the Emperor. Yikao handed the orangutan a jade castanet and an ivory stick. The orangutan hit the jade tablet gently, producing a fragilely pleasing cracking rhythm. Short of a human voice, he sang the most beautiful tunes imaginable. Lacking the expressive countenance almost exclusively possessed by the human race, the albino orangutan more than made up for his deficiency with the eloquence of his fickle voice. He tapped the jade tablets softly to produce a timely beat as he chanted. In the sadness of his tune, he mimicked the gentle and timeless flow of a murmuring stream. In his passionate moments, he sang the love calls of canaries. In his exhilaration, he would sing the most empathetic voice reminiscent of a victory march. With his eyes closed, the alluring voices projected an imagined, enchanted garden and Emperor Zoe was completely spellbound in a spiritual mood of levitation. He closed his eyes and put his arm around Dar-Gee. The enticing music had taken the Emperor to an enchanted garden, beyond the dusty world, to a pleasant, surreal, nondescript void. He was completely inebriated.

So was Dar-Gee. She had been awakened from her long pretension of being a human by the calls of the wild imbued in the exhilarating voices of the orangutan. She was suddenly back to her past, when she lived in nature, unbound and unrestricted by the artificial rules of the humans. She reminisced about the free life in the wilderness. She had not had the comfort, luxury or power of the palace, but she had not had to abide by the tedious protocols either. How wonderful if she could go back to live a free life again, just for a while. As she was fantasizing, unconsciously she let go of her elfin Tao. The restraint that had resulted from thousands of years of effort of training evaporated, though only for an instant. During this brief instant, the fox form that occupied the human body of Dar-Gee floated without, while her seized human body relaxed in the arms of Emperor Zoe.

Seeing a fox form floating above Dar-Gee in the arms of the Emperor, the albino orangutan suddenly stopped singing. Trained to protect human beings, he charged over the banquet table to attack the fox form to protect the Emperor. The Emperor reacted quickly. With his miraculous strength, he killed the albino orangutan with one single blow.

"He tried to assassinate me! If not for the godsend blow from Your Majesty, I would be dead!" wept Dar-Gee.

"Take Yikao to the execution machine immediately!" ordered the Emperor.

218

"Please, let me explain," Yikao pleaded. "The orangutan was in a cage for a long time and probably was hungry and wanted to grab some fruits from the banquet table. He could not have been planted as an assassin, since he carried no weapon, only his bare hands."

"Yes, Yikao is right. The orangutan could not have been an assassin. It was just the outburst of an animal. You are forgiven." the Emperor concluded after a long period of pondering.

"Since you are forgiven, you must play another tune. This time if any indication of disloyalty is found, you will be executed," Dar-Gee ordered.

Yikao panicked. "I am doomed," he thought. "Trick after trick, she just wants to find an excuse to kill me. Well, if I die, I will die an honest son of my father," he determined. "Yes, I will sing my last song," Yikao replied.

> *A kind Emperor far away spreads his mercy and love,*
> *He never heard of the Pao-Lo execution machine,*
> *Nor the Garden of Corrupt Pleasure*
> *And its adjacent torturous Scorpion Basin,*
> *He never lets his people suffer.*
> *Now cupboards of people are empty,*
> *To fill your fountain of wine,*
> *And to pack your throngs of racks of meat.*
> *I have exhausted my tears,*
> *I am left only with my voiceless cry of sorrow.*
> *I wish my Emperor to return to his senses,*
> *Eliminating those evils around him,*
> *Toadies, sycophants, deviants and calumniators.*
> *Returning his court to justice and mercy,*

War among Gods and Men

> *In peace and prosperity,*
> *His country shall forever endure.*

"You disloyal, worthless traitor! How dare you criticize your Emperor!" shouted Dar-Gee, pointing her finger at Yikao.

"What ... what? The song is pretty good, why do you accuse him?" said the Emperor. Dar-Gee then explained to him the meaning of the lyrics of the song. Now the Emperor was mad. "How dare you criticize me?"

"May I finish my song?" The brave Yikao continued his last song:

> *My voice is weak and my life is coming to an end,*
> *But I want to sing my last verses,*
> *Even in vain must I speak,*
> *To ask the Emperor to overthrow the Queen*
> *To eliminate the elfin smog.*
> *I, Yikao, no longer fear death,*
> *In timeless records on bamboo tablets,*
> *I shall forever be known for my fate,*
> *In my attempt, though in vain,*
> *To eliminate Dar-Gee the Elfin Queen.*

At the end of his song, Yikao threw his lute of Goo at Dar-Gee, knocking her down.

"Send him to the snake pit!" ordered the Emperor.

"No, I have a better way of execution. Nail him to a board and ask one hundred warriors to chop him into pieces!"

*

When a messenger first brought the news from the capital that Yikao had gone to see the Emperor himself, San Felicitous, Chancellor of the court of Duke West, sighed: "His life is in danger. He should not present these gifts to the Emperor to seek pardon for his father; the Emperor has everything, and he can always get anything he wants. These precious gifts he brought will mean nothing to the Emperor. Yikao should have bribed the two greedy and corrupt toadies Yu Whenn and Fei Chung."

When the news of the death of Yikao arrived, Chancellor San immediately asked Chi-Fa, the second son, now the eldest prince and hence the Crown Prince apparent, to summon a court session. San the Felicitous first informed the court officers of the sad news. He then concluded: "As a result of the death of Yikao, the life of the duke is in even more grave danger. We must act now to save him."

"By his evil deeds, Emperor Zoe is no longer fit to be our emperor. We must immediately start a revolutionary campaign to rid us of the tyrant and to save our duke." interjected a general by the name of Nangong Gua (Swift).

"Great idea! Emperor Zoe is a tyrant. We have to save the duke and deliver people from tyranny," seconded another warrior, then another until the court was filled with noises of war cries demanding an immediate invasion to save the duke.

"Silence! Silence!" Chancellor San shouted, while making repeated gestures to quiet down the officers. After the commotion subsided, San the Felicitous turned to Chi-Fa. "Your Excellency, may I suggest that General Nangong Swift be executed first, then we can continue our discussion of how to save our duke."

"Why?" said Chi-Fa, astonished.

"I do not dispute the tyranny of Emperor Zoe, and I also wish him to be eliminated as soon as possible," San Felicitous explained, "however, the purpose of our conference is to save the duke. If we start a revolutionary war right away, before we even reach the nearest frontier pass, the duke will have been put to death because of our rebellion. He is a hostage now. This is why I ask you to execute all officers who want to start a revolutionary war now as a measure to save the duke. They are not saving the duke; they are murdering the duke."

This reasoning quieted down everyone in the court. After a long silence, Chi-Fa said, "What do you suggest?"

"I tried to dissuade Prince Yikao from going to the city of Morning Song to see Emperor Zoe himself. He made the strategic mistake of not bribing first the two greedy toadies Fei Chung and Yu Whenn whom the Emperor trusts, and he tried to accomplish the feat by himself. This is why he was killed. With your permission I will send letters to each of the two corrupt officers and offer them gifts. We must do this secretly and discreetly. I think I can get our duke back safely."

"Your suggestion is excellent. What kind of gifts shall we prepare?" said Chi-Fa, now much more relieved after Chancellor San had presented a detailed analysis of the situation and a workable plan.

"Nothing fancy, but the gifts themselves must be expensive. I suggest large and brilliant pearls, round white jade ornaments, colorful silk, gold ingots, and belts richly decorated with jade to complement their court dress. Two messengers should be dispatched separately to offer the gifts to the two without their mutual knowledge. The messengers must disguise themselves as merchants to avoid suspicion. With my letters and gifts, the duke will be back in no time," San the Felicitous proposed.

Two trustworthy court officers were selected as messengers. Disguised themselves as merchants, they passed through the five frontier passes without a hitch and soon they arrived at Morning Song. They did not dare stay at official guesthouses, so they stayed in a hostel for commoners.

The next day, the two messengers went their separate ways to see Fei the Corrupt and Yu the Adulator. The messenger who went to the residence of Fei the Corrupt had no difficulty obtaining an audience with Fei himself.

"Who are you?" said Fei Chung.

"I am officer Tai Tien from the court of Duke West. I am here to deliver a letter and some gifts from my superior, Chancellor San Felicitous. Chancellor first wants me to thank you on his behalf for the kindness you extended to Duke West. Without your kind words, he would have long been dead," the messenger said.

"Sit down. Let me read the letter first," replied Fei the Corrupt. The letter read:

From the humble Chancellor San Felicitous of the court of Duke West,

To the most distinguished Your Excellency Fei.

Over these years I have often heard of your great virtue but I have never had the honor of meeting you in person. My duke, by his careless words, offended His Majesty and only through your great kindness was his life spared. During his imprisonment, he has never expressed a word of complaint against his Emperor nor the treatment he has received. All of us in the fief are thankful to you for your care of the duke. People of the fief have prepared some

223

humble gifts for you, to thank you for your kindness and consideration: a pair of white jade ornaments, one hundred gold ingots, four colored silk rolls, and other ornaments for your personal use. These are but a small token of our gratitude.

We would like to ask you for a favor. The duke is aging and his life in the world will not be long. His mother is now in failing health. May I respectfully plead to you to extend your kindness once again to persuade His Majesty of the sincerity of the duke's repentance, and to release him back to his fief? The family of the duke and the people of Duchy Zhou will forever be grateful to you.

Again, let this humble Chancellor thank you for your kindness.

Looking at the gifts, Fei the Corrupt contemplated: "The gifts are worth at least ten thousand silver pieces. I must do something. How? Let me give this request some thought." He turned to the messenger. "Please convey my thanks to Chancellor San for his generous gifts. It is not appropriate for me to write a letter of reply. However, I can promise you that I will find an opportune time to ask the Emperor to release the duke."

The other messenger encountered almost the same reception. Having accomplished their missions, the two messengers returned to Duchy Zhou.

Neither Fei the Corrupt nor Yu the Adulator told each other of the gifts. One day, Emperor Zoe invited Fei and Yu to play chess with him. The Emperor won two games in a row and was extremely pleased. A banquet of celebration ensued. During the banquet, the topic of Duke West came up. The Emperor casually commented: "He could not even prognosticate that his son was to be killed. Had he been able to do so, he would have warned his son to stay away from his misfortune. He must be a fake."

Seizing this opportunity, Fei the Corrupt quickly assented: "Indeed so. I planted some secret agents to watch Duke West. I have received reports that he offers daily prayers for the health and well-being of Your Majesty. He has never had a word of complaint during the entire seven years of imprisonment. I think he is loyal."

"Yes, indeed so," joined Yu the Adulator. Now they realized that they both had been given expensive gifts.

"You told me previously that Duke West was a scheming and treacherous person. Now what makes you change your opinions," asked Emperor Zoe.

"I was told by others that he was a scheming and treacherous person," Yu the Adulator said. "However, only time can tell the truth. He has been watched by me also, and he surely is as loyal as my friend Fei Chung said. I was also about to inform Your Majesty of my finding when Fei Chung spoke." Yu the Adulator was quite eager to show Fei the Corrupt that he, too, had earned his gifts righteously.

"If both of you say that Duke West is a good and loyal officer, I am thinking of granting him a pardon. What is your opinion?"

"I cannot offer my opinion whether to pardon the duke or not," replied Fei the Corrupt. "All I can say is that he has not shown any indication of disloyalty during his imprisonment. I believe that his loyalty will be further enhanced if he is released and sent back to his fief." Now that he had almost succeeded in getting the release of the duke, he did not want to assume the responsibility should the Emperor change his mind in the future.

War among Gods and Men

Not wanting to let Fei the Corrupt get all the credit for persuading the Emperor to release Duke West, Yu the Adulator added: "Since there is rebellion in the east and the south, maybe Your Majesty can grant Duke West a title and some military authority, so that he can lead his army to battle the rebels. In this way you not only show your kindness, you also gain an army to fight for you against the rebels."

"Excellent idea," the Emperor said. "Release Duke West immediately. In addition, he shall be given the title of my Proxy during his campaign against these rebels. A Yellow Fur Flag and a White Axe symbolizing the delegation of my authority shall be awarded to the duke. He is free to take whatever action he deems necessary to squash the rebels. A three-day parade shall be authorized to celebrate his release and his new title." An imperial order was quickly drafted and formalized.

Before adjournment, Emperor Zoe told the two toadies: "You two are the greatest officers of the court. How could I rule my country without you!" Thus, bribery not only got Duke West out of his imprisonment, but also get him a title, a Yellow Fur Flag and a White Axe symbolizing royal military power, and a three-day parade on main streets of the city of Morning Song to celebrate his new position.

People from Yeau Village felt happy for the duke, that he was pardoned, but they also felt sad that they would lose a good friend and teacher. The entire village's inhabitants followed the duke for several li before they bid him the final farewell.

Suddenly, the duke had been elevated from the status of a prisoner to an important officer, with a parade to celebrate. Curious people from Morning Song crowded the city streets to watch their respected duke riding on a royal float in the parade. On the second day of the parade, Flying Tiger returned to the city from a several-day military exercise, and was aroused by the commotion. He was surprised to see the duke sitting on a magnificent float and waving at well-wishing people on the street. He was then informed of the release of the duke and the award of a new title. Flying Tiger went forward to greet him. "Congratulations! I did not know you had been released or promoted. I have not seen you for a long while. I want to talk to you. Can you come to my home for lunch?"

"I cannot possibly decline such a great honor." Duke West stepped down from the float and bowed to Flying Tiger.

They had not seen each other for seven years, so the lunch dragged into the afternoon tea, and then into a dinner when dusk fell. When the dinner was about over, Huang analyzed the situation for Duke West. "Don't you know that the Emperor does not have any opinion of his own and he only listens to the two toadies and Dar-Gee? Your release must be the result of briberies offered to Fei Chung and Yu Whenn. The Emperor may change his mind any time. Now that you are out, you should go back to your land as soon as possible. The longer you stay, the more likely you will be rearrested. Then you are in real trouble."

"How can I get out," asked the duke, who now realized his new danger.

"As the chief military commander, I have in my possession military passes which will enable you to get out of any frontier pass. You must leave tonight. Do not delay any more."

"Thank you." The duke then went back to the official guesthouse and packed his most important belongings in a travel bag. With the authoritative military pass, the city gate opened and Duke West escaped. He trotted his horse into the darkness of the night and, guided by star light, he was on his way to freedom.

Unfortunately this was a miscalculation of Flying Tiger. Had the duke stayed for the full parade, he could have leisurely departed. His sudden departure in the middle of the parade was easily interpreted as a sign of guilty apprehension. Surely enough, the next day when Fei the Corrupt and Yu the Adulator learned of the midnight flight of the duke, they concluded that he must be scheming something. After they conferred with each other, they both went to report the flight of the duke to the Emperor.

"It is you two who talked me into releasing him. Now explain to me nicely, otherwise I will have you both beheaded," angrily charged the Emperor.

"As Your Majesty knows, in his imprisonment we both sent agents to watch him," pleaded the two toadies. "He was a good pretender and he fooled us. We learned of his flight only this morning. As loyal officers we came here right away to report to you his flight. We have a plan to remedy the situation. We will send two warriors, Ying Po-bei and Lei Kai to arrest Duke West and bring him here for execution."

"All right, since you came to me as soon as you discovered his flight, I believe your loyalty and I pardon you both. Now send the two warriors you named to arrest Duke West." A solution had been found. Emperor Zoe was eager to go back to his indulgence, so he forgave the two.

In his flight, Duke West traveled almost the same path as Jiang Sarn. However, not long after he crossed the Yellow River at Meng Gin, he saw rising dust behind him. It looked like a cavalry speeding towards him. Duke West immediately sensed that they must be pursuers. "I am dead if I am caught. Let me run," sighed the duke as he galloped his horse. Nevertheless, twenty li from the first frontier pass, Tong, the gap between him and the pursuing cavalry was shortened to the point that even the countenances of the two leaders became discernible. He immediately recognized them as Yin Po-bei and Lei Kai, the two cruel warriors who had earlier arrested the two princes.

After taking over the responsibility of fostering Lei Thunder, who had been found after thunder and was thus named, Son of Clouds raised him according to Taoist tradition in Cavern Jade Columns, Mount End South. One day, during his daily mental exercises, Son of Clouds sensed something and he prognosticated. He found that Duke West had been released but he was facing an impending danger. Keeping his words that Lei Thunder would one day meet the duke to save him, he summoned Lei to his presence. "You have been here for seven years and it is about time for you to meet your father for the first time. He just escaped from the capital city Morning Song and he is heading towards his fief. However, he is being chased by a cavalry led by two warriors and in a day or two they will catch up with him. It is your duty to save him from his pursuers. You will need some weapons. Go and find your weapons in the mountain."

This was the first time Lei had ever heard the word "father." Son of Clouds had to explain to him the meaning of the word.

Although it was already late autumn, this mountain was still covered with green foliage. Lei Thunder saw rabbits and deer running around, and occasionally some foxes, but no weapons. "How am I to find a weapon in this mountain? There is nothing here except trees and wildlife." Strolling around, suddenly he saw two bright red apricots on an odd-looking tree. In late autumn all the fruits had already fallen down from the other trees. These two fruits stood out conspicuously. Thirsty and hungry from his searching efforts, he decided to try them. The apricots were delicious, but soon after he ate them, two giant wings began to grow under his armpits and he suddenly grew taller, accompanied by a tremendous increase in his muscle strength. His facial features also changed: his nose grew bigger, his hair turned red, and his complexion became tinted with a shade of blue. He saw his reflection from a still pond nearby and he was so scared that he forwent his weapon hunt and hurried back to see his teacher.

"I thought you would never find them. Those two apricots you ate came from a tree given to me by a Taoist friend ages ago. He told me it would take a millennium for the tree to bear fruit. So this is the magic power he promised me. Now let me teach you how to fly and also give you a weapon."

First he wrote the two words "Wind" and "Thunder" in Taoist inscriptions on the left and right wings, then he recited a long series of incantations. After he had completed his preparations, he uttered: "Up!" Suddenly Lei Thunder found himself flying, upside down with his feet pointing towards the sky. After a few minutes of practice under the direction of Son of Clouds, Lei Thunder began to master the Tao of flying upside down, with his feet pointing towards the sky. After a few minutes of practice under the direction of Son of Clouds, Lei Thunder began to master the Tao of flying upside down and he quickly learned to use the magic power instilled by the two words "Wind" and "Thunder" on his wings. He could generate strong winds and loud thunder as he flew. Next the Son of Clouds selected a golden shaft from his rack of weapons and taught Lei Thunder the art of shaft-play. Lei then practiced under his teacher's guidance. Soon he mastered the combination of shaft play and his newly acquired flying skill, generating wind and thunder occasionally to flaunt the powerful thrusts of the golden shaft.

After practicing for a day, Lei Thunder was again summoned to his teacher's presence. "Your father will be somewhere twenty li from the Frontier Pass Tong, and the pursuing cavalry is about to close in on him.

Go there, repel the cavalry of men, and deliver him to his fief. Afterwards, come back immediately. Also, under no circumstances should you kill anyone. Now go."

Somewhere outside the Frontier Pass Tong, Lei Thunder saw a man on a galloping horse. He landed in front of him and asked: "Are you Duke West?"

Stopping his horse, the duke saw a strange man with red hair, bluish complexion, two wings, and holding a golden shaft. "Bad luck today. I am chased by a cavalry from behind and now I am stopped by this monster," thought the duke. "Yes, I am. Who are you?" the duke said wearily. "Will you please let me pass since I am chased by a cavalry of men?"

"My dear father, how glad am I to find you! My teacher asked me to meet you here and to save you from your pursuers," replied Lei Thunder.

"You are very kind, but I do not recall having a son like you," the duke politely responded, not wanting to offend his would-be rescuer.

"Oh, yes. I am the baby born of thunder whom you adopted." Replied Lei Thunder. "My teacher Son of Clouds fostered me and trained me in Tao. It is a long story about how I acquired the two wings. Let me save you first."

Duke West then remembered the incident. He was surprised that the baby he had found in Swallow Mountain had grown to an adult height in seven years. However, he did not have the time to elaborate, because the cavalry was closing in. "I am glad you come here to save me," said Duke West. "But please do not kill anyone, just scare them away. I do not want any killing; I have already offended Emperor Zoe by running away and I do not want to commit any further offense against him."

"Don't worry, my teacher also told me not to kill anyone. Let me go and scare these pursuers away."

Figure I- 16. The rescue of Duke West
Lei Thunder came to the rescue of his father

Lei Thunder then flew away and descended in front of the pursuing cavalry, and shouted: "Who is your leader?"

"We both are," Yin Po-bei and Lei Kai replied. "Just what do you think you are doing to stop the imperial army from arresting that man over there?"

"Go back, and no one will be hurt," commanded Lei Thunder. "I can kill you all easily, but I will first demonstrate to you my power. If you do not go away, I will crack your heads like this. Don't move." Lei Thunder then flew to the nearest hilltop. As he flew he released wind and thunder from his wings. With a single strike from his golden shaft, a large boulder was knocked off its base and rolled down towards the cavalry, who immediately dispersed to avoid the fast-rolling boulder.

"Do you want to fight or get the hell out of here?" roared Lei Thunder.

Without even waiting for the two leaders to issue a command of retreat, in a seemingly concerted motion everyone in the cavalry turned around and ran their horses back. In no time the pursuing cavalry was out of sight. Lei Thunder then went back to the duke, who was already scared off his horse, and picked him up. Lei carried the duke and his bag and flew over the five frontier passes, Tong, Lin Tong, Penetrating Clouds, Boundary Marker and Vast Water. Finally they arrived at Ridge Golden Rooster. Gently putting the duke down, Lei Thunder bid his father farewell.

"But this is nowhere. Can you fly me to my capital, the city of West Branch?" appealed the duke.

"My teacher told me to deliver you to your fief and then go back to the cavern right away. Now I have extended his order by delivering you to the first village outside the last frontier pass. I must not disobey his order any further. However, my teacher promised me that we will be united soon. Now, farewell." With these words, Lei Thunder parted and flew back to Cavern Jade Columns.

The duke, who had escaped in plain clothes, went to the nearest hostel. The next morning, he realized that he did not have any money with him. He apologized to the hostel owner and promised to pay as soon as he arrived at West Branch City.

"Are you trying to cheat me? How are you going to send money back to me from such far away place? You know our government is fair and just. People are honest. Any infraction of law will be punished. Do you think you can get away with this kind of plain lie?"

"No, I am not a liar. I am the duke who just escaped from the territory of Emperor Zoe. Please help me back to West Branch City."

"You know it is a very serious offense to impersonate a government official, not to mention the duke himself. Are you serious?" said the hostel owner.

"Of course I am telling the truth. Get me some transportation to take me back to the capital. You will be amply rewarded," replied the duke.

"It is true that the duke had been imprisoned by Emperor Zoe of the central government for some time," thought the hostel owner. "This man does not look like an impostor. If he insists that he is the duke, then there might be truth in it. I will go with him to West Branch. If he is a liar, he will be punished. In any case, I have already warned him." The hostel owner half-believed what he had heard, but he was a cautious man. So he bowed to the plain-clothed duke: "Your Lord, I humbly request your pardon for my impudence. However, the only transportation I can provide is the donkey which pulls our millstone. I hope you will not mind the rough ride on a country donkey."

They soon left Ridge Golden Rooster and they traveled the narrow passes to cross Mount First Morning Sun. It was late autumn, and the mountain path was already covered with fallen leaves. The weather was quite chilly at night and in the morning the ground was covered with a thin layer of frost. In a few days of time, they arrived at the vicinity of West Branch.

A month after the dispatch of the two messengers to bribe Fei the Corrupt and Yu the Adulator, Chancellor San Felicitous stationed a patrol outside West Branch to wait for the arrival of the duke. One day, a scout reported that he saw an elderly man resembling the duke riding a donkey over a mountain path approaching the city. A prognostication with three coins confirmed that he had escaped. Chancellor San decided that this old man must be the duke. He thus gathered his officers and princes outside the city, all dressed in official attire in brilliant red, the color of celebration, to form a welcome procession. Meanwhile the city also prepared its welcome atmosphere by hanging red ribbons over door arches, and incense was burned along the road leading to the duke's palace.

A messenger was sent to meet the duke to inform him of the welcome party. Led by Nangong Swift and Chancellor San Felicitous, the procession approached the duke, and San Felicitous delivered a short speech of welcome on behalf of the party. "We are ashamed that we could not get our Lord back sooner. We are extremely pleased to see you. Long live our Lord!"

The duke changed to court dress suitable for the occasion and the procession returned to the palace. Even the hostel owner was given a prominent position in the procession for his service to the duke. As promised, he was amply rewarded, and he was escorted back by two petit officers.

After a few days of resting, a court session headed by the duke, the first in seven years, took place. First the duke related his experience of imprisonment. He mentioned that he had known about the attempt of his eldest son, Yikao, to try to redeem his freedom and his subsequent tragic death, but he had not dared say anything. He then related his subsequent release, promotion, and the three-day parade, and how on the second day of the parade, Flying Tiger had given him a military pass for the five frontier passes. And that he was chased by the two generals Yin and Lei, but then a savior had come. "The savior was a baby I adopted seven years ago when I went through Swallow Mountain. He was fostered by a Taoist Son of Clouds. This baby was named Lei Thunder. It was this adopted son who saved me from the pursuers."

San Felicitous said: "The five frontier passes are all heavily guarded. How did Lei Thunder managed to help Your Lordship pass through?"

"It is a long story. Speaking of the appearances of Lei Thunder, my god, he has an astounding look! The first time I saw him I was nearly scared to death. It is unthinkable that in seven years he has grown to an adult, over seven feet tall, and with a husky build. He has bright red hair and his facial complexion is bluish. His two eyes are huge and forceful. But the most remarkable thing is, he has a pair of two giant wings under his armpits. He used a golden shaft as his weapon. He flew to a small hill top, and with a strike, a giant boulder rolled down and scared the pursuers away. He carried me on his back and flew over the five frontier passes, then let me down at Ridge Golden Rooster, saying that his teacher forbade him to enter West Branch City. Then I found a hostel and the owner accompanied me to come home."

236

During the seven years, West Branch had continued to prosper and nothing exciting had happened. Therefore all the officers listened attentively to the saga of his escape, like a story of adventure.

After the duke finished, San Felicitous said: "Your Lordship, the wrongful and horrendous ouster and murder of the Queen, the unjustified execution of her father, Duke East, and of Duke South and other loyal officers, plus the heavy taxation and coerced hard labor to construct Emperor Zoe's pet project, the Elk Tower, have caused great dissatisfaction among nobles and hatred from common people. Since you were away, political situations have changed drastically. I do not think that the regime of the central government can last very long ..."

Before the Chancellor could finish, Nangong Swift exclaimed, "Now the duke has come back. It is time for us to avenge the bloody murder of Prince Yikao, and to remove the tyrant. We in Zhou Duchy have several hundred thousand brave soldiers and sixty courageous warriors who are ready at your command to commence a revolutionary war to deliver the people from misery."

"Wait! Wait! Be patient!" the duke replied. "My eldest son died because he would not listen to the advice of Chancellor San. As for revolution, I cannot disavow the promise of fealty I made when I succeeded my father. Besides, now that I am back, I must rest my people, avoid conflict, and enrich the people and the treasury so that we can enjoy peace and prosperity, so that my country can endure. Let us not talk about this subject now. However, I had an odd dream last night. I dreamed of a flying bear and a fire around the altar in the temple of this Duchy. What is the foreboding?"

After a few moments of silence, Chancellor San responded, "According to my prognostication based upon the Eight Fold Way developed by you when you were away, the presage is as follows: Fire, the fourth form of the universe, is used by man to extract metallum, the first form, from terra. The west direction is associated with metallum. A flying beast symbolizes ability. My Lord, I think you shall acquire a very capable man to assist you in ruling your country. This man is in this duchy now."

With the ability of the duke to prognosticate, it would have been a trivial matter for him to interpret his dream. But, although during most of the time he was away he had been imprisoned in the cultural desert Yeau Village, he had had plenty of contacts with officers in Emperor Zoe's court. He knew, even though Emperor Zoe was evil, that his court officers were capable and, in fact, there was no comparison between the quality of officers in his court and those in Emperor Zoe's. Yet his officers had been extremely loyal to him. He could not replace them arbitrarily. Using his dream as a hint was the best approach.

After the interpretation of the dream by Chancellor San, the duke said, "Your analysis is very correct. Then, let all of you be aware of the existence of a capable man in our territory. Look out for him." With this statement the court session ended amiably.

Meanwhile, Jiang Sarn led a reclusive life in a hut in Parn Chi Village. To pass his time, he reviewed daily the sutra of Tao, Huang Ting (Yellow Court). To relieve his boredom, he often fished by Wei Water. Even so, he could not forget the happy years he had spent in East Kwen Ren Range, in Palace Jade Abstraction. He often recalled the prediction made by his teacher Primeval: "You are destined to be a great man, enjoying wealth and power in the world of dust. You shall lead a revolutionary army to commence a great period of history." Each time when he recalled this prediction, he always sighed: "Several years have since gone by, and time never returns. When shall the prediction of Primeval come true ...?"

One day, to relieve his boredom, he went to fish as usual. He sat under the shade of a weeping willow. He looked at the river water rapidly flowing eastward and never to return, just like time. He could not help lamenting his own fate. Just then, a woodcutter by the name of Wu Chi (Serendipity), carrying a load of two bundles of firewood on a shoulder pole, passed by. He stopped and sat down on a piece of rock to take a rest. He started to strike up a conversation with Jiang Sarn.

"Mr. Old man, I often pass by here and I have seen you many times fishing in this river. The combination of us two could be a beautiful theme in a painting: 'Fisherman and Woodsman.'"

"Indeed so." Jiang Sarn was pleased that the woodsman appeared to know some culture.

"What is your name, sir," the woodsman asked.

"My given name is Jiang Sarn, my literary name is Flying Bear. I migrated here from the capital to escape from tyranny."

The woodsman laughed heartily. Then he stopped laughing and said, "My name is Wu Serendipity. My ancestors have lived here for several generations."

"Why do you laugh," Jiang Sarn asked.

"I am laughing at you. You have a literary name. That's funny."

"What is so funny about that? Many scholars and accomplished men of letters have literary names," Jiang Sarn replied.

"Yes, indeed. Only scholars and accomplished men of letters have literary names. But you also have a literary name! Ha! Ha! You don't look like a scholar or a man of letters. This is why I am laughing. From what I observe, you are without a profession or trade, so you pass your time fishing and doing nothing. You try to imitate accomplished scholars by adopting a literary name. This is why I feel funny about you." Wu Serendipity then walked over and pulled the fishing line from the water. He took a look, then said, "Just what I thought. You are goofing around. You do not even know how to fish. You use a straight hook. You will never catch any fish that way. You are stupid enough to fish with a straight hook. Yet you are so arrogant as to adopt a literary name and call yourself Flying Bear. You have no common sense. Let me teach you how to fish. First you bend a sewing needle to form a hook in a candle flame, then you put bait on the hook. When the fish bites, you pull it up. It will take some practice ..."

"I am not really interested in getting any fish," Jiang Sarn interrupted. "You know nothing about me. I am waiting here like the sky waits for clouds to disperse. I am waiting to be appointed to an important position to fulfill my lifelong ambitions."

"What are your lifelong ambitions?" Wu Serendipity said.

"I am waiting to be appointed the prime minister," Jiang Sarn replied.

"Ha! I do not think you look like a person who will be any more important than I am, a woodcutter."

"You don't look too good today," Jiang Sarn said.

"Oh yeah? I am a carefree woodsman. What is bad about that? I am not rich, but I am happy. I have composed a song to picture my life. Do you want to hear it?"

240

"Yes, please go ahead."

> *An axe hangs on my waist,*
> *Over mountains and ridges I tramp,*
> *I work amidst nature,*
> *Blue pine, peach flowers, azaleas,*
> *Countless birds and animals I befriend.*
> *Thump, thump I chop woods down,*
> *But I only cut dead branches.*
> *A load of firewood*
> *In exchange for a bag of rice.*
> *With wild vegetables and home-brewed rice wine*
> *I never worry about food.*
> *Ten thousand pieces of silver*
> *Will not make me give up my freedom.*
> *To roam in nature, to pursue the clouds,*
> *To drink to the moon, to live free,*
> *Happily I stay unknown,*
> *In solitude, in companionship.*

Other than my material poverty, I am happy. Why do you say I do not look good today," Wu asked.

"I can prognosticate for you," Jiang Sarn offered.

"Let me hear your prognostication," Wu Serendipity said.

Jiang Sarn put down his fishing pole and divined the fortune of Wu Serendipity. After a few moments, he told him: "You will kill somebody in West Branch City today. The killing is accidental."

"Nonsense. I, Wu Serendipity, am always friendly with my customers, whether they buy firewood from me or not. I never quarreled with anyone in my life." With these words Wu Serendipity angrily left, apparently upset by Jiang Sarn's remarks.

Wu Serendipity arrived at the city without incident. After passing through the city gate, he let his shoulder pole down to relieve himself momentarily of the heavy load of firewood. Just then, the duke was returning after a tour to the countryside to see how the peasants were doing. As his envoy entered into the city, people moved aside to let the envoy through. In a hurry to avoid the convoy, Serendipity swung his shoulder pole around. It happened that a veteran soldier was standing next to Wu and the swinging shoulder pole hit him in his temple, instantly killing him. Bystanders quickly grabbed Wu and took him to the nearest constable. Wu was locked up.

A few days later, Chancellor San personally came by to investigate, since murder was such a rarity in this peaceful city. Wu wept and said, "It was a true accident. I beg you to pardon me."

"We have our laws, and you must receive the proper punishment without exception, even though witnesses said that it was a true accident."

"But my mother will starve if I do not bring food and money to her. She needs my attention. Give me a few months, then I will come back to face the law," pleaded Wu.

"How long have you been living here," asked the Chancellor.

"Since I was born. My family has been living in the same hut for several generations. I do not have any other place to run away to. I promise you I will come back here to face charges if you will let me go back for a few months to take care of my mother first."

"Well, you are right that you cannot run away. I will give you half a year to make arrangements for the livelihood of your mother. If you try to run away, remember that the duke has developed a new method of divination, the Eight Fold Way. It is extremely accurate and I can always locate you with this new method, no matter where you hide. Keep your promise." Thus Wu Serendipity was freed on his own cognizance to go home to take care of his mother.

"Where have you been? I was worried to death! I thought you might have been hurt in a fall, or attacked by wild beasts. What happened to you ...?"

"Mother, disaster!" interjected Wu Serendipity. "The other day I gathered a load of firewood for sale in the city. Just after I passed the city gate I killed a veteran soldier by accident and I was arrested and locked in jail for several days. Chancellor San came to investigate and I begged the merciful Chancellor to let me come back home to take care of you. He gave me six months and he told me that if I try to run away, he can always find me with a new method of divining developed by the duke. This accident must have been caused by the curse of that wretched, crazy old fisherman I met the other day. That crazy man fished with a straight hook. I conversed with him. He said I did not look good that day and he divined for me, and told me that I would kill a man that day, and I did. He must be a sorcerer, and he planted this incident with some sort of magic."

"Oh no, my son. Listen to me. This is indeed a disaster. However, do not blame the fisherman. If he can prognosticate so precisely that you would kill a man that day, he must have a way to absolve you. Go and find him. Beg him to absolve you of your offense." The mother, though in grief, was in a more sober mode than her son.

Wu went to the creek and found Jiang Sarn there, still fishing with his straight hook. "The most revered demigod Jiang," Wu Serendipity beckoned.

"You are the woodcutter who was here the other day. Did you kill anyone that day?" Turning around, Jiang Sarn found Wu kneeling in front of him.

"The most revered demigod, I have unknowingly offended you. You were right. After entering the city, I put down my load of firewood. Just then, to avoid the convoy of the duke, I swung my shoulder pole around and I accidentally hit a veteran soldier in his temple. He died instantly. I was arrested and put in jail for several days until Chancellor San came to investigate. Through his kindness I was given six months to take care of my mother, then I have to go back to face the trial and punishment. I probably will be executed as a murderer. Please save me," pleaded the woodcutter.

"How can I save you? It is you who did not heed my advice," Jiang Sarn responded, without the slightest indication of any emotion.

"Please forgive me for my imprudence, please save me. Only you can save me," pleaded Wu, in tears.

Jiang Sarn took a deep look at Wu Serendipity. After pondering for a while, he said, "You look intelligent. You might contribute to my future cause. I will save you on the condition that you must submit yourself as my disciple."

"Indeed I will," Wu quickly responded.

"All right. Go back to your home and dig a trench around four feet deep in front of your bed. Lie down there at dusk, and ask your mother to scatter a handful of rice over you and light two candles, one around your head, the other around your feet. Sleep in the trench until dawn. I will take care of the rest. Tomorrow morning, you can just tend to your usual business, as if nothing ever happened."

The order of Jiang Sarn was faithfully carried out. During that night, Jiang Sarn put on his Taoist robe, took out his Taoist sword, disheveled his hair, and danced Taoist steps of incantation to set up a pattern of stars. The purpose was to generate an artificial prognostication around Wu.

The next morning, Wu Serendipity went to see Jiang Sarn at his usual fishing spot. He said, "Your disciple is here, waiting for your order." A simple but solemn ceremony to inaugurate Wu as a disciple of Jiang was exercised. According to the traditions of Middle Kingdom, from this day on, Wu would be a disciple of Jiang Sarn for life.

"In the morning you will cut firewood to support your mother and yourself as usual. In the afternoon, come to my hut. I will teach you literature and martial arts. My prognostication indicates that I will be discovered soon. The Shang Dynasty, with the plentiful evil deeds committed by Emperor Zoe, cannot last for long. You must be prepared for the forthcoming campaign against this tyrant." From that night on, Wu Serendipity began learning literature and martial arts.

Half a year passed by and Wu did not go back to face his charges. A year later, Chancellor San remembered Wu and he used the new procedure of the duke to prognosticate the whereabouts of Wu. The answer came, that Wu had committed suicide by hopping over a precipice for fear of punishment. San sighed: "What a waste of life. His punishment for accidental manslaughter could not have been more than a few years of imprisonment."

War among Gods and Men

Spring came. The duke decided to take his court officers outside the city for a spring trot through the countryside. As the procession proceeded, they saw parties and parties of people strolling with their picnic baskets along a river path to relish the first of the spring. Extremely pleased at this peaceful sight, the duke said to Chancellor San as their horses paced along, "This is a different sight from Morning Song. While people there are being taxed to death and loyal officers are being exterminated by torture, I am glad to see people in my land enjoying peace, tranquility and prosperity. I hope we can extend the same to people in the capital and elsewhere."

"Yes, the city of West Branch surpasses utopia." Chancellor San responded, bowing slightly from his horse-riding posture.

As they moved along, a group of fishermen passed by, and one of them sang:

> With eleven campaigns of righteousness,
> The founder of Shang delivered people from tyranny.
> Six centuries went by,
> Now virtues subsiding, atrocities prevailing,
> People are hungry.
> Their food, clothing, and nourishment
> Go to fill fountains of wine,
> And throngs of racks of meat,
> To please the Emperor.
> Blood flows freely beneath Elk Tower.
> In their suffering pain,
> Innocents fulfilled the enjoyment
> Of the Emperor and his woman.
> I, a man of four seas, roam among waves in the day,
> Nightly stars and constellations I watch.

With a bare pole, lonesomely I fish.
Forgetting heights of heaven,
Forgetting depths of the earth,
Forgetting time and space,
Lonesomely I fish,
Lonesomely I fish.

"This is an unusual song. There must be a learned man among them. Ask them who composed the song," the duke said to Chancellor San.

"Who among you composed this beautiful song?" said the Chancellor to the group of fishermen.

"None of us. We learned it from a crazy old man living in a hut over there. He always fished with a straight hook, saying that he is not interested in fish. He said an important position is awaiting him to fulfill his ambitions," responded one of the fishermen.

"This might be the man we are after," said the duke. They followed the directions given by the fishermen and proceeded towards Jiang Sarn's hut. As they paced their horses along, they encountered a woodcutter passing by. As the woodcutter passed, he sang a folk tune:

Spring sun warms the air,
Blue water flows leisurely.
Flowers and green leaves
Eagerly compete for attention.
World has no knowledge of a talent
Withering away by a creek
Fishing with a straight hook.

The duke said to Chancellor San, "The verses of the song are similar to the song sung by the fishermen. Maybe they were authored by the same person."

Chancellor asked one of the attendants to summon the woodcutter over. As the woodcutter approached, Chancellor San suddenly recalled that this woodcutter resembled Wu Serendipity. "Come closer, you woodcutter. You look like an escaped criminal. What is your name?"

Unable to hide any more, Wu Serendipity approached Chancellor San and begged for forgiveness. He told Chancellor San the whole story, starting from the prognostication of the accidental manslaughter, to the promise of immunity by the same elderly man, Jiang Sarn, who was also known by the literary name Flying Bear, and that Jiang Sarn knew how to nullify the new method of prognostication developed by the duke.

After the full story was told, Wu pleaded: "I beg you to pardon me. I am only a woodcutter, I meant no malice ..."

A zealous guard immediately seized Wu Serendipity. "You dared to conspire to nullify the power of prognostication of the duke ...."

"Wait, do not arrest him. Let him off," the duke ordered. Then he turned to Chancellor San. "What a coincidence! This Flying Bear must be the man we are after. Let us find him first."

"Where does your teacher live," asked the Chancellor. "You will be pardoned if you take us to him."

"He lives in a hut just around the corner. Let me take you there."

Arriving at the hut and finding it empty, Wu trembled. "He was here just a moment ago. Maybe he was afraid of the official procession."

"We will come back. In any case, this is the wrong protocol to visit a great talent. We must prepare a proper gift," the duke said. Then he turned to the woodcutter. " Wu, you are pardoned. Inform your teacher that I am the duke. I will come back three days from today to invite him to come to my palace to be my adviser." Then the procession left.

After returning to his palace, the duke summoned all his high officers to his court and they stayed over. During the next three days they were served only vegetarian food, and they were to meditate to cleanse their minds of worldly thoughts in preparation for another visit to persuade Jiang Sarn to serve in the duke's court.

This ritual performed, the next day they departed for Jiang Sarn's hut. One or two li away from the hut, the duke ordered the procession to stop and he walked with a few of his closest court officers for the rest of the way. But Jiang Sarn was not in his hut. The duke and a few attendants strolled towards a creek in back of the hut, and they saw that Jiang Sang stood by the bank of the creek, fishing.

The duke slipped quietly towards him from behind. Jiang Sarn was aware of the approach of the duke, but he pretended not to notice. He began to chant:

> *West winds blow white clouds above.*
> *Lamenting time wasted, an old man fishes by the creek.*
> *Five phoenixes sang together in unison,*
> *Foretelling the arrival of a truly benevolent monarch.*
> *With a lonely fishing pole,*
> *I enjoy my solitude.*

"Is my sage friend happy here," gently asked the duke.

Figure I- 17. Jiang sarn and Duke West

Turning around, Jiang Sarn saw him. He pretended to be startled and let fall his fishing pole. He began a slow movement to assume a kneeling posture as salutation of a commoner to a duke. Before he could even start to bend his knees, his arms were caught by the duke. Softly, the duke spoke with a sincere, apologizing tone. "Please forgive

250

me for my imprudence last time when I dropped in to visit you. This time we have prepared ourselves according to ancient rituals to come to pay you a formal visit. I would like to invite you to come to my court as my advisor. I beg you to accept my invitation. Please do not turn me down."

"I am only a crazy old man passing his time fishing here. I do not have any useful talent to contribute to your court." Politely Jiang Sarn declined the first-time offer, as was the custom of Middle Kingdom.

"No, your talent is well-known. Please do not refuse me." Turning around, he commanded: "Attendants, present the gifts of acquaintance." The gifts of acquaintance were largely ceremonial in nature, as tokens of respect, and were never meant to be of high value.

The acceptance of the ceremonial gifts would also signify his acceptance of the much more important offer of a position in the palace of the duke. Thus Jiang Sarn asked his valet boys to accept the gifts from the attendants. The mission was accomplished, so the procession began the return trip. To honor Jiang Sarn, the duke's personal sedan chair was offered to him for the return trip. "No, I cannot accept your generous offer. It would make me an inconsiderate and imprudent person."

After the usual bickering over ceremonial trivialities traditional to the ancient culture of Middle Kingdom, Jiang Sarn finally accepted a ride on the duke's horse while the duke used his personal sedan chair. The duke's dream was fulfilled and the procession returned to the palace with his prize, Jiang Sarn. The words of the Primeval had finally come to fruition.

Over the next few days, Jiang Sarn briefed the court about what he had learned in Emperor Zoe's court and his views of political situations of the world, which at that time, meant the Middle Kingdom, her feudal lands and the neighboring barbarians. His eloquent presentation and detailed analysis impressed every officer in the court. Jiang Sarn was appointed deputy vice premier of the court. Now he was able to use the Tao he had learned from Primeval to carry out his ambitions. Wu Serendipity, being a disciple of Jiang Sarn, was also appointed a military rank. At last, the promise of wealth and power made by Primeval had come true.

9. Consequences of a Banquet for Elves

While Jiang Sarn was running down the steps of Starplucker Pavilion, Dar-Gee had realized that in order to keep the Emperor's confidence she had to find an officer who could successfully supervise the construction of the Elk Tower. She came up with several candidates within the Emperor's court, but she rejected them all. Because of the dimension of this project, high taxes as well as compulsory labor had to be imposed upon the people, as Jiang Sarn had stated. Almost all officers of the court competent enough to be assigned this task would persuade the Emperor to give it up – and worse than that, to get rid of her. On the other hand, whoever was assigned to head the project would also assume enormous power, and the project itself also offered a vast opportunity for pilferage. This person had to be greedy, ruthless, corrupt and vicious, but at the same time competent. A name immediately occurred to her.

After the commotion of Jiang Sarn's escape was over following his fake suicide, she was not surprised at Emperor Zoe's question: "Who else can we find to build this Elk Tower for me?" The answer came readily: "I think Duke North, Tsung Migratory Tiger, is the ideal person." It must be admitted that this was a good choice for an evil project like this one. As had been done many times before, without calling a court session to discuss this matter, an imperial order was rapidly drafted to summon Duke North to the capital to head the construction project.

The imperial order was sent to the Office of Secretary to formalize it into an official document. The chief of the Office of Secretary was a rotating job, and that day a senior officer of the cabinet level, Yang Zen, was in charge. When he saw the contents of the imperial order, he was puzzled. He asked the messenger who brought it in: "What is this Elk Tower?"

The messenger replied, "It is a giant and elaborate palace raised off the ground by fifty feet, with several stories."

Yang Zen said, "I heard the Emperor wanted to start a new construction project, but the project was stopped after the officer, Jiang Sarn, whom he wanted to commission the task committed suicide." He then pondered for a while, then commented, "the Emperor already has a luxurious building, the Starplucker Pavilion. Why does he need one more?"

The messenger replied: " I do not know. Jiang Sarn said it would take 35 years to complete the task, but Queen Dar-Gee said it could be completed in only two years, and she has suggested that Duke North, Tsung could do it, so here is the imperial order to commission him to oversee the project."

"A thirty-five year project to be finished in two years! And Duke North again! He already caused immeasurable suffering to the people during the construction of the Starplucker Pavilion. This project sounds ten times bigger than the Starplucker Pavilion project. That is sheer madness!" Yang Zen thought. "All right, leave the imperial order here, I will take care of it." Yang then dismissed the messenger.

Yang Zen took the order and asked to see the Emperor, mentioning that he had an important suggestion to make regarding the construction of Elk Tower. Emperor Zoe was in the middle of his indulgence. When he heard that senior officer Yang Zen had some suggestion to make on the construction Elk Tower, he thought the suggestion was about how to shorten the time period needed to finish the project, so Yang Zen was admitted.

"Your Majesty," Yang Zen said, "this country is under a great financial strain now. Both Dukes East and South have rebelled and they have engaged in fierce fighting against our defense forces for years. Imperial Teacher has been leading an army on a campaign to squash rebellion for over a decade and he has not returned yet. The treasury of the country is depleted. May your loyal officer suggest that you postpone this project until peace once again reigns and people have an adequate period of recovery?"

"Another Jiang Sarn," angrily thought Emperor Zoe. "This project is of utmost importance to me. Construction work must begin at once. I do not want to hear any more," he said.

"If you construct this Elk Tower, the Shang Empire will be destroyed!" Yang Zen persisted.

"If I let this kind of argument go on, I will never have a day of rest and enjoyment. I will punish him so that no other officers dare come forward to argue against me," thought Emperor Zoe. "You idiot! You dare insult me!" he shouted in anger. "I will forgive you this time, but I want your eyes pulled out!"

The deed was carried out instantly. The wound proved to be fatal, but as Yang Zen was lying on the ground dying, a gust of wind blew and the sky darkened. When the gust of wind quieted down, the body of Yang Zen had disappeared. A rumor began to circulate that Emperor Zoe's evil deeds had offended Heaven, and the disappearance of the body of Yang Zen was yet another omen that Heaven was angry.

When the news of the disappearance was reported to the Emperor, he was not impressed. "This sort of thing happened before. Just before their scheduled execution, the two princes also vanished amidst a dust storm. There is nothing to worry about."

As recommended by Dar-Gee, Tsung Migratory Tiger was granted the ultimate authority in matters related to the construction of the Elk Tower. To meet expenses, under the authority granted to him, Migratory Tiger immediately raised taxes and imposed new ones. To meet labor requirements, he issued a law mandating compulsory labor from citizens. As the project proceeded, expenditures skyrocketed and taxes were even more drastically increased. As labor requirements grew, still more compulsory labor was imposed. Eventually, each household was required to supply two thirds of its male adults as laborers and those with less than two had to supply all. Needless to say, it was the poor who were drafted, since wealthy households could bribe Tsung Migratory Tiger to avoid the draft. Because of the tight schedule, the workload was intense and, as a result, many laborers died. The dead were buried hastily under the foundation of the Elk Tower.

With the heavy taxation and merciless compulsory labor, two years and four months after the commencement of the project, the Tower was completed. Emperor Zoe and Dar-Gee were invited to come over to inspect the finished product. It was a tower over 50 feet high, built almost exactly as in the drawing supplied by Dar-Gee. Magnificence was but a poor word to describe the grandeur of this Tower. The exterior was covered with white marble, inlaid with agate. Numerous partitions divided each story into rooms of various sizes. The walls of all the rooms were inlaid with pearls and semiprecious stones. Gold, silver or jade bric-a-brac of immense value were seen everywhere. As the two inspected the tower, they never gave even a single thought to the fact that the elegance and beauty had been paid for by the unbearable suffering and even deaths of tens of thousands of innocent people.

A banquet celebrating the successful construction of the Elk Tower took place. Vice Premier Bee Gahn and Tsung Migratory Tiger were invited to attend. Bee Gahn was extremely upset at the sight of the Tower; he knew how much people had been caused to suffer to satisfy the indulgence of a single person. After a perfunctory congratulation, Bee Gahn asked to be excused. Migratory Tiger, being alone in his rank, also left.

Figure I- 18. The Elk Tower

War among Gods and Men

As the Emperor drank and feasted with Dar-Gee, he remembered a promise and he said, "My dear, you promised that after the completion of the Elk Tower, deities would come to visit. Can you tell me when will they come?"

The original purpose of Dar-Gee in submitting the engineering diagram for the Elk Tower to Emperor Zoe had been to entrap her enemy Jiang Sarn in a project that she thought he could not complete so that he would be executed for disobedience. She had not counted on Emperor Zoe's determination to carry it through. Now that it was finished, it became her responsibility to furnish the deities that she had promised. How could she? She knew of no gods, goddesses or fairies who would accept her invitation. She needed to find some convincing impostors. Yet it was not that easy to find impostors. For naturally, gods, goddesses and fairies must descend from heaven and certainly would not knock at the door of the palace to ask to be admitted. Vaguely, she responded, "Gods, goddesses and fairies are from heaven, where the sky is clear, and the moon shines forever. They would not descend to the world of dust unless the sky is also clear, and the moon full."

"Well, that is no problem. I can wait. Today is the tenth of the lunar month. By the fifteenth the moon should be full, so fairies should descend to my Tower by the fourteenth or fifteenth. Wouldn't you say so, my dear," Emperor Zoe generously and enthusiastically asked her.

"Certainly, Your Majesty," replied Dar-Gee.

After two restless nights, by the night of the thirteenth of the lunar month, an idea came to Dar-Gee. She waited for the Emperor to fall asleep, then she transfigured herself back to her fox form, she flew back to her old habitat, an ancient tomb around 35 li from the city boundary of Morning Song. She gathered all the other fox elves she could find, plus the nine-head female pheasant elf, who was taking charge of the old habitat on her behalf now, and said: "I left you some time ago, but I have never forgotten you. Recently the Elk Tower was completed and the Emperor wishes to meet deities in this Tower. I suggest that all of you who know how to transfigure into human form do so and descend on the terrace at the top of the Elk Tower at dusk the day after tomorrow. A banquet will be waiting for you."

Pheasant Elf said, "I have some errands to tend to that day so that I cannot accept your invitation. However, I know we have thirty-nine elves among us who know how to transfigure to human form and fly. Will they be enough?"

"Certainly." After the successful recruitment of an assembly of elves who would pass as gods, goddesses, and fairies, Dar-Gee went back to the palace and retransfigured back to her human form.

Dar-Gee told the Emperor the next day that thirty-nine heavenly guests would come to visit him on the fifteenth of the lunar month, the next day. Emperor Zoe was overjoyed. He ordered thirty-nine guest tables to be set up in the Elk Tower, each tended by two ladies-in-waiting. He said to Dar-Gee, "I still need a senior officer to circulate among the heavenly guests on my behalf. Who could do it?"

"Vice Premier Bee Gahn, who is known for his drinking capacity."

An imperial order was sent to the Vice Premier that he should circulate among heavenly guests on behalf of the Emperor. "What an idiot Emperor! The country is weakening day by day due to the lack of his attention and he thinks of nothing but gods, goddesses and fairies. This is yet another proof of the elfin smog theory," he thought. Further, during his long and fruitful life, he had never learned how to circulate among deities.

War among Gods and Men

By the next day, the fifteenth of the lunar month, Emperor Zoe waited for the whole day for the sun to set. He waited for the full moon to rise, then he waited for the arrival of his heavenly guests. Finally, around eight o'clock by our reckoning, a gust of wind blew around the Elk Tower, shaking everything. "What happened?" said the startled Emperor.

"Nothing, only the arrival of deities."

A real god or goddess, by virtue of his or her Tao, usually flew gracefully and silently. Elves, because of the poor imitation of the elfin Tao, would usually generate a strong gust of wind, blowing dust, sand and small pebbles as they flew. Finally, as the winds subsided, people dressed in various Taoist fashions appeared. Half of them were in female form. One of them, apparently the leader of the group, spoke. "On behalf of our entire group, I salute to the Emperor. May you live forever!"

The Vice Premier was asked to come up to greet the heavenly guests. He was impressed by their apparently stately manner. After he was introduced, the leader said, "As a gift to you, I will grant you an additional thousand years to your life span." The Vice Premier was quite perplexed by this rather intangible and improbable gift. He began to have doubts.

"Let the party begin. Start serving the guests," ordered the Emperor.

Upon this order, the Vice Premier began his duty to circulate among the guests. After several rounds of drinking, some elves of lesser elfin Tao started to lose their control. The air began to be filled with a foul animal body odor. "It is odd. I heard that the presence of gods and goddesses purifies the air surrounding them. Where does this foul animal body odor come from? Maybe they are not gods and goddesses, but elves," the Vice Premier thought, as he continued his duty of filling the empty cups of the guests.

Figure I- 19. Drunk guest elves
Imposter "fairies" got drunk and revealed their "fox tails"

As the banquet proceeded, toasts were made from time to time. These "heavenly guests" apparently had never been entertained with this kind of luxury, and they feasted and drank heartily, quite unbecoming to Taoists who had made vows to give up worldly pleasures. By the time the last course was served, most of the guests were more than half-drunk. Those with the least elfin Tao struggled hard to keep their human forms, but in their efforts to keep their faces human, they had to let go of control over some parts their bodies. As the Vice Premier circulated around, he saw that several fox tails had crept out underneath the otherwise impressive Taoist dresses. "Indeed, these are fox elves. That explains the nature of the foul animal body odor. How could I, Vice Premier of this powerful country, be downgraded to the demeaning position of serving fox elves? This regime is really coming to an end!" mutely grumbled the Vice Premier.

Dar-Gee began to notice the gradual disintegration of the power of transfiguration of her guests. She said to Bee Gahn, "Thank you, Vice Premier. You have accomplished a great feat. Now you may retire." Turning to the Emperor, she continued, "It is quite late, we should bid farewell to our heavenly guests." Being almost drunk himself, the Emperor raised no objections. After a series of perfunctory court manners, the guests left amidst a gust of dusty wind.

As the Vice Premier left the palace, he encountered Nobleman Huang Flying Tiger, who was leading a detachment of warriors and soldiers doing another round of security check around the palace.

"Why is the Vice Premier out so late at night? Is there an emergency? Can we help?" said Flying Tiger.

"I am so glad to see you." The Vice Premier related his adventure with the so-called gods, goddesses and fairies, and his discovery that they were actually fox elves.

262

Nobleman Huang Flying Tiger said, "Thank you for your information. Please go back and rest. I will take care of the elves."

Immediately, Nobleman Huang dispatched his four best warriors each to bring a team of twenty strong scouts, waiting at the north, east, west and south city gates, to track the whereabouts of these so-called deities and, if found, to see where they were heading.

The one stationed in the southern direction saw a group of shadowy figures in human clothes half-falling and half-descending from heaven. He and his men followed. Finally these drunken elves lost their ability to fly altogether when they hit the ground and they decided to walk back the rest of the way. Those with the least elfin Tao reverted back to their fox form, dragging their elegant Taoist clothes along as they crawled on their four limbs. Some 35 five li from the capital, the leader of the scout team saw these shadows disappearing into a crevice near an ancient tomb. He made a mark at the location. The next morning, he reported his finding to Nobleman Huang Flying Tiger.

"Round up three hundred men and prepare a cartload of firewood. Go to this ancient tomb, and seal all nearby holes and crevices with fire wood. Burn them out. When they come out, kill them all," ordered Nobleman Huang the Flying Tiger.

In the afternoon, Nobleman Huang invited the Vice Premier to go to the site to inspect the progress of the extermination of the elves. By the time they arrived, all the fires had already been extinguished. Using long hooks, Huang's men dragged out nearly a hundred dead foxes. Many were burned beyond recognition, but some of them had merely suffocated to death, with some still wearing the Taoist dresses of the previous evening. "Skin them and use their fur to make a cape for the Emperor who can use it to fend off high winds in the Tower. This will certainly discourage Dar-Gee from inviting other so-called heavenly guests," suggested the Vice Premier.

Months went by and winter came. One day during a heavy snowstorm, the Emperor and Dar-Gee drank and feasted as usual at the top of the Elk Tower, enjoying the scene of heavy snowfall. An attendant reported that the Vice Premier was there to see the Emperor. Dar-Gee retired to a back room to observe the court protocol that Queen should not be seen by court officials.

"Why aren't you home enjoying the snow scene, but rather here amidst a snow storm?" said the Emperor.

"In this snowy weather, I came here to present you a cape made of fox fur. This cape will shield you from the elements at the height of this high Tower."

"You are an elderly man and you should keep it for your own use. However, since you are here, let me try it on."

The gift was presented. It was a very large cape, made from at least a dozen fox furs of mixed color ranging from brown to white. The color-matching had been artistically done and the craftsmanship was superb. The Emperor was readily pleased. "As rich as I am, owning treasures of four seas, I do not have a fox fur cape yet. This is exactly what I need for this weather," he said, while attendants put the cape on him. "This is a really great gift. Pour some wine for the Vice Premier, attendants." After gracefully acknowledging the Emperor's thanks and finishing the goblet of wine with compliments to the health of the Emperor, the Vice Premier went back home.

Emperor Zoe went to the back room to show Dar-Gee the cape. "I never owned a fox fur before. See how beautiful and how useful it is?"

Dar-Gee was shocked to see the cape, for she could even recognize the original owners at several patches. She was extremely upset to see her former colleagues in the form of a fox fur cape. Suppressing her grief, she told the Emperor: "A fox fur cape is becoming dress for a hunter, but not for a dignified Emperor. It seems that you are demeaning yourself by covering your body with animal fur."

Thinking for a moment, Emperor Zoe said, "You are right." The fox fur cape was then sent to storage.

Meanwhile Dar-Gee was enraged with distress. "When I proposed the construction of the Elk Tower, I meant only to avenge the death of Jade Pee-Pa. I did not realize that my scheme would lead to the extermination of my old companions. I must avenge the deaths of my colleagues by killing the Vice Premier."

One day, a scheme came to Dar-Gee. She removed her heavy makeup and put on a simple dress similar to the one she had worn when she came for the first time to the palace. Instead of wearing the usual heavy and luxurious makeup customary of a Queen, she presented her natural self with practically no decoration, just like the first time she met the Emperor. This sudden change immediately aroused the attention of the Emperor. He looked at her over and over again, as if he had just discovered something new. Indeed, it was a pleasant sight that had long been forgotten. The Emperor reminisced about the first time he saw her, her shy appearance when he had dinner with her, the first bath, and the first love encounter. A forgotten sweet memory revisited him. He had rediscovered a beauty. He stared at her, remembering the pleasant experiences of bygone days. Meanwhile, Dar-Gee pretended not to notice, and asked in an innocent tone: "Is there anything wrong with me? Why are you staring at me so conscientiously and attentively?"

"You have always been extremely beautiful. However, today you look even more beautiful than ever. As my best possession, I cannot help looking at you over and over again."

The opportunity had arrived. "I am no comparison to a sworn sister of my youth, Hsi Charming. She is now a Taoist in Palace Purple Firmament," Dar-Gee responded.

Hearing that there was someone else even more beautiful than Dar-Gee, the Emperor's erotic desire was aroused. "Is there any way I can get to see her?"

"She went to study Tao since her youth, and she is now in Palace Purple Firmament. She has sworn to give up amenities of the world of dust and lust to become a Taoist. How could I persuade her to come here merely because you would like to see her?"

"Please, find some way to invite her here for me at least to take a look at her beauty," the Emperor pleaded.

While secretly rejoicing that her bait had been bitten, Dar-Gee pretended that she could not do anything to persuade a devoted Taoist to abandon her religious belief to come back to the world of lust and dust. Finally, after some haggling, she reluctantly consented. "There might be a way. In our youth we used to do practice needlework together almost daily. When she was about to depart for Palace Purple Firmament, I was extremely grieved at our separation because I thought we would never see each other again, and I was ready to kill myself. She consoled me. `Don't worry', she said, `after I have learned the Tao of five forms, I will send you a signal incense, which can be sensed thousands of li away. Whenever you want to see me, you need only

266

burn this signal incense. I will immediately come to your presence.' Two years later, a messenger brought me a box which contained the promised signal incense. A year after that, I was summoned by you to your palace to serve you. Since then I have spent all my time serving you at your pleasure and I have nearly forgotten about this signal incense, until now."

"Can you burn the incense right away to summon her here?" The Emperor, always impatient and presumptuous of his royal power and authority, suggested it in a commanding tone.

"No. She is a demigod now. To summon her, proper rituals must be exercised first. I have to wait for a full moon. A table with fruits and tea as offerings shall be set. After a prayer to the founding teacher of her Sect, then the signal incense may be burned to beckon her to come."

Late that night Dar-Gee again exited her human body and went to the ancient tomb to visit Pheasant Elf.

"Do you know that your invitation caused the extermination of your kind in this tomb? They even skinned them," wept Pheasant Elf.

"I knew. This is the reason why I came here." Dar-Gee replied in weeping tones. "I have made a plan to avenge my companions. At the same time my plan also offers you an opportunity to enter the palace to relish the luxury and power that I have been enjoying all along. You are a part of my plan."

Pheasant Elf hesitated. She had been living as a free elf in the wilderness for most of her conscious life since she had acquired the elfin Tao. When the three elves were summoned to the presence of Lady Goddess Woman Wa, she had been the most reluctant one to accept the task. However, under the authority of Woman Wa, she had no choice but to submit herself to the holy order of vengeance. Now she was asked to abandon her carefree life as a freely-roaming elf in the infinite expanse of wilderness and to submit herself to the binds of human decree and precept. She hesitated and sank herself in an ambivalent mood of indecision.

Sensing the indecision of her companion, Dar-Gee said, "What is the reason you do not want to share the ultimate luxury and power of the human world? It is the dream of almost every human."

"What is the use of the luxury and power? I do not have material needs. I am free. I am not used to being attended to by others in every detail of my life. I can find a mate any time I want. Once I go to the palace I have to stick with the same one, sharing him with you."

"But to be a human is a very different experience." Dar-Gee tried to relate her human experience to her elf companion. "Humans do not live for the sole purpose of subsisting and propagating the species. A great part of life as a human is devoted to his or her relationship with fellow humans; he or she derives the most pleasure of life in this kind of relationship. To tell the truth, it is not the material luxury of the palace that pleases me most, it is the authority that I can exert on other humans that I like best.

"Take our relationship with male companions, for example." After hesitating for a while, Dar-Gee continued. "It is very different. We copulate to propagate our species. Male companions find us to satisfy that need and we accept the males for the same reason. But inside a human body there is such a thing which they call 'love.' It is a feeling that we as animals can never comprehend. It is so wonderfully satisfying. As animals, after we satisfy ourselves we part and we find another one the next time. In humans, it is the beginning of a wonderful relationship. When the Emperor first embraced me, I could feel him inside me and I
268

could feel he also had the same feeling. We can feel our mutual presence in our bodies. Do you remember that the reward Lady Goddess Woman Wa promised us was to give us real human forms? Why did she promise us real human bodies if it were not worth anything? Besides, it is also your responsibility to fulfill the holy vow of vengeance of Lady Goddess Woman Wa. You must join me in the palace. You must also acquire a human body."

"But where am I going to get a beautiful human body? You waited for so long to acquire yours." The Pheasant Elf was somewhat convinced, so she would give this idea a try.

"You are in the middle of a popular cemetery. Many men died recently during the construction of Elk Tower. Many of their young wives and fiancees died of heartbreak. The cemetery was always busy during the daytime burying their women. Use your power of telepathy to find a pretty one. Even if hers may not be as pretty as my body, I can help you overcome the shortcoming. Love is not just an appreciation of beauty; men always like women of certain types and styles. I know Emperor Zoe inside out. I can tell you what type and style of woman he likes best. Be selective and find a beautiful one. Show her to me and I will tell you if she is of the right type. Enter her body. When you are ready, let me know. I will help you with your makeup and coach you on your style. I will select the right dress for you when you enter the palace. You will be the beauty that I promised Emperor Zoe."

It was not difficult for her to find a beautiful female body of the type that Dar-Gee approved. Using her power of elfin Tao, she revivified the body and entered her. True to her words, Dar-Gee came and briefed Pheasant Elf how to use the delicate qualities of a beautiful human female, and trained her to assume a certain personality. Pheasant Elf soon became familiar with her newly acquired assets.

"There will be a full moon the day after tomorrow. I will set up a table with offerings on the terrace of Elk Tower. You should descend upon the terrace some time after I have burned an incense. By the way, I have given you a new name, Hsi Charming. You must dress in the two piece Taoist suit that I picked up for you the other day. Wear light makeup. You must carry a flair of stately elegance. Remember you must also carry a disposition of innocence because you have lived almost your entire life in Palace Purple Firmament, located in a high mountain far away from humans. However, at the same time you must also carry an indication of weakness against temptation. Also, remember that you are supposed to be seduced by the Emperor against your struggle to retain your purity of Tao."

On the day of the full moon, Emperor Zoe waited impatiently for the sun to set, and after sunset for the moon to rise. Beginning at dusk, he kept on asking Dar-Gee over and over again, "Is it time yet?"

Using one excuse or the other, Dar-Gee purposely delayed the burning of the signal incense. Finally, around eight o'clock by our reckoning, she said, "Now is the time. However, you should hide yourself behind a curtain, otherwise she may be scared away by your presence." Emperor Zoe unwillingly exited behind a curtain, peeping.

After washing her hands to show respect to her "demigod sister", she knelt in front of the table of offering, facing a northeast direction. She then opened a small, finely carved wooden box and took out a piece of scarlet-red incense and burned it in an incense burner. Within minutes, a gust of wind blew hard, gathering dark clouds and fog which covered the moon entirely. In darkness, sounds of tinkling bracelets and ornaments were heard, followed almost immediately by the thumping sound of a person dropping on the terrace. Dar-Gee quickly urged Emperor Zoe to recede to an inner chamber so that she could converse with the visitor in private.

Figure I- 20. Arrival of Hsi Mei

After the winds subsided, the clouds dispersed and the fog dissolved, and moonlight again bathed the terrace. A female figure materialized. She was dressed in an exquisite two-piece red Taoist robe suit decorated artfully with patterns of Taoist inscriptions. A colorful silk ribbon belt flowed from her waist. She wore a pair of sandals skillfully knitted from flax. The simple flax was a beautiful match to her white and dainty feet. There she stood, mysteriously beautiful. Her hair was done in a Taoist fashion, with part flowing down around her neck. She stood near the edge of the terrace, majestically, with a grandiose sweetness. The feeble and passionate moonlight, complemented by the light from fickle flames of several candles on the table of offering, further added a mystique to her beauty. Evidently caused by the exertion of her recent flying, her countenance was tinted by a slight shade of rosy sunset. Her two large black eyes shone like pearls. Her two cherry-like lips blended with the other features of her face into a beauty which, when combined with the mystery of her appearance, created a sensation far beyond the initial expectation of Emperor Zoe, who had managed to find a tiny opening in the wall of the inner chamber to peep at her during the entire episode of her arrival.

Dar-Gee moved forward to greet her, "My dear sister is here finally."

Hsi Charming responded, "May I, an unworthy Taoist, salute to you."

Hand in hand, they went to the reception hall. After another round of salutation and offering of tea, they sat down.

"You mentioned that you would come to my presence as soon as I burned the signal incense. You have kept your word. I am extremely pleased that you have given me an opportunity to renew our old relationship," said Dar-Gee.

272

"I have been waiting for your signal incense ever since I dispatched a messenger to deliver it to you. As soon as I detected your signal, I came right away without delay. I hope I have not intruded upon you," replied Hsi Charming.

This kind of chitchat went on and on while Emperor Zoe paced back and forth in the back room, continuing to peep at Hsi Charming over and over again. The more he looked at her, the more he was aroused. "I would give up my throne just to have her sharing my bed for one night," muttered the Emperor to himself.

Finally, Dar-Gee asked her sworn sister, "Would you like to have a vegetarian dinner or meat dinner?"

"Vegetarian dinner." A vegetarian banquet was ordered and served.

The chitchat continued as they tasted the various vegetarian delights. Dar-Gee pretended to have completely forgotten about Emperor Zoe, who in the course of waiting became more and more impatient. Louder and louder he coughed and coughed, trying to attract Dar-Gee's attention. Realizing that the Emperor was about to reach his limit of patience, Dar-Gee spoke to Hsi Charming. "My dear sister, may I say something?"

"Anything you like, my dear sister."

"This is the palace of Emperor Zoe. I have mentioned often to him that I have a sworn sister, who is also my best friend. The Emperor mentioned to me several times that he wants to see you. This is why I burned the signal incense to ask you to come here. Will you meet him?"

"I think it is inappropriate. First, when I went to Palace Purple Firmament to study Tao, I swore a solemn vow to give up my worldly desires. Second, it is not usually our tradition to get involved with affairs

273

of the world of dust. Third, he is a man and according to proper protocols, unrelated men and women must not sit at the same table to eat. In addition, this is a palace where the propriety of protocols is of utmost importance. Thus it is extremely difficult for me to comply with your request." Hsi Charming, following the traditional custom of Middle Kingdom, had politely declined the first-time offer.

"I do not think so. You, an accomplished Taoist, are already above the usual protocols of conduct with regard to contacts with the world of dust. These protocols are applicable only to newly ordained Taoists. Besides, he is our Emperor. He derived his authority from Heaven to take charge of earthly affairs under the sun. Even deities and demigods should show some respect because the Emperor derives his authority from Heaven. In addition, we were sworn sisters since our youth. Our passion for each other equals or exceeds that between siblings; you are my relative. Since I am serving the Emperor now, there is nothing wrong about my relative meeting the Emperor. In homes of ordinary citizens, relatives of both sexes can sit together to eat. There is nothing wrong with his joining us."

"You are right. Would you ask the Emperor to join us, please."

Before the word "please" was uttered, the Emperor was already out. Hsi and Dar-Gee both stood up, ready to perform the necessary protocols of salutation to greet the Emperor, but he hastily excused them both from carrying out the protocols. Eagerly, and against rules of conduct prevailing at that time, the Emperor sat by the side of Hsi Charming. Using all the charms she could muster, Hsi Charming conversed with the Emperor in a subdued but articulate voice. As the two sank deeper and deeper into conversation, Dar-Gee knew that the time was ripe, so with an excuse to exit herself temporarily to the powder room, she left Hsi Charming to the Emperor. Before she left, she asked Hsi Charming to tend to his needs.

Heeding this request, Hsi Charming innocently, so it seemed, offered to refill the empty wine goblet for the Emperor. Emperor Zoe seized this opportunity and gently grabbed her hand. Hsi Charming made a faint attempt to retrieve her hand but did not resist his hold. He gently laid down her hand on her lap and moved closer to her. She sank her head down, blushing, and said nothing. The Emperor then whispered words of admiration of her beauty and his adoration of her. To these words Hsi Charming responded only with restrained giggles.

After a while, the Emperor suggested they go out to the terrace to enjoy the city view under full moonlight. Upon the terrace, still holding her hands, the Emperor propositioned: "My Taoist demigod, why don't you give up your simple life and come to my palace to share with your sister the wealth and power here? Nights are short and years go by. Why do you have to chastise yourself by living in solitude? Come and enjoy my love, my power and my wealth." Hsi Charming did not respond, but lowered her head, as if meditating. She then raised her head, staring at the distant horizon as if she were dreaming. The Emperor moved closer to her. With one hand around her waist, his other hand moved towards her breast. At these movements of intimate love play, Hsi only offered encouraging resistance. As the Emperor intensified his hand movements, Hsi resisted no further and leaned her body against his and cooed in pleasure.

With an almost jolting action, the Emperor quickly lifted Hsi up and place her on his two powerful arms and went to the nearest resting room. Putting her down on a long couch, he started to undress her. Hsi closed her eyes and responded with a moaning of pleasant surprise. As the Emperor lowered his body upon her, she lifted her arms and embraced him. In a whisper she begged, "Please spare me, my Tao will be destroyed if I lose my chastity." The Emperor responded with more deep kisses.

She was in a dreamy mood. As he entered her body, she began to feel the warmth of passion. Her breath hastened as the Emperor continued his thrust. Her breath further hastened as she enjoyed the experience which Dar-Gee had claimed to be uniquely human. In her animal form, she had never experienced embracing; to her male companions she was always a passive entity. Now, for the first time she learned how to participate. Finally the electrifying sensation that Dar-Gee had described to her came. "If this is to be part of the holy order of vengeance, I will gladly submit myself to do it," thought Hsi.

The Emperor was not satisfied yet. Once more he thrust his powerful body against Hsi and the second electrifying sensation came. By this time Hsi was totally exhausted, her breath short, her heart pounding heavily, and her pulse so fast that her blood seemed to be exploding out of her veins.

Dar-Gee had been watching the entire scene between the crevices of a curtain. After giving the couple some time to rest, she made a slight noise and at this warning, Hsi told the Emperor, "My sister will come back soon, please get up and let me put on my dress."

No sooner had Hsi put on her wrinkled dress than Dar-Gee entered the room. Hsi was still short of breath, trying to recover from her exhilarating experience, while the Emperor was still half-naked. Pretending to be angry, Dar-Gee accused Emperor Zoe, "You have deceived me. You said that you only wanted to meet my sworn sister, but now you have destroyed her Tao by violating her. She can no longer go back to Palace Purple Firmament. You have wrecked her, my poor

276

darling sister..." Dar-Gee began to weep emotionally and moved over to caress Hsi Charming.

Figure I- 21. Caught in the act
Dar-Gee pretended annoyance at Emperor Zoe

"Don't worry. She is destined to stay in this palace and this is why she came here. She can stay here forever. From now on you and your sister will never be apart. She will enjoy the same luxury as you. I love you both and I need you both," the Emperor promised with sincerity.

"In this case, you must formalize her status as your concubine queen of the first rank as soon as possible. I do not want my beloved sister to reside in the palace without a proper title."

"Of course, but we must wait for an appropriate occasion. Meanwhile, she will stay in the palace with you and me." The three then slept together that night in the Elk Tower.

After acquiring the second elf-woman, the Emperor spent even less time tending to affairs of the country. Huang Flying Tiger had the entire army of 480,000 under his capable command, but he could do very little to persuade the Emperor to move away from his indulgence in pleasure-seeking activities and to pay more attention to affairs of the country. To make things worse, the new Duke East, the son of the late Duke East, had already begun a rebellion. With an army of 100,000, he launched an attack against Ridge Mustang as the precursor campaign to overtake the strategic Frontier Pass Chien Tang (which at one time was guarded by Li Militaris, the father of Nata). Unable to tend the defense of Ridge Mustang himself, Nobleman Huang dispatched Ru Brave with an army of 100,000 to fend off the invaders. Meanwhile, the life of indulgence went on as usual in the palace.

One morning during breakfast, Dar-Gee suddenly fell ill and became unconscious with blood flowing out of her mouth. Shocked, the Emperor said to Hsi Charming, "My Queen never fell ill like this before. What happened?"

Hsi Charming sighed: "It is the same old ailment again."

"What kind of old ailment? I never heard of it," the surprised Emperor said.

"She has always had a weak heart," Hsi Charming sighed. "One day during her childhood she had a heart attack. Just then, a passing Taoist diagnosed that her heart needed a new part. With his Tao, he could replace the damaged part with a new one. Just at that time, a child in our neighborhood died and her heart was acquired. The damaged part was replaced and Dar-Gee recovered. However, the Taoist warned that the same ailment might recur when she grew up. This was also part of my reason to study Tao, so that one day when this happened I could save her. We need another heart."

"That is easy. With my power and authority I can get one for you," quickly offered the Emperor.

"Not every heart can be used. It must be the right kind of heart, otherwise her body might reject it and she will certainly die."

"Do you know how to select the right kind of heart?"

"Yes, I know how to prognosticate who has the right kind of heart. I need a quiet room, a cushion to sit down on, a low table, incense, and three coins," Hsi Charming said.

"Consider it done."

In no time the room was prepared and Hsi Charming went in and closed the door behind her. Half an hour later she emerged, looking sad.

"Well?" asked the Emperor eagerly.

"I think Dar-Gee is doomed," Hsi Charming responded while weeping.

"You mean that you cannot find one single heart in my country that can be used to save my dear Dar-Gee?"

"I found one, but he is an important person. You cannot rule your country without him," replied Hsi Charming.

"Nonsense. I have so many capable people under my rule. No person is indispensable. Just name him and I will have his heart pulled out to save my dear Dar-Gee."

Hsi pretended to be reluctant to tell the truth. After repeated prodding by the Emperor, she reluctantly named the qualified donor — the Vice Premier.

"No problem. I will issue an imperial order asking him to give me his heart."

The Vice Premier could not understand the wording of the imperial order: "Your heart is urgently needed. Please have someone deliver it to the palace immediately."

"Why, he already has my whole heart. I have served two emperors before, now I am serving him with all my heart. What is the meaning of this order?" He was perplexed.

Another imperial order arrived. This time the wording was explicit: "I, Emperor Zoe, need your heart to cure my dear Queen Dar-Gee." There could not be any mistake, now. What he wanted was the death of the Vice Premier so that his heart could be used to cure the wretched Queen Dar-Gee.

Without any other choice, he bade his wife farewell. "You must take care of my children after my death, since there will be no just and straight officers left in the court."

His wife wept: "You have been a loyal officer to three generations of emperors of this dynasty, now see what kind of treatment you get as a reward for your loyalty!"

At this time, one of his sons reminded him: "Father, when Jiang Sarn bade you farewell, he left an envelope with you. He said that you may need it some day. Why don't you open it up now and see what it says?"

Vice Premier opened the envelope. There was an instruction and a piece of paper drawn with Taoist talismanic inscriptions. In a hurry, the Vice Premier read only the first part of the instruction: "Burn this talismanic inscription in a bowl, and drink it with water. You shall be immune to what shall befall you."

This done, he went to see the Emperor. Emperor Zoe coldly told him: "You now have an opportunity to show your ultimate loyalty. Give me your heart."

"You idiot Emperor, you want to kill a loyal officer who has served flawlessly three generations of Shang's emperors just to save your woman of pleasure?"

"Give me your heart or I will have the guards do it," commanded the Emperor angrily.

"I will take it out for you." With a dagger in his hand, he cut open his chest, took out his heart and threw it to the ground. There was no blood. Without a second word, the Vice Premier immediately left the court.

Nobleman Huang Flying Tiger met him on his way out, and said: "Why are you so pale today?" Again without a word, the Vice Premier mounted his horse and left.

War among Gods and Men

"Hollow heart vegetable for sale!" a country woman vegetable peddler yelled as she walked along with a basketful of hollow heart vegetable.

When the Vice Premier passed by, he suddenly remembered that his heart had been taken out. He asked the woman: "What do you mean by hollow heart vegetable?"

"Vegetable with a hollow stem, without a heart."

"What will happen to a person if his heart is taken out?" Suddenly the Vice Premier was worried.

"This person will certainly die," the country woman answered.

Upon this answer the Vice Premier immediately fell down off his horse and blood started to stream out of his open chest and he died instantly. Unfortunately the Vice Premier had never finished reading the instruction, the last part of which said that he should go back to his residence immediately without stopping and he should lie down. By the power of divination, Jiang Sarn would find out his misfortune and he would come to his rescue. If he conversed with anyone on his way home and if any one reminded him that a person without a heart would die, the magical spell would fail and he would die.

A state funeral was held to honor the passing of the Vice Premier by his sad colleagues in the court. The funeral ceremony was held in a temporary pavilion just inside the north gate of the city and would last for a month. During this mourning period it happened that Imperial Teacher Wen Zhong triumphantly returned from his campaign, after squashing the rebels in the North Sea. He was surprised to see the funeral pavilion for his old friend, the Vice Premier, because he knew that Bee Gahn had always been in excellent health. Looking up at a distance, he saw the Elk Tower. As he trotted along the familiar streets

282

of the city of Morning Song, he saw the magnificent Elk Tower more closely. He had no idea what this tower was for. As he trotted through the Gate of Noon into the palace, he was greeted by a congregation of court officers, who, upon learning of the return of Imperial Teacher, had spontaneously gathered to greet him.

The Imperial Teacher dismounted his riding beast, Black Unicorn, and returned the greetings. "My respected friends," he said, "I spent years away from the capital, carrying out a long and bloody campaign in the North Sea. By the blessings of the ancestors of the Shang dynasty, I succeeded in my mission. Upon my return, I have found many changes. Please brief me of these changes." Dismounting his horse, Imperial Teacher smiled to his welcoming party.

Nobleman Huang Flying Tiger, being the most senior officer, responded on behalf of the rest: "When you were in the North Sea, did you hear that affairs of the state had been left unattended, the country led astray, and many feudal lords had abandoned their fealty to this court and rebelled?"

"Yes, I received news now and then. However, until I had successfully squashed the rebellion in the North Sea, I could not do anything to help the situation in the capital."

As they strolled into the main hall where court used to be held, the Imperial Teacher was grieved to see the empty tables which, before he left, had always been piled with documents to be discussed in daily court sessions. Now many of his former colleagues were dead. He pointed to the gigantic yellowish pillars at the east side of the hall and asked: "What are those contraptions?"

The officer in charge of the main hall answered: "These are new; they are execution machines, called Pao-Lo."

"What is meant by Pao-Lo," asked the puzzled Imperial Teacher.

Nobleman Huang Flying Tiger answered: "My dear Imperial Teacher, this punishment machine is a tube made from bronze. There are three fire traps. Any officer who opposes Emperor Zoe, who criticizes the Emperor on account of the welfare of the country, who argues against the Emperor, is immediately put to death on the Pao-Lo machine as follows: First the bronze tube is heated to red-hot by burning charcoal in the traps. The prisoner is brought in and his four limbs are then tied around the red-hot tube. Within instants his body is reduced to ashes. The foul odor of burnt flesh will stay in the hall for days and weeks, reminding others not to follow the example of the executed. As a result, the capable resigned, the articulate escaped, the apt retired to seclusion, and the loyal died for their cause. We are trying to hold on to our responsibilities as long as we can."

The blood of the Imperial Teacher now boiled. The color of his face reddened. His middle eye, derived from his dedicated study of Tao as well as from his character of righteousness and loyalty and which was normally closed and not visible, now opened up. In his rage, a white ray emerged from his middle eye, distinctly visible for more than a foot. "Ring all gongs to get the Emperor here," ordered the Imperial Teacher.

Dar-Gee, who had just recovered after the "transplant" of the heart of the Vice Premier by Hsi Charming in a secluded room, was convalescing when the gongs rang. "Which idiot dares ring the gongs at this critical moment of recovery of my dear Dar-Gee?" angrily thought the Emperor, and he ordered one of his attendants: "Find out who ordered the gongs to be rung."

284

The attendant soon returned. "Your Majesty, the Imperial Teacher has just returned from his triumphant suppression of the rebellion in the North Sea! He is the one who ordered the gongs to be rung!"

"Another of those," thought the Emperor. But this time it was different. The Imperial Teacher had been his teacher, his prince regent during the early years of his early reign, and his benefactor. He had spent close to 15 leading a difficult campaign against rebels in the North Sea. He had to be shown respect and his voice had to be heard. After a long silence, the Emperor ordered: "Prepare for my passage to the main hall of the court."

After the Emperor arrived, the Imperial Teacher Wen Zhong approached him and said, "Through the blessing of ancestor emperors of Shang, after a bloody campaign which lasted fifteen years, finally I have successfully squashed the rebellion in the North Sea. However, I have heard from many sources that the palace is now manipulated by toadies who have caused decadence and degeneration against which many lords have rebelled. Is what I heard true?"

"Duke East, Jiang Huan-Chu attempted to assassinate me to seize my throne, Duke South conspired with Duke East, so they both were executed. As a result, their heirs rebelled against me. This must be the rebellion you have heard of." Emperor Zoe responded mindlessly, trying to cover up what he had wrongfully done.

"Is there any evidence to indicate that they attempted assassination? Who can testify that they attempted to seize your throne," asked the Imperial Teacher.

The Emperor had no good answer to offer. After a while, the Imperial Teacher continued, "For years I have been fighting a terrible war in the northern frontier against rebels. Upon my return, I find many things have changed for the worse. Within the government, justice is forgotten and you have indulged yourself in wine and women. These are the causes for the new rebellions. May I ask, what are those yellow pillars?"

Emperor Zoe replied, "Those so-called loyal officers insulted me, argued against me. This punishment machine, called Pao-Lo, is explicitly used to silence my critics."

The Imperial Teacher went on, "As I entered the city, I saw a tall tower, what is that?"

"That is Elk Tower. In summer, I have no place to go, so this tower was built to allow me to enjoy the summer high winds. Also, I can get a good view of the city and its surroundings." Emperor Zoe gave yet another faint excuse.

Feeling extremely frustrated, the Imperial Teacher said, "Fields are withering, people are starving to death and rebellion is rampant outside the capital. The root of these problems is your lack of concern for factual reality. You have distanced yourself from loyal and straight officers, surrounded yourself with toadies, indulged yourself in wine and women day and night. You have usurped people of their livelihood for your own luxury. When the late Emperor was in reign, all barbarians showed respect to his country, people were wealthy and happy, and all lords swore their fealty without any doubt or fear. Now you have turned prosperity to recession, caused lords to rebel against you and common people to hate you. My years of hard effort to suppress rebellion are being nullified. Now that I am back, I want to submit a new policy to turn things around. Emperor Zoe, for the time being please go back to the palace, I will come back later with a plan of reform."

Having nothing valuable to say, Emperor Zoe retired to his residential palace. Before the court session was adjourned, the Imperial Teacher beckoned the officials to stay. "Do not return to your homes yet. Come to my official residence with me, let us have a conference there."

In the reception hall of his residence, the Imperial Teacher asked all the court officers present: "Gentlemen, I have been away for fifteen years and I do not know the current state of affairs. As the prince regent who was given the responsibility to supervise the current Emperor during the early years of his reign, I have my moral obligation to the late emperor. I know of many violations against charter laws of the Shang dynasty. Gentlemen, please tell me what has happened during the last fifteen years. Please report to me fairly. Do not exaggerate. I will weigh all opinions and arrive at a fair conclusion."

An officer suggested: "It is well-known that the Emperor has done many ill deeds. Opinions are varied. If you hear from everybody, you might become confused. Let me suggest that we delegate Nobleman Huang Flying Tiger, the most senior officer here, to speak on our behalf. We will supplement his description should the need arise."

"This is a good suggestion. Nobleman Huang, may I hear what you have to say?" said Imperial Teacher.

"So many events have taken place since you were away. It is impossible to tell you all of them," Flying Tiger said. "Since you wish to know the truth, let me summarize the most important events to you. Since you left, the Emperor acquired Dar-Gee, the daughter of Lord Soo Defender, as his concubine queen. Ever since, court affairs of the court began to go astray." He then went on to describe the death of the Imperial Astronomer Du Yuansee, and the construction of the Pao-Lo torture machine to execute loyal officers who spoke against the

287

Emperor, the overthrow of the former Queen Consort Jiang under a false charge of attempted assassination and the circumstances leading to the disappearance of the two princes, the luring of four dukes to the capital and the subsequent execution of the two, Duke East and Duke South, and the banishment of Duke West, and other evil doings such as the snake pit to torture innocent ladies-in-waiting, the fountain of wine and racks of meat to perform orgies, the construction of the Elk Tower with forced labor, and forcing the Vice Premier to commit hari-kiri and take out his heart to cure his evil Queen Dar-Gee's heart ailment. "You just saw his casket and the funeral when you returned to the city. I have heard that when a country is prosperous, good omens appear and when a country is doomed, disasters manifest. We have submitted numerous communiques to the Emperor, but these communiques were never read. Now you have returned in triumph. You are our only hope. Only you can turn things around. For the sake of the people and the country, please take action."

At the end of this long summary, the Imperial Teacher was in a mood of great rage and depression. "Gentlemen, I thank you for your detailed information. Give me three days and I will come up with a communique. I will present it to the Emperor myself. Please be there three days from now."

The Imperial Teacher ordered that his official residence be sealed for three days, during which no guests or communications would be received, so that he could concentrate on preparing the communique. Three days later, he asked that a court session be held so that he could submit the communique. All the officers of the court knew of this submission and they arrived at the court early, ready to hear the communique. After the usual court protocols were exercised, the communique was submitted. It read:

Consequences of a Banquet for Elves

To Your Majesty, Emperor of Ten Thousand Years,

May the humble Imperial Teacher, the Prince Regent, Wen Zhong, submit a communique for your consideration:

The purpose of this communique is to discuss recent changes in national policies, which have caused a degradation of public morals, a shift of power from the loyal and the straight to toadies, and the creation of horrendous punishment by torture machines. This shift of policy will not be sympathized with by Heaven and may cause unknown danger to weaken the foundation of this country.

I have read that the Sage Emperor Yao considered his throne a seat to fulfill a responsibility mandated by Heaven to his people, and not a position for him to indulge in pleasure. Thus, he eliminated all toadies from his court and promoted the just, loyal and straight to prominent positions. His reign was regarded as a role model of reign by a sage king. After seventy years of rule under Yao, he decided to pass his ruling power to another sage, Suan, and not to his son, whom he regarded as incompetent. Again, Suan passed his throne to another sage, Yu, because of Yu's ability to cure the flood problem of Yellow River. During Yu's rule, music was created and in subsequent rules civilization developed and prospered. A number of very capable emperors have since ruled the country. People ruled by capable emperors enjoyed prosperity and justice. Your Majesty has succeeded to a throne on which once upon a time these sage kings sat. You are obligated to the cause of common people, by spreading righteousness, mercy and prosperity. You have the responsibility to respect lives, to promote literature, to revere the destructive power of arms and to follow the natural tendency of Heaven and Earth. If you fulfill these obligations, the country shall endure and people shall respect you and show their loyalty to you.

Now, you have indulged yourself in wine and women, surrounded yourself with toadies, promoted hatred and forgotten love and mercy. You have tortured your Queen to death by pulling out her eyes and burning her hands, and gotten rid of your own children thus terminating your own lineage. I wish Your Majesty to henceforth distance yourself from these toadies, accept righteousness and justice, and return this country to its previous grandeur and greatness. People will then restore their faith, respect and loyalty to you. The world shall enjoy a lasting peace. Even facing the danger of offending you, it is my obligation to you and to the ancestor emperors of Shang to submit a ten-point program to restore this country to a righteous course. The ten points are:

1. Dismantle the Elk Tower and distribute its wealth back to the people.

2. Abolish the Pao-Lo torture machine so that loyal and straight officers can offer you their constructive criticisms.

3. Destroy the snake pit so that the palace shall be free from evil.

4. Dismantle the wine fountain and the racks of meat to reduce taxation and to restore staple food supply to the people.

5. Banish Dar-Gee and select another queen of virtue.

6. Remove all toadies from office. Execute Fei Chung and Yu Whenn immediately to quench the ill feeling of the people and to discourage future sycophants.

7. Open your grain storage to feed the poor and the hungry.

8. Send messengers to the east and the south to discuss terms of peace and to settle their grievances.

9. Dispatch envoys to search for talents in your country to serve in your court.

10. Solicit public opinion and constructive criticism as basis for your policies.

While Emperor Zoe was reading this communique, the Imperial Teacher stood by his side with a brush pen, ready for the Emperor to mark the communique for execution. Emperor Zoe hesitated.

"First of all, an enormous amount of money and manpower has already been spent on the construction of the Elk Tower. It would be a pity to dismantle it now. Let us discuss this first item later. The second item, the abolishment of the Pao-Lo punishment, is approved. The third item, the destruction of the poisonous snake pit, approved. The fourth item, approved. The fifth item, the expulsion of Queen Dar-Gee, needs further discussion. Queen Dar-Gee is known for her virtue; how could I dethrone her? Item six, the execution of Fei and Yu, needs further discussion. They are my loyal officers and they have committed no crime; how could I execute them just like that? All other items you have submitted are approved except for these three."

"I know the immense effort exerted to construct the Elk Tower. But it has become a symbol of the suffering of the people; the dismantling of this tower and the distribution of its treasures among poor people will quench their grudge. Queen Jiang was put to death because of her loyal and honest criticism of you. Justice will never be done unless you dethrone Queen Dar-Gee and select another Queen of virtue. The execution of Fei and Yu will eradicate evils from the court and restore justice. These are three most important items, and I hope that you will approve them," the Imperial Teacher insisted.

Under the intense pressure of the Imperial Teacher, Emperor Zoe had no alternative but to continue his delaying rhetoric, "Let us discuss these three items later."

"No. These items are of such fundamental importance to the welfare of this country that their discussion cannot be delayed," said the Imperial Teacher again.

Just at this time, an officer left the rank and wanted to speak. "Who are you," asked the Imperial Teacher.

"I am Fei Chung."

"Oh, it is you. Come closer. What do you have to say?"

Fei Chung moved closer and said, "Although the Imperial Teacher is the highest-ranking officer here and is the prince regent, he shows no respect to the Emperor. He forces a pen to the Emperor's hands to ask him to approve his proposals; he wants the Emperor to expel the Queen without justifiable cause; he wants to execute innocent officers. These are evidences of his lack of respect for the Emperor."

Hearing Fei Chung's words, the Imperial Teacher became so angry that his middle eye opened up and the white ray emerged again. "You have enraged me. You toady, you sycophant! You will learn a lesson today." Without further words and with a single punch, Fei the Corrupt was thrown 20 feet out of the platform where the Emperor and the Imperial Teacher were arguing.

Another officer stepped out of the rank, moved forward and reproached the Imperial Teacher. "You are not hitting Fei Chung. You are hitting the Emperor. You are assuming the authority of the Emperor in this court."

"Who are you?"

"I am Yu Whenn."

"Ha, the team is complete." With another punch, Yu Whenn also was thrown twenty odd feet away. "Guards, take them to the Gate of Noon and I want to see their heads here immediately," ordered the Imperial Teacher.

The two toadies were tied up and taken out to the Gate of Noon, ready to be executed. "These two asked for it," Emperor Zoe thought.

"Would you please give the order to have them executed," repeated the Imperial Teacher.

For a while Emperor Zoe did not utter a word. Finally, he spoke. "I agree with you in principle, but the three items you insisted upon must wait. As for Fei and Yu, they did offend you but their crimes do not deserve the death sentence. I will have my justice department looking at this matter."

Now, after having exerted as much pressure as he could, the Imperial Teacher began to soften. He thought, "After all, he is still my Emperor. My further effort of insistence will make me an unreasonable person." He thus agreed, "Yes, all I want is to restore the authority of your throne and prosperity to the country."

Emperor Zoe readily ordered: "Put Fei and Yu in prison and turn this case over to the justice department. The seven points in the communique of the Imperial Teacher shall be carried out immediately." The court session then adjourned.

Unfortunately, as usual, good luck did not last long. A lord in the East Sea area, by the name of Ping Ling, started a rebellion. A few days after the court session, messengers brought the news to Nobleman Huang Flying Tiger, who immediately went to confer with the Imperial Teacher.

"It looks like one of us must go. Do you want me to go or do you want to go?"

The Imperial Teacher asked.

"It is up to you, Your Excellency." replied Flying Tiger.

Since the Imperial Teacher was Flying Tiger's superior, and had won the highest respect from Flying Tiger, his intention to leave the decision to the Imperial Teacher was out of his respect. However, Imperial Teacher misunderstood his intent. After pondering for a while, Imperial Teacher said: "Let me go, you stay at home to take care of things here. You are more familiar with things in this court than I do."

The next morning, the Imperial Teacher and Nobleman Huang Flying Tiger went to report the rebellion to Emperor Zoe.

"Another rebellion! What shall we do?" the startled Emperor said.

"My loyalty to the throne obligates me to go to take care of the rebels in the East Sea. I have delegated Huang Flying Tiger to take charge of the defense of the capital should anything happen. I sincerely wish that from now on Your Majesty will pay more attention to the affairs of this nation. The three remaining points in my communique will be discussed when I come back. I reckon I will not be away for more than half a year."

Emperor Zoe was extremely delighted to see the Imperial Teacher go away, so that he would not have to listen to his so-called "good advice."

"I shall delegate the Imperial Teacher the royal power of my throne by issuing him the tokens of royal power, a White Axe and a Yellow Fur Flag," announced Emperor Zoe, who could not wait for Imperial Teacher to leave so that he could continue his life as before.

The next day, the loyal Imperial Teacher started preparation for yet another campaign against the rebels. Days later, all military preparations were made. A provident day was selected to sanctify the battle flag, an important ritual that must be performed immediately prior to the commencement of a long campaign. Emperor Zoe and his court officers attended this important ritual. After the ritual was performed, Imperial Teacher marched his army eastward. Once again the Imperial Teacher was on the road to squash another rebellion.

War among Gods and Men

10. First Revolutionary Campaign

After Jiang Sarn was invited to serve in the court of Duke West in the capacity of deputy vice premier, he soon showed his ability. As time passed, more and more responsibilities were piled upon him. Eventually he became indispensable, so he was promoted from vice deputy premier to assume the full title of the premier. He frequently dispatched spies to the capital to keep in touch with affairs of the city as well as those in the court of Emperor Zoe. First he received report that Emperor Zoe's indulgence in wine and women had become worse and that the two toadies – Fei the Corrupt and Yu the Adulator – were almost in complete charge. Next he learned that Duke North, Tsung Migratory Tiger, had successfully finished the construction of the Elk Tower project, and that, during the construction, people were heavily taxed and enslaved as forced laborers. Another spy reported that Vice Premier Bee Gahn had been forced to commit hara-kiri to take out his heart to cure an ailment of Dar-Gee. Jiang Sarn was especially enraged at the death of his colleague and friend. Even the Vice Premier, probably the last just and straight civilian officer left in Emperor Zoe's court, had been eliminated.

"Tsung is a capable man. He was able to complete the huge project in two and half years and I estimated it would have taken thirty-five! He is also a very wicked man. He must be removed first," swore Jiang Sarn.

The next day, during the regular court session, Jiang Sarn briefed the court of recent affairs in the capital. "To cure the ailment of the wicked Queen Dar-Gee, Emperor Zoe murdered Vice Premier Bee Gahn. Duke North, Tsung Migratory Tiger, successfully constructed the Elk Tower but during the construction he caused people in Morning Song to suffer intolerable taxation and forced labor. Many people died while he enriched himself through embezzlement and taking bribes. It is time for us to start a campaign against injustice and tyranny. Let us begin by first eliminating Tsung Migratory Tiger."

Duke West replied: "Your analysis is right. However, Duke North is at the same rank as I am. How can I justify myself to take action against him?"

"First of all, every person in the world has the responsibility and the moral obligation to set things right. Secondly, you have been given the royal authority. Before you left from the capital, Emperor Zoe awarded you the title of his Proxy and you were issued the tokens of royal authority, a Yellow Fur Flag and a White Axe. Under the power granted by the decree, you have the authority to take whatever actions you see fit. Further, by eliminating Tsung Migratory Tiger, perhaps you can awaken Emperor Zoe from his evil deeds so that he will accept reform," Jiang Sarn said. As if his arguments were not convincing enough, he added, "If, through your action, Emperor Zoe accepts reform, he might even become another great sage emperor like Yau or Suan. This feat, if accomplished, will make you immortal, to be remembered by posterity forever." Knowing the weakness of Duke West to hope to rank himself among sage kings of the past, Jiang Sarn presented further argument.

Duke West was entertained by the thought that he could reform Emperor Zoe through an action to eliminate an officer who had caused people great sufferings. The duke readily consented to this campaign. "You have convinced me. It seems a good idea. Now, who can take the command to subjugate Tsung Migratory Tiger?"

"I recommend myself to take the command," offered Jiang Sarn. This offer was unanimously seconded by the officers of the court.

298

Still wary that Jiang Sarn might overact during this campaign, the duke said: "I accept your offer. But I will also go with you. This way we can always keep in touch with each other."

"Indeed, all people under the sun will follow you and help you in your endeavors if you are personally involved," Jiang Sarn quickly agreed.

A Yellow Fur Flag and a white Iron Axe were issued to Jiang Sarn as tokens of delegation of authority by the duke. By the authority granted to him, Jiang Sarn became the commander-in-chief of the army and has the power of absolute command. Although the duke was with the army throughout the mission, he can only offer advice but must leave all military decisions to the commander-in-chief. The relationship between a Jiang Sarn, the chief commander and the duke is much like the relationship between the captain and the owner of a modern day merchant ship. The owner of the ship can order the captain to sail to any destination, but he has no authority to direct the operation of the ship even if he is on board.

On a provident day, after a traditional ceremony of offering sacrifices to sanctify the battle flag, an army of 100,000 soldiers and warriors, under the command of Jiang Sarn, marched towards North Duchy, the fief under Duke North. Nangong Gua the Swift, who had always been enthusiastic for a campaign against tyrants, was appointed the vanguard. The first revolutionary campaign thus began.

Days later, a scout reported that Tsung City, the capital of North Duchy, was within sight. Jiang Sarn ordered encampment set and defense obstacles erected. An assault was planned.

War among Gods and Men

A scout from the city of Tsung reported the arrival of the army of the duke. At this time, Tsung Migratory Tiger happened to be in Morning Song and his son, Tsung Tiger Cub, was in charge of Tsung City. Tiger Cub called a conference. He told his warriors: "The rebellious Duke West escaped from Emperor Zoe's court some time ago. On several occasions Emperor Zoe talked about sending armies to subjugate him but was persuaded to leave him alone by my father. We never intrude or encroach upon him and now he comes here to invade us. We must punish him. Prepare for a defense war."

The next day, Tiger Cub sent a letter to challenge Duke West either to fight or to withdraw. Jiang Sarn accepted the challenge of war on behalf of the duke. Instead of waiting for the enemy to take the first offensive, Jiang Sarn asked Nangong Swift to challenge the city.

Leading a regiment of foot soldiers, Nangong Swift approached the west city gate of Tsung and confronted the defense: "Ask the bandit Tsung Migratory Tiger to come out to face his punishment!" A warrior, Huang Yuan-Chi, was dispatched to respond to the challenge. Nangong Swift reiterated his insult. "You incompetent idiot, don't waste your life. Go back and send the bandit Tsung Migratory Tiger out to face me!" Enraged, Huang Yuan-Chi rolled his horse forward, waving his weapon, a scimitar with a long handle. Nangong Swift ran his horse forward to match his challenger and he too used a long scimitar as his weapon. Weapons clanked for around 30 rounds, then Huang Yuan-Chi began to show weakness. He tried to retreat back to the city, but his escape path was blocked by Nangong Swift. Finding a slip in his enemy, Nangong Swift swung his long scimitar and cut Huang into halves. Nangong Swift triumphantly returned to his encampment.

The death of warrior Huang was reported to Tsung Tiger Cub. "We must avenge the death of Huang Yuan-Chi!" he proclaimed. "Prepare all our warriors and men for a decisive battle tomorrow!"

The next day Tsung Tiger Cub, fully armored, led a sizable troop of soldiers and warriors out of the city to face the invading army. Under his enemy's flag, the Tiger Cub saw the leader of the invading army, a Taoist carrying a pair of swords and wearing a long Taoist robe embroidered with talismanic inscriptions. "Who are you to dare invade my territory," asked the Tiger Cub.

"I am the premier of Zhou Duchy, under the flag of command of Duke West. You and your father have committed horrendous evil deeds against the people. Even a child can recount your evil deeds and hates you. To deliver people from misery, we, the army of righteousness, come here under Emperor Zoe's authority to subjugate you. The Emperor has delegated Duke West royal military authority. Duke West has received a Yellow Fur Flag and a White Axe as tokens of this authority. Surrender now to avoid bloodshed," Jiang Sarn threatened.

"Ha! I know you. You are an old, useless, rotten fool from Parn Chi. I can easily kill you, right now and right here." Tiger Cub cursed and shouted, and commanded his soldiers and warriors forward in an attacking formation.

Jiang Sarn's warriors and soldiers also rushed forward to combat against the challengers. A melee ensued as warriors and soldiers from both sides engaged in fierce combats. After the dust settled, four out of six of Tsung's warriors were dead while none of the six warriors of Jiang Sarn's army was injured. Under the heavy attack, Tsung Tiger Cub had to issue a retreat order.

After they were safely back to the city, Tsung decided to stay inside the fortified Tsung City, waiting for reinforcements to arrive.

Jiang Sarn wanted to order an immediate attack against the city and he ordered the preparation of scaling ladders, catapults and other devices needed to overcome high walls of defense. Then, Duke West interceded. "We come here to deliver people from misery and suffering. If we order a full-scale attack against the city, innocent people will be either wounded or killed. We must not launch any direct attack against the city if we can avoid it."

Jiang Sarn thus withdrew his plan to attack the city. He devised another plan. He wrote a letter and asked Nangong Swift to deliver it personally to Tsung Black Tiger (who was a younger brother of Migratory Tiger and a lord of lesser rank). A few days later Nangong Swift arrived at the home city of the Black Tiger, the city of Tsao, and delivered the letter.

The letter read:

Under the flag of your command, the humble Premier of Zhou Dukedom in the city of West Branch submits salutation.

To the Great Lord, General Tsung:

I have read: As a responsible officer, one must direct his emperor to the path of righteousness by offering proper advice so that his emperor will scatter his mercy among people, propagate peace and prosperity. I have never seen or heard of a high officer like your brother, who ingratiates his emperor by performing evil deeds to please him. In the process people suffered, and he profited himself. Earlier, Duke West has been delegated the royal power to take military action against injustice and has been issued the tokens of royal power, a Yellow Fur Flag and a White Axe. In turn, the duke has delegated his military to me, Jiang Sarn, the Premier of Zhou Dukedom. To eliminate your brother, we have assembled an army and now we are at the outskirts of Tsung City. However, we do not want to launch a direct attack against this city for fear of causing unnecessary casualties of the common people in the city.

You have always been just and straight. Please arrest your brother and deliver him to our encampment, to Zhou Duchy, so that the people of Tsung City may be spared from further conflicts of war. By cooperating with us, you will be able to dissociate yourself from his evil deeds, and to clear your family's name. Otherwise, when your brother is overthrown, you may be considered an accomplice of his evil deeds through no fault of yours. I hope you will not consider me as a stupid fool offering you this advice.

Again Jiang Sarn salutes you for your kind consideration.

Tsung Black Tiger read this letter several times. The implication and the message were clear: either to cooperate or to be an enemy of the powerful Zhou Duchy. The letter did not imply any territorial ambition. Instead, the sole purpose appeared to be just to get rid of his brother because of his evil deeds, and it even mentioned the continuation of his family's lineage. He pondered: "Indeed my brother has committed many evil deeds. I saw how my brother behaved when he engaged in the unnecessary battle against Soo the Defender. During the construction of the Elk Tower many forced to perform forced labor died, people suffered and hated him. In the mean time he enriched himself with bribes and pilferage. I would rather offend my brother than people of the world. In doing so I at least can hope to sustain and to preserve the lineage of my ancestors. Besides, Jiang Sarn even invites me to he his ally." So he made up his mind.

He then said, "General Nangong, I understand what your premier said in his letter. I do not need to write a reply. Please ask him to wait for the delivery of my brother to his encampment." After a formal banquet of welcome and departure, Nangong Swift departed.

Tsung Black Tiger asked his son Tsung Yinrun (Responsive Bird) to take charge of Tsao City. He immediately departed for Tsung City with his crow army of 3000. He was greeted warmly by his nephew, Tsung Tiger Cub. Black Tiger asked Tiger Cub: "Do you know why Jiang Sarn come here with a sizable army to invade this city?"

"I really do not know. However, the other day I had a bad defeat and I lost a number of my best warriors. I am glad that you, my uncle, decided to come here to help me," replied the Tiger Cub.

The next morning, Black Tiger, leading his crow army of 3000, marched to the front gate of Jiang Sarn's encampment and challenged. Jiang Sarn ordered Nangong Swift to respond, because Nangong had established an understanding with Black Tiger.

After a short exchange of insults, combat commenced. As weapons clanked, the two gradually moved away from their soldiers. Black Tiger whispered, "This is all the fighting I am going to do for now. Please pretend that you are defeated and run back to your camp. I will chase you but I will let you run away. Tell the premier I will keep my promise."

At this hint, Nangong Swift pretended that he had tired himself from fighting, so he turned his horse back while shouting, "I am defeated, do not kill me." Black Tiger did not chase Nangong Swift for long. He and his crow army returned to Tsung City.

"You are the only one here who can overcome Nangong Swift. He killed several of my warriors and many soldiers. Why didn't you use your magical iron-beaked eagle to catch him? The siege could be over if he is captured," asked the Tiger Cub.

"My dear nephew, you are too young to know the intricacies of warfare. Jiang Sarn knows Tao well. I do not want Jiang Sarn to know that I have this ability yet. I will use it when there is an urgent need. Now, although I have won this battle, I think we still need your father here. Please ask him to come home as soon as possible. I will also write a letter to him and ask him to come back to join us to defend the city. Please provide a messenger to deliver my letter and yours to him."

In days the letter was delivered. Upon learning that his city was under siege by an army of Duke West, Tsung Migratory Tiger became exceedingly enraged. His aggravation was further exacerbated when he learned that the commander of the invading army was none other than Jiang Sarn, the petit officer who'd proclaimed that it would take thirty-five years to complete the Elk Tower while he'd finished it in two and a half! In his rage he left instantly for the Palace and asked to have an audience with the Emperor right away. The request was granted.

Migratory Tiger came directly to the point: "This rebel Duke West, Chi Chang, invaded my territory and my city is under his siege. Please advise me what to do."

"The wicked Chi-Chang escaped from me, and now he is invading you! Let me see. Go back to your city to take care of your defense first. I will dispatch an army of three thousand to go with you to aid your defense. Then I will discuss with my officers dispatching additional forces to assist you." With the Emperor's promise and this small reinforcement, Migratory Tiger left Morning Song for his home, Tsung City.

War among Gods and Men

A few days later, a scout reported the return of Migratory Tiger. Black Tiger secretly asked one of his warriors to set up a trap with a team of 20 armed men with short weapons just behind the city gate through which Migratory Tiger was expected to pass. Another team was dispatched to arrest the rest of Tsung's direct family and to deliver them to the Zhou encampment. Black Tiger then asked Tiger Cub to join him to greet Migratory Tiger at the city gate. As Migratory Tiger saw the greeting party, he dismounted his horse and walked towards them, not suspecting anything. As soon as Migratory Tiger stepped inside the city gate, at a prearranged signal of Black Tiger, the 20 armed men quickly ambushed the father and the son, disarming both of them, and tied them up.

"What are you doing," the startled Migratory Tiger asked.

Black Tiger responded coolly, "Delivering you, the evil cause of suffering of people, to the camp of Duke West to face justice. You, a high officer, should advise the Emperor to promote good deeds. Instead, you build the wretched Elk Tower for him. During this project, you have broken families, caused deaths of their beloved ones, and enriched yourself with bribes. All other three dukes are against you now. I would rather face my ancestors for my betrayal of you than the rest of the world as your co-conspirator against the people. There is nothing more to say." Upon hearing this accusation from his own brother, Migratory Tiger merely sighed, without saying another word.

By the time they arrived at the encampment of Duke West, Migratory Tiger saw his wife, Ms. Lee and his daughter standing on one side of the tent office, as prisoners. He now realized that everything was lost. "I never expected that I would be betrayed by my own brother," wept Migratory Tiger.

Since the party was now complete, Jiang Sarn began a military court session to determine the fate of the prisoners. As the commander-in-chief, he presided the court. Duke West was also present. First Black Tiger went forward and spoke to Jiang Sarn.

"I have delivered my evil brother to you for your disposal," Black Tiger said.

Duke West was not happy at all to see the betrayal of a sibling against another, even though the cause was a justifiable one. He sank into a deep pensive mood, pondering.

Jiang Sarn, being quite aware of the soft heart of Duke West, immediately ordered: "Bring the father and son Tsung in." The two prisoners were brought in and they looked at the duke with pleading eyes, and the duke looked at them with compassion.

Sensing that the duke was about to pardon both of them, Jiang Sarn decided to act fast. Using the authority of absolute military command granted to him for this mission, without even giving a chance to allow Migratory Tiger or his son to plead for their lives, Jiang Sarn ordered: "This is the time to end their evil deeds. Execute them immediately and bring their heads here to show to me." The duke was so startled that he did not know how to respond. By the time he wanted to say something, the executioners had already come back with two bloody heads. "Good! Display them on a post at the outer gate of this encampment!" ordered Jiang Sarn.

The poor Duke, who for all his life had never personally ordered the execution of anyone, including murderers, was completely stupefied by the bloody display of the two newly cut human heads. His face turned extremely pale. "I am scared to death! Take the heads away from me!"

He scowled and trembled. He was so upset that he immediately retired to his residential tent and asked Jiang Sarn to continue the court session on his behalf.

"What do you want me to do with his family members, the duchy and Tsung City," asked Black Tiger.

"His family has nothing to do with the evil deeds committed by Tsung Migratory Tiger. Further, his daughter eventually will marry and assume her husband's family name, so she is of no concern to us. Release the mother and the daughter, and it is your responsibility to see that their wants are met and that they are treated with respect as the family of your brother," said Jiang Sarn. "As for the duchy and the city, you may annex them and place them under your reign. In fact, I would like to advise you to move your capital from Tsao City to Tsung City and to assume the title Duke North. Assign someone you can trust to take charge of your old home city Tsao. From now on, you are Duke North."

Thus, the only duke who had remained loyal to Emperor Zoe, Migratory Tiger, was eliminated and replaced by his brother, who, having gained his new status from his collaboration with Duke West through Jiang Sarn's advice, was now also an outcast of Emperor Zoe's court and thus would accept Duke West as his better, if not his king.

Days later, the triumphant army returned to West Branch. However, ever since he had seen the bloody display of the two freshly cut heads of the father and son Tsung, Duke West had been very upset, and he fell ill on the way home. After his return to West Branch, he could not eat much or sleep well. Upon closing his eyes, he often saw the two bloody heads of father and son standing in front of him, pleading for mercy. No medicine was of any help. As he withered away day by day, he realized that his life in the world would soon come to an end.

308

One day when he felt a little better, he summoned Jiang Sarn to his sickbed.

"This loyal Jiang Sarn is here. May Your Highness feel better! Is there any service this humble serf may perform for you?" Jiang Sarn said.

"I do not think I will ever recover again. I think I am dying. Before I die, I want you to promise me one thing. I have held the position of Duke West and ruled this duchy for many years, governing people in my duchy and supervising the two hundred other lords under a decree set forth by the founder of the Shang dynasty. Although Emperor Zoe was not behaving as a good emperor should and it was necessary to take actions to right some of his wrongs, he is still our Emperor and I am still a duke under him. I have never rebelled in my life. The elimination of Tsung was justifiable – exterminating evil officers and bandits is the civic responsibility of all, as sages said in the past. However, this action against Tsung was carried out without an explicit order from the Emperor and further, Tsung was of the same rank as I am and I trespassed my authority by killing him. I can never escape the bad name from these two offenses. Ever since the execution of the two Tsungs, I frequently hear their sobbing sounds and voices pleading for their lives at night. As soon as I close my eyes trying to sleep, images of the two always appear in front of me. I am weakening day by day and I do not think I will be in this world for long. The reason I call you here is to make you promise me one thing: Whatever evil deeds the Emperor commits, you must not follow the examples of other lords to revolt against him. It is against the code of loyalty to revolt against one's emperor. Please do not disobey me, otherwise you will have difficulty facing me in the underworld." When Duke West finished, his face was already covered with tears and his breathing short and rapid.

Kneeling down, also in tears, Jiang Sarn attested: "I have received an enormous amount of great favors from you, to place me in the prominent position of premier in your court. How dare I disobey your order? I will be unfaithful to you if I ever disobey your requisition."

At this moment, the duke's now eldest son, Chi-Fa, came in to inquire about his father's health.

"Good, I was just about to send for you. Come here." The Duke then turned to Jiang Sarn. "My son is young. After my death, please take good care of him. Instruct him. Do not let him be incited by others to start a revolution against the Emperor. Jiang Sarn, you sit over here. My son, come over here and kowtow to the premier. After my death the premier will be your proxy father. You must listen to everything he says."

Jiang Sarn was very much moved. He knelt down next to the sickbed and said with a trembling voice, "Even if I break every bone in my body, shed every drop of my blood from my veins, I cannot repay you for your trust in me. Please rest, you will recover soon."

"No, I feel I am dying now. My son, please take this advice: Do not rest yourself from doing good deeds, have no doubt to carry out feats of righteousness, and never let yourself be led astray by temptations. Remember these three things, then you shall be a good ruler." With these last words, Duke of West expired, at an age of ninety-seven, during the twentieth year of Emperor Zoe's reign. Having been a very cultured person who had always been considerate of his people, his subordinates, and his colleagues, he was given the posthumous title: "Wen Wang," or "King of Literature." As was the custom in Middle Kingdom, this posthumous title was always used as a respectful reference to him in all subsequent writings.

Following the last will of Duke West, Chi-Fa was enthroned as the new Duke West, but no request was made to Emperor Zoe to ask for the official sanction of Shang dynasty (so no pledge of fealty was made to him). Instead of the old title Duke West, he assumed a new title, King of Arms. After the enthronement, heeding to the last wish of King of Literature at his deathbed, Jiang Sarn was officially titled "Proxy Father" by King of Arms. As was the custom of Middle Kingdom, all officers of the court were promoted by one rank following the enthronement.

War among Gods and Men

11. Mutiny of Flying Tiger

No sooner had the Imperial Teacher departed to quash the rebellion in East Sea than Fei the Corrupt and Yu the Adulator were released from the prison under a special order of Emperor Zoe. An uncle of Emperor Zoe, Wei Tzu, argued against the release: "Fei and Yu were put in prison by the Imperial Teacher and they should be tried for their wrongdoings in accordance with the law of the land. To me, their release is highly out of order, especially right after the Imperial Teacher's hasty departure to quash rebellion on your behalf."

Emperor Zoe replied, "These two are my most loyal officers. There is no substance in the charges the Imperial Teacher brought against them." Upon hearing this highly biased reasoning, without further words Wei Tzu left the court. With the absence of the only voice of criticism, that of the Imperial Teacher, Emperor Zoe continued his life of indulgence.

It was the apex of spring, and peonies blossomed everywhere in the imperial garden. The Emperor decided to give a banquet party for his court officers. As was the custom, Emperor Zoe sat separately. He sat in the balcony of his residential palace, the Starplucker Pavilion, accompanied by Dar-Gee and Hsi Charming (who was now formally installed as a queen to reward her for healing Dar-Gee of her "heart attack"). The officers sat at tables placed in the garden for the occasion. As was the custom, the seating reflected rank and seniority. When Flying Tiger came to the banquet, he remarked to Wei Tzu and Chi Tzu (who was another uncle of Emperor Zoe), "At this time, when rebellion is rampant everywhere and prosperity is fading, this Emperor thinks of

313

nothing but parties, banquets and enjoyment of peonies. I hope he will institute reform soon, otherwise the days of his reign may be numbered." Wei Tzu and Chi Tzu said nothing but shook their heads and sighed.

At the insistence of Emperor Zoe, the banquet did not end at noon as was scheduled, but continued into midnight. The Emperor circulated among officers and exchanged toasts, leaving Hsi Charming and Dar-Gee in the Starplucker Pavillion. By midnight, Dar-Gee and Hsi Charming were completely drunk, lying on couches and dozing half consciously. Even the thousand year elfin Tao of Dar-Gee could not cope with her state of drunkenness, and Dar-Gee reverted back to her fox form. She slipped off her clothes and began flying around. Her old instinct of eating humans during earlier days of her elfin Tao came back. In her fox form and her drunken state, she flew around the garden to find some poor victim to eat. At the sight of the shadow of a half-fox and half-human flying in midair, the chief wine marshal cried out: "A bugaboo! A bugaboo is coming!"

At this warning, being a warrior, Huang Flying Tiger immediately broke loose a banister to defend against the monster (all weapons were banned inside the palace except those of the palace guards). As the fox form approached, he went forward to challenge it. After one or two rounds of engagement, Flying Tiger suddenly remembered he had a hunting eagle with him. "Release my hunting eagle!" he shouted. Immediately the cage confining the eagle opened and the eagle, trained to hunt foxes, swiftly flew up and charged at the fox form. The fox, unaware of the eagle, was hooked by its iron claw in the face and with a shriek scream, disappeared under a flat stone bed and escaped.

Emperor Zoe ordered the stone bed overturned. Underneath, a huge pile of human bones was found. Obviously the fox form had been

314

feasting on palace ladies-in-waiting since her arrival, and the mystery of missing women was now solved. "The elfin smog theory was not without some truth," Emperor Zoe thought. Because of this incident, the banquet ended rather unhappily.

The next morning, Emperor Zoe discovered the scratched face of Dar-Gee. "What happened?"

"I was not careful when I took a walk in the garden last night. I was scratched by a falling twig."

Unaware that his woman of pleasure was the very fox form he had seen with his own eyes the previous night, the Emperor continued: "Don't go near the garden anymore. Last night a monster resembling a fox attacked General Huang. He had to use his hunting eagle to chase it away. It then disappeared underneath a flat stone bed. When the stone bed was overturned, a pile of human bones was found. The elf must have eaten them."

"I will avenge this. Just you wait, you Huang Flying Tiger," swore Dar-Gee in her thoughts.

Han Yung (Glory), the defense commander of Frontier Pass Vast Water, dispatched a report to the capital detailing the invasion of the Tsung duchy by Duke West under the command of Premier Jiang Sarn, the execution of both the father and the son, the appointment of the brother of Migratory Tiger to succeed the post of Duke North, and the subsequent natural death of Duke West and his succession by his relatively young son who now called himself King of Arms. A new Chancellor by the name of Yao Zong read the report and he immediately consulted with Wei Tzu. Yao Zong wanted to bring this matter immediately to the attention of Emperor Zoe. Wei Tzu commented:

"You are just wasting your time reporting this matter to the Emperor. He won't pay any attention."

Yao replied, "But I have to perform my duty." So Yao went to the Starplucker Pavilion to see Emperor Zoe. He was coolly received and was told to state his business as concisely as possible. Yao reported: "Duke West has expired. His eldest prince succeeded to his father's position and called himself King of Arms without asking for your permission or your sanction. You must dispatch an army to subdue this new duke."

"The new duke is nothing, he is only a young boy," the Emperor replied.

"He may be young, but he is aided by very capable officers, including Jiang Sarn." Yao insisted.

"Jiang Sarn? The sorcerer who escaped from the Palace some time ago? He is only a magician, a sorcerer. He is nothing." the Emperor then waved Yao to leave.

Unable to convince the Emperor that the Zhou Dukedom would eventually become a potential threat, Yao went back to his office and sighed, "Sooner or later the Shang dynasty will be terminated by King of Arms. He has already indicated his ambition, and he has capable hands in his court."

The New Year came. As was the custom, wives of high-ranking officers were obliged to go to the Middle Palace to present their New Year's greetings personally to the reigning Queen Consort. Following this custom, Huang Flying Tiger's wife, Ms. Chia, went to the palace to fulfill this ritual obligation. She planned first to present her salute to the Queen Consort in reign, now Dar-Gee, then to visit Queen Huang, her sister-in-law and the sister of Huang Flying Tiger.

"Ms. Chia is here to present her New Year's salute to you," Dar-Gee's lady-in-waiting reported.

"Who is she?"

"The wife of Huang Flying Tiger."

"Great! My opportunity of revenge is here now," Dar-Gee secretly rejoiced. "Show her in."

The usual protocols were exercised. As they chatted, Dar-Gee was impressed at Ms. Chia's beauty. A devious scheme suddenly materialized in her mind. "I would like to know more about you," said Dar-Gee. Then she ordered a banquet table prepared for Ms. Chia. Unable to decline this offer from Queen Consort, Ms. Chia had to accept the impromptu invitation, though rather reluctantly. After several rounds of drinks, ladies-in-waiting reported, "The Emperor is coming."

"I must not be here when the Emperor arrives. I must adhere to the strict protocol that wives of officers must never meet the Emperor in person. Let me leave," begged Ms. Chia.

"Don't worry, you can retire to one of the back rooms. After the Emperor leaves we can continue our conversation and develop our acquaintance." The sound of the approach of the Emperor became louder and louder. As time was pressing, with no other choice, Ms. Chia retired to one of the back rooms.

"With whom were you drinking and feasting," asked Emperor Zoe.

"With Ms. Chia, the wife of Huang Flying Tiger."

"It was very nice of you," responded the Emperor.

They sat down around the banquet table and after a few rounds of drinking, Dar-Gee asked the Emperor, "Have you ever met her? She is exquisitely beautiful."

"You cannot suggest this. The protocol is very strict that an emperor must not see or meet wives of court officers," replied the Emperor.

"Normally this is true. However, she is also a relative of yours. Her sister-in-law is currently a queen of yours residing in the West Palace. Commoners always mingle their relatives at the same table when they dine. So can you. Why don't I use some excuse to get Ms. Chia to the top balcony of the Starplucker Pavilion, where you can meet her. You can see for yourself how beautiful she is." Knowing Emperor Zoe's weakness not to be able to pass by a pretty face easily, Dar-Gee furthered her scheme.

"A good idea!" seconded Emperor Zoe, who always wanted to meet another new pretty face.

After the Emperor left, Dar-Gee asked Ms. Chia to step out of the room and suggested, "Before you leave here to visit your sister-in-law, I would like to show you the Starplucker Pavilion." Again, Ms. Chia refused. But Dar-Gee was very insistent and Ms. Chia could not overcome her persistence, so together they went to the top balcony of the Starplucker Pavilion.

As they were standing there enjoying the city view around, an attendant accompanying Ms. Chia reported the arrival of Emperor Zoe, as planned. Ms. Chia was now in a panic, because the top balcony had no other rooms just a roof over it. "Don't worry, after the Emperor comes, you can just present the usual pleasantries. Then you can leave," Dar-Gee reassured her.

After entering the balcony, the Emperor said, "Who is the lady over there?"

"The wife of Nobleman Huang Flying Tiger," Dar-Gee replied.

Without any other choice, Ms. Chia had to turn around, and presented pleasantries to the Emperor. Surely enough, he was very impressed by the beauty of Ms. Chia and he immediately decided he wanted her, too. "Please sit down," insisted the Emperor.

"Your Majesty Emperor, please let me go. The protocol is very strict that wives of officers must not meet the Emperor. I have already violated this code, please do not embarrass me further by detaining me," pleaded Ms. Chia, who now realized she had fallen into a trap set by Dar-Gee.

"If you do not want to sit down, I will come over and stand by your side." As the Emperor approached her, she retreated towards the edge of the balcony. The Emperor then poured wine into a goblet and extended it towards Ms. Chia. "Please, drink this cup ...." As he said these words, he moved closer. This was an unmistakable first indication that the Emperor was prepared to make a pass.

Ms. Chia could tolerate it no further. "You idiotic Emperor! My husband has fought countless wars to defend your throne. Now by Dar-Gee's scheme, you have insulted me and my husband." Blushing, Ms. Chia shouted at the top of her lungs. She was also now at the very edge of the balcony and had no space to retreat further. In her rage, she grabbed the goblet of wine from the Emperor's outstretched hand, and threw it at his face. "I would rather commit suicide than subject myself to your insult and violation!" With these words, she jumped over the railing of the balcony and fell nearly 50 feet below to her death.

Meanwhile, Queen Huang was eagerly awaiting the visit of her sister-in-law. After Ms. Chia fell to her death, the messenger Queen Huang had sent to find out the whereabouts of her sister-in-law quickly ran back and reported to her the tragic event. "This is yet another evil scheme of that wicked woman Dar-Gee."

She departed immediately for the Starplucker Pavilion, and ran upstairs quickly to the balcony. Pointing her finger at the Emperor, she denounced, "You jerk Emperor! Do you know to whom you owe your throne? My elder brother fought many wars to defend your throne, and my father defends the Frontier Pass Boundary Marker for you. Today, my sister-in-law came here to pay her respect to your Queen, in adherence to protocols of the Palace. Then your evil woman tricked my honorable sister-in-law to this pavilion, and you, lewd and licentious Emperor, indiscriminately let your carnal desire run wild! You have insulted your ancestor emperors and you are destroying your empire, and you are unseating yourself from the throne!" Emperor Zoe, having no good reply to these words, sat there and said nothing. Turning to Dar-Gee, Queen Huang continued, "You dirty and wicked woman. You have tarnished and tainted this Palace. Let me give you a lesson." She pulled Dar-Gee from her chair, threw her down on the floor and beat her repeatedly.

Although Dar-Gee could have easily overpowered her opponent by her elfin Tao, she did not dare use it in the presence of the Emperor. She screamed in pain, and asked Emperor Zoe for help. The Emperor stood up and tried to separate the two. However, accidentally Queen Huang hit the Emperor in the face. Now the Emperor was enraged. "How dare you hit me!" Lifting her up, he threw her out of the Starplucker Pavilion and amidst a shrieking cry she also fell to her death below.

Ms. Chia's attendants quickly exited the Palace and ran back to the residence of Huang Flying Tiger to report the tragedy. "Mistress fell down to her death from the top of the Starplucker Pavilion. Queen Huang went there to argue with the Emperor, and she was thrown out of the Pavilion to her death!"

At this moment, Huang Flying Tiger was in the middle of the traditional New Year celebration with his family, relatives and close friends, among them his two warrior brothers Flying Tiger Cub, and Flying Leopard, his sons the Heavenly Blessing, Heavenly Lord and Heavenly Auspicious, and his four sworn brother warriors Zhou Chi, Long Quan, Wu Chien and Huang Ming. The news was so shocking that tears immediately flowed from the eyes of the three children and they cried and cried.

The four warriors angrily proclaimed, "It is quite clear the lewd Emperor tried to violate your wife, and she committed suicide to avoid the loss of her virtue. Your sister, in defense of her sister-in-law, was also murdered by the Emperor. There is nothing to argue about. We have heard: `If an emperor is not righteous, his officers may leave for another country.' Over these years, we have been the most fervent and ardent defenders of his throne and his dynasty. We never rested; we slept with swords under our pillows and armor by our bedsides, ready to defend his throne at any time. Look what kind of reward you get! This kind of emperor is not worthy of our loyalty. We must leave this country in search of a just and fair king." Drawing their swords, they swore their determination to rebel against the Emperor.

The mood became very tense and Flying Tiger tried to defuse the explosive situation. "I will never allow a woman to become the cause of my rebellion," shouted Flying Tiger.

"You idiot, you blockhead!" one of the four shouted back. "No one can take this kind of insult! You have no regard for your honor or your family! If you do not leave, then we will." Then the four warriors, angry at the indifference of their master sworn brother, jointly walked out of the house.

Afraid that the four might cause undue trouble, Flying Tiger chased after them. When he caught up with them, he argued, "My dear brother warriors! If you want to rebel against this Emperor, you must at least have a plan. Come back, let us discuss this." The four warriors looked at each other and decided that they indeed needed a plan. They went back with Flying Tiger to the house they had just left.

Inside the house, Flying Tiger drew his sword and denounced the four. "My wife and my sister's deaths are of no concern to you. I, Huang Flying Tiger, have been a loyal officer of the court and my family has served the Shang dynasty for over two hundred years. I cannot rebel against Shang on account of two women. What do you think you are doing? Becoming a gang of bandits?" The four warriors had no good reply to this rather idiosyncratic statement. They looked at each other and felt embarrassed.

A few moments later, one of them, Huang Ming, responded with a smile, "Yes, master brother, you are right. It is of no concern to us." Turning around to his three comrades, he said, "It is New Year's Day, let us drink and be merry." He summoned attendants to set up a banquet table. Moments later, a table of food and wine was brought. The four sat down, drank, ate and joked as if nothing had happened. The noise of their merrymaking became a drastic contrast to the incessant cries of sorrow of the three sons of Flying Tiger.

"Why are you four so merry and why do laugh so loud? There is a tragedy in my house. What kind of manner is this?" Huang Flying Tiger admonished.

"Yes, you have a tragedy in your family. But as you said, it is your own affair and is of no concern to us. We do not have anything to lament about. Besides, this is New Year's Day. Isn't it the day of year to celebrate and to be merry?" one of them replied.

Extremely mad at their inconsideration, Flying Tiger further admonished the four, "When tragedies happen to my household, as sworn brothers and as friends you should at least show some sympathy. Instead, you are laughing and making merry. This is not right."

"We are not making merry. We are only laughing at you," Zhou Chi said.

"There is nothing in me for you to laugh at. I am at the top of all ranks. In the court I am second to practically none," boasted Flying Tiger.

"My elder brother warrior, your only concern is to stay at the top of the ranks. Those who know you well might say that you are a forgiving person, that you would pardon offenses against your family. Those who do not know you well would say that you achieved your rank by subjugating your wife to the pleasure of your Emperor."

The impact of this statement was ultimate and final. Rage finally conquered reason. "To hell with the Emperor! Let us rebel against this tyrant.... But where can we go?" Flying Tiger said.

"Let us join the Zhou Dukedom. They already have the support of two-thirds of the highest-ranking Lords," responded Huang Ming.

"Good, pack up and let us leave at once," ordered Huang Flying Tiger.

Fearing that Huang Flying Tiger's determination to revolt against the Emperor might be the result of a momentary anger and thus short-lived, Zhou Chi decided to instigate further. "How about challenging the Emperor to a combat?" In ancient Middle Kingdom, to challenge an emperor to a combat was essentially an irreversible declaration of rebellion, usually not pardonable.

At the height of his anger, Huang Flying Tiger agreed. "Good idea. Let us go to the Gate of Noon to challenge the Emperor to a combat."

Mounting his Five Color Godspeed Ox, Huang Flying Tiger marched his private army of one thousand, his brothers, his children, and the four warriors and all their families to the Gate of Noon. "Ask the idiotic Emperor to face me," Huang challenged.

The Emperor was very upset over the deaths of Ms. Chia and Queen Huang. As he was deploring himself, a Palace guard came in and reported: "Huang Flying Tiger just mutinied against you. He is now outside the Gate of Noon with an army, challenging you to a combat."

"Get my horse and my weapon. I will face these rebels." The Emperor, angry at the open rebellion of Flying Tiger, accepted the challenge.

Flying Tiger was still a little embarrassed to face the Emperor in arms. Noting the embarrassment of Flying Tiger, Huang Ming denounced the Emperor loudly. "You shameless Emperor. You are immoral. You tried to make advances to the wife of a great officer, causing her to commit suicide. Your evil deeds shall be punished! I am coming to get you." He then ran his horse forward and engaged the

Emperor in a weapon-to-weapon combat. Now the code of fealty had been broken. Zhou Chi joined the attack against the Emperor.

With no other choice, Flying Tiger also joined in. Although Emperor Zoe was noted for his strength, he could not face the simultaneous attack from three fierce warriors. Thirty rounds later, he was defeated, and he retreated. Huang Ming wanted to give chase, but Flying Tiger stopped him and said, "Let him go." Thus the Emperor was allowed to escape through the Gate of Noon back to his Palace.

The news of the mutiny of Huang Flying Tiger spread fast to all parts of the city. Stores were closed and people boarded up their windows and doors to avoid becoming casualties of the conflict. Huang and his men had already packed all the belongings they could carry on horse-drawn carts, and the convoy easily exited the city.

The court officials heard about the rebellion of Huang Flying Tiger, so they all went to the Palace to inquire. An impromptu court session was held. Not wanting to admit his guilt, the Emperor explained, "Ms. Chia offended the Queen when she came in to present the customary greeting, so she committed suicide to avoid my punishment. Queen Huang beat Queen Dar-Gee, and she fell down to her death through a mistake. Huang Flying Tiger suddenly went mad and mutinied against me. He even came to the Gate of Noon to challenge me to a combat." No officers dared express any opinion, so they just stood there, silently. No one dared utter a word.

Conveniently, at this moment of awkwardness, a messenger reported that the Imperial Teacher, having accomplished his mission of suppressing rebellion in the East Sea, was returning triumphantly to the capital, and he would arrive at the city gate soon. This timely incident ended the silent embarrassment in the court and using the excuse to greet the Imperial Teacher's return, the officials left for the city gate. There they formed a procession to greet his triumphant return.

Riding his Black Unicorn, the Imperial Teacher trotted into the city and he thanked all the officials who greeted him. He then asked them to accompany him to see the Emperor immediately.

Inside the meeting hall, he could not find his friend Flying Tiger. "Where is Nobleman Huang?" said the Imperial Teacher.

"He just mutinied against me. Now he is on his way out of the country," answered the Emperor.

"Why?" The Imperial Teacher was very astonished, so he asked.

"His wife, Ms. Chia, offended the Queen at the time when she went to the top balcony of Starplucker Pavilion to present the customary New Year salute, so she committed suicide to avoid my punishment. Queen Huang came up to the balcony in her anger and she beat Queen Dar-Gee. Accidentally I knocked her over the railing so she fell to her death. I have no idea how Huang Flying Tiger got the idea that I was responsible for these two tragedies. He suddenly went mad and mutinied against me. He even went to the Gate of Noon to challenge me to a combat. Fortunately I escaped in time. I am glad that you, the Imperial Teacher, came back just in time. Please arrest this rebel for me so that he can receive the proper punishment."

A long silence ensued. Finally, in a stern voice, the Imperial Teacher responded. "According to the opinion of this loyal officer, I believe that Your Majesty Emperor violated your loyal officer. Nobleman Huang has always been the most loyal among your officers. It is an appropriate protocol for his wife to go to the Middle Palace to present her salutation to Queen Consort on New Year's Day, but there

326

was no reason for her to offend Queen Dar-Gee nor to commit suicide. Besides, the Starplucker Pavilion is your residence and no one is allowed there, especially ladies of her rank. How did she get there? There must be someone who is behind this scheme. You must have attempted to violate her, thus causing her to commit suicide. Queen Huang must have felt injustice for her sister-in-law's death and she went up to the Pavilion to argue with you and then, because of your intolerance of opinions against you, you threw her out of the Pavilion to her death. You have violated a just officer. Huang Flying Tiger did not offend you. There is a saying: `When an emperor is not righteous, officers move to other countries.' Huang Flying Tiger has always been loyal to you all his life; he never hesitated to sacrifice his life for you. Now, he could not even keep his wife from being slighted by you. He could not protect his sister from her horrible death. My sympathy is with him. Please issue an absolute pardon for Huang Flying Tiger so that I can persuade him to come back. Your country needs him."

"The Imperial Teacher is right. Your Majesty the Emperor, please issue an order of absolute pardon," all the officers concerted.

The Imperial Teacher paused for a while, then added, "What I have said refers to wrongs I think Your Majesty the Emperor did to Huang Flying Tiger. I do not know if Huang has also done anything wrong against Your Majesty. If so, I must also listen to the counterargument, too."

At this moment, a junior officer came out of his rank and asked to be heard.

"May I hear your opinion?" said the Imperial Teacher.

"The Emperor is certainly wrong to have committed the offenses you mentioned. However, Huang Flying Tiger is also wrong to have led his personal army to the Gate of Noon to challenge the Emperor. This is very wrong."

"Is that so?" the Imperial Teacher pondered. All the officers concurred with the accusation. "In that case, this is a serious offense that cannot be pardoned, at least according to existing laws." He turned to his attendants. "Quickly, send urgent messages to all frontier passes to stop the flight of Huang. Send relay messengers to the following frontier passes: Tong, Good Dream, and Blue Dragon. Ask them to send armies to rendezvous at a location that I will specify. I will personally bring Huang back to find the truth to settle this matter."

Following virtually the same route as Jiang Sarn during his escape, Huang's convoy went through the city of Meng Gin but bypassed the city of Ming Pond (Ming Tze) to avoid confrontation with the sentry commander of the city, Chang Kwei (Giant Step). They then headed towards the Frontier Pass Tong. As they moved along, suddenly they saw rising dust from three directions, from behind, directly ahead, and to the right. These rising dusts were from galloping horses of cavalries. The high-flying flag of the leading horseman pursuing from behind soon became discernible as that of the Imperial Teacher.

"I am doomed! With so few men how can I fight the almighty Imperial Teacher and other pursuers?" said the saddened Flying Tiger. "I am doomed to perish here." All the members of the convoy were saddened, too, and the air around Flying Tiger, his children, his warriors and his men was filled with anguish and indignation.

At this moment his rescue came. A demigod, Lord Gracious Virtue, who resided in Cavern Purple Sun in the Green Peak Mountain, happened to pass by the vicinity of Frontier Pass Tong at this particular moment. The air of sadness and indignation of Flying Tiger and his convoy had risen above the clouds and caught his attention. Years ago Lord Gracious Virtue had taken one of Huang's sons when he passed by his garden, and claimed the son as one of his disciples. The son, who was three when he was taken, would later be returned to Flying Tiger to join the revolutionary campaign. Finding the father of his disciple in grave danger, Lord Gracious Virtue decided to give a hand. He took out his Pennant Shroud, and with it he camouflaged Huang's convoy. As the Pennant Shroud covered Huang and his convoy, they found themselves enshrouded underneath a white canopy of foggy substance. They were puzzled, but they could not freely move. The Pennant Shroud generated a false scenery, creating a road that was far from the Huangs. Lord Gracious Virtue next cast a spell to distort the power of prognostication of the Imperial Teacher. Moments later, the Imperial Teacher and other pursuing armies converged together on the false road, and they found that Huang and his convoy had disappeared. A cloud of dust like that raised by a rapidly moving cavalry was seen at a distance moving towards Morning Song. The Imperial Teacher prognosticated the whereabouts of the Huangs. Because of the spell cast by Lord Gracious Virtue, the divination was distorted and the Imperial Teacher was informed by his prognostication that Huang's convoy had turned back to attack the capital city Morning Song, and this prognostication was verified by the rapidly moving cloud of dust. The Imperial Teacher hurriedly turned his troops back to chase the moving cloud of dust, and the rest of the pursuing troops were sent back to their points of origination.

After the pursuit was diverted, the Pennant Shroud was removed and Huang's convoy found themselves once again in the same location as before they were engulfed underneath the mysterious white canopy. "A bad dream this must be," mumbled Flying Tiger. After a recuperating rest, the whole convoy continued its flight.

Days later, Flying Tiger's convoy arrived at the vicinity of Frontier Pass Tong. The urgent message sent from the capital to intercept Huang had already arrived. The sentry commander, Chang Fung (Phoenix), who had previously refused Jiang Sarn's request to let a crowd of refugees escape through his frontier pass, was in full armor, waiting for Flying Tiger with an army in battle formation. "Please let my convoy pass. We are in distress," the Flying Tiger, on his Five Color Godspeed Ox, pleaded.

"For the sake of merely two women, you rebelled against Emperor Zoe? Your father and I are colleagues. Even so, I cannot let you pass. The best you can do, let me advise you, is to surrender and let me take you back to the capital. I will plead to the Emperor to have mercy on you. Perhaps he will pardon you. This is the best chance you have," Chang Phoenix arrogantly challenged.

"My dear Uncle Chang. You know how loyal I have been to the Emperor and to the Shang dynasty," pleaded Huang Flying Tiger. "I have performed my duties faithfully. You know that for some time the Emperor has long been indulging himself in wine and women, that he has distanced himself from virtuous and straight officers, and surrounded himself with sycophants of the court. I have engaged in hundreds of battles to defend his throne and the country. Not only has the Emperor not expressed appreciation for what I have done for him, he also wanted to violate my wife. My wife refused him and committed suicide. My sister argued with him and he threw her over the Starplucker Pavilion to her death. I only ask you, the brother colleague of my father, to let me through this frontier pass. I will forever be grateful to you."

"Nonsense." Angrily, Chang Phoenix hacked forcefully with his long-handled scimitar.

With his long spear, Huang deflected the thrust of the long-handled scimitar while pleading again for an understanding. "Please, my dear uncle colleague. If you were in the same position as I am now, you would do the same thing. Besides, there is the old saying : 'When the Emperor is not righteous, officers move to other countries.'"

"You rebel! How dare you argue against me!" Another thrust of his long scimitar followed.

Now, finally at the limit of his patience, Flying Tiger decided that this was as far as his observance of the protocol of respect for his father's colleague would go. He lunged his spear at Chang Phoenix. After 30 rounds of weapon clanking, Chang Phoenix weakened. He turned his horse around and escaped back towards the frontier pass. Flying Tiger chased him and as he was closing in, Chang took out a hidden weapon – a hammer ball with a long silk rope. Waiting for Flying Tiger to come close, Chang suddenly swung this hammer ball at him. Being an experienced warrior who had been exposed to all kinds of tricks and hidden weapons, Huang quickly drew his sword and with a fast swing, the rope was cut and the hammer ball flew harmlessly to the ground. Hopelessly defeated, Chang ran his horse back to his compound. Huang did not pursue any further.

After Chang Phoenix returned to the frontier pass, he sat down and think. "Flying Tiger is really as fierce a warrior as his reputation says. Let me take him by surprise." A scheme came to mind so he called one of his secondary warrior generals. "Where are you, Hsiao Silver?" beckoned Chang Phoenix at his best warrior.

Hsiao Silver quickly came forward. "At your command."

"Huang Flying Tiger defeated me in combat, and he destroyed my hidden weapon. But I must eliminate him. At dusk, bring three thousand archers with long bows and sneak as close to Huang's camp as possible. At the signal of a war rattle, you order these archers to shoot as many arrows as they can at the enemy's camp to kill them all."

Unknown to Chang Phoenix, Hsiao Silver at one time had served under the command of Flying Tiger. Under his fair and just supervision, Hsiao had advanced in rank and was finally transferred to his present position. Being a grateful person, and being dissatisfied with the current politics in the capital, Hsiao decided to inform Huang of his imminent danger. Dressed in black clothes suitable for night mission, Hsiao Silver sneaked to Huang's camp and asked to be shown to Huang.

"Who are you?" said Flying Tiger.

"You may not remember me. I used to serve under you. I know you are a just and righteous commander. You are in imminent danger now. I have been ordered by Chang Phoenix to lead three thousand archers to come here to shoot you and your men to death. You must get away as soon as possible," briefed Hsiao Silver.

"How can I escape," the startled Flying Tiger asked.

"At the second round of the night watchman's signal bang, I will wait for you at the main gate of the frontier pass. Bring your convoy to the gate quietly. I will open it to let you pass. There is no time to lose now. Quickly you must act," offered Hsiao.

Without waiting for a second, Huang ordered all his men to wake up and to prepare for immediate departure. Surely, at the second round of the night watchman's signal bang, Hsiao Silver was waiting at the pass.

The gate quietly opened. Flying Tiger and his convoy passed through without a hitch.

The noise of the passage of the convoy alerted Chang Phoenix and he discovered that Huang's convoy had already exited the frontier pass. "Damn me! I should have known that Hsiao used to serve under the command of Flying Tiger. All of you! Get out and chase them!" ordered Chang Phoenix.

Chang Phoenix was not aware that Hsiao Silver was waiting behind the gate ready to ambush him. As Chang appeared at the gate, Hsiao lunged his two-pronged spear at him, instantly killing him, and Chang Phoenix fell dead without even knowing who had ambushed him. Hsiao Silver then ran his horse towards the fleeing Huang and shouted, "I have killed Chang Phoenix and now you are safe. I do not know when we will meet again!"

"How can I reciprocate your great dispensation?" Flying Tiger thanked Hsiao Silver.

"Never mind. Take care!"

The danger was not over yet. This was but the first frontier pass, and there were four more to be negotiated. Eighty li beyond lay the Frontier Pass Lin Tong. Flying Tiger asked around to find out who the leader of defense was.

"Chen Tong, Your Highness," Flying Tiger was told.

Huang said nothing for a while. A warrior asked, "What's the matter?"

"Chen Tong used to serve under my command. He committed a serious infraction and he was supposed to be beheaded," replied Flying

333

Tiger. "His colleague warriors pleaded with me to spare him. I spared him but I also discharged him and threw him out. Now he is the commander of this frontier pass. He is certainly going to avenge this past discord."

Surely enough, Chen Tong was waiting in front of the gate of the frontier pass. He had been waiting for this day to come, to be able to carry out his vengeance. He cursed at Flying Tiger, "I am really glad that I have a chance to meet you here. Now I am under the command of the Imperial Teacher to arrest you. You can save yourself a lot of agony and trouble by surrendering to me peacefully."

"To hell with you. You were punished justifiably when you were under my command. It was too bad that I was too lenient and spared your life, at the pleading of your colleague warriors. If you want to avenge yourself, you just go ahead. I am waiting," responded Flying Tiger.

Chen Tong charged forward and thrust his long spear at Flying Tiger. Weapons clanked for around 20 rounds, then Chen Tong decided that he was no match for the weapon play of Flying Tiger, so he turned his horse around and retreated towards the frontier pass. Flying Tiger chased after him and as he closed in, Chen took out a hidden weapon from his purse – a poisonous dart called Fire Dragon Dart, a device taught to him by a traveling Taoist some time before. Chen Tong aimed the Fire Dragon Dart at Huang. The dart shot forward at a fantastic speed, drawing a trail of heavy black smoke behind. By the time he was aware of it, the Fire Dragon Dart had already hit Flying Tiger, instantly felling him to the ground. Huang's brother, Flying Tiger Cub, rushed to his rescue, but by the time he got to Flying Tiger, he was already deeply unconscious and presumed dead. One of the sworn brothers, warrior Zhou Chi charged forward to chase after Chen Tong. Another Fire

334

Dragon Dart was fired, leaving another trail of black smoke. Zhou Chi also fell. The rest of the warriors and soldiers from Flying Tiger's camp stampeded forward to rescue their wounded leader. It happened that dusk was setting in. With two major hits, Chen Tong decided to call it a day and retreated to his compound without further engagements.

Although Chen Tong had been chased away, Flying Tiger's camp was now without a leader. They were at a critical moment of anguish and torment; they could not pass through this crucial frontier pass, neither could they retreat.

Lord Gracious Virtue, who'd rescued Huang earlier in his flight, was alerted to the misfortune of Flying Tiger during his daily mental exercise. "It is time for the son to meet the father." Summoning his disciple Heavenly Compliance to his presence, the Lord said, "It is time for you to go to your father's rescue."

"Who is my father?" the surprised Heavenly Compliance said.

"I took you from your father when you were three, while you were playing in his back garden. I took you because we have a destined teacher-disciple relationship that must be fulfilled. You will soon join your father, but not yet. However, your father, Huang Flying Tiger, is now in grave danger of death. You must rescue him. As soon as he is safe, do not linger; come back immediately. But I do not intend to keep you here forever; you will have an important mission to accomplish and you will join your father not too long after this rescue effort."

Heavenly Compliance, a tiger-build youth with forceful eyes, was instructed in the use of various magical devices his teacher entrusted to him. "Now you are ready to go. He is some twenty li from Frontier Pass

Lin Tong. You will recognize his camp easily as there are no other inhabitants nearby," Lord Gracious Virtue said.

Applying the Tao of terra-trekking, Tien-hua arrived at the vicinity of Frontier Pass Lin Tong around midnight, and without any trouble he found his father's camp.

"Who are you, Taoist," the guard at the encampment asked.

"I am from Cavern Purple Sun in the Green Peak Mountain. I know that your master is in trouble. I am here to save him. Please admit me," replied Heavenly Compliance.

Flying Tiger Cub, brother of Flying Tiger, quickly went to meet this Taoist. "Can you really save my brother," he asked, while surprised at the likeness between the Taoist and his mortally wounded brother.

"Yes, take me to him as soon as possible," responded Heavenly Compliance.

When Heavenly Compliance saw his father, pale and unconscious, he felt a sense of sadness. "My father, what are you doing here? Where is your fame, your glory, and your power?" thought Heavenly Compliance, who had been educated under Taoist principles to abandon all worldly amenities. He took a look at his father, then looked at the other wounded warrior. "Who is the other?" he said.

"He is a sworn brother of mine and also of my wounded brother," responded Flying Tiger Cub.

"I will heal them both. Fetch me some water," Heavenly Compliance said. Taking two balls of decoction made of herbs from a basket he was carrying, he mixed the medicine with water. He then forced the mixture down the throats of the two wounded. Lo and behold, minutes later, the two yelled in pain and regained consciousness.

"Where am I? Did he get away? — Who is this Taoist here?" said Flying Tiger.

"Father, I am your lost son. I was taken by my teacher when I disappeared from your back garden thirteen years ago. I was only three then. My teacher, Lord Gracious Virtue, said that I was destined to be his disciple, so he took me to his cavern, raised me and taught me Tao. He knew you were in danger so he dispatched me to save you. Now we are reunited again, and I am glad to have an opportunity to meet my brothers, my uncles and your sworn brothers. Now where is my mother? How could you have left her behind?"

"She is the reason that I mutinied against this evil Emperor Zoe. On New Year's Day, she went to salute the Queen according to protocols of the kingdom. Emperor Zoe tried to violate her and she committed suicide by jumping over of the railing of the balcony of the Starplucker Pavilion. Your aunt went to the Pavilion to argue with the Emperor and he threw her to her death." Stomping his feet heavily against the ground, in tears Flying Tiger briefed his newly reunited son of his misfortunes.

"Gods damn him ..." before finishing the sentence, out of his rage and grief Heavenly Compliance fainted. After regaining consciousness, he swore, "I will give up my study of Tao in the Green Peak Mountain to avenge my mother and my aunt. Let us go back to the capital to eliminate the evil Emperor."

While they were conversing, the late night had turned into dawn. Not long after the sun rose, guards reported that Chen Tong was

337

challenging for combat. Upon this challenge, the face of Flying Tiger immediately turned pale.

"Don't worry, just go out to face his challenge. I am here. I will protect you," Heavenly Compliance assured his father.

Half-believing what Heavenly Compliance said, Flying Tiger put on his golden armor and mounted his Five Color Godspeed Ox to face the challenger. "Today is my day of revenge against your dart!" shouted Flying Tiger at Chen Tong.

Ten or fifteen rounds of weapon clanking later, Chen Tong turned around and retreated. Flying Tiger also stopped.

"Go and chase after him, I am here to protect you," said Heavenly Compliance.

Flying Tiger, though afraid of the Fire Dragon Dart, reluctantly began his chase after Chen Tong. Again, a Fire Dragon Dart was fired. Heavenly Compliance uncovered his basket and turned it towards the dart. Suddenly it changed its course and fell harmlessly into the basket. Another one was fired and again it harmlessly homed into the basket. One by one, the Fire Dragon Darts homed towards the basket. Finally, Chen Tong exhausted all his darts. "Any more?" the encouraged Flying Tiger said.

Chen Tong, finding that his Fire Dragon Dart ineffective, charged towards Heavenly Compliance. "You damned Taoist, you have destroyed my Tao. I am going to get you."

Unsheathing a sword that he carried on his back, the Heavenly Compliance pointed it at Chen Tong. A little star of light, the size of a plate, emerged from the tip of the sword and moved swiftly towards Chen Tong. The little star of light passed through his neck. After the star of light passed, Chen Tong's facial expression suddenly froze and a moment later, his head fell off his shoulders and his body collapsed onto the ground. This sword, by the name of "Precious Sword of Moya", was a mascot treasure of Cavern Purple Sun. It was capable of killing an enemy from a great distance with its flying star of light.

With the death of the sentry commander, Huang's fierce warriors had no difficulty dispersing Chen Tong's army. Chopping down the lock on the main gate of Frontier Pass Lin Tong, they emerged on the other side, free and well.

"I must bid you farewell now, my dear father," wept Heavenly Compliance.

"Can't you come with us," asked Flying Tiger sadly.

"No, I must not disobey my teacher. My teacher promised me that we will be reunited soon," responded Heavenly Compliance.

"Where and when are we going to meet again?" said the father.

"In West Branch City, soon. Farewell." With these words they parted sadly, but with the faith that the promise of reunion would be fulfilled.

Another eighty li later, Flying Tiger's convoy arrived at the vicinity of Frontier Pass Penetrating Clouds. Escaped army remnants of Chen Tong had already reported the anticipated arrival of Huang's convoy to Chen Woo, the sentry commander of Frontier Pass Penetrating Clouds, who happened to be a brother of Chen Tong. Chen Woo was saddened by his brother's death and wanted to have an immediate confrontation with Huang and his convoy to avenge his brother. Collecting all his warriors, he made known his plan.

An officer went forward and asked, "May I say a word?"

"What do you have to say?" responded Chen Woo angrily and impatiently .

"In my humble opinion, you must not rush into action. It is true all of us want to help you to avenge the death of your brother, but please remember that Flying Tiger is a very fierce warrior, and he is aided by four equally fierce warriors who are his sworn brothers. We must use a scheme to trap them unguarded. Let me present you a plan," Warrior Hou San suggested.

"Tell me your plan," Chen Woo said.

"You should do this and that ..." said Hou San.

"Great! It is a fantastic scheme," consented the elated Chen Woo.

As Huang and his convoy approached, Chen Woo ordered his warriors to mount their horses, unarmed, and wait at the gate of the frontier pass to greet Huang.

"General Huang, I offer you my most sincere greetings and welcome. I offer you free and unobstructed passage through this frontier pass." said Chen Woo.

Flying Tiger had not expected that he would be welcomed by Chen Woo, especially after killing his brother Chen Tong to get there. "I apologize for my encounter with your brother, General Chen Woo. I apologize that he was killed in his action against me and my men. You are a reasonable man. I will forever remember your grace," said Huang Flying Tiger.

"You have a justifiable cause to escape the evil deeds and the tyranny of the Emperor. My brother was stupid to try to stop you. He deserved whatever fate fell upon him. Your mutiny is justified; for generations your family has served the dynasty with loyalty and you have been treated unjustly. Now may I offer you and your men a repast before you leave this frontier pass?" Chen Woo asked obligingly.

"What a difference between the two brothers," muttered Huang Ming, sworn brother of Flying Tiger.

A banquet was served to Huang and his warriors. The thousand men were also fed an equally delicious meal. Chen Woo ordered music to be played, and dances to be performed. Soon dusk fell and the banquet went on, into the darkness of night.

"Since it is too late for you to leave today, will you stay here for the night? You can leave at daybreak," Chen Woo politely suggested.

"This might not be a good place to stay for too long," thought Flying Tiger. However, Huang Ming, who had enjoyed this dinner thoroughly, seconded the suggestion of Cheng Woo: "It is too late, and General Chen is so earnest. We must not decline his hospitality."

After the past few days of toil and camp food, Flying Tiger's convoy took advantage of the banquet and they accepted the offer of a good night's rest under a real roof and not tent tops. Soon snores were heard everywhere. Huang Flying Tiger, with heavy thoughts upon him, could not sleep too well. As the night watchman patrolling the streets with the banging of a bamboo rattle came by the second time (around ten o'clock by our reckoning), he woke up from his nightmares and could sleep no further. He decided to read, so he lighted a candle. Just then, the feeble candlelight suddenly flickered and a hand, coming out of nowhere, extinguished the flame. Startled, Flying Tiger said, "Who are you? Are you a demon?"

An agonizing female voice feebly screamed, "No, I am not a demon. I am the spirit of your wife. Your life is in danger now. This guesthouse will soon be on fire. Act quickly to save my children and the others. I am a spirit now and cannot stay with you for long. I must depart now." Immediately afterwards, the candlelight miraculously came back.

Slapping his palm hard on the desk, the alarmed Flying Tiger shouted, "Get up! Get up!"

Huang Ming and the rest of the sworn brothers woke up, and said, "We are resting from these days of hardship, why do you wake us up?"

"Our lives are in danger!" Flying Tiger then briefly related the message delivered through his wife's voice.

Flying Tiger Cub, brother of Flying Tiger, agreed. "I would rather believe this warning even if it may turn out to be a false alarm." Surely enough, they found that the gate of the guesthouse was locked from the outside.

Quickly waking up the rest of his men, Flying Tiger, his brothers, and his sworn brothers broke open the door with axes. They found piles of fire wood outside the residential hall, soaked with oil, ready to be kindled. Gathering his men and his carts outside, Huang's convoy was ready to escape.

At this moment, Chen Woo arrived – unfortunately for him, a little too late.

"You treacherous thief! You tried to deceive me with your false kindness!" Flying Tiger accused.

"You thing! You murdered my brother. Unfortunately my scheme failed. Now it is the time for us to settle things once and for all!" challenged Chen Woo. As he rolled his horse forward, Flying Tiger had already mounted his Five Color Godspeed Ox and with his long spear in his hands, he was ready for action.

Naturally Chen Woo was no match for the fighting skill of Flying Tiger. In less than five rounds, Chen Woo was pierced through his heart and he fell dead. The gate of the Frontier Pass Penetrating Clouds was opened and once again Flying Tiger and his men were on their way to freedom.

Another seventy or eighty li later, they arrived at the outskirts of Frontier Pass Boundary Marker. "This should be an easy one, since the sentry leader is my father," announced Flying Tiger.

To their surprise, the group was greeted by 3000 fully armed soldiers in a battle formation, with his father Huang Gwen (Roll) also in full armor. Alongside there were ten prisoner transport carts.

"It does not look good. What does my father want to do with the army and the prisoner carts?" muttered Flying Tiger.

As Huang Flying Tiger neared, he tried to find out what was going on. He gently approached and bowed slightly on the saddle of his Five Color Godspeed Ox. He then said, "My dear father, I haven't seen you for a long time, how are you doing? Is there any reason that you have to greet me, your most accomplished son, with a full display of military power?"

"You traitor! The Huang family has served Shang emperors with unquestioned loyalty for over seven generations. Our family is proud never to have had a criminal under its family name. Now you, for the sake of a woman, have mutinied against the Emperor. How dare you face me?"

While Flying Tiger still pondered between loyalty and vengeance, Huang Ming, one of the four sworn brothers, shouted, "The Emperor is corrupt and evil. He never expressed gratitude for our fealty and service. He deserves to be overthrown. We already fought numerous combats to get here; why should we give up now?"

Huang Roll angrily shouted back, "You traitors, you thieves! You want to persuade my son to continue his mutiny? Watch out for my scimitar!"

Quickly, Huang Ming deflected the thrust of the long-handled scimitar with his long-handled battle-ax.

"You are within your right to yell at your sons. But we are not your sons or your subordinates. As for your intention to take your son prisoner, my Senior General, you are utterly wrong. Even a poisonous snake does not bite its offspring. A ferocious tiger does not eat its own cubs. Your son just suffered the great loss of his virtuous wife and his righteous sister. You suffered the loss of a devoted daughter and daughter-in-law. And you still think of nothing but fealty! Haven't you seen enough corruption and evil doings in the court? All you speak about is fealty. You haven't thought of the horrible death of your daughter-in-law, and the murder of your daughter by the evil Emperor. We are doing the right thing, like the old saying: 'When the Emperor is not righteous, officers move to other countries. When the father does not take care of his children, children go away.' Wake up, you old man."

"You devil and your evil words!" Huang Roll continued his thrust of his long scimitar against Huang Ming, who deflected the thrust once again. "I have been trying to reason with you. I am stronger and younger than you are. Stop this nonsense before I hurt you."

The long scimitar and the long battle-ax clanked. The three other sworn brothers joined in the combat, surrounding the senior Huang. As the combat proceeded, Flying Tiger hesitated and debated which side he should join. Sensing this indecision, Huang Ming bellowed at the top of his lungs to the rest of the convoy, "You idiots, what are you waiting for? Quickly, run your men and carts through the gate of the frontier pass while we are engaging this old man in combat! Go! Go!" Before Flying Tiger could make up his mind, the rest of his brothers and followers knocked down the guards at the gate and they all rushed through the frontier pass.

As soon as the entire convoy had exited through the gate, the four sworn brothers stopped their combat against the senior Huang.

"You treacherous traitors. You have destroyed my career. I am finished. I am going to commit suicide now." Drawing his sword, Huang Roll was prepared to kill himself by slashing his own throat.

"You cannot do this." Huang Ming jumped out and knocked down the sword before the senior Huang could hurt himself. "Don't you know that your evil son threatened to kill all of us if we do not go along with him? I tried to send you a message, but you kept on arguing against me. You missed your chance to arrest him because of your engagement in combat with us."

Though this explanation was apparently a transparent lie, after all the recent excitement and the emotional strain that followed, unconsciously the senior Huang was more than eager to have a way out, and this explanation, though illogical, was as good as any in the midst of a confusion. The senior Huang asked, "What are we going to do now?"

"I have a scheme for you," Huang Ming offered. "Go out of the gate of the frontier pass. Ask your son and his convoy to come back. Tell him that I, Huang Ming, convinced you to leave your post to join him to go to West Branch City together, but you want to have some time to pack up. He will come back. You then feast him and his convoy. I will round up my sworn brothers and some men to prepare to ambush them during the feast. When you ring a signal bell, we will come out from hiding places and arrest your sons and their followers. How does this scheme sound to you?"

"An excellent idea."

The senior Huang thus rode his horse out of the main gate and chased after his son. He beckoned them to come back, giving the reasons he was instructed. Knowing that Huang Ming was scheming something, Flying Tiger collected his men and they went back to the frontier pass. Meanwhile, Huang Ming had asked his sworn brothers to organize a group of men to pack up all the precious belongings of the senior Huang and load them onto carts.

A banquet was served. After several rounds of toasts were made, the senior Huang rang the signal bell. Nothing happened. He rang the bell again, and again nothing happened. Huang Ming pretended not to notice. The senior Huang asked an attendant to summon Huang Ming to come to his table, and said, "I rang the bell several times. You did not make any move. Why?"

"We have not completely assembled our hatchet men yet and we are not quite ready. We must be absolutely sure of our readiness, otherwise your son may notice irregularities."

Just at this time, the senior Huang saw smoke and fire rising from the warehouse where military supplies were kept. "You deceived me! You schemed against me!"

"To tell you the truth, this evil Emperor will never reform. If you do not leave with us, you are also doomed since the military supply under your command is on fire. You will have to face a court martial and you know the penalty. You had better join us," persuaded Huang Ming.

"I am forced to abandon seven generations of fealty to the Shang throne. It is not my fault, but I have no other alternatives," sighed the senior Huang.

Leading his private army of 3000, the senior Huang joined his son's mutiny against Emperor Zoe. As they moved along, the senior Huang briefed his son and other warriors, "In another eighty li we will arrive at the last Frontier Pass, Vast Water. The commander of the guarding regiment is Han Yung the Glory. Under his command is an invincible warrior general by the name of Yue Hua Variant. He studied elfin Tao in his youth and he is a master of this art. He is thus nicknamed 'Seven Head Warrior.' He rides a Fiery-Eyed Golden Pupil Beast, and uses a long two-pronged spear as his weapon. He has invincible magic power. I do not think we can defeat him. You should have let me take you back to the capital; at least I could have pleaded for mercy for your lives. Now, he certainly will catch all of us, and if we are delivered to the capital, we will be just as good as dead."

Having gone this far, and having encountered numerous hardships which were eventually overcome, all the warriors of the group were rather unimpressed by this warning and in fact annoyed by the senior Huang's briefings.

War among Gods and Men

The next morning, having received the report that the mutineer Huang Flying Tiger had convinced his father to join his rebellion, Han Glory ordered Yue Variant to stop the Huangs. Riding his Fiery-Eyed Golden Pupil Beast, Yue Variant challenged the Huangs for combat.

Mounting his Five Color Godspeed Ox, Flying Tiger, with his long spear, went out to face the Seven Head Warrior.

"Who are you?" Said Yue Variant.

"I am Nobleman Huang. Emperor Zoe has done me wrong and now I am on my way to join Duke of West. Please let me pass. I will be forever grateful to you," answered Flying Tiger.

"I have my duty to defend this frontier pass. You are now a traitor. I cannot let you pass. Let me advise you to surrender now. You have many friends in the court; they will plead to the Emperor for a pardon. It is useless for you to plead with me. I am only doing my duty," responded Yue Variant.

"Ha! I have already gotten through four of the five frontier passes. Do you think you can stop me? Watch out!" The Flying Tiger on his Five Color Godspeed Ox marched forward to challenge Yue with his long spear. Ten rounds later, Yue was no match to Flying Tiger's fighting skill. Turning around, he ran back towards the frontier pass.

Flying Tiger chased him. As Flying Tiger neared, Yue took out a black flag, called "Soul Snatching Flag," given to him by a heresy Taoist, Demigod Unique Essence. With an incantation, Yue raised the black flag and, amidst several dark columns of smoke, Flying Tiger disappeared. When he woke up, he was already tied up facing Han Glory.

"The Emperor did not do you wrong. You have all glories that any one can dream about. Why do you rebel?" said Han.

"The Emperor is evil and his dreadful deeds are beyond description," responded Flying Tiger. "You know nothing about the corruption and the brutality that go on in the court. You should be ashamed of yourself for being faithful and loyal to such an evil emperor. You are only usurping the power given to you by the evil Emperor. You did not defeat me honorably over a fair combat; you used your elfin Tao to catch me. I am already prepared to die for my cause."

"I do not want to kill you. I will deliver all of you to the Emperor for his disposal and at his pleasure," laughed Han.

The next morning, the Seven Head Warrior again went to challenge. The two sworn brothers, Huang Ming and Zhou Chi, volunteered to face the challenge. Thirty rounds later, again Yue turned back. Again, he used his Soul Snatching Flag and captured the two.

The remaining warriors, including the brothers of Flying Tiger, rushed forward to the rescue of the two. One of the brothers pierced the left leg of Yue Variant with his long spear. However, this wound did not disable the magical power of Yue. Again, he used his Soul Snatching Flag and captured them all. They were put in the same prison with Flying Tiger.

With no more warriors, the senior Huang decided to beg Han Glory to let at least one of his grandchildren escape to West Branch City, to preserve the lineage of the family of Huang. Packing all his valuable assets, he went to see Han Glory and begged him to let one of his grandsons leave, in exchange for all his valuable assets.

Han Glory merely laughed. "You the Huangs, you have gotten the utmost prominence, position and wealth from the Emperor. Why do you want to rebel? There is no way I can let you off. Guards, imprison them all."

Thus all Huang's family was arrested and all Huang's soldiers and followers were taken prisoner. Transport carts were readied to take the prisoners back to the capital, the city of Morning Song. Yue Variant, having recovered from his wound by application of a magical herb given to him previously by his teacher, Demigod Unique Essence, volunteered to escort the prisoners to the capital.

Two days later, the procession with the prisoners arrived at Frontier Pass Boundary Marker. Street people rushed to see their former governor and his family in prison transport carts. They all felt sorry because the senior Huang had been a good governor.

Meanwhile, during his daily mental exercises, Demigod Great Unity, the teacher of Nata, sensed the danger to Flying Tiger and his convoys. Summoning Nata to his seat of meditation, he instructed him to go to the rescue of the Huangs. "Go there and save them. Deliver them outside Frontier Pass Vast Water, then come back. You will soon join them, but this time you should only perform a rescue mission."

After several years of studying Tao, the unruly behavior of Nata had been tamed. However, having lived the rather rigid life of a Taoist in a high remote mountain, he was more than eager to go out to the world of dust, even just for a little while. Immediately, after stuffing his magical devices into his leopardskin bag, he mounted his Wheel of Wind and Fire to go to the Frontier Pass Boundary Marker.

When he arrived, Yue's procession had already passed the Frontier Pass Boundary Marker and was on the second leg of the trip to the capital city, Morning Song. Having learned manners during his study of Tao from Demigod Great Unity, Nata had become more rational. "How can I provoke a conflict without reason? I must find an excuse first," he told himself. He devised a simple scheme. Standing on the narrowest part of the mountain path, he declared, "This is my territory. All passersby must pay me a toll at my discretion." As Yue approached, Nata started to sing a song:

> I was born of heaven,
> But heaven I fear not, only my teacher.
> Yesterday my old man passed by,
> And a gold brick he had to leave as toll.

"Who are you? What do you mean by paying you a toll?" said Yue.

"I own this place now. Pay me your toll and I will let you pass," answered Nata.

"This road is owned by the Emperor and no one is authorized to collect a toll. I am on an official mission to deliver a batch of prisoners to the capital. You had better let me pass, otherwise I will have to kill you," Yue Variant declared, affirming his authority.

"I see. You are a government official," said Nata. "All right, I will give you a special discount. Pay me a toll of ten large gold bricks, then I will let you pass." Finally, the excuse to provoke a conflict had been found.

"You idiot! You asked for it." On his Fiery-Eyed Golden Pupil Beast, Yue charged forward with his long two-pronged spear.

With his fire-tipped long spear, it was a relatively easy task for Nata to overpower Yue. Turning around, Yue again took out his Soul Snatching Flag. Unknown to Yue, Nata did not have the usual soul that this flag was designed to snatch – he had been revivified by Tao and reincarnated from lotus flowers, stems and leaves. Opening up his

351

leopardskin bag, at Nata's beckoning, the Soul Snatching Flag together with its several black columns of smoke converged and disappeared into the bag. "Any more worthless tricks?" said Nata.

Figure I- 22. Nata and Seven Head Warrior Yue

Yue immediately turned around and ran back towards his procession. Fearing that Yue might decide to harm the prisoners, Nata took out his boomerang gold brick and with a quick throw, it crashed through Yue's rear armor plate and instantly he coughed out blood. He

352

escaped on his Fiery-Eyed Golden Pupil Beast to the wilderness, and ran his beast as fast as he could to escape from the powerful Nata.

After chasing Yue for a while, Nata reminded himself of the purpose of his mission and he turned back. He next threw the boomerang gold brick at the prison guards, who immediately dispersed in all directions. After knocking down the locks on the prisoner transport carts, all the prisoners were freed. Nata then introduced himself and told them, "I will go with you to overtake Frontier Pass Vast Water."

"Thank you. We will forever be grateful to you." Picking up the weapons left by the fleeing guards, the entire group marched on foot towards Frontier Pass Vast Water.

Meanwhile the defeated Yue Variant rode his Fiery-Eyed Golden Pupil Beast back to the frontier pass as fast as he could and he arrived the next day.

Surprised at his swift return, Han Glory sensed something wrong. "You appear wounded. What happened?"

"The procession marched effortlessly to the vicinity of Frontier Pass of Penetrating Clouds. Suddenly a Taoist, mounting a pair of Wheels of Wind and Fire, intercepted us. He blocked our movement on a rather narrow mountain pass. Without even telling me his name, he demanded ten pieces of large gold bricks as the toll of passage. I told him to get lost. He then engaged in a weapon combat against me and I was losing. I took out my Soul Snatching Flag, but he overpowered the Tao of the Flag and took it away from me. Then he threw a piece of yellow metallic thing at me, and nearly broke my neck. I ran back as fast as I could," Yue Variant answered, rather distressed.

"What happened to the Huangs," asked Han.

353

"Don't know."

"All our efforts are in vain! I will be blamed by the Emperor as careless! Now I am in trouble," sighed Han Glory fretfully.

"They haven't escaped back through this frontier pass yet. Maybe we should send an urgent message to the capital to ask for reinforcements," suggested Yue Variant.

Unfortunately for them, their time had just ran out. "A Taoist riding on a pair of wheels just appeared, and he demanded to meet the Seven Head Warrior." reported a guard.

"It must be the same guy," said Yue Variant.

"I will meet him myself," vowed Han Glory angrily. With several thousand soldiers behind him, Han went out to face the challenger.

"I want Yue Variant, not you," challenged Nata.

"Who are you?" said Han Glory.

"My name is Li Nata. I am a disciple of Demigod Great Unity, of Cavern Golden Ray in Mount Genesis. My teacher instructed me to rescue the Huangs. I just encountered Yue Variant, and I only wounded him. I am here to finish him."

"You rebel! You have committed a capital crime to have intercepted imperial prisoners. I am going to kill you," charged Han Glory.

"You stupid idiot! The Shang dynasty is rapidly coming to an end," retorted Nata. "The idiotic Emperor even forced their key general, Huang Flying Tiger, into rebellion. Now the dynasty is opposed by all four dukes. You must realize that you are opposing the wishes of the heaven to continue to defend this decaying dynasty."

354

Han Glory spoke no further but ordered his army on a fullscale attack against Nata. The powerful thrust of Nata's fire-tipped spear felled many warriors on Han's side. As the fighting went on, Flying Tiger and his group arrived on foot. Seeing their enemy, their eyes turned red and they all fought as mightily as they could. "Get Han Glory! Don't let him escape!" they shouted angrily. Nata took out his boomerang gold brick and with a single throw, Han's breast armor was broken. Another throw at Yue Variant broke his arm. Both of them ran towards wilderness and soon disappeared. A few days later, after Han Glory learned that the Huangs had left, he came back to the frontier pass. However, Yue Variant never came back and was presumed dead.

The Huangs then took over the frontier pass. First they released their soldiers and followers from prison, they then recovered all their belongings from Han's residence. While they were at it, they also removed whatever valuables they could find from Han's possession. They rested for one night while Nata stood on guard. The next morning they opened the gate of the frontier pass and exited.

Nata escorted the convoy to Ridge Golden Rooster, then he bid them goodbye. "You are in the territory of Zhou Dukedom now. You do not need me anymore. But I will join you soon when the revolutionary campaign begins. Farewell."

"How can we thank you?" Huang said gratefully, on behalf of the entire group.

"We will be colleagues in the near future. There is no need for you to thank me. Take good care of yourselves and I will see you soon."

With no further incidents, the entire convoy trekked through the hilly paths of Mount First Morning Sun and crossed Ridge Peach

Blossom. Thirty li from West Branch City, Flying Tiger stopped the convoy. "We are in a new territory and a new country now. Let me go into the city alone to ask the king to admit us. If they welcome us, we can go in. Otherwise we have to consider other alternatives."

"Very good idea. We will wait here," the senior Huang answered.

Flying Tiger trotted his Five Color Godspeed Ox and entered West Branch City. The city was evidently orderly governed; people were prosperous and polite. "What a difference!" muttered Flying Tiger. Flying Tiger stopped a passerby. "May I ask where is the official residence of Premier Jiang?"

"Just across the Little Golden Bridge over there. You can't miss it," the passerby answered.

Arriving at the official residence of the premier, Huang knocked at the door. "Please report to the premier that Huang Flying Tiger from the capital city of Morning Song asks the favor to have an audience with the premier." Flying Tiger then handed over his visiting card.

Jiang Sarn was surprised. He muttered to himself, "The only Huang Flying Tiger in Morning Song I know of is Nobleman Huang. How and why is he here? What happened?" Putting on his official dress, he went to the formal reception hall and asked the guards to admit Flying Tiger. However, Flying Tiger did not enter the hall and only stood at the entrance of the reception hall under the eaves.

Jiang Sarn approached the entrance and bowed. "I am extremely honored by your visit. Unfortunately I did not know in advance so that I could personally greet you at the city gate. Please forgive me. Please come in."

356

Flying Tiger bowed deeply but did not enter. "I am grateful for your courtesy to allow me to see you. I am in distress."

Jiang Sarn again bowed and extended his invitation to Flying Tiger once again to enter the hall. This time Flying Tiger accepted the invitation. Upon entry to the hall, he was offered the seat reserved for the most honored guest. He declined politely. "I am a rebel officer from the court of Shang. It is more than my pleasure just to stand here to talk to you."

"When I served in the Shang court, my rank was far below yours. It is certainly proper for you to sit at the most honored guest seat. Please," insisted Jiang Sarn.

"Thank you for your kindness." Flying Tiger then sat down.

"May I hear the reason why you abandoned the Shang court?" Jiang Sarn said.

"As you know, Emperor Zoe has distanced himself from righteous officers and surrounded himself with toadies and sycophants. He indulges himself in wine and women. He slaughters loyal officers merely because he disliks their criticisms. During the past New Year, my wife went to the court to pay the annual tribute to the Queen, in accordance with the proper protocol. Queen Dar-Gee schemed against her and forced her to jump from the Starplucker Pavilion to commit suicide. My sister, who was the reigning queen of the West Palace, went to the Starplucker Pavilion to reason with the Emperor. Out of rage, he threw my sister out of the Pavilion to her death. As the saying goes: 'When the Emperor is not righteous, officers move to other countries.' I therefore mutinied against Shang. I fought through the five frontier passes to get here. I wish to offer the service of my entire family and my men to accommodate the desires of the king and you."

"It will be a great honor to have you as my colleague. Your ability is well-known. Please stay here while I go to the palace immediately to inform the king of your arrival. I am sure that he will be as glad to see you as I am. I will be back as soon as is feasible." Extremely excited by the possibility of the addition of a very capable general, Jiang Sarn immediately departed for the palace.

Jiang Sarn was admitted to the presence of the new king in no time. "My proxy father the premier, may I be of service to you?" King of Arms said.

"Congratulations! Nobleman Huang Flying Tiger just abandoned Emperor Zoe to come here. He asks for your permission to serve you."

"Is he *the* Nobleman Huang, who is an in-law relative of Emperor Zoe?" said King of Arms.

"Indeed he is. On many occasions the late duke expressed gratitude for Huang's help in his flight from the city of Morning Song. Please accommodate him," Jiang Sarn answered.

"Of course. Ask him to come to the palace immediately." An official invitation was issued.

Moments later, Flying Tiger showed up. Kneeling down in front of King of Arms, Huang Flying Tiger saluted. "Salutations to the king of a thousand years!"

"Please rise. I have often heard about your kindness and consideration for people. It is my pleasure to be able to meet you in person," King of Arms said.

"Thank you for your kindness. I wish to have the honor to serve you faithfully," the grateful Flying Tiger responded.

"What was General Huang's rank in the Shang court," King of Arms asked Jiang Sarn.

"He had the title of Master Lord of National Poise."

"Let me offer him the same rank. I will only change a word in his title: Master Lord of National Constituent," suggested the king.

Flying Tiger thanked the king. A banquet of celebration followed, and during the banquet Flying Tiger related to the king the evil deeds of Emperor Zoe. At the end of the banquet, the king asked Jiang Sarn to select a provident day to start construction of an official residence for Flying Tiger.

The next day, Flying Tiger attended his first court session, during which he was introduced to all officers present. At the end of the court session, he bid to speak. "My father, my brothers, my sworn brothers, my sons and four thousand men are awaiting thirty li from the city gate. May I have your permission to bring them into the city?"

"Indeed so. All of them will be granted the same title and position as they had in the Shang court," King of Arms said and all officers concurred with a warm applause.

Thus King of Arms gained not only Flying Tiger as a capable general, but also an assembly of competent warriors. However, most importantly, he gained much inside information about the court of Emperor Zoe that would be needed in the forthcoming revolutionary campaign.

War among Gods and Men

12. Quest of West Branch City

During his pursuit of Flying Tiger, through a momentary slip-up, somehow the Tao of the Imperial Teacher did not overcome the distortion cast upon his power of prognostication. This slip-up was likely an omen of the destined fall of the Shang dynasty. Normally, the Imperial Teacher, being an accomplished disciple of Holy Mother Golden Spirit of Palace Green Roam, and having been thoroughly trained in the wisdom of Tao, should have easily detected this distortion. By the time he and his troops chased the moving cloud of dust to the vicinity of Morning Song, the cloud mysteriously disappeared and he soon discovered that Flying Tiger and his men had never returned to attack the city as he had prognosticated. Now they must be long gone. He had no explanation for his failure. As he narrated his unsuccessful mission to court officers who gathered to hear about his quest for the Huangs, the crowd fell silent. To lessen his embarrassment, the Imperial Teacher said, "Huang has no way to get out of this country; the southern escape route is secured by the almighty Chang Kwei Fang the Fragrant Cassia at Frontier Pass Blue Dragon, the northern passage by the four Mo brothers. If he tries to go westward, he will encounter five invincible frontier passes. If he tries to escape eastward, he has to pass us first. I am sure that it will be a only a matter of time before he is captured." The court session ended in subdued silence.

Days later, a messenger reported: "A secondary warrior Hsiao Silver killed the sentry commander Chang Phoenix of Frontier Pass Tong and let Flying Tiger escape." The Imperial Teacher said nothing. Soon afterwards, another report came: "Chen Tong, the sentry commander of Frontier Pass Lin Tong, was killed by Flying Tiger." Before the Imperial

Teacher could act, another report came: "Flying Tiger also killed Chen Woo, the sentry commander of Frontier Pass Penetrating Clouds." Another report soon followed: "The sentry commander of Frontier Pass Boundary Marker, Huang Roll, joined the mutiny party of his son." Then another message came from the sentry commander Han Glory of Frontier Pass Vast Water: "Urgent request for reinforcements to stop the flight of Huang and his convoy." Finally, the most devastating report arrived: "An unknown Taoist rescued the Huangs and defeated the defender of Frontier Pass Vast Water to let Huangs escape to Zhou Dukedom. Flying Tiger is now appointed the Master Lord of National Constituent of Zhou Dukedom."

Sitting in his office, the Imperial Teacher became extremely frenzied. He shouted loudly at himself: "I, the prince regent, was entrusted by the late Emperor with the well-being of the current Emperor. Now, unfortunately because of the evil deeds of the Emperor, rebellions abound. Deplorably, the tragedy during the New Year's Day caused an important officer of the court to defect. Yet as the highest-ranking officer of the court, I failed in my effort to stop his flight. The fate of this country is now in jeopardy. I must not fail again. I must not fail the trust my late Emperor placed upon me. I am ready to die for my duty."

He then called his disciples to his presence, and gave the order: "Bang war drums to summon all warriors and generals to my conference hall." Soon enough, war drum signals were heard all over the city to request all ranking warriors and generals to report. They soon gathered in the meeting hall of the residence of the Imperial Teacher.

"Gentlemen, we are here to discuss an urgent matter," announced the Imperial Teacher. "As you know, Flying Tiger has mutinied against the Emperor. He has sworn his loyalty to Chi-Fa, the new Duke West.

362

We know the ambition of Chi-Fa. We must do something to stop him. In the first place, Flying Tiger is now a rebel and must be caught and brought to the capital to be tried for treason. In the second place, if we do not stop the expansion of Zhou Dukedom now, we will soon suffer the consequences. What is your opinion? I wish to hear anything you have to say."

Ru Brave, the general who had successfully defended Mustang Ridge some time before, spoke first. "Let this unworthy general present his opinion to the Imperial Teacher. For years Duke East, Jiang Wen-huan, has been at war with us since the Emperor executed his father. Their military campaign has strained our defense in the east front and for years the sentry commander Doe Yung Splendor at Frontier Pass of Drifting Spirits has been battling against him. Duke South, Er Shun, has also been on our back for years. He has caused great uneasiness for the defending general Deng the Ninth Lord of that region. Although Flying Tiger has escaped from this country to join Duke West, for the time being he is not able to do very much. The best strategy, in my opinion, is to strengthen defense of the five crucial westward frontier passes as well as the two others, the northward and southward Frontier Passes Blue Dragon and Good Dreams. While we are still at war with these two other rebel dukes, we must conserve our strength — we must strike a balance between urgency and our capability. Our treasury is already being depleted quickly by the existing conflicts. Please think thrice before you commence another campaign."

"The opinion of my senior general is certainly correct," the Imperial Teacher replied. "However, I am afraid that the ambition of the new Duke West does not stop at his boundary. If they start a rebellion, I want to be prepared. We all know the fierceness and the combat quality of their chief warrior, Nangong Swift, the scheming ability of Chancellor San Felicitous, and the Tao of Jiang Sarn. Now a very capable general of our court, Flying Tiger, has just defected and joined their camp. We must make preparations. As the saying goes, it will be too late if we wait to dig a well to get water when we are dead-thirsty."

"If you are still pondering between action and no action, let me make a suggestion," Ru the Brave said. "You first dispatch one or two of your warrior generals to bring a sizable army to the vicinity of West Branch City to investigate. If they find activities indicating an imminent rebellion, they are authorized to take action. Otherwise they should do nothing to provoke war and come back right away. What do you think?"

The Imperial Teacher pondered for a while and agreed. "It is a very good suggestion and I will take it." He then asked the warrior generals present: "Who will volunteer to carry out this mission?"

"I volunteer," a high-ranking general, Zhao Tien (Field), quickly responded. "I will investigate the activities in Zhou Dukedom. While I am there, I will also try to probe their weaknesses and strengths."

"Very good. I will place an army of thirty thousand under your command. Be careful." The meeting thus ended.

Zhao Field then asked his brother Zhao Lei (Rumble), who was under his command, to join him. On a provident day, after the traditional ceremony to sanctify the flag, the two Zhaos and an army of thirty thousand crossed the Yellow River, went through the five frontier passes and in days they arrived at the eastern border of West Branch City.

Scouts were sent to sneak into the city and they reported their findings: "There does not seem to be any indication that they are starting a rebellion, nor are they prepared for war."

The two Zhaos discussed the situation with each other: "We are already here with a sizable army. Since they are unprepared, maybe we can overcome them by surprise and bring the rebel Flying Tiger back. This feat will add high merits to our war records." The two brothers thus disobeyed the instruction of the Imperial Teacher by provoking Zhou Dukedom to war.

As the Zhaos were discussing various strategies, the noise of activities of the army was heard inside West Branch City. A scout from West Branch reported to Jiang Sarn: "A sizable army from the capital, the city of Morning Song, is now stationed at a distance from the East Gate. I have not been able to find out the reason why they are here."

"Are they invading us?" wondered Jiang Sarn. "Sound war drums to summon all warriors and generals to my conference hall." Soon all the warriors and generals had gathered, and a conference began.

"Does any of you know why Shang's army is here," asked Jiang Sarn.

"No, we surely don't have the slightest idea," one after another replied.

"Be prepared. They might start action soon," said Jiang Sarn. The meeting was thus adjourned.

Meanwhile, the Zhaos made up their minds to surprise the defense of West Branch City. Zhao Field, fully armored and carrying a long-handled scimitar, challenged the defense of the city for combat.

"Who will volunteer to encounter this challenger?" asked Jiang Sarn.

"I will," Nangong Swift, who had been waiting all along for this day, immediately volunteered.

"Go," Jiang Sarn consented.

An army was placed under the command of Nangong Swift. He recognized the challenger, Zhao Field. Nangong Swift first asked: "Is there any reason for you to bring a sizable army to invade our territory?"

"I am under a direct order of the Imperial Teacher to punish you for your rebel activities," Zhao Field announced. "King of Arms succeeded the late duke without asking for an endorsement from Emperor Zoe nor affirming his loyalty to the Emperor. In addition, you sheltered and accommodated a rebel from the capital, Flying Tiger. You are ordered to submit Flying Tiger to us immediately. Otherwise I will attack your city. You will be responsible for all consequences!"

"Nonsense! Your Emperor is evil." Nangong Swift shouted back. "Your evil Emperor killed loyal officers, created instruments of torture, murdered the faithful Vice Premier to take his heart to cure his evil Queen, and on top of it all, tried to violate the wife of his most loyal and capable general. Your Emperor has disregarded all moral principles. We in West Branch City abide by laws and observe high moral principles. Our people are happy and prosperous. All other lords and dukes look upon us as their role models. Now you dare invade us! You are asking for your own extermination!"

Having waited for this day of combat against Emperor Zoe's force, Nangong Swift outperformed himself and in 30 rounds Zhao Field was dead-tired and could hardly deflect the heavy thrusts of the long scimitar of his enemy. Finding a slip in his opponent, the powerful warrior lifted Zhao Field off his horse and threw him to the ground. Soldiers of Nangong Swift quickly tied Zhao up and brought him back to West Branch City.

Zhao Field was brought directly to the presence of Jiang Sarn. Defiantly Zhao stood, his head up, facing the premier.

"Aren't you going to beg for mercy for your life?" Jiang Sarn said.

"Me? A high-ranking general of the court of Emperor Zoe? No! You are nothing but a noodle monger and a skimmer peddler in the city of Morning Song. You are asking me to surrender to you? You can kill me but I will not yield to you!" Zhao Field declared even more defiantly.

At this moment, Jiang Sarn sensed the scornful opinions of his officers regarding his low background before he became premier in the dukedom. "I do not regard the statement that I was a noodle monger and a skimmer peddler in the capital city Morning Song an insult. We know of many high-ranking officers who started their careers from trivial positions. For example, the premier who helped Shang to establish the current dynasty, Yee-Yin, was nothing but a poor country farm hand before he was discovered. This is no insult to me. However, since Zhao Tien does not want to surrender, I have to execute him. Carry out the execution!" Jiang Sarn ordered and Zhao was taken away.

Just then, the new Master Lord of National Constituent, Flying Tiger, came out of his rank and pleaded, "Please, give me a chance to convince him. Zhao Field knows only Emperor Zoe and nothing about our country. I knew him before. I think I can convince him to surrender. He will be a very useful source of information when we begin our revolutionary campaign. Give me a chance to convince him."

Jiang Sarn consented. Outside the hall, Flying Tiger found Zhao Field tied up, ready to be executed. He approached him, and beckoned, "General Zhao!" Looking up, Zhao recognized Flying Tiger. He then silently lowered his head, without a word. "General Zhao," Flying Tiger repeated. "You do not know what has been going on outside your capital. Of all territories in the world, two-thirds are already under the control of Zhou Dukedom, and your Emperor has the control of only the remaining third. The four major dukedoms, East, West, North and South are all against Emperor Zoe. The Emperor is still strong, but he is near the end of his fate. He has offended people of the world. As you know, rebellion has been going on for some time in the east and the south. Since I came here, they have accommodated me to my heart's content; they even retained my title, changing only one word, from Master Lord of National Poise to Master Lord of National Constituent. I am here to persuade you to surrender. You will see for yourself what a great regime we have here! This is the regime for the people! Please reconsider."

Thinking it over again, Zhao Field began to have second thoughts about his stubbornness. As a warrior, he never thought about intricacies of human affairs. Besides, it was his unauthorized provocation that had gotten him into this current situation. Even if he was released, an investigation might disclose his disobedience of the explicit order of the Imperial Teacher. After pondering for a while, Zhao Field replied, "I am willing to surrender now, but I have just insulted the premier Jiang Sarn. He surely will not forgive me for my insolence."

"On the contrary. He certainly will forgive you," Flying Tiger reassured Zhao Field. He then ordered Zhao Field untied.

As soon as Zhao Field reentered the conference hall, he apologized for his rudeness. Jiang Sarn merely nodded and gave the order: "Bring all your men here and surrender to us."

Zhao Field requested, "My brother is still there. I have to go back to persuade him to surrender."

"All right, you may go," Jiang Sarn permitted.

368

Just as Zhao Rumble was worrying about his brother's fate, he was relieved to see Zhao Field come back. "You were reported captured, how did you get out?"

"I was indeed caught, by Nangong Swift. I insulted Jiang Sarn and he wanted to execute me. However, Flying Tiger came to see me and he convinced me to surrender. They sent me back to convince you to surrender, too," replied Zhao Field.

"What? You have surrendered? We are under a military order to come here. Do you know what will happen to our family and our parents if the Imperial Teacher finds out that we have surrendered? Our parents and families will all be killed," Zhao Rumble cursed.

"Then what shall we do," asked Zhao Field.

"There is only one way out. Do this ...", Zhao Rumble schemed.

Zhao Field went back to West Branch City, empty-handed. "What happened," asked Jiang Sarn.

"My brother is willing to yield. However, he is still a commander under Emperor Zoe. He wants to have an assurance that you will accept him. He wants you to send a messenger with me to bring your order of pardon to him, then he will formalize his surrender," replied Zhao Field.

"I will issue the order. Who will volunteer to be the escort?" said Jiang Sarn.

"I will, since I also know his brother," volunteered Flying Tiger.

As Flying Tiger and Zhao Field galloped into the camp, Flying Tiger was immediately ambushed and taken prisoner.

"Ha! We got the rebel. We must leave at once," ordered Zhao Rumble. In no time the army of 30,000, who had already packed, headed out eastward.

Thirty li later, when they came across a narrow pass on the treacherous mountain path by the name of Dragon Mouth, suddenly rumbles of battle drums were heard and two generals, Hsin Chia and his brother Hsin Mian, were waiting with an army of men. "Free the Master Lord. We know of your trick. Premier Jiang ordered us to wait here to intercept you. Surrender immediately."

"Leave me alone and I will not hurt you," shouted Zhao Field as he rolled his horse towards his opponents, waving his long scimitar. Twenty rounds of weapon clanking later, Hsin Chia, using a giant battle-ax, began to gain an upper hand over Zhao Field. Hsin Mian, also using a giant battle ax, ran his horse towards Zhao Rumble. Knowing that he was no match to the challenger, Zhao Rumble escaped into the wilderness and Flying Tiger was immediately set free.

"You forgetful rascal! I saved your life and you repay me by entrapping me!" Flying Tiger cursed loudly. Picking up a short scimitar left behind by fleeing soldiers, he hopped on a wandering horse and quickly caught up with Zhao Field. A few rounds later, Zhao Field was pulled off his horse and captured.

In darkness Zhao Rumble ran his horse as fast as he could to escape his pursuers. Soon he saw lights and he thought they were from a village. He was wrong. An army of men, led by Nangong Swift, was waiting for him with brightly-lit lanterns. "Please let me go. I am already defeated," pleaded Zhao Rumble.

"No, we have been waiting for you here for some time. We are ordered to take you prisoner." After a short engagement, Zhao Rumble was also captured.

By the morning, the victors and the two captives were gathered in the official residence of Premier Jiang. Flying Tiger first privately thanked Premier Jiang Sarn for his thoughtfulness in his arrangement of an ambush-rescue mission. When the two Zhaos were brought in, Jiang Sarn said: "I know from the beginning that you were scheming something against me. I know the geography of this area very well so it was a relatively easy matter to station my army at strategic points to wait for you. You have betrayed our trust in you. You are to die." Turning to the guards, Jiang Sarn ordered: "Execute them both."

As Zhao Rumble was carried out, he pleaded loudly, "I am innocent!"

Jiang Sarn laughed, "What a lie. Bring him back. Let me hear what kind of scheme he has this time!" Zhao Rumble was thus brought back to face Jiang Sarn. "You promised to surrender. Instead, you set up a trap to capture your guarantor, Flying Tiger. I saw through your trick from the very beginning," Jiang Sarn angrily charged. "You are now caught. The punishment for your scheme is death. What is so innocent about it?"

"We know the political situation: the Zhou Dukedom already has the control of two thirds of the world." Zhao Rumble pleaded, "We really wanted to surrender, but our families and our parents are still in the city of Morning Song. If news of our surrender reached the capital, then our parents and families would all be killed as a revenge against us.

This is the reason why we schemed against you. Please have mercy upon us."

"If this is the only reason, then you should have discussed your problems with me first. I have a scheme to get them out. Why didn't you tell me your difficulties first?" Jiang Sarn said.

"We are stupid. We are ignorant. We cannot see that far. Please forgive us," Zhao Rumble continued his appeal.

"I hope you are telling the truth this time." Turning around, Jiang said, "General Flying Tiger, is it true that the parents of Zhao are still in the city of Morning Song?"

"Yes, it is true," responded Flying Tiger.

"All right. I will keep Zhao Field here as a hostage. Zhao Rumble, you must show your good will this time, otherwise your brother will be executed. Take this envelope. Open it when you are back in the city of Morning Song. Follow my instructions and you will be able to move all your families here," ordered Jiang Sarn.

With a small convoy of soldiers, Zhao Rumble went back to the capital city Morning Song. He then opened up the envelope and studied the instructions. He went to the official residence of the Imperial Teacher. Zhao Rumble reported: "Your Highness, we arrived at West Branch City some time ago. The city of West Branch is already prepared for war. A number of engagements were fought without decisive victories on either side. We did not anticipate that our mission would last this long, and when we set out we did not bring enough supply. Now our food is almost depleted. We went to the nearest frontier pass, Vast Water, to ask for help. The sentry commander, Han Glory, claimed that he was also short of supply too so we didn't get much from him. I come back to ask you to allow me to bring additional military supplies to my encampment."

"It is odd that the sentry commander Han Glory did not supply the Zhaos what they needed in full. Maybe he really is short of supplies himself," the Imperial Teacher pondered. "Well, Zhao Rumble, I will give you the supply you need. Take the supply and go back right away. I will join you later."

Military supply was prepared and an escort of an army of 3000 was placed under the command of Zhao Rumble. Secretly, Zhao disguised all his family members as military personnel. Thus his parents and other family members, including those of his brother, were sneaked out of the city of Morning Song as a part of his envoy.

A few days later, the Imperial Teacher was still puzzled about the military supply problem of Frontier Pass Vast Water. He pulled out some records and discovered that a fresh supply had recently been delivered to the frontier pass. Immediately he knew something was wrong and he prognosticated and discovered that Zhao Rumble had just defected with all his family members. "God damn me! How could I let him slip by my grasp just like that!" the Imperial Teacher cursed. However, this was already several days after Zhao Rumble had left the capital city, and presumably he had already gotten through all the frontier passes and arrived safely at Zhou Dukedom.

Indeed, Zhao Rumble, with the new military order issued by the Imperial Teacher, smoothly went through the five frontier pass passes without any trouble. As soon he entered West Branch City, he went directly to the official residence of Premier Jiang Sarn to present his thanks. He thanked him again and again. "Your scheme worked without a hitch. The Zhaos will never forget your kindness and we owe you our lives." He then briefed Jiang Sarn on his interview with the Imperial Teacher.

It was obvious that the war was going to be escalated. Jiang Sarn thus issued orders all around the city: "Imperial Teacher himself or his warrior generals will be here soon. Be prepared."

The rescue of the families of the two Zhaos further strengthened Jiang Sarn's reputation among his subordinates. The handling of Zhao's episode established Jiang Sarn's credibility as a good military commander who mastered the art of war, as a generous leader who was concerned with his comrades' welfare, and as a great statesman who placed the interest of his country above his own.

13. Escalation of War and a Roll of Deities

After the Imperial Teacher discovered his slip of letting Zhao Rumble escape with the family members of the two Zhaos, he wanted to organize a campaign immediately against the regime of West Branch. He discussed this intention with his staff.

A disciple of the Imperial Teacher, Yue Chin (Fiesta), offered his opinion. "You are needed here. West Branch is only a small city and their strength is not great. You do not have to lead the campaign yourself. You can delegate this mission to some one you can trust."

Another disciple, Chi Li (Erect), seconded and proposed: "Maybe you can dispatch Chang Kwei Fang, the sentry commander of Frontier Pass Blue Dragon to head the campaign. He is perfectly suited for this task."

After pondering for a while, the Imperial Teacher agreed. "Excellent idea!"

An arrow of command, a token of military authority, and a fire table, a document containing urgent commands and messages (both were widely used as authorizations for field military command communications in ancient Middle Kingdom), were dispatched to the sentry commander of Frontier Pass Blue Dragon, Chang Kwei Fang, or Fragrant Cassia. Immediately Fragrant Cassia mobilized an army of 100,000. He appointed Fong Lin (Wind Forest) as his vanguard, who was a direct descendant of the ancient Queen Wind (a ruling empress sometime after the founding emperor of Middle Kingdom, Huangdi). The assembled army commenced their mission without delay and days later the force of Fragrant Cassia arrived within five li of West Branch City.

Scout patrols from West Branch City reported to Jiang Sarn the approach of a rather large and hostile force under the command flag of Chang Fragrant Cassia. A conference took place in the official residence of Premier Jiang Sarn. The premier said, "General Huang, do you know anything about this Chang Fragrant Cassia?"

"If you insist, I have to tell you the truth," answered Flying Tiger.

"What do you mean by the `truth'? Aren't we all working together now?" the perplexed premier said.

"He served under my command at one time. Then he told me, in his youth, he received training from a heresy Taoist. He knows a magical trick which may be quite fatal," responded Flying Tiger.

"May I hear what kind of magical trick Fragrant Cassia is expert in," asked Jiang Sarn.

"It is an unusual trick. As a rule, usually before warriors combat against each other, they always exchange their names. However, if Fragrant Cassia knows his opponent's name, all he needs to do is to yell `So-and-So, get off your horse,' then his opponent will became mesmerized and will automatically fall off his horse and become unconscious. Therefore, the most important thing to remember in your combat against Chang Fragrant Cassia is not to reveal your name. If you do so, then you have already lost," Flying Tiger replied.

None of the warriors attending this conference believed in the existence of this kind of magical power. "Never heard of it. Does this mean that if we give him a list of names of all of us, then all he needs to

376

do to defeat us is merely to read over the entire list and we will all be captured? Nonsense!" one of the warriors sarcastically remarked.

Chang Fragrant Cassia ordered his vanguard, Wind Forest, to challenge for an encounter.

"Who will volunteer to meet this challenger?" said Jiang Sarn.

"I will," responded a younger brother of King of Arms, Chi Su-chien.

Wind Forest used a short shaft as his weapon while Chi Su-chien used a long spear. Chi was extremely good at his defense, and, finding a slip in the shaft play of Wind Forest, Chi pierced his left leg. Wind Forest immediately turned around and ran his horse back to his encampment in an apparent defeat. Unfortunately, Chi chased. Seeing that Chi was closing in, Wind Forest stopped and turned around. Opening his mouth and chanting a spell, suddenly a red ball shot out from his mouth, trailed by a black column of smoke. This ball hit Chi Su-chien and knocked him off his horse. Turning back, Wind Forest swung his shaft and immediately killed him.

The next day, Chang Fragrant Cassia spread his army of men into a military formation ready for battle, and he asked to talk to Jiang Sarn. Jiang Sarn and his army of men and warriors came out of the city gate. Chang Fragrant Cassia challenged: "Jiang Sarn, you have been an officer in the court of Emperor Zoe. Why do you rebel against him? Why do you shelter the rebel Huang Flying Tiger? I am now under an imperial order to take the traitors back to the capital to face proper punishment. If you resist, I will level the entire city of West Branch."

"You are utterly wrong," Jiang Sarn laughed. "Haven't you heard that a wise bird carefully chooses a good branch to make its nest, and an intelligent man selects the right king to serve? Flying Tiger and I came here because the King of Arms is just and fair. You are a loyal and good officer, but even with your honesty you cannot redeem the evil deeds of the Emperor. We have violated no laws; it is you who come here to invade us. We only want to live peacefully within the borders of our territory. Please go back, otherwise you will be punished for your act of invasion."

"I heard that you learned Tao in East Kwen Ren Range. However, I also heard that you have not learned any useful skill. Do you think you can resist me?" Turning to his vanguard Wind Forest, Fragrant Cassia ordered: "Arrest Jiang Sarn for me."

As Wind Forest charged forward, Nangong Swift rushed forward to intercept him. Flying Tiger, on his Five Color Godspeed Ox, also joined in and engaged in combat against Fragrant Cassia. Not even 15 rounds later, Fragrant Cassia used his trick. "Huang Flying Tiger! Get off your horse!" Surely enough, Flying Tiger's facial expression froze and moments later he fell off his Ox. As Chang's foot soldiers were ready to tie him up, his two brothers, Flying Tiger Cub and Flying Leopard, jumped forward and pulled Flying Tiger back. A sworn brother, Zhou Chi, rolled his horse forward to fend off Fragrant Cassia during the rescue effort. Chang knew him from a previous occasion and hence his name, so he used the same trick again. "Zhou Chi, get off your horse." This time, Zhou Chi was not so lucky and he was captured by Chang's foot soldiers.

Meanwhile, Wind Forest was no match for the fighting skill of Nangong Swift. Retreating, he used the same ball trick again. A red ball trailed by a column of black smoke emerged from his mouth and knocked Nangong Swift off his horse and he was captured. Both Wind Forest and Chang Fragrant Cassia returned triumphantly to their encampment.

378

Neither of the two captives begged for their lives and they stood there defiantly and looked sarcastically at Fragrant Cassia and Wind Forest. "We have been captured not through a fair fight, but through your heresy Tao. If you want to kill us, go ahead. We will never surrender," one of the two said, and the other one nodded.

"Imprison them first. We have to deliver them to the capital for the Emperor to decide what to do," Fragrant Cassia ordered.

The next day, Wind Forest and Fragrant Cassia went to the front of the city gate of West Branch and challenged. Afraid of the heresy Tao of the two, Jiang Sarn had ordered that a tablet of temporary truce be hung high over the city walls above the city gate – this tablet was an indication that Jiang Sarn's party was for the time being not ready to engage in combat for one reason or the other. This was a military tradition of the Middle Kingdom and this tradition was usually honored by most warring parties. "Ha! A mere engagement already caused them to ask for a temporary truce! We will wait them out," Fragrant Cassia declared.

During this critical moment, in his daily mental exercises, Demigod Great Unity, of Cavern Golden Ray in Mount Genesis, sensed that Jiang Sarn was in trouble and it was an opportune time for Nata to enroll formally in Jiang Sarn's camp. "Ask your brother student Nata to come here," Demigod Great Unity ordered a disciple who happened to be nearby.

Approaching the seat of meditation of his teacher, Nata asked: "Do you want me to do anything for you?"

"Yes. The time has come for you to formally join Jiang Sarn's camp and to be part of his revolutionary campaign. You have been well-trained to carry out all necessary feats. If you encounter any trouble, come back here to ask for my help. Take care," said Demigod Great Unity.

"Finally, after all these years of a rigid life of a Taoist on a remote mountaintop, the promise of action has come true. This is really my day!" Nata's delight was undescribable. After bidding farewell to his brother Taoists in the mountain, he packed all his devices in his leopardskin bag. Taking his weapon, the fire-tipped spear, he mounted his Wheels of Wind and Fire and rolled swiftly towards West Branch City.

Moments later, he dropped inside the city. He stopped a passerby and asked: "Where is the residence of Premier Jiang Sarn?"

"Right across the Little Golden Bridge." The passerby pointed at the direction.

"I wish to see the premier," Nata said to the guard at the door.

Being an ex-Taoist himself, Jiang Sarn always had a respect for Taoists. "Show him in," he ordered. "What is your name and where do you come from," Jiang Sarn asked Nata.

"My name is Li Nata. I am a disciple of Demigod Great Unity, of Cavern Golden Ray in Mount Genesis. I have been ordered by my teacher to come here to join your command."

Jiang Sarn was naturally extremely pleased at any extra help he could get. Meanwhile, Flying Tiger showed up. He recognized Nata and again he reiterated his thanks for Nata's help in saving his family from the hands of the sentry commander Han Glory at Frontier Pass Vast Water. Jiang Sarn was even more impressed when he learned how Nata had managed to save the Huangs.

"There is a large military encampment outside the city. What are they here for?" Nata said.

"This is the force of Chang Fragrant Cassia," Flying Tiger replied. "He was dispatched by Emperor Zoe to invade us. He has an unusual ability and he already captured two of our best warriors. This is the reason why the premier ordered the tablet of temporary truce hung above the city wall."

"Since I am here to help, I will volunteer to take a look at the enemy," Nata said to the premier. "May I have your permission to remove the tablet of temporary truce? I can handle them." Jiang Sarn gave the permission.

The tablet of temporary truce was removed. The removal was reported to Fragrant Cassia and Wind Forest. "They might have gotten some help. Go and find out," Chang Fragrant Cassia said to Wind Forest. Wind Forest thus went to the front of the city gate, and challenged for a combat.

"Be careful. You are the only one we have now," Jiang Sarn, rather concerned, advised Nata.

"I will be careful. I shall find out their weaknesses first," Nata promised. Mounting his Wheels of Wind and Fire, he went outside the city gate to face the challenger.

"Who are you?" challenged Wind Forest.

"I am a disciple of Premier Jiang Sarn. My name is Li Nata. Are you Chang Fragrant Cassia – the one who can get people off their horses just by calling their names?" shouted Nata.

"No, I am his vanguard, Wind Forest."

"I will spare your life if you will get the real Fragrant Cassia to face me," Nata demanded arrogantly.

"You insolent thing! I will kill you," Wind Forest angrily replied, and the engagement began.

Twenty rounds later, Wind Forest began to weaken under the heavy thrusts of the fire-tipped spear. "I'd better use my trick again, otherwise I'll be defeated," he thought. During his retreating flight, he turned around and opened up his mouth. Again a red ball shot out, trailed by a black column of smoke.

"This is heresy Tao, nothing to it," laughed Nata. Pointing his finger at the ball, the black smoke dispersed instantly and the red ball fell harmlessly to the ground. "Now I will let you have a taste of my dharmaratna!" Nata said. Removing the Bracelet of Zion from his leopardskin bag, he threw it at Wind Forest. The bracelet marked a direct hit and broke the shoulder of the opponent. Wind Forest, with the help of his foot soldiers, barely made it back to his encampment. Nata, having incapacitated Wind Forest, demanded to have an engagement with Chang Fragrant Cassia. Chang came out and engagements began almost instantly.

Although Fragrant Cassia was a very strong warrior, he felt he was losing ground as the engagement continued. He decided to use his supreme trick. He yelled, "Nata, get off your wheel!"

Nothing happened. "This trick never failed before. Why?" wondered Fragrant Cassia. He yelled again, and again, and again. Nothing happened.

By this time, Nata had already lost patience and he laughed at Chang. "I am my own master. If I wish to get off my wheel, I will do it myself. Why do you think you can yell me off my wheel? You idiot coward!"

Unknown to Chang Fragrant Cassia, his trick — equivalent to the technique of instant mesmerism — had been developed only to work with ordinary persons. The reason for the failure of his trick on Nata was exactly the same as for the failure of the Soul-Snatching Flag — Nata did not have the usual soul and body constitution; his constitution was lotus flowers, stems and leaves.

Again, Nata took out his Bracelet of Zion and cast it at Fragrant Cassia. It marked a direct hit and broke his left arm. He narrowly escaped back to his camp. Now it was his turn to hang up a tablet of temporary truce. Messengers were dispatched back to the city of Morning Song to ask for urgent reinforcement.

Although Jiang Sarn was victorious, he realized that the recent victory hung on one individual — Nata. Anticipating further reinforcements from the city of Morning Song, he decided that he should seek the help of his teacher, Patriarch Primeval. After performing appropriate rituals to ready himself to see his teacher, he went to see the King of Arms.

"I want to take a temporary leave of absence for a few days to visit my teacher, Mentor Primeval, in East Kwen Ren Range to ask for his help. I sense that the regime at the capital is about to send fresh reinforcements to attack us. We must be prepared," Jiang Sarn reported.

"Please do not linger. Come back as soon as possible. We are under siege now," King of Arms anxiously pleaded.

"Indeed. It will not be long. I should be back within three or four days," he promised.

Before he left, he gave specific instructions to Nata and his disciple Wu Serendipity. "Do not engage any further combat. Just concentrate on defense. I will be back shortly." Jiang Sarn reiterated his instructions.

Figure I- 23. Palace of Abstraction
Jiang Sarn arrived at a precipice overlooking his former Temple

"We will obey your order faithfully," promised Nata and Wu Serendipity.

Jiang Sarn terra-trekked and he soon arrived at East Kwen Ren Range. He stopped his terra-trekking at Precipice Unicorn, where he had begun his return trip to the capital city Morning Song nearly ten years before. The scenery had not changed much; wild deer and rabbits still hopped amidst wildflowers and bushes and the only sound was the gentle roar caused by soft winds brushing over high tips of pine trees. "It has been ten years since I saw the scenery of my home of forty years. What a great life I used to live here." As he reminisced over those pleasant memories of the good old days, he sank into a pensive mood, relishing the nostalgia of the time long gone. He was awakened from his nostalgic thoughts by the messenger boy White Crane. "Patriarch Primeval knows you are here. He wants to talk to you."

They entered Palace Jade Abstraction and went directly to Eight Trigram Seat, the seat of meditation of Primeval.

Jiang Sarn saluted to the teacher, and bowed. "Your disciple, Jiang Sarn, wishes His Holy Teacher ten thousand blessings!"

"Please rise. Your presence here is most opportune," said Primeval. "I was just about to send a messenger to summon you here." Primeval then paused and turned to an elderly Taoist on his left. "Senior Demigod South Pole, please bring me the Roll of Divinities." The elderly Taoist went to a cabinet, opened it and removed a scroll. He handed the scroll to Primeval. "Thank you, Senior Demigod," Primeval said. He then turned to his disciple. "Jiang Sarn, this Roll looks blank, but it already contains the names of those who are destined to be part of it. Take this Roll and go back to West Branch City. Build an earthen platform in a nearby mountain, to be named the Platform for Appointment of

385

Divinities. Hang this Roll at the center of this terrace platform. You will receive further instructions about how to complete your mission. This will be the most important task in your life."

"But I am in deep trouble now," Jiang Sarn pleaded. "West Branch City is under siege. We are victorious at present but I envisage that our victory might be short-lived. My Tao is shallow. I need your help. This is my main purpose in coming back to East Kwen Ren Mountain."

"Now you are a premier, with the most impressive title `Proxy Father Premier,' enjoying all glories and advantages of your rank. West Branch City is ruled by men of virtue and guarded by good providence; there is no need for you to fear heresy Taoists. If you are in real danger, help will always arrive in time. You cannot ask me to solve all trivial problems of your affairs. Now go." Primeval merely waved his hands to signal Jiang Sarn to leave.

Jiang Sarn was perplexed by the indifferent reaction of his teacher to his plea for help. Nevertheless he obeyed the order of his teacher-mentor and moved toward the exit of Palace Jade Abstraction. However, just before he stepped out, he was stopped by the messenger boy White Crane. "Primeval wants to see you once more." Thinking that Primeval might have changed his heart, eagerly Jiang Sarn returned to Eight Trigram Seat.

"When you leave this mountain, do not respond to anyone beckoning at you. If you respond, you will regret it. The man who beckons at you will incite thirty-six enemies to feud against you. Also, there is a person waiting for you in East Sea. Now go." Primeval again waved his hand.

Even more perplexed, Jiang Sarn left. Senior Demigod South Pole saw him out. Jiang Sarn complained to Senior Demigod: "Senior

Demigod, the purpose of my visit was to seek help from my teacher. Now he just ignored me totally. What can I do? What shall I do?"

"You should keep up your faith. Everything in the world is ordained according to the wishes of Heaven. By destiny, everything will be all right with you. Also, please heed the advice not to respond to anyone beckoning at you, whoever he may be. Do not disregard this advice. This is as far as I can accompany you. Now, farewell." Senior Demigod of the South Pole stopped and made a gesture of goodwill.

Holding the Roll of Divinities in his arms, Jiang Sarn walked slowly towards Precipice Unicorn where he would begin his terra-trekking trip to go back to West Branch. Just then he heard a voice beckoning at him: "Jiang Sarn!"

"Surely enough, Primeval was right. Some is beckoning me now. Let me ignore him."

The voice continued: "Mr. Jiang Sarn!" Again, Jiang Sarn ignored it. The voice came again: "Premier Jiang." Jiang Sarn again did not respond. Finally the voice became very angry, and yelled: "Jiang Sarn, you forgetful snob! Now that you are a premier, you want to forget all your old buddies? I was a fellow disciple of yours for over forty years in the Palace Jade Abstraction. Just because you are a premier now, do you think you can ignore the beckoning of an old friend?"

Being a humble person who hated to be called a snob, he turned around and saw the source of the voice, his old buddy, a younger fellow disciple by the name of Sen Kungpao (Buck Panther), who was riding a tiger to chase after him. "My dear brother of Tao, I did not know it was you," Jiang Sarn apologized. "My teacher told me not to respond to any beckoning, so I followed his order. Had I known that it was you who beckoned, I would have responded."

"What is the scroll you are holding," asked Buck Panther.

"The Roll of Divinities," responded Jiang Sarn. "I was ordered by our Patriarch to build a Platform for Appointment of Divinities near West Branch City. This Roll will be hung on the Platform."

"Why do you serve that master in West Branch," asked Buck Panther scornfully.

"My dear brother student, I do not know what you have in your mind," Jiang Sarn replied. "I am now the premier of Zhou Dukedom. I have also been appointed prince regent by the late King of Literature to assist the current king, King of Arms. Zhou Dukedom already controls two-thirds of territories of the world. My mission to assist King of Arms is justified by prognostications indicated by current astronomical arrangements of stars and constellations of the sky. You very well know that the Shang dynasty is about to end; just take a look at what evil deeds Emperor Zoe has committed in recent years. You should know better."

"You said that the Shang dynasty is about to end," retorted Buck Panther. "I disagree. I am on my way to assist Emperor Zoe. I will oppose you."

"You go ahead. I cannot disobey the instructions of my teacher-mentor." responded Jiang Sarn.

Buck Panther persisted and continued his persuasion: "I have one suggestion that will avoid a conflict between you and me. You should give up your position of premier and come with me to Emperor Zoe's court. You can work with me. I will treat you well."

Figure I- 24. Sen the Buck Panther
He was in an awkward situation with his head backwards

"No, I cannot disobey my teacher-mentor. Besides, you are on your own to help the Shang dynasty. Our teacher-mentor did not authorize you to do so," Jiang Sarn retorted.

Buck Panther now became angry. He threatened, "Your Tao is no match to mine. I have learned more Tao than you have. I know how to tame dragons and rein tigers, I can move mountains and empty seas. What have you learned? Nothing that can match mine."

"You have developed your own line of Tao, and I have developed mine. You may have studied Tao a few more years than I, but that does not mean you are superior. The Patriarch promised me he will always come to my aid if I need it," Jiang Sarn said.

"Never mind our Patriarch. You, with your meager ability of Tao, are bound to fail. You have only forty years of study of Tao, during which you wasted most of your time on nonessential subjects. I have a few more years of study of Tao than you. I have mastered more ploys and stratagems of Tao than you can imagine. How can you expect to match my skill?" boasted Buck Panther.

"My Tao may be different from yours, but I have mastered mine. It is not a mere number of years of study that counts," Jiang Sarn retorted.

"I know what you have learned," Buck Panther also retorted. "You have only mastered the Tao of Five Forms. You can only move mountain or sea, but me? I have mastered many other skills. For example, I can cut off my own head and throw it to the sky. My head will wander around the universe while my body stays here. At my signal my head will come back to join my body at any time, completely unharmed. This is the kind of Tao you missed! You think with your Tao of Five Forms you can overthrow Emperor Zoe? Forget about it! You should submit yourself to my Tao and serve Emperor Zoe with me."

Jiang Sarn's faith weakened. He thought: "My teacher never taught me these important and utilitarian skills. I need these skills now more than ever to defend West Branch City. If Buck Panther is against me, I will never win. Maybe I should go with him." He then said to Buck Panther, "If you can cut off your head and perform miracles as you just said, I will burn this Roll of Divinities and go with you to assist Emperor Zoe."

"Do not renege on your promise." Without further words he unsheathed his sword and cut off his head – and not a single drop of blood was shed. He threw his head up, and surely enough, the head floated and flew away.

Jiang Sarn was stupefied; he had never seen this kind of trick before. Mesmerized, he watched the dancing movements of the head intensively, and in astonishment his mouth being completely open.

Senior Demigod South Pole did not go back to Palace Jade Abstraction right away. As he saw Sen Buck Panther riding a tiger to chase after Jiang Sarn, he sensed something wrong. He followed Buck Panther and he saw at a distance that the two were arguing. Later, he saw the head of Buck Panther rising and floating among the clouds, flying without wings. He beckoned the messenger boy White Crane: "Quick! Transfigure yourself into a giant white crane and carry the head of Buck Panther with your beak to South Sea and wait there for further orders."

A giant white crane suddenly materialized from nowhere and with its giant and powerful beak, it effortlessly picked up the floating head of Buck Panther and flew southward. Soon the white crane and the head of Buck Panther disappeared amidst the clouds.

Startled, Jiang Sarn began to curse at the white crane. "This is the head of my brother of Tao. Come back! Come back!" At this moment Senior Demigod appeared. "Oh, look what happened! Please help me get back the head of my fellow student, Buck Panther," pleaded Jiang Sarn.

"You idiot! You have been fooled by the heresy Tao of Buck Panther which he learned from elsewhere, unauthorized by Primeval. You will commit a heavenly crime if you burn the Roll of Divinities. I will let the giant white crane stay in South Sea for one and three-quarter hours. This heresy Tao to float his head only lasts that long. Afterwards he will die instantly," said Senior Demigod.

"Please spare him. After all, he is still my fellow student. We have been buddies like brothers for forty years. Please spare him," pleaded Jiang Sarn.

"I can spare him, but he won't spare you. He is extremely jealous of your accomplishments and your position as premier. This is the reason why he devised this scheme to deceive you to abandon your position as premier and to destroy your career. If I spare him now, he will continue to use stratagems to feud against you. He will cause thirty-six enemies to cause conflict against you," warned Senior Demigod.

"Well, I guess I have to take the consequences. Meanwhile, if you do not spare his life, right away I will have to bear the blame as the cause of his death. Please give him back his head," pleaded Jiang Sarn again.

The time was certainly running out. The headless body of Buck Panther paced here and there, back and forth, and his anxiety was obvious, even without a head. Finally, the giant white crane reappeared, and the head was dropped. Unfortunately the head landed the wrong way, with its face towards the back of the body. It took him some doing to reposition his head the right way.

"You deceitful elfin Taoist!" Senior Demigod cursed. "You tried to deceive Jiang Sarn with your heresy Tao, to persuade him to burn the Roll of Divinities. You traitor to your teacher! He never asked you to assist Emperor Zoe's regime! You jealous slug! Get out of here!"

Embarrassed at the failure of his heresy Tao, Buck Panther hatefully pointed his finger at the vanishing figure of Jiang Sarn. "I swear I will cause blood to flow like water in a river, human bones to pile mountain-high in West Branch City!"

After terra-trekking for a while, Jiang Sarn was stopped by a body of water at the side of a mountain. This mountain, full of sharp peaks, presented a magnificently impressive view against the peaceful body of water. "I wish I could shed my responsibilities in the world of dust and come here to study Tao for the rest of my life." Jiang Sarn sighed as his thoughts wandered back to the many unresolved problems at West Branch City. Before he could finish his thoughts, suddenly great waves commenced, a gust of wind blew hard and the sky was soon covered with dark clouds. "What happened!" Jiang Sarn was really startled. Very soon, the water separated, and a naked man appeared.

"Demigod, this wandering spirit has had no home to go to for thousands of years. The other day, Lord Gracious Virtue passed by here and told me that today at this hour, a high priest of Tao would pass by and he was to be my savior. Please, save my spirit from wandering forever!"

"Who are you," Jiang Sarn asked, collecting as much courage as he could.

"The name of this wandering spirit is Pah Gian the Mirror. I was a commander under Huangdi eons ago, during the dawn of civilization. During the decisive battle against the barbarian leader Chi You, he launched uncountable projectiles of fire balls against Huangdi's army and I was hit by one of them. In desparation I ran and ran, and eventually I jumped into this body of water. Since then I have been not been able to get out of it. Please help me. I will forever submit my service to you if you deliver me from this body of water," pleaded the naked wandering spirit.[2]

"He did not know he was already dead when he ran and it was his spirit who jumped into this water. No wonder he could not get out of it," Jiang Sarn thought. "I will release you," he said. Writing a talismanic symbol on his left palm, he aimed his palm towards the body of water. A succession of thunderbolts commenced. Then the water receded and the spirit was set free.

The spirit ran ashore and thanked Jiang Sarn. "What is the command of my savior," the spirit asked.

"Wait for me at Mount West Branch," said Jiang Sarn. Pah Mirror left right away.

Continuing his interrupted trip, Jiang Sarn terra-trekked to Mount West Branch. He was greeted not only by Pah Mirror, but also by the five gremlins whose lives he had spared long before, when they were subdued in the garden of Sung Remarkable, near the capital city Morning Song. "We have been diligently following your order and we haven't hurt a soul ever since. We are at your command," the five gremlins reported.

---

[2]This great battle was described in the chapter *Creation*.

"I need your service now. Also, since you have reformed, I will grant you five a joint title of Five Gods of Roadways. I need to construct an earthen platform, to be named the Platform for Appointment of Divinities. You will carry out the construction work for me. General Pah Mirror will be your supervisor. In addition, I will appoint Pah Mirror the God of Prevalent Blessing. I will soon select a provident day according to Tao to commence this construction project. Meanwhile, keep the Roll of Divinities for me. It shall be hung on the Platform when it is finished. Now rest yourselves, but be prepared to start this task soon."

Jiang Sarn then returned to his official residence in West Branch City. "Did Fragrant Cassia provoke combats since I was gone," he asked his disciples, who were extremely happy to see their leader back.

"No," Wu Serendipity replied. Jiang Sarn then went to see the king.

"How did your trip to the East Kwen Ren Range go?" the king said. Jiang Sarn didn't dare tell the exact truth about the Roll, so he said a few irrelevant things.

The next morning, signal drums sounded in West Branch City, beckoning all warriors to come to Jiang Sarn's official residence for a conference. After all the warriors gathered, Jiang Sarn issued secret orders to four, Flying Tiger, Nata, Hsin Chia and Hsin Mian. They were told to be ready by the evening.

Since his defeat, Fragrant Cassia had been resting quietly to recuperate from his wounds as he patiently waited for reinforcements from the capital. During Jiang Sarn's absence, no war activity was detected around the city of West Branch, and the defense of Fragrant Cassia began to grow lax. He did not anticipate any activity of war for the time being. To his surprise, around eight o'clock in the evening by our reckoning, under the cover of darkness, the four warriors of West Branch City named above, each leading an army of men dressed for a night mission, launched a synchronized sneak attack against the encampment of Chang Fragrant Cassia from four sides.

Suddenly, loud and rapidly palpitating sounds of war drums were heard, and heavily armed soldiers bearing insignia of Zhou Dukedom rampaged through Chang's camp, setting everything along their path of stampede on fire. Chang's soldiers and warriors were totally surprised and all they could do was run from this melee. On his flight path, Fragrant Cassia saw Nata, and immediately turned around and ran in the opposite direction to avoid engagement. Wind Forest saw Flying Tiger coming on his Five Color Godspeed Ox. Grabbing two shafts, he engaged in combat against Flying Tiger. Just then, the invaders located the two captives, Nangong Swift and Zhou Chi, and set them free. These two also joined the attacking forces on foot. Under the fierce attack from all sides, Fragrant Cassia and Wind Forest had to abandon their defense and escaped along with their soldiers.

After the fight was over, he regrouped his army. After a cursory count, of the 100,000 men Fragrant Cassia had brought with him, half had either been killed or captured, or had deserted. The defeated army resettled in an encampment 30 li from the city, near Mount West Branch. Again an urgent message was dispatched to the Imperial Teacher to ask for immediate reinforcements.

Quite shocked by the defeat of Chang Fragrant Cassia, the Imperial Teacher wanted to lead the reinforcement himself. However, because of rampant rebellions in the east and in the south, he was reluctant. His disciple Chi Li again suggested: "The situation is indeed urgent, but you are needed here. You are the only one who can defend the capital now. During your study of Tao you have established friendship with many colleagues. Some of them surely can help you. Why don't you look them up?"

This suggestion reminded Imperial Teacher of the many demigod friends he had made during his study of Tao. After delegating his authority to his two most trusted disciples Chi Li and Yue Chin, he was ready to leave. "I will be gone for three days at most."

Mounting his Black Unicorn and carrying his weapon – a pair of golden whips – off he went to visit his old friends. Patting the head of his Unicorn, the beast bellowed once then it rose from the ground to the heights of the clouds. It moved effortlessly high above as if it were gliding on an invisible rail.

Soon the Imperial Teacher arrived at his first intended stop, Nine Dragon Island in West Sea. Upon his arrival, he saw a Taoist lad collecting herb medicine outside the residential cavern of his friends. He asked the lad: "Is your teacher-mentor in?"

"Yes, he is with his friends playing chess."

"Please report that Wen Zhong the Imperial Teacher from the capital, the city of Morning Song, is here and wishes to see him."

Moments later, four Taoists emerged from the cavern and welcomed him warmly. "My dear brother colleague, how and where did you come from?"

"I decided to pay you a visit, after all these years," the Imperial Teacher replied.

"This is a desolate island. We decided to study Tao in seclusion, so we moved here years ago. This is no place for you, a Premier and Prince Regent. Do you have some need for our service?" said one of them.

War among Gods and Men

"Indeed, I have a pressing need," the Imperial Teacher responded. "This matter is urgent so I will skip all perfunctory protocols and come right to the point of the purpose of my visit. As you know, I went to the world of dust some time ago. I have served two emperors of the Shang dynasty and I am serving the third one. I am now his Premier. Now, Jiang Sarn, a disciple of East Kwen Ren Range, serving King of Arms as his premier in West Branch City, in Zhou Dukedom, has incited rebellion against my Emperor. I asked one of my best generals, Chang Fragrant Cassia, to squash Jiang's rebellion but he was repeatedly defeated and I have received several requests for reinforcements. I want to go myself to his aid. However, there are other rebel activities in the east and the south. If I personally undertake the task to squash this westward rebellion, I fear for the security of the capital. Will you help me to squash the westward rebellion?"

"I will certainly volunteer my service to help you," one of them, Wang Mo (Devil), said.

"Don't you think that you are the only one willing to help our friend the Imperial Teacher!" another Taoist said. "Count me in!"

Then the remaining two said enthusiastically, "Me too!" "Me too!"

Wang Devil nodded, then he said to the Imperial Teacher, "All of us will go together."

The names of the other three Taoists were Yang Seng (Forest), Kao Yuechien (Friendly Sovereign) and Lee Hsinbah (Hegemony). They told the Imperial Teacher: "Please go back to the capital first, we will join you there really soon." The Imperial thus rode his Black Unicorn back to Morning Song, relieved.

The four Taoists hydro-trekked to Morning Song. They were surely a fierce bunch. All four of them were extremely tall, over seven feet by our reckoning. Wang Devil had an enormous face, Yang Forest was pitch-black, with red beard and yellow eyebrows, Kao Friendly Sovereign had a bluish complexion and bright red hair, and Lee Hegemony had a heavy face colored dark brown, wearing a long beard. They were dressed as traveling Taoists. Their enormous robes were decorated with various Taoist talismanic symbols and the street rumbled as they trampled through with their heavy footsteps. Passersby only dared glance at them with awe and fear. The four asked around: "Where is the official residence of the Imperial Teacher?" A brave passerby gave them the direction.

They were warmly received by the Imperial Teacher.

The next day, the Imperial Teacher brought the four for an interview with Emperor Zoe, who was so scared by their appearances that he asked Imperial Teacher to entertain them on his behalf. After the ceremonial banquet, the four thanked Imperial Teacher and bade farewell: "We have a mission to accomplish. We will come back here to drink again when we squash the westward rebellion." They then departed for the encampment of Fragrant Cassia in West Branch Mountain via hydro-trekking.

The riding beasts for the four had already been brought by their respective disciples to the encampment of Fragrant Cassia. Wang Devil rode a huge and horrible-looking dog of enormous size called Canis Terribilis, Yang Forest a great lion of a horrendous build called Leo Ferus, Kao Friendly Sovereign a giant spotted panther with long teeth called Panthera Immensus, and Lee Hegemony a nondescript, extremely fierce-looking beast called Zeng Ning. All these beasts were not of the ordinary variety; they were one-of-a-kind mythical beasts, as we say. The presence of these four beasts caused great uneasiness among the ordinary war horses. One of the four Taoists, Wang Devil, drew talismanic symbols on a number of sheets of paper and asked Fragrant Cassia to give them to his warriors to paste over their horse saddles. "These talismanic symbols will keep your horses from being scared off by the fierce looks of our riding beasts," Wang said.

"The wounds of Wind Forest and myself have not yet healed. Please help us if you can," Fragrant Cassia pleaded to his saviors.

"Don't worry, you will recover in no time at all." After taking a look at their wounds, Wang Devil opened up a large gourd bottle and poured out a number of different herb pills. Selecting two from the pile, he gave one each to Fragrant Cassia and Wind Forest and asked them to crush them in water and apply the paste over their wounds. Surely enough, moments later, all the wounds healed and they were ready for action.

The next day, Chang moved his encampment back to the vicinity of the east gate of West Branch City. Patrols reported this movement to Jiang Sarn. Jiang Sarn called a conference and told his warriors: "Chang Fragrant Cassia must have gotten some extraordinary help. Be careful."

Surely enough, the following morning the fully armored Fragrant Cassia emerged from his camp, and challenged to meet Jiang Sarn.

"You are already defeated, why don't you just go back?" Jiang Sarn said.

"I may have lost a battle or two, but I have not lost the war. In fact, I am going to win all battles from now on..." Before Fragrant Cassia could finish his words, the four Taoists, on their fierce beasts, lunged forward.

At the sight of these odd-looking beasts, war horses on the side of Jiang Sarn – without the protection of talismanic symbols prepared by

Wang Devil – were frightened and jolted many warriors and Jiang Sarn off their horses, except Nata, who was unmoved from his Wheels of Wind and Fire, and Flying Tiger, whose Five Color Godspeed Ox was itself a mythical beast. At the sight of the disarray, the four Taoists laughed their hearts out and said: "Take your time to get back to your horses. We will be patient."

After recovering from the "fierce beast shock" and remounting his horse, Jiang Sarn said to the four: "May I ask from which caverns and from which mountains do my Taoist colleagues come? May I be of service to you?"

Wang Devil replied on behalf of the four: "We are Sublimators of Essence from Nine Dragon Island in West Sea. You and we are fellow Taoists. At the invitation of the Imperial Teacher of the court of Emperor Zoe, we come here to try to resolve his difference with you. Will you agree to three terms of our proposal?"

"Of course. We will even agree to thirty terms, not mentioning a mere three," Jiang Sarn politely responded.

"The first term of our demand is: King of Arms must swear his fealty to Emperor Zoe," Wang Devil said.

"You are wrong to accuse the king of being disloyal. My master, King of Arms, is a subordinate under Shang's rule. Of course he will swear his fealty to Shang's court. He will reiterate his fealty if you wish," Jiang Sarn answered.

"Second, this army has suffered a great loss. Although we will not force you to compensate for all the losses, at least you should generously award them gratuities. Third, you must deliver Flying Tiger and his father to us so that we can send them back to the capital to face punishment for their mutiny," Wang Devil said.

"Your three terms are very clear. We agree to all of them. However, please allow us some time to prepare all the necessary documents, gratuities, and the prisoners you named. Give us three days. There will be no further arguments," Jiang Sarn consented.

"Good. We will wait for your action. Meanwhile, we will not disturb you." The four Taoists, Chang Fragrant Cassia, and the army of soldiers then returned to their encampment.

Upon their return, Jiang Sarn summoned an emergency conference. Flying Tiger first approached Jiang Sarn and said, "Please deliver myself and my father to the camp of Fragrant Cassia to avoid further conflicts."

Jiang Sarn immediately left his seat and personally assisted Flying Tiger back to his seat. "Please. The purpose of my agreement to his three demands was to gain time. Didn't you see that our war horses couldn't even face their fierce-looking riding beasts? If I had not promised them what they demanded today, they would would have started a combat, and I am certain we would have been defeated. By promising them our agreement to their demands, we gain some time for action." Flying Tiger thus thanked Jiang Sarn gratefully. Afterwards, Jiang Sarn asked Wu the Serendipity and Nata to strengthen defenses of the city, and after performing appropriate rituals to East Kwen Ren Mountain, went to visit Palace of Jade Abstraction for the second time to plead for help from his teacher-mentor, Primeval.

White Crane messenger boy reported to Primeval that Jiang Sarn was outside waiting to see him. "Send him in," he said.

"I know the purpose of your visit, that you have run into difficulties with the four Taoists from Nine Dragon Island. Let me tell you the origin of their riding beasts. They were offspring of cross-breeding between dragons and various earthly beasts during early epochs of the Universe. White Crane messenger boy, bring my riding beast here."

Although he had studied Tao on this mountain for 40 years, Jiang Sarn never even knew that the Primeval owned a riding beast. It did not look like anything Jiang Sarn had ever seen in his entire life, including the four fierce-looking riding beasts from his enemy's camp. It had a head resembling that of a unicorn but the horn was much shorter, a snakelike tail, and a body of a dragon covered with golden scales.

Primeval told Jiang Sarn: "The name of this beast is No-elephant, which is also a one-of-a-kind beast. It can take you anywhere and it will not be scared off by the riding beasts of the four. I am giving you my riding beast because you shall fulfill the mission of appointment of divinities on my behalf. You need this riding beast to accomplish your mission. In addition, let me give you a dharmaratna, a Deity-Pounding Whip. It can deliver a forceful and fatal blow to anyone, including demigods, whose names are on the Roll of Divinities." This Deity-Pounding Whip was made of wood, consisting of twenty-one flexible sections. On each section four talismanic symbols were inscribed, so that there were eighty-four talismanic symbols altogether. "When you go back, take a detour through North Sea. Someone is waiting for you there," Primeval added. "Use this yellow flag and read the instructions when you encounter difficulties with him. This yellow flag is the Mascot Flag of this Palace. It is also known as Almond Yellow Flag. It will protect you on numerous occasions in the future."

Jiang Sarn, pleased at the change of mood of his teacher, left after presenting the nominal thanks and farewell. He then mounted this beast No-elephant. He gently patted the short horn on its forehead.

Immediately four rays of red light beams emerged from its four hoofs and lifted the beast No-elephant up to the sky. It then moved swiftly and smoothly. Jiang Sarn discovered quickly that the beast could be directed with his thoughts.

After a while, he arrived at the North Sea, and he decided to stop by a mountain near the shore of this huge body of water. After he landed, suddenly a gust of wind blew hard and fog gathered. A strange-looking thing appeared. It had a head like a camel, with a long neck like a goose, and long whiskers as thick as pencils shot out from all directions of his head, like those of a shrimp. It had ears like those of an ox, feet like a tiger, hands like the claws of an eagle, and two large, protruding eyes.

"Jiang Sarn, I have been waiting for you here for some time. I want to eat you! I have been told that if I eat you, I will live forever," this thing shouted.

"I don't even know you. Why do you want to eat me," Jiang Sarn asked.

"Never you mind. I just want to eat you." This thing hopped over.

Stepping aside to avoid the thing, Jiang Sarn unwrapped the Almond Yellow Flag Primeval had given him and read the instructions. Planting the Almond Yellow Flag in the ground, he challenged this thing: "All right, I probably am destined to be eaten by you today. However, I challenge you to lift up this Almond Yellow Flag. If you can lift it up, I offer myself as your meal of the day."

The little yellow flag suddenly grew to a height of 20 feet. This thing used both claws to lift it up. He couldn't. He lowered his claws to ground level to try to lift it up. Again he could not. At this moment, Jiang Sarn drew a talismanic symbol on his palm, then made a fist. He then

404

pointed his arm at the beast and opened his fist. Lo and behold, thunder and lightning commenced and this thing tried to remove his claws from the flagpole. Unfortunately his claws were now glued to the flagpole and he could neither get off nor lift the flagpole up.

"All right, it is my turn," said Jiang Sarn. Drawing his sword, he was ready to pierce the heart of this thing.

"Spare my life! I was stupid to have listened to Sen Buck Panther!" this thing pleaded.

Surprised at the name of Buck Panther, Jiang Sarn asked the thing: "You wanted to eat me. What does Sen Buck Panther have to do with your intention to eat me?"

"Mighty demigod, my name is Dragon Whisker Tiger. I was born long ago during an early summer not long after the creation of the world. Since then I have gathered essences of Yin and Yang to become immortal. The other day Sen Buck Panther passed by here and told me that you would travel through here sometime soon. He told me that if I ate you, I would live forever! I was too stupid and believed in him! Please spare me," this thing, Dragon Whisker Tiger, pleaded.

"All right, I will spare your life but you must become my disciple," Jiang Sarn said.

"Indeed I will," Dragon Whisker Tiger consented.

"Close your eyes," Jiang Sarn said. He then cast an incantation. A loud thunder commenced, and Dragon Whisker Tiger was freed from the flagpole.

After the thing performed the ritual to honor Jiang Sarn as his teacher-mentor, Jiang Sarn accepted Dragon Whisker Tiger as his disciple. Jiang Sarn then asked: "Do you know any Tao?"

"Yes. I know some. I know how to throw stones with accuracy. I can throw stones the size of a home millstone. I can throw stones in quick succession," Dragon Whisker Tiger said.

"He might be very useful during future night sneak attacks against enemy camps," Jiang Sarn muttered to himself.

They arrived at West Branch City and Jiang Sarn dropped his No-elephant to the ground. All the warriors were startled at the look of Dragon Whisker Tiger. "Where did he get a thing like this," one of them asked.

"He is Dragon Whisker Tiger from the North Sea. He is my newest disciple. Any irregularities since I was away?" Jiang Sarn said.

"Nothing," Wu the Serendipity answered.

"Then prepare for a major engagement," Jiang Sarn ordered.

Fragrant Cassia waited for five days. Jiang Sarn did not deliver gratuities to his army, nor Flying Tiger and his father to his encampment. He discussed this with the four Taoists. "Honorable teachers, five days have passed since you delivered your demands to Jiang Sarn. Nothing has happened. Would he cheat us?"

"He made a promise to us. I do not think he will renege on his promise. If he deceives us, we will level his city, fill his city streets with corpses and blood," Wang Devil boasted.

Another three days passed by and they heard nothing from Jiang Sarn. Yang Forest said to Wang Devil, "It has been eight days since Jiang

Sarn made his promise and he has delivered us nothing. Let's go and demand an immediate response."

Fragrant Cassia joined in: "He might have sensed that he could not win us the other day, so he agreed to all our demands. He appeared sincere, but he never struck me as a honest person."

Yang Forest said, "Let's go to demand an immediate response. If he deceives us, we will strike. It will not take long for us to wipe them out. You can then return to your capital triumphantly."

The soldiers quickly formed an attacking formation and marched towards the city gate. Jiang Sarn, riding his No-elephant, brought Nata, Dragon Whisker Tiger and Flying Tiger, out of the city gate, facing the attackers.

"You deceitful Jiang Sarn! You used the time we gave you to prepare for surrender to go to East Kwen Ren Range to borrow this No-elephant! Do not think the addition of a mere riding beast can turn things around. All right, we will wipe you out today," Wang Devil shouted, while forging his Canis Terribilis forward, waving a sword in his hand.

Nata intercepted Wang Devil with his fire-tipped spear. "Get away from my uncle-teacher!" The short sword of Wang Devil was no match for the long, fire-tipped spear. Yang Forest, seeing that Wang Devil began to show signs of weakening under the powerful thrusts of the fire-tipped spear, took out a fetish ball and threw it at Nata, immediately felling him. As Wang Devil waved his sword trying to kill Nata, Flying Tiger ran his Five Color Godspeed Ox forward and engaged Wang Devil in combat. Again Yang Forest used the same fetish ball and knocked down Flying Tiger.

407

At this moment, Dragon Whisker Tiger rushed forward. "You get away from my fellow warriors."

"What kind of devil is this?" Even Wang Devil was startled. At this moment, Kao Friendly Sovereign rode his Panthera Immensus forward and threw a fetish ball at Dragon Whisker Tiger, hitting him in his neck. However, before anything could happen to the three, foot soldiers rushed forward and quickly pulled the three wounded back to the city. Alone and defenseless, Jiang Sarn ran his No-elephant towards wildness to escape from the melee.

Seeing that Jiang Sarn had escaped, Lee Hegemony chased him and threw his Ball of Earth at him, cracking his breast armor and wounding him. Jiang Sarn turned his No-elephant around, heading towards the direction of the North Sea. As the four red beams of light lifted No-elephant up to escape, Wang Devil laughed, "Don't think you are the only one who can fly." He also patted the head of his Canis Terribilis and the beast also flew to the sky. Taking his Ball of Creation out, he knocked Jiang Sarn off the saddle of No-elephant. Jiang Sarn fell down and landed on a slope, face up, unconscious.

As Wang Devil was about to kill Jiang Sarn with his sword, a Taoist came by, singing:

> Gentle winds flutter by weeping willows,
> In this desolate wilderness I roam.
> Fallen flowers float on a quiet pond.
> Where is my home?
> High above and deep among clouds.

Raising his head, Wang Devil saw and recognized the singing Taoist, who was Demigod Grand Bodhi Manjusri, of Cavern High Clouds in Five Dragon Mountain. "Why are you here?"

"To save Jiang Sarn. Under the directive from Palace Jade Abstraction, I have been waiting here for some time for your arrival. Jiang Sarn has the important mission to appoint deities at the end of the forthcoming war. You, an accomplished Taoist from Sect Interceptus, should roam freely and happily within your territory. You should not be involved in affairs of the world of dust, otherwise your name will be included in the Roll of Divinities."

"Grand Bodhi Manjusri, you are arrogant! Although we belong to different sects of Tao, we are still fellow Taoists. What do you mean by asking me not to be involved? I have been asked by the Imperial Teacher to come here to defeat Jiang Sarn. It is an obligation I cannot refuse. I am also backed by my Sect," Wang Devil retorted, as he started to approach Grand Bodhi Manjusri with his sword.

"Don't try to start any violence. Here I come," interceded Suvarnata, son of Li Gin and the eldest brother of Nata, also a disciple of Grand Bodhi Manjusri. Wang Devil turned his sword to Suvarnata and a sword-to-sword duel began. As the combat went on, Grand Bodhi Manjusri took out the Pole of Dragons – the one that had confined Nata before – and planted it in the ground. With an incantation, Wang Devil suddenly found himself restrained to the Pole. A gold ring bound him at his neck, another at his waist, and the third one around his two legs. With a single strike, Suvarnata cut Wang Devil into halves. His spirit then wandered towards the site of the Platform for Appointment of Divinities. Using the Banner of All Souls, Pah Mirror, now God of Prevalent Blessing, directed this spirit to a temporary holding area, waiting for the arrival of the Appointment Day. The first deity candidate had been sequestered.

After Wang Devil was killed, Grand Bodhi Manjusri knelt towards the direction of East Kwen Ren Range and prayed: "Please forgive me.

This disciple has just broken the code of abstinence from carnage." After this brief repentance, he asked Suvarnata to carry Jiang Sarn on his back to the top of the mountain. Taking out an herb pill and dissolving it in water, he forced the medicine solution down Jiang Sarn's throat.

Moments later, Jiang Sarn moaned and woke. "How did I get to meet you here?" he asked.

Grand Bodhi Manjusri related to Jiang Sarn the entire episode. After a short rest, he told Suvarnata: "You should now accompany Jiang Sarn back to West Branch City and stay there to assist him. Take the Pole of Dragons with you. I will join you later when the time comes."

After burying the body of Wang Devil, the two went back to West Branch City, which was already in a turmoil, looking all over for Jiang Sarn. The return of the premier was celebrated. Jiang Sarn then introduced Suvarnata to King of Arms. Afterwards, Suvarnata was reunited with his brother Nata.

Worrying about the overdue Wang Devil, Yang Forest prognosticated and found out about his tragic death. "Damn it. Thousands of years of study of Tao ended, in an untimely death at the hands of Taoists from Five Dragon Mountain. We must avenge his death." The three remaining Taoists waited impatiently for dawn to come to carry out their vengeance.

Early the next morning the three Taoists rode their fierce beasts to the city gate of West Branch and demanded an encounter with Jiang Sarn, who was still recuperating from his wounds. Suvarnata said to Jiang Sarn: "Don't worry, go out and face them. I will protect you."

Jiang Sarn, riding his No-elephant and escorted by Nata and Suvarnata, went out of the city gate to face the three challengers. Uttering words of curses, the three Taoists charged forward with their swords drawn at Jiang Sarn. Both Nata and Suvarnata intercepted the attackers. "Let me try the Deity-Pounding Whip my teacher gave me," Jiang Sarn muttered to himself, and the Whip was released. Thunder and lightning commenced and the Whip whisked at Kao Friendly Sovereign, instantly cracked his skull and killed him. Yang Forest, roaring his anger, turned to Jiang Sarn with his sword. To divert Yang's attack, Nata cast his Bracelet of Zion at Yang Forest. Before Yang Forest could catch the Bracelet of Zion, Suvarnata took out the Pole of Dragons and confined Yang to the three gold rings and cut him into halves. The spirits of both Kao and Yang were steered towards the site of the Platform for Appointment of Divinities and were guided into the temporary holding area by Pah, God of Prevalent Blessing.

Watching their side in defeat, Fragrant Cassia and Wind Forest charged out of their encampment to the aid of the remaining Taoist, Lee Hegemony. A melee commenced. At this moment, from West Branch City emerged a young warrior who was in a silvery suit of armor and helmet – a son of Flying Tiger, by the name Huang Heavenly Blessing. He lunged towards Wind Forest. Amidst rapid movements of his spear, Heavenly Blessing pierced Wind Forest and dragged his body to the ground. The spirit of Wind Forest was also directed to the temporary holding area at the site of the Platform for Appointment of Deities.

Fragrant Cassia and Lee Hegemony retreated. Jiang Sarn, having won the battle nearly decisively, let them retreat back to their encampment.

After they had returned to the safe haven of their encampment, Lee Hegemony suggested: "Out of the four of us who came to help you, three have already died. We must send a messenger with an urgent message to the Imperial Teacher asking for help. There is no time to lose."

In West Branch City, congratulations poured to Heavenly Blessing – it had been his first experience of a real combat and he had done it so well. Jiang Sarn gave high praise to his spear play. All warriors reported their hits, which were then recorded. Suvarnata suggested: "We have nearly decisively won this long engagement. We must ride on the crest of our victory to eliminate the enemy altogether. Tomorrow, let us finish them off." Jiang Sarn and the other warriors agreed.

The next morning, in high victorious spirits, Jiang Sarn's entire army went out of the city gate to challenge their enemy. Fragrant Cassia, having never been defeated in his life, went out to face his challengers. "Sink or swim, this is it." he determined. However, his enemy was equally determined. In order to prevent him from using his mesmerizing magic to get people off their horses, all the warriors from Jiang Sarn's camp – no less than 20 – unified their combat against Fragrant Cassia.

In the meantime, Jiang Sarn ordered Suvarnata to challenge Lee Hegemony. "I will use my Deity-Pounding Whip to help you," he said. As Suvarnata combated against Lee Hegemony, Nata also joined in. When Jiang Sarn took out his Deity-Pounding Whip, Lee Hegemony knew the power it had. Patting the head of his riding beast, Zeng Ning, wind and clouds formed under its four hoofs and it flew up to the sky, escaping towards Nine Dragon Island. Nata let Lee escape, for he had another mission to accomplish. He joined the combating warriors against Fragrant Cassia. Among the encircling warriors was Zhao Field, who had defected during his unsuccessful campaign against West Branch City. Zhao Field bellowed at Fragrant Cassia: "Give up and yield, we will share peace and prosperity!"

"You shameless traitors! Do you expect me to follow your example? I have already dedicated my life to my Emperor," Fragrant Cassia proudly refused. The combat then continued from morning to noon, and Fragrant Cassia could not get out of the heavy blockade of warriors. He was tired and his strength was fading. He roared for the last time: "My Emperor Zoe! I failed my mission, but I will not yield. I would rather die for my cause!" Turning his spear towards himself, he pierced his own heart and fell to the ground. His spirit, too, was guided to the temporary holding area in the site of the Platform for Appointment of Deities.

A part of the defeated army of Chang Fragrant Cassia surrendered to West Branch City, but many managed to escape back to their home camp, Frontier Pass Blue Dragon. Jiang Sarn, having wiped out the last of the invaders, returned to the city triumphantly. Needless to say, banquets of celebration followed.

As for the escaping Taoist, Lee Hegemony, after flying his beast away as fast as he could for a while, he paused his Zeng Ning and dropped it to the side of a mountain when he was sure no enemy was pursuing. Leaning the beast against a pine tree, he sat on a piece of rock, thinking. "The four of us studied Tao in Nine Dragon Island for thousands of years without any mishap. Now in this West Branch City three brother Taoists have been killed. How can I go back to the Island to face my other colleagues? Maybe I should go to Morning Song to confer with the Imperial Teacher first." As he was pondering, a young Taoist passed by.

"Good day." The young Taoist presented a Taoist greeting. Lee Hegemony responded with a similar greeting. "May I ask where is your cavern and your mountain?"

"I am from Nine Dragon Island. I am just resting to recover from my recent defeat by Jiang Sarn of West Branch City. Where do you come from?" Lee Hegemony said.

"Ha! I couldn't find him in a thousand years and in this place in the middle of nowhere I encounter him unexpectedly!" the young Taoist muttered to himself. He then declared loudly: "I am no other than Li Moksa, a disciple of Demigod Pu Hsian Prevalent Sage, of Cavern White Crane in Mount Nine Palaces. He sent me to the aid of Jiang Sarn, to help him terminate the reign of the evil Emperor Zoe. Before I departed, he asked me to catch Lee Hegemony and deliver him to Jiang Sarn. I didn't even know how and where to begin! You have just made my day! Completely unexpectedly!"

"You dire evil! How dare you nudge me around!" Lifting his heavy sword, he charged towards Moksa. Moksa responded to the challenge with his sword. After ten rounds of dueling, Moksa pulled from his back a dharmaratna sword by the name of Woo Hook and released it up the sky. Woo Hook Sword sped to the sky and then whisked down rapidly towards Lee Hegemony and slashed his throat while he was still engaging his rounds with Moksa. The temporary holding area of the Platform of Appointment of Divinities had just received another spirit.

After burying the body of Lee Hegemony, Moksa continued his trip to West Branch City. He easily located the official residence of Jiang Sarn and asked to be admitted. Jiang Sarn received him, and asked Moksa: "Where do you come from?"

Suvarnata answered for Moksa. "He is my brother. He studied Tao under Demigod Prevalent Sage, of Cavern White Crane in Mount Nine Palaces."

414

"I am glad that you three brothers are united. I am very pleased that you are all members of this command," Jiang Sarn commended.

West Branch City thus survived its first major attack by Emperor Zoe's forces. The city suffered virtually no loss, and it gained three capable young Taoists. However, compared to what was to come, the war had not even begun.

War among Gods and Men

14. Mo Brothers

With most capable officers either executed or exiled, the Imperial Teacher had to take complete charge of affairs in Emperor Zoe's court and in the city of Morning Song. He was a very systematic person. Under his guidance the city and the court were run efficiently and smoothly. The two toadies, Yu the Adulator and Fei the Corrupt, having learned a lesson from their near execution, became much less arrogant and less visible. Emperor Zoe did carry out his promise of fulfilling some of the seven points of reform he agreed to and he actually sat in more court sessions than ever. The Imperial Teacher, meanwhile, assumed that with the help of his powerful former colleagues from Nine Dragon Island, the rebellion of West Branch City would be squashed in no time.

Instead, an urgent message from Han Glory, the sentry commander of Frontier Pass Vast Water, arrived at the capital informing the Imperial Teacher of the death of his three Taoist friends and the imminent danger that shadowed the remaining Taoist and Chang Fragrant Cassia. Slapping his palm hard on his desk, the Imperial Teacher roared in grief and frustration: "My poor Taoist brothers! How could you have died just like that? It should have been me. I could not get away from my office to take care of this rebellion so I asked you to help me. Now you have sacrificed your lives on my behalf! I vow vengeance!" He then ordered his attendants to sound signal drums to summon all warriors and generals to the conference hall in his official residence.

When all the warriors and generals had congregated in the meeting hall, the Imperial Teacher announced: "A few months ago I sought the help of my four Taoist friends from Nine Dragon Island to help Chang

417

Fragrant Cassia to squash the rebellion of West Branch City. Unfortunately three of them and one of our warriors, Wind Forest, perished during this quest. We must take action before the strength of the rebels grows further. Which one of you will volunteer to reinforce Chang Fragrant Cassia?"

"I will," Ru Brave volunteered.

"If you will excuse me, you are quite old, to be frank. I have doubts that you will be able to accomplish this feat," the Imperial Teacher politely declined.

"Your Excellency. It is true that Chang Fragrant Cassia is much younger, but he is arrogant and he relies too much on his magical power. Wind Forest is a brave warrior but he has little brain. This is the reason why he perished. To be a good military general, one must first carefully study local geography and weather patterns. In assignment of duties, one must recognize and utilize meritorious qualities of his warriors. He must utilize these qualities in a most efficient manner and he must avoid exposing his weaknesses to enemies. He must have the disposition of patience, but at the same time he must always be on the alert and always be ready for action. I have all these qualities. An army of one hundred thousand will be adequate for this mission. An army of this size, if well-commanded, can accomplish a great deal. In addition to this army, I only need one or two consultants or advisors. I can assure you of my success," Ru Brave argued.

The Imperial Teacher was impressed by the eloquence and reasoning of the general. "You have convinced me that you really know the art of military deployment," the Imperial Teacher agreed. "In addition, you are extremely loyal. You said that you needed two consultants and advisors. These consultants must be cunning and alert. I propose the names Yu Whenn and Fei Chung." Ru enthusiastically endorsed this choice. The meeting was thus adjourned.

Yu Whenn the Adulator and Fei Chung the Corrupt were summoned to the presence of the Imperial Teacher. "You two have been appointed military consultants and advisors to aid General Ru Brave to reinforce Chang Fragrant Cassia. If you do well in your job, you will be amply rewarded upon your return."

This was a tremendous shock to the two. To calumniate against loyal officers and to adulate the Emperor? Yes! They knew how to do these evil deeds well. To advise a loyal general on a real military mission? No! They had never done anything useful in their entire lives! Quickly the two pleaded: "Your Excellency. We are civil officers and we know of no military skills. Please excuse us from this military duty."

"No. Your abilities are well-known to His Majesty Emperor. You two are known to have provided excellent advice to him, because he often listens to you. You have the ability to recognize quickly intricacies of a situation and to change your views accordingly. This is a very good quality and it can be gainfully applied to situations involving complex military operations. Besides, you two have often maintained yourselves as the most loyal officers and have reiterated over and over again that you will not hesitate to sacrifice your lives for the Emperor. Do not renege on your pledge of loyalty!" The Imperial Teacher then ordered his junior officers to bring the official seals and insignia of the rank of military advisors. These official apparatus were immediately issued to the two. The Imperial Teacher would not hear any further arguments offered by the two toadies so they were appointed military advisors after the seals of authority and insignia of their new rank were passed to them. Silk flowers were pinned on their dresses as tokens of congratulations to their newly appointed posts.

A copper tablet of command – similar to the fire tablet described earlier, but carrying less urgency – was issued to General Ru as a token of military authority. An army of fifty thousand was mobilized and placed under his command. This, together with the 50,000 army under the command of Chang Fragrant Cassia then would make up the 100,000 Ru Brave requested. A provident day was chosen and after the usual sacrifices to sanctify the battle flag, the army marched towards West Branch City. However, this was late summer and the weather was still very hot. The heavy armor the soldiers wore multiplied the torture of the heat from the late summer sun.

After the army passed through the last frontier pass, Vast Water, scout patrols reported: "The entire army of Chang Fragrant Cassia has been wiped out. His head is on display at the east gate of West Branch City. There is no one for us to reinforce."

"What?" Ru Brave was startled. "Stop here. Now where are we?" he asked.

"This is West Branch Mountain," a scout reported.

Ru Brave decided to station his troops by the mountain while he contemplated what to do next. Besides, there was a forest nearby, which would shield the incessant heat from the sun. He thus ordered: "Set up our encampment inside the forest under tree shade, as the weather is hot." Meanwhile, an urgent message was sent back to the Imperial Teacher to inform him of the liquidation of the army of Chang Fragrant Cassia, and the death of Chang himself, as well as to request reinforcements since Chang's army was completely gone.

Concurrently, in West Branch City, Jiang Sarn had already selected a provident day according to Tao to start construction work on the Platform for Appointment of Divinities. Under the guidance of the God of Prevalent Blessing and through the hard and dedicated work of the Five Gods of Roadways, the Platform was completed in no time, together with a new holding area to house those poor souls who had lost their earthly lives because of their beliefs. It remained for Jiang Sarn to dedicate the Platform to formalize its function.

Before Jiang Sarn could plan for the ceremony, his scout patrols reported the arrival of an apparently hostile army which had already set up an encampment in West Branch Mountain. In response, Jiang Sarn ordered Nangong Swift and Wu Serendipity to station an army of 5,000 at a strategic location – a narrow part of a mountain path – to stop further movements of this hostile army towards West Branch City.

The defending force soon arrived at the foot of West Branch Mountain. They could see clearly in the distance the color and insignia of flags of their enemy – distinctively those of Shang. The weather was extremely hot and this part of the mountain was almost barren. There was no shade to shield the soldiers from the incessant scorching heat of the sun. They became irritated at the tormenting heat. Wu Serendipity conferred with Nangong Swift: "We have been ordered to encamp our army here. Yet there are no convenient water sources nearby and there is no shade. Soldiers will start to complain really soon."

The next morning, Warrior Hsin Chia brought a personal order from Jiang Sarn: "Move the encampment to the top of West Branch Mountain." All were startled: "The mountaintop is barren without any water supply. If we set our camp there, we will all perish of thirst soon." However, a military order was a military order; one must obey the order no matter what. The encampment was moved. Soldiers complained about the enormous difficulty involved in fetching water for essential purposes, such as preparation of meals and so on.

Inside the forest under tree shade, Ru Brave observed the movements of his enemy and laughed at the stupidity of the commander to encamp his soldiers at the top of a barren mountain, especially during such hot weather. "Within three days they will all die of thirst and we won't even have to bother to fight against them!" Thus Ru Brave decided to wait for reinforcements to arrive to complete his mission.

The next day, Jiang Sarn arrived, leading an army of 3,000 to reinforce Nangong Swift and Wu Serendipity. The reinforcements also set up their encampment at the top of the mountain. "Go and construct an earthen platform, three feet high. Complete it as soon as possible," Jiang Sarn ordered.

Meanwhile, warrior Hsin Mian escorted shipments of supplies to the camp. The supply consisted of seemingly irrelevant items such as heavy winter cotton jackets and umbrella hats. Each soldier was issued a heavy winter cotton jacket and a giant umbrella hat. "With these heavy winter jackets, we are going to die of heat stroke even sooner," muttered some of the soldiers.

By early evening Wu Serendipity reported: "The earthen platform is completed."

"Very good." Jiang Sarn commended.

Later in the evening, Jiang Sarn readied himself to perform the ritual to cast Taoist incantations. First he changed into a different Taoist robe. Next he disheveled his hair to disperse, symbolically, the dust of vanity that he had accumulated in the world of mortals. He then knelt

422

down towards the direction of East Kwen Ren Range and prayed to his teacher-mentor. He next danced Tao steps of incantation, and with his sword of Tao he drew signs of talismanic constellations on the sky while he danced the incomprehensible Tao steps. He then read verses from a book of spells, while sprinkling holy water around and drawing talismanic signs around him. Lo and behold, gusts of wind gathered instantly, which first blew mildly, then became stronger and harder. The sky was soon covered with dark clouds.

"Excellent. The Imperial Teacher's reinforcements will not encounter the same hardship of hot weather as we suffered on our way here," Ru Brave rejoiced as the wind cooled down the incessantly hot weather.

"The weather turned favorable because of the blessing heaven bestows upon the Emperor," the two toadies, Yu the Adulator and Fei the Corrupt, who had been conditioned by their habits of adulation all their lives, instinctively added.

However, unknown to General Ru, the change of weather was not a blessing. The winds blew harder and harder. After three days of cloud gathering, a cold front arrived and the air temperature suddenly dropped to below freezing.

"Maybe the punishment for evil deeds of the Emperor has come. This is extremely unusual weather for this time of year. We have severe winter weather at the end of summer!" some soldiers in Ru's camp mutely prophesied.

The worst was yet to come. Snow began to fall heavily and gusts of wind turned the heavy snow fall into a severe snowstorm. "We did not bring any winter clothes with us," complained Ru's soldiers.

"Do you have any idea how to get us out of this current difficulty," Ru Brave asked the two toadies, Yu the Adulator and Fei the Corrupt. Naturally these two had no idea why the weather pattern had changed, nor did they have any good advice to offer.

Meanwhile, the problem of water supply at the mountaintop was solved, due to the accumulation of snow. With the heavy winter jackets issued earlier, Jiang Sarn's army did not suffer from the cold weather as Ru's army did. "How much snow do we have now," Jiang Sarn finally asked.

"Two feet at the top of the mountain and probably four or five at the foot," Wu Serendipity replied.

"Very good," Jiang Sarn muttered to himself. By the evening, he again changed to a Taoist dress, disheveled his hair, danced the incomprehensible Tao steps and cast yet another incantation on the earthen platform. The next morning, the snowstorm stopped and the sun reappeared. Within hours, the snow melted under the irradiation of the normal late summer sun. This sudden thaw caused the bottom of the mountain to be flooded. By now soldiers in Jiang Sarn's mountaintop encampment appreciated the foresight of the earlier military order to station them at the top of the mountain.

A day or two later, almost all the snow had melted and the valley was flooded with water. Once again, in early evening, Jiang Sarn performed the proper rituals and danced the Tao steps to cast yet another incantation. This time the weather merely turned freezing cold. Within days the flood water at the bottom of the hill was frozen into solid ice. Ru's army became completely immobile.

Jiang Sarn then ordered Nangong Swift and Wu Serendipity: "Take twenty armed men with you down the mountain and bring Ru Brave and the two toadies here." As all the soldiers were suffering from the freezing weather and could not fight, the two accomplished their mission without any difficulty and they delivered the three to Jiang Sarn's presence at their mountaintop encampment.

Ru Brave stood defiantly, while the two toadies Yu the Adulator and Fei the Corrupt knelt down and begged for their lives. Jiang Sarn ignored the two toadies and addressed Ru. "General Ru, you must know that with all the evil deeds Emperor Zoe has done, Shang dynasty is about to come to an end. Now you are our captive. You are single-handed. You are a lone supporter of this evil Emperor. Why do you have to act against the wishes of the heaven? Will you yield," Jiang Sarn asked.

"You rebel!" Ru Brave shouted defiantly. "You once served in Emperor Zoe's court but you have betrayed him. I shall not disavow my fealty towards Emperor Zoe. Unfortunately I am your captive now. As a loyal officer I would rather die than surrender. I am ready to die."

"If it is your desire to sacrifice yourself for the evil cause of your Emperor, then I cannot stop you." Ignoring the pleading of the two toadies to spare them and their repeated assertion of their willingness to serve with unquestioned loyalty the "premier of the people", Jiang Sarn ordered his guards: "Imprison them for the time being."

During the evening, Jiang Sarn, after performing proper rituals, cast another incantation to restore the weather to its normal pattern. By the next morning, the late summer sun reappeared. The ice melted and the ground thawed. Two to three thousand of the fifty thousand troops brought by Ru had died of exposure during the recent sudden change of weather and as soon the ground was thawed enough to walk, the rest escaped to Frontier Pass Vast Water. The battle was won without a combat.

Jiang Sarn did not pursue the fleeing army remnants. He had a more important mission to complete. He asked Nangong Swift to go back to West Branch City to invite King of Arms to West Branch Mountain.

Upon the return of Nangong Swift, King of Arms was somewhat concerned about the hot weather. "My proxy father premier suffered through the torturous weather on my behalf. How is he doing now?" King of Arms said.

"He is doing fine. He asked me to invite you to go to West Branch Mountain," Nangong Swift responded.

"Do you know why he wants me there," asked the King of Arms.

"No, the premier did not tell me his reason, but he does want you there," replied Nangong Swift.

The snowstorm commanded by Jiang Sarn's incantation had certainly been only a local phenomenon, for around West Branch City the weather was as hot as ever. Twenty li from the city, the King of Arms was surprised to see blocks of ice floating in nearby creeks and trenches. Nangong Swift briefed the king on the alteration of the weather by Jiang Sarn to defeat the invading army.

Another 50 li later, they arrived at the top of West Branch Mountain. After a brief official welcome ceremony, the King of Arms said: "May I ask my proxy father premier, what is the purpose of my visit here?"

Jiang Sarn did not want King of Arms to know that this was to be the dedication ceremony of the Platform for Appointment of Divinities.

426

He merely said: "I would like Your Highness to perform a ritual to honor West Branch Mountain."

Although puzzled, King of Arms agreed. "This mountain has been here for eons of time and my people have been benefited by its resources for time immemorial. It is certainly appropriate for me to perform a ritual to honor this mountain and its gods."

A table of offering was set. Jiang Sarn prepared a document of dedication, but he showed it to no one. He first placed this document on the table of offering. Next he ordered the execution of the three prisoners. The heads of the three prisoners were then presented as sacrifices of offering. Thus, the prognostication by King of Literature that Yu and Fei would eventually die amidst snow and frozen water was fulfilled.

"We are here to perform a ritual to honor this mountain, why do you have to use human sacrifices?" the startled King of Arms said.

"Two of them are Yu Whenn and Fei Chung, wellknown toadies in the court of Emperor Zoe," Jiang Sarn replied, without naming the third one, the loyal officer Ru Brave.

"These two were obsequious sycophants of the court of Emperor Zoe. Their executions are rightfully justified," King of Arms, knowing the reputation of the two, agreed.

The dedication of the Platform for Appointment of Divinities was thus completed. Without realizing what he had done, the King of Arms had dedicated the Platform with the sacrifice of three prisoners. And with the addition of three new spirits, who did not need to wander far to be guided to their places in the new holding area, the Platform was open for business, so to speak.

War among Gods and Men

In the capital, the Imperial Teacher first received the good news that Deng the Ninth Lord had almost decisively defeated the Duke of South. He became very happy. However, his happiness did not last long. After the remnants of Ru's army escaped to Frontier Pass Vast Water, the news of the defeat of Ru Brave was promptly transmitted by the sentry commander Han Glory to the Imperial Teacher. The Imperial Teacher instantly became furious.

Trampling his feet heavily on the floor of his office, Imperial Teacher roared in anger and in frustration: "I never expected Jiang Sarn to be so difficult an enemy. Not only has he killed Chang Fragrant Cassia, he also completely defeated a very experienced general, Ru Brave. I must head the next campaign myself against him." Then he lamented, "Damn! There is still rebellion in the east. In addition, although a nearly decisive victory has been achieved, rebellion in the south is not completely squashed yet. What should I do? What should I do?" In desperation he almost cried, shouting his discontent to Heaven, as if help might come thence.

His loyal disciple Chi Li tried to console the Imperial Teacher. He again suggested: "Your Excellency, West Branch City has many capable warriors and military advisors. Even as capable a general as Chang Fragrant Cassia was, he could not overcome them. Even with the help of the four very powerful and capable Taoists from Nine Dragon Island, he was defeated and killed. We must overcome the evil city of West Branch, even though they are riding on the crest of their recent victories. We must draw our trump card and ask the four sentry commanders in Frontier Pass Good Dreams to lead a campaign against them. These four sentry leaders are brothers, of the family name of Mo. They have invincible magical powers and they are known never to have lost a

428

single war or battle. These four Mo Brothers should be able to eliminate Jiang Sarn and the rebellion."

"You are right!" The Imperial Teacher was extremely elated at this suggestion. "I should have thought of this myself! Thank you! My head has been muddled by so many recent events and I cannot think clearly. I thank you for this excellent suggestion. I will immediately dispatch an order to ask the four Mo Brothers to suppress the rebellion of the Zhou Dukedom."

A copper tablet of command was issued to order the Mo Brothers to commence a campaign to crush the rebellion of West Branch City. Two warrior generals, who were brothers, Hu Lei (Thunder) and Hu Seng (Ascension), were dispatched to temporarily take over the defense of Frontier Pass Good Dreams until the return of the Mo Brothers from their campaign.

Upon receiving the order from the Imperial Teacher to ask them to squash rebellion of the Zhou Dukedom, the four Mo Brothers laughed. "The Imperial Teacher is overreacting. The enemy in West Branch City consists of incompetents such as Huang Flying Tiger and Jiang Sarn. Why does he have to engage us? It is nothing for us to overcome them. Like cracking a small nut with a sledge-hammer! Nevertheless, since he has ordered us to go, we will obey his order." After transferring the authority of command to the Hus, the Mo Brothers departed for West Branch City with an army of 100,000.

Days later, the Mo Brothers and their army crossed the last mountain, Ridge Peach Blossom, and arrived at the northern vicinity of West Branch City. Scouts reported: "The north gate of West Branch City is just beyond the horizon."

Figure I- 25. Mo Brothers

"Stop the troop movement and set up our encampment here," the Mo Brothers ordered.

During the time when the Mo Brothers and their army were mobilized to move towards West Branch City, Jiang Sarn had been enjoying his popularity, because he had successfully frozen West Branch Mountain with his Tao to defeat the most recent invasion efforts of Emperor Zoe's forces. His prestige grew tremendously and many capable warriors and scholars from different parts of the land joined his command. During one of his frequent conference sessions with his staff members on civil matters of the city, a scout reported to Jiang Sarn the approach of the Mo Brothers and their 100,000 troops. The meeting was interrupted and an emergency meeting on the defense of the city was called instead.

After all the high ranking warriors had gathered in the conference hall of his official residence, Jiang Sarn briefed them on the circumstances, the name of the invading warrior generals and asked for opinions on how to fend off this invasion. Huang Flying Tiger left his rank and said: "Your Excellency, may I have your permission to say a few words?"

Jiang Sarn replied, "Of course, please go ahead."

"Thank you for your kindness," Flying Tiger continued, "The four Mo Brothers learned various magical tricks from masters unknown to me and they possess an assortment of powerful magical weapons. The name of the eldest of the four is Mo Li Blue, an extremely tall man over seven feet. His face is like a crab with whiskers as stiff as copper wires. He uses a long spear as his weapon and he fights on foot. He has a fetish sword, called the Sword of Blue Clouds. It has four talismanic inscriptions, Earth, Water, Fire, Wind. When the power of Wind is commanded, the Sword generates a black column of smoke blowing thousands of spears and hooks at the enemy. If the magic of Fire is summoned, the Sword sends out thousands of fire snakes spewing fire and smoke and as these snakes roam around, they burn anything in sight. The second eldest brother is known by the name of Mo Li Red. He has a fetish device known as Umbrella of Primeval Pearls. It is embroidered with primordial pearls of nature. When this Umbrella is opened, it sucks all other magical devices of lesser Tao into it, rendering many of our dharmaratna devices useless. In addition, it darkens the sky, shakes the earth, and commands hurricanes. The name of the third brother is Mo Li Sea. He uses a long spear as his weapon. He carries a Pee-Pa harp with him. This Pee-Pa has four strings, tuned to four talismanic tones of Earth, Water, Wind and Fire. When its respective strings are plucked, this Pee-Pa yields the same terrible power as the Sword of Blue Clouds. The youngest brother, by the name of Mo Li Longevity, uses two stiff whips as his weapons. He has a mythical beast, known by the name of Spotty Foxy Sable, which when kept in a storage bag assumes the likeness of a small white ferret. When this beast is released, however, it grows into the size of a gigantic elephant with the ability to fly as swiftly as a sparrow. It can swallow thousands of soldiers in one single gulp. I am afraid we do not have countermeasures against these fetish devices."

"How do you know all this?" Jiang Sarn was a little surprised at such a detailed description of the four Mo Brothers.

"The four used to be under my command when I led a campaign in East Sea years ago. This is how I learned about their capabilities," Flying Tiger responded.

Since information supplied by Flying Tiger in the past had been correct almost on every occasion, his opinion had to be trusted. Thus Jiang Sarn and his staff were quite depressed to learn that the new enemies were much more powerful than anyone they had encountered so far, and, as nearly as they could tell, invincible.

The next day, the four Mo Brothers advanced their army to the north gate of West Branch City and challenged the city. Knowing the enormous magical power they had, Jiang Sarn was hesitant to face them. However, Moksa, Suvarnata and Nata disagreed. Nata said: "Teacher, we cannot avoid facing them. General Huang has already briefed us on their capabilities. However fierce and invincible they are, we still have to respond to them. My teacher promised to help me in case of difficulty and so did your teacher. We have many demigod friends who will also help us. In addition, prognostications indicated by current astronomical arrangements of stars and constellations of the sky favor us. We cannot stop here. We must face their challenge."

Jiang Sarn was reminded of his teacher's promise. Yes, there had been ups and downs before, but he had always managed to get through all the past difficulties without harm. Besides, he was the leader and he could not bear the name of a coward. "Yes, we must face them," decided Jiang Sarn. He ordered all his warriors to be ready for action.

The north gate of the city opened. Jiang Sarn's army marched out and a well organized battle formation materialized almost instantly. Riding his beast No-elephant forward, Jiang Sarn faced the Mo Brothers.

"Are you the four Mo Commanders," Jiang Sarn asked politely, slightly bending his riding posture.

"Yes," Mo Li Blue responded. "Jiang Sarn, you invaded the territory of Shang. You rebelled against our Emperor. You sheltered rebels, violated Shang's laws. You executed our generals and officers and displayed their heads in your city gates. Now we, the officially designated force of vengeance under an order from Emperor Zoe, are here to subdue you. If you do not surrender right away, we will level your entire city and slaughter every person in your country. You will not even have an opportunity to regret."

"My dear Commanders, you are utterly wrong," replied Jiang Sarn. "We are law-abiding citizens. We are still officers of the court of Shang, our people still pledge loyalty to Shang. Our land was granted by the founder of the Shang dynasty to our founding king as a dukedom under Shang. We have never rebelled against Shang. Your source of information is wrong. So far we have been invaded by your forces, and not even one soldier from our side has crossed our boundary to violate the territory of Shang. You have wrongly charged us as rebels. We will not accept your false accusation."

"You wise guys! You think you can convince us of your innocence by your distorted reasoning? You don't even care if your country is about to be exterminated! Brothers, charge forward!" Mo Li Blue furiously roared. The four Mo Brothers thus charged towards Jiang Sarn.

Nata rolled his Wheels of Wind and Fire forward to meet the challenge of Mo Li Sea, while Nangong Swift intercepted Mo Li Blue, and Wu Serendipity tangled with Mo Li Longevity. An altercation of confusion resulted. As the fighting continued, Nata took out his Bracelet of Zion and threw it at Mo Li Sea. Unfortunately Mo Li Red saw it and he opened up his Umbrella of Primeval Pearls and the Umbrella immediately gulped up the Bracelet. Moksa took out his Pole of Dragons, which again was also gulped up by the Umbrella of Primeval Pearls. Likewise, Jiang Sarn's Deity-Pounding Whip was also gulped up. Now that all the magical devices of Jiang Sarn's side were gone, the Mo Brothers released their magical weapons. The Spotty Foxy Sable flew swiftly around and swallowed up warrior after warrior, soldier after soldier. Spears and hooks flew down like rain while fire snakes roamed everywhere, spewing out fire and smoke. Under the heavy attack of

434

these magical weapons, Jiang Sarn's army was defeated. Moksa and Suvarnata escaped back to the city via terra-trekking, while Nata whirled his Wheels of Wind and Fire towards wilderness to escape from the rain of swords and the vicious fire and smoke spewed by the fire snakes. Dragon Whisker Tiger fled into the nearest body of water. Jiang Sarn narrowly escaped by flying his No-elephant back to the city.

An assessment of casualties was made and the dead and wounded count was as follows: Over ten thousand soldiers were killed, nine warriors of lesser rank died, six brother princes of the King of Arms perished and half of all the engaging warriors were either wounded by spears and hooks released from the Sword of Blue Clouds and the magical Pee-Pa, or burnt by fire spewed out by fire snakes. This was certainly a sad occasion in Jiang Sarn's camp since it was the biggest defeat thus far.

The Mo Brothers returned to their camp triumphantly. Mo Li Red suggested: "Let us attack the city tomorrow. We must ride on the crest of our recent victory," All agreed.

The next day, scaling ladders and all paraphernalia available to scale city walls were assembled and an all-out assault on the city was launched. Jiang Sarn ordered that tablets of temporary truce be hung, but this time the Mo Brothers completely ignored the time-honored tradition and continued their assault. Jiang Sarn ordered all warriors not severely wounded to join in the defense. Lime bottles, rolling stones, fire-tipped arrows, crossbows, boiling water, and anything they thought might be useful was used to defend the city. Three days of intensive efforts to scale the city wall resulted only in severe casualties for the attacking forces. The Mo Brothers then decided that the losses were too great to be acceptable. They decided on an alternate scheme: to lay siege to the city. Sooner or later the city would run out of food, water, supplies, or patience, the brothers reasoned.

Two months later, the defense of West Branch City was as strong as ever. The Mo Brothers began to become impatient so one day they conferred among themselves. The eldest Mo, Red, argued: "We have been here for over three months now. We have used up a great deal of the supplies we brought with us in this engagement and we have not yet accomplished our mission. The Imperial Teacher may regard us as inefficient. I suggest that tonight we coordinate our magical weapons to release their power concertedly. In our unified effort, we can certainly wipe out the city instantly." This suggestion was seconded by the other three brothers. A night attack was planned.

While Jiang Sarn was conferring with his warriors on the situation of siege of the city, a strong gust of wind suddenly blew, breaking the main mast which displayed the flag of the premier. Startled at this omen, Jiang Sarn prognosticated and discovered the scheme of the Mo Brothers. His face turned pale. Immediately, he changed into a Taoist robe and knelt towards East Kwen Ren Range, praying to his Patriarch. Then he danced the proper steps of incantation according to Tao. At the end of his incantation, he moved North Sea over, suspending it above West Branch City as a shield against the power of the magical devices to be unleashed by the Mo Brothers.

Primeval heard Jiang Sarn's prayer. To aid him, he added a layer of holy water on top of North Sea. This holy water further increased and strengthened the shielding power of the body of water. Not knowing that West Branch City was shielded by North Sea, around eight o'clock in the evening by our reckoning, the four Mo Brothers quietly emerged from their encampment and in unison they unleashed the maximum power of the Sword of Blue Clouds, of the Umbrella of Primeval Pearls,

436

and of the Pee-Pa, while the Spotty Foxy Sable was released to fly into the city searching for victims. During the entire night, fire, smoke, rain of spears and hooks, fire snakes and lightning descended upon the city, but these projectiles and snakes were stopped and neutralized by the protective water shield. All night the Spotty Foxy Sable flew around the city but could not penetrate the water shield either.

At dawn, all devices were withdrawn. When things quieted down, Jiang Sarn sent the North Sea back and began to inspect the city for damage. After a sleepless night during which the earth had rumbled and bright flashes of light were clearly visible through the body of water above, Jiang Sarn and his warriors were greatly relieved at the effectiveness of the shield against the almost invincible attacking forces. Not a single blade of grass had been disturbed at the top of the city walls.

Scout patrols reported to the Mo Brothers that apparently no damage has been inflicted on West Branch City. The Mo Brothers were startled and upset at the ineffectiveness of their supposedly invincible magical devices, but they could not figure out why they had failed. After further conferring among themselves, they only came up with the plan to continue their siege of the city.

Another two months of siege passed by. One day the officer in charge of military supply in West Branch City reported to Jiang Sarn: "Only ten days of supply of food for the army remains in the warehouse." Jiang Sarn was shocked.

Flying Tiger suggested: "I know that the city is well-stocked. Perhaps we can display notices around the city to solicit the help of wealthy citizens to lend the government their stock of food. We can promise to pay them back with interest after the siege is over."

Jiang Sarn thought it over and decided: "There are still ten days of food supply left. We do not need to ask for loans of grain from citizens as yet. If we indicate to our citizens that we are short of food for our army, they may start a rebellion for fear of defeat. Let us wait first."

Eight days later, as the shortage would soon become a reality, Jiang Sarn began to ponder whether to take up the advice of Flying Tiger. Just then, two young Taoists showed up at the gate of the official residence of Jiang Sarn and asked to have an audience with the premier. They were admitted.

The two saluted. "Respectable teacher of Tao, we are here to help you."

"From which cavern and mountain do you come, may I ask?" Always heeding to the possibility of the unexpected presence of Taoists of a rank higher than his, Jiang Sarn responded politely.

"We are disciples of Demigod Mighty Tao, from Cavern Jade Edifice in Mount Golden Court," one of the young Taoists said. "My name is Han Doolong, and his name is Shiue Oahu the Ferocious Tiger. We have been ordered by our teacher to deliver to you the needed grain supply for your army and to join your command." He then handed a letter to Jiang Sarn.

After reading the letter, Jiang Sarn became greatly relieved. He announced to his officers: "My Patriarch promised me that, when I am in difficulty, he will send help. He has kept his promise. My fellow officers, we are saved." He turned around to the two, "Please deliver the grain you brought to the warehouse." One of the two took out a two-gallon-sized basket, showing Jiang Sarn and the attending officers its contents, around half a basketful of rice. At the sight of this scanty supply, which supposedly was to fill up the nearly empty food storage

438

warehouse, the warriors did their best to keep their composure to refrain from laughing.

Moments later, Han Doolong (Poisonous Dragon) returned and reported: "We have just delivered the rice we brought with us. It will take some time to fill up the warehouse."

Two hours later, warehouse keepers came and reported: "The warehouse is filled to capacity. Rice grains even flow out of the ventilation holes." The crisis of food for the army was thus resolved.

With a fresh food supply, the city was able to continue its defense and the siege of the city continued without any decisive victory on either side for nearly a year. The Mo Brothers finally decided to send the Imperial Teacher a message reporting their failure to capture the city, that the city was still under siege but no decisive victory was in sight.

While the message asking for help from the Imperial Teacher was on its way, one day a Taoist showed up and asked to be admitted to see Jiang Sarn. "Your Excellency the premier, a Taoist is at the door to see you," a guard reported.

"Show him in." Having derived so much help from his Taoist associates, Jiang Sarn never refused the request of any Taoist for an audience with him. This one, of ordinary build and look, wore a beret in the shape of a fan and was dressed in a rather mundane-looking robe. Having tied a silk rope around his waist and wearing a pair of sandals woven from flax, this Taoist somehow showed a kind of indescribable neatness and commendation.

After the usual salutation, Jiang Sarn said: "Where do you come from?"

"My name is Yang Jian the Exterminator. I am a disciple of Demigod Jade Cauldron, of Cavern Golden Sunset Clouds in Mount Jade Spring. I am here to join your command," Yang Exterminator replied gently.

Impressed by the calm composure carried by Yang Exterminator, which imparted a depth of self-assurance, Jiang Sarn introduced him to all the warriors and then to King of Arms. After the nominal rituals of acquaintance were over, Yang Exterminator asked Jiang Sarn: "Who is the leader of the assembly of battalions outside the city? They seem to be determined to stay here for some time judging from the farming activities around their encampment."

Jiang Sarn then briefed Yang Exterminator on the past episodes of their defeat and their endeavor to defend against the invaders and their superior magical devices. Yang listened quietly. At the end he requested: "Is it possible for you to remove this tablet of temporary truce so that I can size up the Mo Brothers?"

After nearly a year's display of the tablet of temporary truce as a de facto permanent fixture (which could have been called, appropriately, a tablet of inaptness), Jiang Sarn was more than glad to remove it. "Be careful," he felt obliged to say.

The Mo Brothers were more than excited to see some action. The four came out of their encampment and were rather unimpressed to see that their opponent was a timid looking Taoist on a white horse, holding a three blade-spear as his weapon.

"Who are you?" the Mo Brothers roared.

Figure I- 26. Yang Jian the Terminator

"My name is Yang Exterminator. Jiang Sarn is my uncle-teacher. What kind of idiots are you, relying on your heresy Tao to enter our territory to lay a siege upon us? I will show you immediately that you are about to be exterminated, as my name says," Yang Exterminator challenged.

War among Gods and Men

A melee ensued. With a long spear Yang Exterminator fought the four bravely, without any sign of weakening. As the fighting continued, a military supply commander of West Branch City happened to pass by and decided to join in the battle. Unfortunately for him, Mo Li Longevity did not like having another enemy so he released his Spotty Foxy Sable. Half of this commander was immediately bitten off by the flying beast.

"Ha! So this is your trick," Yang Exterminator secretly rejoiced.

Mo Li Longevity next commanded his Spotty Foxy Sable to attack Yang Exterminator. The Spotty Foxy Sable swiftly descended and in one gulp, bit off half the body of Yang Exterminator, and with another gulp, Yang Exterminator totally disappeared. Nata, who was intensely watching the battle, reported this disaster to Jiang Sarn, who felt even more depressed than before that this new help was no better than what he had.

The Mo Brothers went back and rejoiced over another hit, the first in a seemingly long time. They feasted and drank wildly. In high spirits Mo Li Longevity offered: "Why don't I send my Spotty Foxy Sable back to the city to rampage around the town? If it eats Jiang Sarn or King of Arms, then the war is won. We can start our triumphant return march right away. What do you think of my idea?"

"Indeed a great one. Why didn't we think of it before? Do it right now." The three brothers, after some drinking, were equally elated at this suggestion.

The Spotty Foxy Sable was released. Unknown to the Mo Brothers, Yang Exterminator was an unusually intelligent person and he learned his Tao well — he had mastered the Tao of Nine Turn Primeval Deployment, a Tao that permits seventy-two different ways of transfiguration. When used in combination, these seventy-two ways of

442

transfiguration enabled him to transfigure himself virtually into anything. In fact, he was almost indestructible. Inside the body of the Spotty Foxy Sable, he had heard every word the Mo Brothers said. As the Spotty Foxy Sable flew towards West Branch City, Yang Exterminator snatched the heart out of the Sable and killed it instantly. He then split the body of the Sable into two and got out. Restoring himself to his own image, he went back to West Branch City and knocked at the door of the official residence of Jiang Sarn, around midnight.

"A ghost is here!" the startled door guard screamed, having heard the fate of Yang Exterminator earlier.

Nata went out to investigate and saw Yang Exterminator. "You are already dead," he exclaimed.

"Our Taos are different. I am not dead. Please report to the premier that I want to see him," Yang Exterminator replied.

The Exterminator went into the conference hall with Nata. Jiang Sarn was very startled: "You were killed this morning, how did you revivify yourself?"

"I was not dead. It was my scheme to destroy the Spotty Foxy Sable." Yang Exterminator then related to Jiang Sarn the schemes of the Mo Brothers. "I just killed the Spotty Foxy Sable to come here." After chatting for a while, Yang Exterminator wanted to leave. "I am leaving now. I have to go back to the encampment of the Mo Brothers," Yang Exterminator said.

"You have just escaped, why do you have to endanger yourself again," Jiang Sarn asked, rather surprised.

"I have to return to Mo Li Longevity his Spotty Foxy Sable."

"How?" Jiang Sarn said.

Suddenly Yang disappeared and a small white ferret materialized and hopped around. The small white ferret then suddenly grew into the likeness of the Spotty Foxy Sable, flying here and there. Again, without any warning, the Spotty Foxy Sable vanished and Yang Exterminator reappeared. "How is that for a trick?" he said.

"Fantastic! Wait! While you are there, can you steal the sources of their invincibility, the four fetish devices?" Jiang Sarn said.

"I will do my best," Yang Exterminator replied as he vanished.

Yang Exterminator transfigured himself into the reduced form of the Spotty Foxy Sable and dropped into the bed of Mo Li Longevity. In his sleepy drunkenness, Mo Li Longevity sensed that the Spotty Foxy Sable had not succeeded in its mission. Putting the Sable back into the storage bag, he returned to his slumber.

Yang Exterminator sneaked out of the storage bag and removed the four bags containing the powerful magical devices from the hooks on the bedposts. In a slip, he dropped three of the devices on the ground and the noise woke up the four brothers. Yang thus succeeded only in stealing the Umbrella of Primeval Pearls. Opening up their slumbering eyes, the four brothers did not examine the dropped items carefully. They merely hung up the three bags and went back to their slumber, unaware that the Umbrella of Primeval Pearls was missing.

Yang Exterminator delivered the Umbrella of Primeval Pearls to Jiang Sarn. The Bracelet of Zion, the Pole of Dragons, and the Deity-Pounding Whip were also recovered with it. Yang Exterminator then returned to the encampment of the Mo Brothers and after transfiguring himself into the reduced form of Spotty Foxy Sable, he hid himself inside the leopardskin bag of Mo Li Longevity.

The next morning, after the brothers woke, the theft of the Umbrella of Primeval Pearls was immediately discovered. The Mo Brothers blamed it on lax security, but the security officers insisted: "The inner camp where you live is so tightly guarded that not even a dust particle can sneak through without being detected, how could anyone steal things without our knowledge?"

The brothers were puzzled by the disappearance of the Umbrella, but they had no idea how it had disappeared. "How could this theft take place, with the tight security we have around here ...?" The four brothers were very upset. Mo Li Red shouted in despair: "Throughout my career I have depended upon the magical power of this Umbrella to accomplish my feats. Now that it is lost, what will I do?"

Meanwhile, in another corner of the world, in his daily mental exercises Lord Gracious Virtue, of Cavern Purple Sun, Blue Peak Mountain, sensed that it was time to send his disciple, Huang Heavenly Compliance, to unite with his father. "It is the opportune time for you to unite with your father and to formally join Jiang Sarn's command. Let me prepare you for your mission. Come with me." Lord Gracious Virtue gave Huang Heavenly Compliance two large hammers as his weapons. The Tao of hammer play was taught. In addition, Lord Gracious Virtue also gave Huang his own riding beast, a jade unicorn. He also gave him the Fire-Dragon Darts which had been taken away from Chen Tong during his rescue mission to save Flying Tiger. After Heavenly Compliance was ready, Lord Gracious Virtue said: "You are all set to go. My disciple, you must always remind yourself of the origin of your Tao, and its rules. Now go."

Huang Heavenly Compliance mounted the jade unicorn and gently patted its horn. Wind and clouds formed under its four hoofs and the jade unicorn rose to the sky and flew swiftly towards his destination. In a short while Heavenly Compliance landed inside West Branch City. He went directly to the official residence of Jiang Sarn.

"A young Taoist is here to see you," the door guard reported.

"Show him in," Jiang Sarn ordered.

Making a Taoist bow to Jiang Sarn, the young Taoist said: "Uncle-teacher, this disciple Huang Heavenly Compliance is under an order of his teacher to come here to serve you."

"From which mountain do you come," Jiang Sarn asked.

"This boy is a disciple of Lord Gracious Virtue, of Cavern Purple Sun in Blue Peak Mountain. He is my eldest son," Huang Flying Tiger replied for Heavenly Compliance.

"This is worth some celebration! General, let me congratulate you that you have a son who has mastered Tao well," Jiang Sarn complimented.

The father and son were finally united. After they returned to Flying Tiger's residence, the family feasted. Heavenly Compliance had observed vegetarianism when he was studying Tao in Blue Peak Mountain. Now that he was back to the world of dust, he decided that he could forego the rule of a vegetarian diet. He ate meat and fish joyfully during the feast, thus violating his teacher's edict and the code of his Sect, which required total abstinence from diets consisting of living creatures such as meat and fish.

The next morning, Heavenly Compliance changed into dress appropriate to the son of a Master Lord, wearing jade belts and red robes.

446

Jiang Sarn was displeased to see this change of dress. "Heavenly Compliance, you are a Taoist. Why do you abandon your practice of Tao and change to a dress of the world of dust? I am a premier now, but I always keep my appreciation and recognition of East Kwen Ren Range where I learned the wisdom of Tao. It is unbecoming of you to abandon the proper Taoist attire. You should change back to your Taoist dress."

"I just thought that I might have to fight as a warrior, so I changed. But I will change back to my Taoist dress immediately, as you commanded." Huang Heavenly Compliance then changed back to his Taoist dress.

After his change of dress he went to see Jiang Sarn again. "I was ordered to defeat the Mo Brothers." Huang Heavenly Compliance requested permission to face the four mighty Mos.

"Be careful. They have immense powers of heresy Tao," Jiang Sarn said.

"My teacher was confident that I can defeat them," Huang Heavenly Compliance replied.

So the Heavenly Compliance, mounting his jade unicorn and carrying his two hammers, went directly to the front gate of the encampment of the Mo Brothers and challenged. Jiang Sarn appointed Nata as the rearguard for Heavenly Compliance.

The Mo Brothers, while still upset over the loss of their precious weapon, the Umbrella of Primeval Pearls, accepted the challenge. The four emerged, and after exchanging their names, combat began.

Twenty rounds later, Mo Li Blue took out his bracelet, the Bracelet of Golden Jade, and marked a direct hit at Huang Heavenly Compliance, instantly felling him. Nata, mounting his Wheels of Wind and Fire, rushed forward to the rescue of the Heavenly Compliance. The Bracelet of Golden Jade was again cast at Nata and Nata responded with his Bracelet of Zion. The two bracelets clanked in midair. The Bracelet of Zion, being of metallic composition, easily cracked the Bracelet of Golden Jade into pieces since it was of stony constitution. Before the magical power of the Pee-Pa could be unleashed, Nata had already successfully rescued Heavenly Compliance and had carried him back to the city.

Heavenly Compliance was deeply unconscious, and apparently dead. Flying Tiger was extremely upset because their long-awaited reunion had lasted not even a day. Jiang Sarn was also very upset. At this moment, another Taoist showed up. "Where do you come from?" Jiang Sarn said.

"I am White Cloud Lad, a disciple of Lord Gracious Virtue, of Cavern Purple Sun in Blue Peak Mountain. My teacher sent me to bring Heavenly Compliance back to the mountain to save his life." A sense of hope returned to Jiang Sarn and Flying Tiger, and they were pleased.

Back at the mountain, Lord Gracious Virtue took out some herb pills and mixed them with water, and forced the mixture down the throat of Heavenly Compliance. Moments later, he woke up.

"You ungrateful slob! You went to the world of dust not even for a day and you already broke two codes of Tao of this mountain, abstinence from diet of live creatures and the dress code of Tao. If it were not for the sake of Jiang Sarn, I would have let you die!"

Heavenly Compliance immediately bowed, and apologized.

Lord Gracious Virtue took out another device, put it in a silk bag and handed it to Heavenly Compliance. "With this device you will be

448

able to eliminate the four Mo Brothers. The instruction is inside the bag. Now go to West Branch City to complete your mission. Sometime later I will join you there."

Heavenly Compliance terra-trekked back to West Branch City. He reported his encounter with his teacher to Jiang Sarn and his father. Both were pleased. The next day, Heavenly Compliance once again mounted his jade unicorn and went to the front gate of the encampment of the enemy to challenge the Mo Brothers.

The four brothers emerged. After some perfunctory curses and insults, combat began. A few rounds later, Heavenly Compliance retreated. Mo Li Blue chased him. Heavenly Compliance took the device out of the silk bag. It was labeled Heart-Penetrating Nail, a pointed miniature spear in the shape of an oversized nail around seven inches long, surrounded by a brilliant and iridescent light. The Nail was released and it shot forward at Mo Li Blue. The Heart-Penetrating Nail cruised rapidly and homed at his heart. It effortlessly penetrated through the thick breast armor and tore out the heart of Mo Li Blue, instantly killing him. It then returned to the silk bag Heavenly Compliance was carrying. Mo Li Red cursed and chased after Heavenly Compliance. The Heart-Penetrating Nail was again released, and Mo Li Red was likewise killed. Mo Li Sea chased after him. While he chased, he tried to unsheathe his Pee-Pa Harp from its storage bag, but before he could unleash the magical power of the Harp, the Heart-Penetrating Nail was launched again and Mo Li Sea fell dead. The last of the four brothers, Mo Li Longevity, put his hand in his leopard bag to retract the Spotty Foxy Sable. Unknown to him, the real Spotty Foxy Sable was long dead and the one in his bag was an impostor, the transfigured Yang Exterminator. His hand was bitten off by the transfigured Yang

Exterminator and the Heart-Penetrating Nail easily found its target. So the last of the four Mo Li brothers was also dead. The spirits of the four brothers were promptly received by Pah, the God of Prevalent Blessing, and were guided to the holding area in the newly dedicated Platform for Appointment of Divinities.

After the revolution was over, the four Mo Brothers, because of their fierceness, and their loyalty towards each other and towards their Emperor, would be appointed the Four Devarāja Kings, permanently guarding the gates of Heaven. To this day, their icons, together with their magical weapons, are prominently displayed in the entrance halls of almost all large Buddhist temples in Middle Kingdom (which later became known as China), and have been ever since their appointments to the rank of gods.

After the last of the Mo Brothers was eliminated, a Taoist materialized. Heavenly Compliance asked: "Who are you?"

"I am Yang Exterminator. I was sent by Premier Jiang Sarn to hide inside the encampment of the Mo Brothers to destroy them. I am very glad that you have killed all four." As they were talking, Nata rushed over on his Wheels of Wind and Fire, and he congratulated Heavenly Compliance and Yang Exterminator.

The heads of the four Mo Brothers were displayed at the city gates. The long siege was over. Once again West Branch City had survived the assault of fierce invaders.

Figure I- 27. Icons of Mo Brothers
In Chinese Buddhist Temples they are guardians of gates of Heaven,
Devarāja (god king).

War among Gods and Men

15. Imperial Teacher and Matrices of Carnage

Remnants of the army of the Mo Brothers escaped back to the nearest frontier pass, Vast Water, and reported their total defeat to Han Glory. Han Glory was completely startled: "What! The four mighty Mo Brothers were exterminated and their heads hung over the city gates of West Branch? This rebel Jiang Sarn is really powerful. Let me send an urgent message to the Imperial Teacher to inform him of this disaster!" Nonstop relay messengers were dispatched to the capital to report this unfortunate defeat.

After the Mo Brothers had been dispatched to squash the rebellion of West Branch City, the Imperial Teacher had relaxed for a while as good news continued to pour in. The report from Frontier Pass Drifting Spirits was good: "Warrior General Doe Yung the Splendor repeatedly drives away the invasion forces of Duke East." The report from Frontier Pass Three Mountains was also good: "The force led by the daughter of Deng the Ninth Lord, Deng Charn-Yu, the Charming Jade, has repeatedly defeated the army of Duke South and the invaders have retreated."

The Imperial Teacher was pleased. All he needed was the good news he expected to hear from the Mo Brothers. First he was upset by the news that the Mo Brothers had not overcome the defense of the city of West Branch right away, but he reckoned that a long siege would eventually be of more advantage to invaders than defenders. "All I need is some time," he thought.

Unfortunately, his respite was a short-lived one. An urgent message sent through relay messengers by Han Glory from Frontier Pass Vast Water arrived, informing him of the death of the four Mo brothers and that their heads were displayed at the city gates of West Branch. Slapping his palm hard on his table, the Imperial Teacher was furious. "Damn! The four loyal, brave and fierce warrior generals have died in action! As invincible as they were! Who are you, Jiang Sarn! Repeatedly defeating my force!" Again his third eye opened up and a white ray emerged, extending over a distance of two feet. "All right. Now since rebellions in the east and south are more or less under control, it is my turn to lead an army to stamp out the rebellion of West Branch. Tomorrow I will ask Emperor Zoe for a formal order to head this campaign myself!"

The Imperial Teacher immediately prepared a communique to ask for a formal order to appoint him to carry out a campaign against West Branch City. This document was delivered to Emperor Zoe during the now more regular court sessions. The request was gracefully accepted, now that Emperor Zoe realized the seriousness of the matter of rebellion. "Issue to the Imperial Teacher a Yellow Fur Flag and a White Axe as a token of my authority," Emperor Zoe ordered. So the proposed campaign was under way.

A provident day to commence the campaign was selected accordingly. Battle flags were sanctified with appropriate sacrifices. Emperor Zoe personally took charge of the departure ceremony. At the end of a long banquet, just before the Imperial Teacher was about to depart, the Emperor poured a full goblet of wine and offered it to the Imperial Teacher. "I am very grateful to you for your loyalty. I am grateful to you for your endeavor to pacify the west for me. I shall wait for good news from you."

The Imperial Teacher, after accepting the goblet, bowed to the Emperor and said: "This old officer swears to do his best to crush rebellion in the west and to strengthen our boundaries. After I leave the capital to head this campaign, I sincerely wish that you will listen to advice of loyal officers and distance yourselves from toadies. I reckon I will not be away for more than half a year before my triumphant return. Please keep in touch with me so that our normal communication is not broken."

Figure I- 28. Imperial Teacher

After this last toast, the Imperial Teacher prepared to mount his Black Unicorn. The Unicorn, after several years of repose without a rider, became frightened. It reflexively shrugged, throwing the Imperial Teacher to the ground. As the startled attending officers helped the Imperial Teacher brush dust off his clothes, a junior officer, Wang Bian, left his rank and offered his opinion: "This is a bad omen for this quest. I submit the suggestion to assign another commander-in-chief to replace the Imperial Teacher for fear of his safety."

"My respectable officer, I thank you for your concern but I must go because this is an important mission," the Imperial Teacher replied. "In taking up the post as the Premier, I have dedicated my life to this country. When a general mounts his horse to lead an army to defend his country, his life is no longer of his own concern. When a warrior engages in combat, he is prepared to be wounded or die. There is nothing unusual about this incident. My riding beast has not had a rider for some time and this is the reason for his misbehavior. There is nothing wrong. Nothing more needs to be said regarding this incident." The Imperial Teacher then readjusted his clothes and remounted his Black Unicorn. When everything was ready, he ordered: "March on." So the quest of West Branch City began.

The 300,000 troops led by the Imperial Teacher left Morning Song immediately and after crossing the Yellow River at Meng Gin, they arrived at Ming Tze (Ming Pond). Chang Kwei (Giant Step), the commander of the defense force of the city, warmly welcomed the Imperial Teacher. After the usual protocols, the Imperial Teacher said: "I do not want to let West Branch City know that I am going to subjugate them. Is there an alternate route to West Branch?"

"Normally we travel through Frontier Passes Tong, Ling Tong, Penetrating Clouds, Boundary Marker and Vast Water," Chang Giant Step answered. "The southern route through Frontier Pass Blue Dragon is less traveled, but the passage goes through steep mountains."

Eager to reach West Branch as stealthily as possible, the Imperial Teacher chose the southern route instead of the more conventional route through the five frontier passes.

After passing through Frontier Pass Blue Dragon, the mountain path became extremely narrow and many passages were so restricted that two horses abreast could just barely pass. The movement of the 300,000 men with their heavy equipment and supplies through this narrow mountain pass was extremely difficult and torturous. The Imperial Teacher regretted having chosen this stealthy route instead of the other one, which was used by merchants and most travelers. The other path was much wider and did not involve many steep hilly passages. Nevertheless, nothing could be done now. As the troop inched through the difficult path, one day they passed by a mountain by the name of Yellow Flower. This mountain was very steep but it was covered by a primeval pine forest. Its astounding undulating peaks combined with the majestic foliage of the forest presented a setting so attractive to the Imperial Teacher that he could not help but stop his Unicorn. He pondered and wished: "What a nice place to study Tao for the rest of my life! If only I could get away from my earthly responsibilities!"

He stopped the movement of his troops and gave the soldiers a rest while he rode his Black Unicorn to the top of the mountain to take a better look. Looking down, he saw a nearby flat plateau upon which a small army was exercising some kind of battle formation under the direction of a warrior wearing a red robe and a suit of golden armor, using a long battle-ax as his weapon. The Imperial Teacher watched the battle formation and admired. "This warrior surely knows the art of war. If I can, I would certainly like to engage him in my campaign."

Just then, the warrior discovered the presence of the Imperial Teacher. He dismissed his army and ran his horse up the mountain to meet him. "Who are you to come to my mountain to spy on me?"

"I am a Taoist and I like this mountain. I would like to build a hut here to study Tao. Will you allow me to do it?" the Imperial Teacher said in a tone that indicated no fear of the warrior.

The indifference in the tone of the Imperial Teacher annoyed the warrior and he roared, "You heresy Taoist!" Without another word he challenged at the Imperial Teacher with his huge battle-ax. The Imperial Teacher deflected the thrust of the ax with his golden whip.

A few rounds later, the Imperial Teacher thought: "His ax play is not bad. Maybe I can get him and his companions to join my campaign." He turned his Black Unicorn around and retreated. The warrior chased after him.

Pointing his golden whip at the warrior, the Imperial Teacher, a master of Tao, reversed the process of metallum-trekking and entrapped the warrior inside metallum, one of five forms of the universe. The warrior suddenly found himself and his horse tightly surrounded by a metallum wall and he could not move.

After entrapping the warrior by the reverse process of metallum-trekking, the Imperial Teacher sat down and waited. Sure enough, soldiers watching the combat between the two reported the disappearance of this warrior to his two partners: "Disaster! A Taoist generated a yellowish smog, and General Deng disappeared!"

The two warriors, by the names of Zhang Chien (Node) and Taon Yung (Splendid), rushed out to the rescue of their missing colleague. Taking their weapons, they led an army to the mountain top and saw the Imperial Teacher sitting on a piece of rock, leaning against a tree, enjoying the scenery.

"What kind of heresy Taoist are you to make our sworn brother disappear? Send him back otherwise we will have to kill you," the two challenged.

"You mean the one with the blue complexion? He annoyed me, so I killed him with my golden whip. I only want to build a hut here to study Tao. He not only refused me, he also insulted me and tried to kill me. Do you agree to let me study Tao here?" The Imperial Teacher again purposely irritated the two by a request that certainly would be turned down.

The two were furious at the Imperial Teacher. They ran their horses forward and attacked. Again the Imperial Teacher applied the process of reverse trekking, entrapping Zhang Node with reverse hydro-trekking and Taon Splendid with reverse wood-trekking. The two found themselves respectively entrapped by a body of water and by a thickly grown forest.

The stupefied soldiers ran back to report to the remaining warrior, Hsin Quann (Ring). Hsin Ring had a pair of wings under his armpits, just like Lei Thunder. He flew up to the sky and started to attack the Imperial Teacher with a giant hammer.

458

"Ha! This is something new. However, reverse trekking will not work on this one. I will try a new trick," the Imperial Teacher said to himself. Pointing his golden whip at a giant rock, he ordered: "Up!" The rock flew up and forced Hsin Ring down, entrapping him in a nearby ditch.

The Imperial Teacher raised his golden whip and threatened to smash the head of Hsin Ring. Hsing Ring yelled: "Spare my life, demigod Taoist! I am a stupid mortal and I did not realize the kind of power you have! I will forever serve you if you spare my life!"

"You are right. I am no ordinary Taoist. I am the Imperial Teacher from the court of Emperor Zoe. I happened to pass by here, and it was your friend with the blue complexion who provoked me first. What is your intention? Do you want to stay alive?"

"Oh no! If I had only known it was you, I would have already laid down arms to welcome you. I have heard your name many times and I hold the highest respect for you. Please forgive me for my imprudence and please spare my life." Hsin Ring now realized how rude he and his fellow warriors had been.

"I will spare you if you four will become my disciples," the Imperial Teacher replied.

"It will be our honor," Hsin Ring promised.

"All right, you are spared." The giant rock then effortlessly floated away and dropped into a nearby ditch. Simultaneously, the metallum walls entrapping the first warrior, whose name was Deng Zong (Ardent), disappeared. So did the body of water surrounding Zhang Node, and the thick forest entrapping Taon Splendid.

The three warriors joined together and found Hsin Ring talking to the Taoist who had trapped them. "Catch the heresy Taoist for us!" they shouted at Hsin Ring.

Hsin Ring stopped the three and reproached: "You blatant three, stop! This is the renowned Imperial Teacher from the capital city Morning Song. Get off your horses and apologize to him!"

Upon hearing the name the Imperial Teacher, the three rolled off their horses and bowed deeply, apologizing for their rude behavior. "We have heard your famous name for a long time but we never had the honor of meeting you personally. We did not recognize you. Please forgive us."

The four introduced themselves, then said: "We four have been sworn brothers for a number of years. Because of rebellion of many feudal lords, we have organized an army to protect ourselves. However, it is not our intention to be bandits forever."

"I am leading an army to squash the rebellion in West Branch City. Will you join me?" the Imperial Teacher said.

"Definitely," the four agreed. Thus, they informed their followers, an army of 10,000, of their intention to join the campaign of the Imperial Teacher. Their followers were given the choice to join the campaign or to go back to their homes. Roughly two-thirds decided to join the campaign of the Imperial Teacher. All assets accumulated over the years were equally distributed among the followers. After the gang was dismissed or regrouped into the official army, the Imperial Teacher continued the movement of his troops towards West Branch. He was very glad that four warriors had been added to his army. None of the warriors he'd brought with him could match the fighting skills of the four.

A few days later the army arrived at a ridge. A stone tablet revealed its name to be: "Ridge Cessation of Dragons." Upon seeing this tablet, the Imperial Teacher fell silent, his face showing signs of a jolt, and he sank into a pensive mood. Deng Node asked: "Are you upset over something?"

"After fifty years of studying Tao under Holy Mother Golden Spirit in Palace Green Roam, I was sent to the world of dust to assist the

Shang government. Just before I bade farewell to my teacher, I asked her about my destiny. She told me that my life would be filled with success and prosperity but would soon come to an end when I encountered a location marked 'Cessation.' We just passedy Ridge Cessation of Dragons. This is why I was pondering," the Imperial Teacher replied.

The four newly acquired warriors merely laughed and one among them said: "Our dear Imperial Teacher, you are wrong! A real capable person never believes that his fate hangs on the encounter with one single word. You, a man of great talent and capability, have been extremely successful in the past and we have no doubt that you will be successful in your campaign against West Branch. You, a man of commendation, are always insured of your future by your providence." At this statement, the Imperial Teacher smiled, but said nothing in reply.

Not long afterwards, the troop arrived at the vicinity of the south gate of West Branch City. Camp was set. The Imperial Teacher, being an accomplished master of the Tao of military arts, commanded an extremely organized encampment as follows:

The encampment was set in accordance with the ancient art of war. It was stretched along the north and south direction, with the northern gate facing West Branch City. Battle formations were formed along the east and west directions according to the two forms, metallum and wood. Security posts were stationed according to signs of dragons and tigers. Password systems were quickly installed. At night, archers with long bows were stationed around the encampment at critical posts against any possible intruders. Experienced and sharp-eyed observers were posted at strategic points to monitor enemy movements. The security was so tight and the atmosphere of war was so dominant that birds even avoided flying over the encampment. The entire site was as quiet as a still pond. Under an order of strict quietness, conversations were carried out in nearly silent whispers. All unnecessary activities were suspended. The entire encampment was ready for action.

Scout patrols reported to Jiang Sarn the arrival of a huge army led by the Imperial Teacher and that they had set up their encampment within sighting distance in the southward direction.

"When I was in the capital city of Morning Song, I never got a chance to meet the Imperial Teacher. Now he leads an army here to campaign against us. I often heard about his quality in military matters. Let me see how he puts his knowledge of military art into action," Jiang Sarn remarked. He then led his warriors to the highest point of the city and observed.

Figure I- 29. Military encampment

After a long span of observance, Jiang Sarn sighed: "I have often heard compliments on the military capabilities of the Imperial Teacher

Wen Zhong, but none of these compliments came anywhere close to his real ability. Look at the neatness, the order and the arrangement of his battalion formations. His ability is above his reputation."

After returning to his conference hall, Jiang Sarn assembled his warriors and generals and started to discuss means to fend off the huge invading army. Flying Tiger consoled the premier: "My premier need not worry. We have defeated the four mighty Mo Brothers. We have blessing from the heaven, so everything should be fine."

With no better answers, Jiang Sarn replied: "Although it seems so, residents of the city will still suffer through another invasion. People will be disturbed, soldiers will suffer casualties, and battles will tire our warriors and horses. Peace and prosperity will once again not be with us."

As discussions continued, Nata, who was on duty to guard the city, reported: "A messenger from the Imperial Teacher is outside the city gate. He wants to deliver a letter."

"Admit him," Jiang Sarn ordered.

The messenger was admitted. He was one of the four newly acquired warriors in the encampment of the Imperial Teacher, Deng Ardent. The letter read:

The Imperial Teacher of Shang, the Heaven-Protected Commander-in-Chief of Westward Campaign,

Hereby submits a communication, to the attention of Premier Jiang Sarn, under the respectable flag of his command:

It is said that the rebellion of an officer in the court of an emperor is equivalent to anarchy against Heaven. The Son of Heaven is now aware of illegal activities in the land of West, whose rulers have blatantly ignored the laws of Shang. These unlawful activities include the self-appointment of Chi-Fa to the title of king without explicit permission or endorsement from the Emperor. The court of Shang has sent several armies to subjugate your illegal activities and your disobedience. You have not repented, and in fact, you have shown your further disrespect of the imperial authority by your stubborn resistance. Then you further insinuated your intention of rebellion by defeating the imperial army recently dispatched by Emperor Zoe, and by displaying the heads of dead generals and warriors high above your city gates. Where are the laws in your land? I am now under the direct order of Emperor Zoe to subdue your rebellion. If you care about those innocent lives in your city, surrender immediately and face your proper punishments. Otherwise, your fate is sealed. Your forces will be crushed and your entire city will be rendered ruins. Please make your decision upon the arrival of this letter.

Enough has been said. Make a wise decision to avoid blood shed.

After he had read this rather imposing letter, Jiang Sarn did not reply immediately, but said to the messenger: "May I have your name?"

"My name is Deng Ardent."

"General Deng, please go back and thank the Imperial Teacher for his letter. I have marked my answer on the letter. Bring it back to him. Our forces will engage yours three days from today," Jiang Sarn replied.

Deng Ardent returned to his encampment with the reply of Jiang Sarn marked on the letter of challenge. Three days later, battle cries were heard all over in the encampment of the Imperial Teacher.

Jiang Sarn ordered his troops out and arranged them in a five-tiered battle formation. Four of them were installed in accordance with the placement of four dominant positions of the Eight Trigrams, and the fifth placement was planted in between the location of the fifth heavenly stem and the sixth earthly branch. Standing at the foremost tip of the troop formation was Jiang Sarn, who rode his beast No-Elephant and was accompanied by Huang Flying Tiger, the Master Lord of National Constituent, on his Five Color Godspeed Ox. Behind Jiang Sarn and Flying Tiger stood a formidable cluster of warriors. In the middle, directly behind Jiang Sarn, was Nata on his Wheels of Wind and

Fire. Next to Nata was Yang Exterminator on a white horse. Remaining warriors – Suvarnata, Moksa, Han Poisonous Dragon, Shiue Ferocious Tiger, Huang Heavenly Compliance, Wu Serendipity and others – were on horses stationed respectively at the left and right sides of the horizontal formation.

The Imperial Teacher Wen Zhong, on his Black Unicorn and positioned in front of an extremely neat battle formation, was accompanied by a much smaller entourage: the newly acquired Deng, Hsin, Zhang and Taon. Behind the quartet was a huge formation of secondary warriors.

On his No-elephant, Jiang Sarn bowed his head slightly to the Imperial Teacher. "I apologize for not being able to salute to you according to the full code of protocol."

"Premier Jiang Sarn, I understand that you are an accomplished Taoist from East Kwen Ren Range. Why do you behave so irrationally?" the Imperial Teacher challenged.

Jiang Sarn replied: "As a humble student of Tao in Palace Jade Abstraction, I have learned moral principles and rules of Heaven. I have obeyed all laws of the land, guided by the needs of the people, and those under my authority are required to do the same. We have stayed within the borders of our territory and we have ruled people here under laws of benevolence and kindness. Why do you accuse me of any irrational behaviors?"

"You are very good in distorted reasoning," the Imperial Teacher charged. "You have violated many laws of the land. You have enthroned your king without an imperial endorsement from Shang, and you have sheltered a rebel officer from the court of the Emperor. When armies were sent to subjugate you for your disobedience, you not only did not honor the royal authority delegated to the generals, you also resisted and killed them. Now I am here to subjugate you. And you still resist the authority of the court of Shang!"

Jiang Sarn responded gently, with a smile: "The most honored Imperial Teacher, you are wrong. It is true that we have not asked for endorsement to enthrone our king, but it has been an unwritten rule since the establishment of the Shang dynasty that the eldest son succeeds the deceased father. There is nothing wrong about that. The current Emperor of Shang deserves disrespect because he has committed many evil deeds. The departure of a loyal officer from your court was caused by immoral acts of the Emperor, and his action is justified by the adage: 'When an emperor is not righteous, officers move to other countries.' The Emperor not only did not seek penance, he further aggravated all concerned by laying blame on this loyal officer. As for defeating the armies sent here to conquer us, they deserved whatever fate they met – because they have invaded us without any justifiable cause. We have committed no crime, we have not rebelled against you. The only act we did was to defend ourselves. Although many lords have already rebelled openly against the Shang regime because of the evil deeds committed by the Emperor, we have never allied with them. We never even sent a single soldier across our borders to invade you. We never attacked any of your frontier passes. We are not rebels. Now you, the Imperial Teacher of well-established fame and reputation, come here with a huge army to invade us and call us rebels. It is you who infringe upon us. Please leave immediately so that a peaceful relationship may be maintained between Zhou Duchy and the Shang regime. If you will not accept my humble suggestion, and start a war, you must bear all consequences. War is no joking matter; no one knows who will win at the end. Please think thrice before you act."

The Imperial Teacher had never expected to receive a rational reply from Jiang Sarn. He was rather embarrassed, because what Jiang Sarn said was true. He did not have a good answer. While he was searching for a response, he saw Huang Flying Tiger standing behind the flag of Jiang Sarn, so he changed the subject. "You rebel Huang, come out and face me!"

Huang Flying Tiger was a little embarrassed to face his old colleague and friend. "We have not seen each other for several years. I am glad we meet today so that you can hear my side of the story," he said.

Figure I- 30. Battle scene

"Nonsense!" the Imperial Teacher shouted. "The Emperor gave you the utmost in glory, fame, rank and wealth. Now not only have you rebelled against him, you have also helped Jiang Sarn to annihilate imperial generals and warriors. You and your lame excuses!" The Imperial Teacher angrily turned around to his entourage. "Arrest him!"

Deng Ardent immediately volunteered. "I will arrest him!" Running his horse forward, he waved his giant battle-ax and challenged Flying Tiger, who, with a long spear, also ran his Godspeed Ox forward. Zhang

467

Node then rushed forward to help Deng. Nangong Swift also ran his horse forward to stop Zhang Node. Taon Splendid joined in, but was intercepted by Wu Serendipity. A melee followed.

Hsin Ring flew up to the sky to attack Jiang Sarn from above, but he was stopped by Huang Heavenly Compliance, whose jade unicorn also rose up the sky to intercept him. The Imperial Teacher darted his Black Unicorn forward to battle Jiang Sarn, who was no match for his the combat skill. Finding a slip, Imperial Teacher cast one of his golden whips up to the sky, which rapidly whisked at Jiang Sarn and hit him in his left shoulder, felling him off his No-elephant. As the Imperial Teacher rushed forward to kill Jiang Sarn, Nata wheeled forth to intercept him, while Hsin Chia pulled Jiang Sarn back to the city. Again, the golden whip was cast, and it felled Nata off his Wheels of Wind and Fire. Suvarnata, Moksa and Han Poisonous Dragon rushed forward to stop the Imperial Teacher, but they were all knocked down by the two whisking golden whips. Then Yang Exterminator darted his horse forward to fend off Imperial Teacher. The golden whip was against cast, marking a direct hit at the head of Yang. However, the crash of the whip on his head merely produced a series of brilliant sparks without hurting Exterminator at all. The Imperial Teacher was startled. "With conjurers as powerful and remarkable as this one aiding Jiang Sarn, no wonder he won all those previous campaigns!" He could not help but admire the abilities of his deadly enemy.

The battle went on and on. Taon Splendid decided that something must be done, so he took out his fetish, the Wind Gathering Flag, and waved it. Suddenly gusts of wind blew dust and pebbles at Jiang Sarn's army. Unable to see anything, the battling soldiers of West Branch had to retreat hurriedly back to the city. A sizable number of them were killed during the hasty retreat. Amidst victorious drum beats, the Imperial Teacher and his troops returned to their encampment.

Meanwhile, Jiang Sarn called an emergency conference. "We were defeated because we were not organized. We never got a chance to use our magical weapons. The next time, we must be better-organized and prepared,"

Yang Exterminator added, "Let us rest for a few days before we challenge the enemy again. If we are better-organized, we can certainly win the next battle. After we have won the daytime battle, then we should plan a sneak night attack immediately following our victory." This suggestion was approved.

Three days later, the planned counterattack was carried out. Jiang Sarn's troop came out of the city and advanced towards the enemy. The Imperial Teacher, his warriors and his army also rushed out of their camp to defend against the invaders. This time when the Imperial Teacher cast his golden whip, Jiang Sarn also cast his Deity-Pounding Whip, which had been given to him by his teacher-mentor, Primeval. The Tao behind the Deity-Pounding Whip was much more powerful than that of the golden whip, so the golden whip was broken into two pieces. The Deity-Pounding Whip was again cast at the Imperial Teacher and marked a direct hit. The Imperial Teacher fell down from his Black Unicorn, and escaped back to his encampment via terra-trekking. Without a leader, the defending force was in complete disarray. This time it was the army of the Imperial Teacher that suffered defeat.

Following the victory of the day, the planned night sneak attack was carried out as planned. All available warriors were engaged. Huang Flying Tiger, his brother Flying Tiger Cub, and Huang Ming were ordered to lead an attacking force from the left, while Nangong Swift, Hsin Chia and Hsin Mian were sent to attack from the right. Nata and Huang Heavenly Compliance would lead the main assault force in the front. Yang Exterminator, accompanied by Suvarnata, Moksa, Han Poisonous Dragon and Shiue Ferocious Tiger, would sneak to the back to set the military supply of the enemy on fire.

After his daytime defeat, the Imperial Teacher took extra precaution and he prognosticated. He discovered the planned night sneak attack and set up a defense plan. However, his defense plan was severely limited by his lack of competent warriors and was not as strong as he wished. The planned sneak attack took place as scheduled. While his forces were defending his camp against the invading forces from three sides, the Imperial Teacher saw fires rising from his military supply. "Damn, with my military supply gone, I am really defeated," The Imperial Teacher tried to disengage himself from the battlefield to go to defend his military supply, but his opponents would not let him leave. Just then, Jiang Sarn arrived and again the Deity-Pounding Whip was cast. This time it marked another hit at the Imperial Teacher, nearly felling him off his Black Unicorn. His four warriors immediately abandoned their fight and rushed to the rescue of the Imperial Teacher. Under the escort of the four, Imperial Teacher escaped as he fought his way away from the battlefield.

Around this time, during his daily mental exercises, Son of Clouds, of Cavern Jade Column in Mount End South, sensed the battle of the Imperial Teacher against West Branch. "This is an opportune time for Lei Thunder to join his adopted brothers," thought Son of Clouds. Lei Thunder was summoned to his presence. "It is time for you to join your adopted brothers. On your way to West Branch you might encounter a man with a pair of wings. Defeat him if you have the time," Son of Clouds then bid his disciple farewell.

As Lei Thunder flew near West Branch Mountain, he saw an army in disordered retreat, apparently in recent defeat. "This must be the defeated army of the Imperial Teacher," he thought. As he neared, he recognized the Imperial Teacher, who also saw him.

"Hsin Ring, there is someone overhead. Be careful!" the Imperial Teacher informed Hsin Ring.

Hsin and Lei met. An air combat ensued. However, Hsin was no match for the strength of Lei so he had to fly away. Reminding himself that he had been told to go to West Branch, Lei gave up his chase and headed towards the city. Upon arrival he went directly to the official residence of Jiang Sarn.

"Who are you? From which cavern and which mountain did you come?" said Jiang Sarn.

"My name is Lei Thunder. I am a disciple of Son of Clouds, of Cavern Jade Column at Mount End South. My teacher ordered me to come to West Branch to assist you and to rejoin my brothers," Lei Thunder replied.

"Who are your brothers?" said Jiang Sarn.

"King of Arms and the other princes."

"Does any one of you recognize him," Jiang Sarn asked the other brother princes of the King of Arms. No one recalled having a brother like this Taoist.

Lei then narrated a brief history of his life. "I was born in Swallow Mountain. I was born of thunder and was adopted by the late King of Literature. I was fostered by Son of Clouds and became his disciple. When I was seven I rescued King of Literature from his pursuers. After I flew him out of the five frontier passes, I left him at Ridge Golden Rooster,"

Jiang Sarn recalled this incident. "Heaven bless the king! This is wonderful!" So Jiang Sarn brought Lei Thunder to see King of Arms.

"My royal brother, I would like to thank you again on the behalf of my late father. He mentioned you many times during his life. It is a great occasion that we finally meet!" King of Arms said. However, he was hesitant to invite Lei Thunder to stay in his residential palace because of his rather odd appearance – an extremely tall person with a high nose, red hair, bluish complexion and on top of these oddities, a pair of wings. Women in his palace might be rather scared by him. He said to Jiang Sarn, "Please arrange a banquet of welcome on my behalf."

Jiang Sarn replied, "Lei Thunder is a strict vegetarian. He can stay with me in my residence." Thus Lei Thunder followed Jiang Sarn back to the official residence of the premier.

After regrouping his defeated army, the Imperial Teacher counted over 20,000 of his soldiers either perished or missing as a result of the night sneak attack. "I have never suffered a defeat as humiliating as this one in my entire life." The Imperial Teacher was rather depressed. Beyond the four warriors, he had no others that he could call upon. The four were too few compared to the large number of warriors in the camp of Jiang Sarn.

His disciple Chi Li advised: "You have many Taoist colleagues. You should solicit their help."

"Yes, I should have previously solicited their help. I will leave right away. Take care of the camp for me while I seek this help," the Imperial Teacher agreed.

He first stopped at Golden Tortoise Island. He saw no one around. He went to the caverns of his friends. All the doors were locked. "Where could they have gone?" the puzzled Imperial Teacher wondered.

As he was about to leave, someone beckoned: "Brother Taoist Wen!"

The Imperial Teacher turned around and saw an old colleague of his, a female Taoist by the name of Demigod Fragrant Water Lily. Saluting with a Taoist bow, the Imperial Teacher asked: "Where have the rest of the Taoists gone?"

"Some time ago Sen Buck Panther came by this island to solicit help from us to aid your campaign. Several Taoists agreed to offer you help. All the other Taoists of this island have gone to Albino Elk Island to instill magical power into their dharmaratnas of war to assist you. I have stayed behind to complete a device. I stay here only to wait for the completion of it. I have not quite finished instilling my Tao into this device yet; it is still in my Kiln of Eight Trigrams. My Taoist brother, you should go to Albino Elk Island right away to meet the other Taoists of this Island. I will join you there as soon as the instillation process of my device is completed."

Greatly pleased, the Imperial Teacher bid farewell to Demigod Fragrant Water Lily and patted the head of his Black Unicorn to fly as fast as he could to the Albino Elk Island. Upon his arrival, he saw a group of Taoists in different Taoist dresses resting at the foot of a mountain, chatting.

"My Taoist friends, you are really enjoying yourselves!" the Imperial Teacher beckoned to these cheerful Taoists.

Upon seeing the approach of the Imperial Teacher, the Taoists rose and greeted him. Chin Won (Comprehensive) said: "We have heard that you are leading a campaign against the rebels in West Branch City. The other day Sen Buck Panther came by and asked us to help you. Since then we have been working diligently on this island to instill our Tao into ten fetish devices which will become the chief components in ten apparatus of war, known as Matrices of Carnage. These Matrices of Carnage will help your cause. We have just finalized our process of instillation of our Tao into these devices. You come here just in time to see the completion of our work."

"What magical power have you instilled into your ten Matrices of War," the Imperial Teacher asked.

"You will see yourself in more detail when they are set up around your encampment in West Branch. However, we can show what we have got here to you now," Chin Comprehensive said.

After taking a cursory look, the Imperial Teacher said, "I only count nine of them, what happened to the tenth one?"

"It is being prepared by Holy Mother Golden Rays. Her device has a special profundity and it requires a large isolated area for testing so it has to be instilled at a different location. Fellow Taoists, now that we have completed our processes of instillation, I suggest that all of us go to West Branch first to set up our apparatus of war. The Imperial Teacher should stay here for the arrival of Holy Mother Golden Rays." The nine Taoists then departed for West Branch with their devices via hydro-trekking.

473

The Imperial Teacher sat on a flat rock and leaned against a pine tree, waiting. "I am lucky that I have so many trustworthy friends." He relished his pleasant thoughts. Not long afterwards, a female Taoist came from the south direction, riding a large panther with five large spots, apparently skimming over water. She wore a fish-tail-shaped golden beret, a bright red robe of Eight Trigrams with a silk rope tied around her waist, a pair of elevated sandals, and she carried a pair of swords and a large bundle on her back. Swiftly and gently she landed her panther near the rock on which the Imperial Teacher sat.

Holy Mother Golden Rays saluted the Imperial Teacher with a Taoist bow, and asked: "My brother Taoist Wen, where did you come from and where are my fellow Taoists?"

"They have already left for West Branch Mountain. They left me behind waiting for your arrival so that we can go to West Branch together." The two then left together, flying their mythical riding beasts abreast. Soon they arrived at the new encampment of the defeated army near West Branch Mountain, where they joinedthe other Taoists.

"Where are we now?" Chin Comprehensive said.

"We are seventy li from West Branch City. Our army was originally stationed near the city, but after our recent defeat we had to move our camp here," replied the Imperial Teacher.

"You should move your encampment back to your old location as soon as possible, like tomorrow morning," one of the Taoists suggested, and all agreed. So the entire encampment moved back to their old location, near West Branch City.

The sound of military movements during the setting up of the encampment of the Imperial Teacher was heard inside West Branch City. Jiang Sarn said to his entourage of warriors: "Scouts said this noise is caused by the return of the Imperial Teacher and his army. He must have secured fresh help."

Yang Exterminator then added: "After his recent defeat, the Imperial Teacher disappeared from view for nearly half a month. I heard that he is a disciple of Sect Interceptus, which is wellknown for its heresy Tao. He might have secured help from his colleagues. We must be careful."

Jiang Sarn did not quite believe what Yang Exterminator said, so he went to the top of the city tower with Nata and Yang Exterminator to take a look at the revamped enemy encampment. A different atmosphere and appearance were seen and sensed. No one had any idea what went on inside the encampment of their enemy.

After the encampment was set, the Imperial Teacher conferred with his ten Axis Taoists. Yuan Jeau (Horn) suggested: "I heard that Jiang Sarn is a disciple of Sect Elucidatus. We are all fellow Taoists, although we study different branches of Tao. There is no reason that we should demean ourselves to fight against mortals in the world of dust; I suggest that we show them the ten apparatus of war, the ten Matrices of Carnage, to which we have instilled the power of our Tao. As accomplished Taoists, it is below our dignity to compete against mortals on sheer physical strengths. Let us compete our wisdom of Tao against theirs. If we win, he must surrender to us."

"This seems like a good idea. I agree with you," the Imperial Teacher replied.

The next day, spreading his troops in a battle formation behind him, the Imperial Teacher galloped his Black Unicorn forward to ask to talk to Jiang Sarn. In response to the new challenge, Jiang Sarn ordered his troops to march outside the city to forge a battle formation. On his No-elephant, Jiang Sarn once again came face-to-face wiyh his opponent. But this time his opponent was accompanied by ten Taoists, each of whom was of vicious appearance. Their facial colors could be described by the five hues: blue, yellow, orange, white and red. They all rode giant elk except Holy Mother Golden Rays who rode a large panther with five large dots.

Chin Comprehensive rode his elk forward and with a Taoist bow, he saluted: "Fellow Taoist Jiang Sarn, please."

Jiang Sarn also responded with a Taoist bow, and said: "My brother Taoist, please. May I ask from which cavern and mountain did you come?"

Chin Comprehensive replied: "I am a Sublimator of Essence from Golden Tortoise Island. I understand that you are a disciple of Sect Elucidatus in East Kwen Ren Range. We are disciples of Sect Interceptus. Although we are from different Sects, we are all students of Tao and we all observe the same codes. Why did you repeatedly infringe upon my colleague and the government he serves? It is not a right thing to do."

"What makes you think that we have infringed upon your Sect?" Jiang Sarn said.

"You have slaughtered the four Taoists of Nine Dragon Island," Chin Comprehensive replied. "The four Mo Brothers whom you killed and whose heads you displayed in your city gates were also from our Sect. You have insulted and abused our Sect. We decided to leave our caverns to come here to settle our dispute with you in a duel of Tao against Tao. This is a duel of the depth of the wisdom of Tao, and not a duel of physical strengths. It is unbecoming for demigods like us to engage in duels based on a competition of physical strengths."

"You are a competent Taoist and your Tao is not much different from ours," Jiang Sarn retorted. "You know that Emperor Zoe is a tyrant without moral principles. His star is fading fast. An emperor of benevolence and mercy has already emerged in the west. As good Taoists you must know how to interpret patterns of astronomical events. Recent patterns favor us and not Emperor Zoe. Phoenix, a bird that reputedly pays tribute to righteous rulers of the people, already appeared in the west, indicating that a great ruler emperor is in our land. Since eons ago, righteousness always overcomes evil. You have studied Tao from a great Patriarch. You must understand the trend of events ordained by Heaven. Why do you act against the wishes of Heaven to come here to aid Shang?" Jiang Sarn asserted.

"According to you, Emperor Zoe is an evil ruler and the ruler of Zhou Dukedom is the king of people," Chin Comprehensive retorted

476

back. "I do not believe it. We are here to aid Emperor Zoe. Doesn't your statement imply that we are acting against the wishes of Heaven and we are destined to fail? Do you expect me to believe you? We can argue in words indefinitely over this point. Jiang Sarn, we have instilled and infused our wisdom of Tao into ten invincible apparatus of war, called Matrices of Carnage. If you dare, you can come and compete against our Tao by nullifying the power we imparted into these ten Matrices of Carnage. Any one of you who fails in the process of nullification of the power in any Matrix shall die. I advise that you yield. There is no point in you sacrificing innocent lives. Your defense is futile." Chin Comprehensive proudly pointed in the direction where the ten Matrices of Carnage were being set up while he talked.

"If so, please complete the ten Matrices of Carnage. We will first examine them, then we will comply with your request to compete our wisdom of Tao against yours. Remember, you said this is to be a duel of wisdom of Tao. Whoever loses in the competition of Tao shall die. This equally applies to you," Jiang Sarn replied. So it was agreed that the outcome of the duel of Tao against Tao would determine the outcome of the war. Only wisdom of Tao could be used in the competition. Under the oath of death no other physical means of the mortals could be used.

Chin Comprehensive returned to his encampment. Within days, the ten Matrices of Carnage were ready. Chin Comprehensive then went to the city gate to challenge Jiang Sarn. "The ten Matrices of Carnage have been set up. Please examine them carefully for as long as you wish."

"At your service," Jiang Sarn said. He then rode his No-elephant out of the city, accompanied by Nata who stood on his Wheels of Wind and Fire, Huang Heavenly Compliance who rode his jade unicorn, the ferocious-looking Lei Thunder on his wings and Yang Exterminator riding a white horse, in his arrogantly modest Taoist manner.

As they were about to cross the enemy line to examine the ten Matrices of Carnage, Yang Exterminator rode forward and spoke to Chin Comprehensive. "We left our city to enter your compound at your invitation. You must promise not to use secret devices or hidden weapons against us."

Chin Comprehensive laughed, and said, "Our Tao is invincible. If we want you to die in the morning, you will not survive beyond noon. Why do we need to use secret weapons to ambush you while you are examining the ten Matrices of Carnage at our invitation? There is no need for us to use any secret weapon to harm you. We always engage in honorable duels. You have our words that while you are examining the Matrices we will not harm you in any manner. Go ahead."

Nata replied: "We do not completely believe you. In any case, we are not without preparation. We will constantly watch you closely, so no tricks." The four mighty disciples then guarded Jiang Sarn in close proximity and they went through all ten Matrices of Carnage and examined each one of them carefully. The first one was "Matrix of Heavenly Extermination," the second one "Matrix of Earthen Fire," the third one "Matrix of Wind Roar," the fourth "Matrix of Cold Ice," the fifth "Matrix of Golden Rays," the sixth "Matrix of Gore," the seventh "Matrix of Fiery Flame," the eighth "Matrix of Lost Soul," the ninth "Matrix of Red Water," and the tenth "Matrix of Red Sand." After Jiang Sarn and his entourage had thoroughly examined all ten Matrices of Carnage, they left the enemy's compound and rode back to their side. Chin Comprehensive kept his promise, so that Jiang Sarn and his four disciples did get to examine the ten Matrices thoroughly without any interference.

"Have you seen enough of these ten Matrices of Carnage?" Chin Comprehensive said.

"Yes, but I am not impressed by any of them. I understand them all," Jiang Sarn replied.

"Do you think you know how to nullify the power we gave infused into these Matrices?" Chin said.

"Of course. It is well within the capabilities of our Tao," Jiang Sarn replied.

478

"When do you want to come to challenge our Tao," Chin asked.

"As far as I can see, these ten Matrices are not quite completed and they are not operational yet. When they are in full operation, send us a letter of challenge, then we will come to nullify them. Now, please." With a gesture of his hand, Jiang Sarn escorted his battle formation and his entourage of warriors back to the city. The Imperial Teacher and the ten Taoists also returned to their encampment.

After returning to his official residence, Jiang Sarn's mood changed. He put on a long face and frowned. Yang Exterminator said, "Respectable teacher, you just said that you know how to nullify these ten Matrices of Carnage, what is the problem?"

"These ten Matrices are specialties of Sect Interceptus," Jiang Sarn replied. "They use very rare forms of Tao especially developed by the Patriarch, Savant of Heaven. Even their names are completely obscure to me, how can you expect me to nullify them? I had to make the pretense that I knew them all in their presence, but I do not know anything about them."

As Jiang Sarn frowned and felt hopeless, there was a mood of celebration inside the encampment of the Imperial Teacher. "Although Jiang Sarn boasted that he knew how to nullify them, from my observation, he does not have even the slightest idea of what is the Tao involved. He merely bluffed. We will see," the Imperial Teacher said. After making his first toast, he said to his fellow Taoists: "Even I do not understand the Tao of your Matrices. My Taoist friends, what are the powers that you have instilled into these ten Matrices of Carnage? How will these ten Matrices of Carnage enable us to overcome West Branch? Can you tell me?"

Chin Comprehensive first described the power of his Matrix of Heavenly Extermination. "This Matrix was infused with the power of prognostication developed by my teacher-mentor. This power has been transformed into an invincible weapon as follows: There is a flag which consists of three streamers called Flag of Three Heads. These three streamers unify the power of Three Talents, of Heaven, Earth and Man, into a coherent unity. When an enemy enters my Matrix, I will wave the three streamers to activate the Tao. The power of the coherent unity will then snatch the soul out of the body of my enemy. He will immediately fall to the ground and die. Even demigods cannot escape the power of this Tao. There is no defense against the soul-snatching power of the Flag."

The Imperial Teacher was impressed. He asked the next one, Zhao Jiang (River): "What can the Matrix of Earthen Fire do?"

Zhao River described it. "This Matrix is permeated with the essence of the Earth. It has an embodiment which is derived from the extreme heat confined in the depths of the Earth. This heat is stored underneath the ground and is controlled by a red flag. When this red flag is waved according to my prescription, the stored heat is released. Thunder and lightning commence from above while fire from the depths of the Earth entrapped in the embodiment shoots up from below, instantly immolating anything and everything within the confines of the Matrix. The heat is so intense that nothing is known to be able to survive its power. The usual Tao of fire-trekking is useless against this fire. It is not the fire of mortals; it is the primordial fire that was entrapped deep within the Earth during the creation of the Universe."

"May I hear about the Matrix of Wind Roar?" the Imperial Teacher inquired further.

"The power of this Matrix is derived from two of the five forms of the Universe, that is, metallum and fire," Tong Chuan (Entirety) explained. "The power of the two elements is further enhanced by the power of wind that I instilled into this Matrix. When I wave a red flag according to my prescription, fire first commences. This is no ordinary fire; it is Fire of Samadhi, derived from the original primordial fireball. This fire trains metallum into thousands of extremely sharp blades. The wind launches these blades towards the enemy, instantly slicing them into countless pieces. The blades are of such a sharpness that they cut through armor as if it were nothing. There is no defense against the combination of Fire of Samadhi and my wind."

"How about the Matrix of Cold Ice?" the Imperial Teacher continued.

"The power of the Matrix of Cold Ice could not be imbued in one day," Yuan Horn narrated. "I have entrapped coldness in this Matrix. When the controlling flag is waved along with an incantation, two extremely cold ice fields will materialize, one above and one on the ground. The ice field on the ground contains many sharp icicles. The ice field above is similar to that on the bottom, but the sharp icicles are inverted and mate perfectly with those in the ice field below. When an enemy is inside the Matrix, I will activate the two ice fields and they will move towards each other with great force. The ice fields will crush the enemy and pulverize them into cold dust. It is so cold that even demigods lose their magical power, including all usual means of mobility, so they cannot escape."

"What is the power that has been impregnated into the Matrix of Golden Rays?" the Imperial Teacher, greatly pleased so far, continued.

Holy Mother Golden Rays, an elegantly-dressed female Taoist with a command of authority, spoke. "The Matrix of Golden Rays is inculcated with the essence of the Sun and the Moon, and the extract of Heaven and Earth. These essences and extracts are imbued within the Matrix in the form of pure energy, stored in an urn. There are twenty-one mirrors hung high on twenty-one poles. These mirrors are enclosed in individual enclosures and strings are attached to these enclosures. When these strings are pulled according to a preset pattern, the twenty-one mirrors spin once or twice until they are locked onto a target. Then the pure energy stored in the urn is released and focused by the twenty-one mirrors onto the target, in the form of golden rays. The target is cremated instantly. There is no defense against the power of golden rays of my Matrix. The action of the rays is so fast that no one can escape, even if he knows how to fly."

"May I ask about the Matrix of Gore?" The Imperial Teacher, finding each Matrix more powerful than the preceding one, had become intensely interested.

"This Matrix is instilled with an essence derived from the five forms of the Universe, called enzyme," Sun Good answered. "The enzyme is materialized in a form of black power. As a demigod or a mortal enters into my Matrix, by waving a flag and casting an incantation, I can unleash wind and thunder, which blows the black sand into a focused jet onto the target. Upon contact, the black sand turns the body of the demigod or mortal into a pool of bloody water in a matter of moments via a process known as enzymolysis. Hence the name, `gore.'"

It was the turn of Bei Protocol to explain the power of his Matrix. "The Matrix of Fiery Flame is implanted with powers of three kinds of fires, the Fire of Samadhi, the Fire of Air, and the Fire of Rock. These three kinds of fires are instilled by my Tao into a coherent entity and stored inside an urn inside the Matrix. This entity is controlled by three red flags. When a demigod or a mortal enters into my Matrix, these three flags are waved according to a certain pattern. The coherent entity of three fires is unleashed to become an intense jet of invisible flame which instantly engulfs the enemy and reduces his remains into ashes. No incantation is effective against this jet of invisible flame."

"How does the Matrix of Lost Soul work?" the Imperial Teacher urged.

"It is infused with a power that shuts the door of life, and opens the gate of death," Yao Aptitude replied. "It derives its power from the containment of many evil spirits of the Universe. There is an urn of black sand inside the Matrix. When an enemy enters into my Matrix, I can command wind to blow a jet to deposit the sand particles onto the enemy. The sand particles can permeate the body of any demigod or mortal, and drive his soul out of his body. The soul is then collected by a white paper flag which derives its power from a number of talismanic drawings, inscriptions and seals. This flag separates the soul into two basic constituents, anima and umbra, which are then extracted and confined into a gourd bottle inside the Matrix. The enemy instantly becomes a living corpse. Neither mortals nor demigods are immune to the power of this Matrix."

"What is the Matrix of Red Water," asked the Imperial Teacher.

Wang Variance answered: "It is instilled with the essence of the Ninth and Tenth Heavenly Stems and the power of Unity of Heaven. Inside the Matrix there is a platform of Eight Trigrams, on which three gourd bottles sit. The gourd bottles contain a red liquid, which has been instilled with the power of the Ninth and Tenth Heavenly Stems. It contains a powerful substance called enzyme. As an enemy enters, the contents of the three gourd bottles are emptied out. A red sea is created and this sea will instantly consume the enemy, be he a demigod or a mortal. After the enemy is consumed, the red liquid enzyme then returns to the bottle. The Matrix becomes dry afterwards."

The Imperial Teacher finally came to the last Matrix of Carnage. "What is the Matrix of Red Sand?"

"This Matrix is ingrained with Three Talents, Heaven, Earth, and Man. Three urns of red sand are stored inside the Matrix. As an enemy enters, I will throw a handful of red sand at him. Then wind and thunder commence, blowing the red sand particles at extremely high speed. Any person or demigod will be blasted into dust. There is no way to escape its power," Zhang Continuance explained.

The Imperial Teacher was more than impressed at the end of this briefing. "With your help, it will be only a matter of time before the rebellion of West Branch City is completely squashed," he concluded.

"I can speed up your victory." An idea came to Yao Aptitude, who had created the Matrix of Lost Soul.

"How," the Imperial Teacher asked.

"I have a simple scheme to kill Jiang Sarn without the use of force. Within twenty-one days Jiang Sarn will be dead. With their leader dead, the entire rebel group will disintegrate in no time. There will then be no need for our Taoists to defend against their attempts to nullify the Tao of our War Matrices," Yao Aptitude boasted.

"May I hear your scheme," the Imperial Teacher asked.

"Do this and that.... Then Jiang Sarn will be dead in twenty-one days," Yao Aptitude whispered to the Imperial Teacher.

"If your plan succeeds, I will be forever grateful to you. It shall be the greatest blessing of the country." The Imperial Teacher bowed deeply to Yao Aptitude.

"Nothing to it. You owe my success to the blessing of the Emperor," Yao Aptitude responded with an equally deep bow.

The ten Matrices of Carnage were now readied, waiting for action. The first major clash between Sect Elucidatus and Sect Interceptus had begun.

13844868R00285

Made in the USA
Charleston, SC
04 August 2012